THE TORTURED WIND

A**LYCE** C**ASWELL**

First time in print: 2019

ISBN: 978 0 6481626 0 5 (EPUB)
ISBN: 978 0 6485444 0 1 (Print)

Cover design by Hampton Lamoureux, TS95 Studios © 2017, 2019

THE TORTURED WIND

CHAPTER ONE

Callista lashed out and her boot connected with a soft, pliable stomach. Her assailant wavered on his unsteady feet and all it took was a single swipe of her electrified baton against his head to send him down cold. Only when he lay on the pavement, glassy stare directed across the road at her audience, did Callista hear the faint hum of her active weapon.

Tossing a wave over to her fellow Maria clanspeople, she switched off the baton then hooked it onto her faded leather belt where it hung right beside her lasgun, a sleek, silver thing, tapered like a dagger but far more dangerous.

Her companions had challenged her to take down one of their opponents without shooting him outright. Callista knew they'd have respected her even less than they already did if she'd refused. Having proved herself yet again, she unholstered her lasgun and plugged a bolt into the man's head. He was dead long before the weapon was back on her belt.

Callista Krendasta blew stray brown hairs out of her face but they stubbornly returned. She'd tried to bind her hair into a knot but as usual the tie that was meant to be keeping it in place had fallen out. Shaking her head, she jogged across the road, her breath steaming the air. It was cold in Atsa City tonight, a reprieve from the arid desert heat that besieged the streets during the day. She was grateful that she was wearing a jacket, though this had caused her companions to complain about how it was far too easy for her to use it to conceal the symbol on her shirt, the one that revealed her allegiance.

The buildings around her stabbed into the sky like they did in most of Atsa, but here the windows were cheerfully glowing eyes and the base of each towering residence was lit by a web-like scattering of lamps. Callista cast a sardonic chestnut eye at the streetlight nearest her. The city could use more of these in other, less wealthy, sections but then again...the cover of darkness made it easier for her and the rest of the Maria to wage war against the other gangs, who also preferred to call themselves clans. Chasing Primus gang members into this bright, tranquil region had been a mistake, but Callista hadn't wanted to argue with her fellow clanswoman who had been placed in charge of the mission.

One of Callista's companions opened his mouth to crow in triumph, but Callista held up her hand to silence him. She kept her voice low. 'Can't risk making the nice innocent people of Atsa nervous enough to speak to the governor, can we?'

He shook his head, sullenly silent, and joined the small group of Maria clanspeople as they filed away into the streets, retreating from the most respectable part of Atsa, known among the clans as the No-Go Zone. It was meant to be off limits to the gangs; this was one of the many unwritten rules that policed the city at night when the Chippers, those sent by the Galactic Law Enforcement Agency to provide security to the denizens Atsa, vanished from the streets.

If someone heard too much noise and reported it to Governor Jon Garnett, the daytime ruler of the entire planet of Yalsa 5, he might have to retaliate on behalf of his voters. And while GLEA's agents didn't belong to any planet in particular, they were sworn to uphold the laws of any local governing body. They might actually come after the clans in the light of the day if the governor decided to write a law that made it illegal for any gangs to exist in the city.

'Ain't you out past curfew, Dancer?' asked Matron, a slender woman who had earned her name from her habit of counting their number to ensure they were all still alive and kicking.

Callista twisted her bottom lip around her top two teeth. 'It's enough that my street name makes a slight on my inability to glide across the dance floor, but you just had to remind me I still live *with my parents?*'

Her companions snickered. Callista ignored them and started scanning her surroundings. They had walked far enough from the epicentre of Atsa's nicer areas that some of the windows were broken, but they weren't safe yet. And she could sense the hostile energy of several lifesigns — living, breathing people — lurking nearby. She closed her eyes for just a moment and saw them in her mind's eye, firing their lasguns at her and her companions.

But that was in the future. How many minutes away, she couldn't tell.

Opening her eyes, Callista wondered, as she always did, if she should let her fellow clanspeople know what she could see and feel but, just as she always did, she decided against it. They would accuse her of being a Chipper, someone who had willingly entered one of GLEA's temples and stuck a chip in their head. The chip apparently connected them to the Creator God and gave them unique abilities — they could sense the energy of others, which helped them locate lifesigns, and they could generate forcefields which could be used to shield someone or lasso around an object and move it with a form of telekinesis.

Callista had undergone the required scan upon becoming a

member of the Maria gang and nothing had been detected. The sides of her face were completely devoid of a chip. She'd been relieved then, but now she couldn't figure out why. If she just had an explanation for why she could *feel* the way she did...had she been born with it? Were there any others like her?

But even if she'd had a chip, that wouldn't explain why sometimes she caught flashes of the future. No Chipper could do that — or so they claimed. Something to do with them only being able to read the energy that existed in the present; they couldn't sense what *might* exist. Reading thoughts was apparently beyond them too. They might be able to pick up on someone's mood, if the emotion was strong enough, but that was it.

Callista thought it best not to mention that she could sometimes see what people were thinking — her clan's paranoia would condemn her alone. She worked hard not to hear any intimate thoughts when she was outside the interrogation cells, just in case.

'Don't see why you need to be stuck with your folks,' Matron said with a shrug, her voice rising to cover the continuing chuckles of their companions.

Callista winced at the noise they were making and glanced around at the dark alleys surrounding them. She closed her eyes for the briefest of moments — and saw a lasbolt come streaking out of the dark, aimed at Matron's head. The older woman dropped to the ground, dead.

When Callista blinked again, Matron was still standing and prattling away. 'Just take your stuff and leave! And I'm sure Ala'd give you a room back at headquar...'

'Down!' Callista shouted and tackled Matron.

The lasgun bolt screamed overhead, singeing the air and

making it reek of ozone. Time seemed to slow and Callista caught a vision of the next bolt striking the pavement beside her. Her hand curled and crept towards the area. If she could create an invisible shield, the way the Chippers did...

Callista jumped when the bolt hit and swiftly reeled her hand back in.

'Chippers!' Matron hissed.

They took cover behind a dumpster that was rusted shut. Callista stared hard into the night. If their attackers *were* Chippers, they would feel like an ever-present buzz to her senses, like they always did —

'Are you mad?' Matron said, grabbing Callista's elbow and dragging her away from the road.

'They don't feel like...it might not be Chippers — I think it's the Alcazaar,' Callista panted, naming a rival gang. Aside from not *buzzing*, these shooters had been wearing Alcazaar colours in the brief vision she'd had of them. This wasn't exactly something she could mention. She swiftly ducked as more lasbolts whizzed overhead.

'Don't matter who it is, just that they're out for us!' another Maria clansperson said.

He was right. Callista unhooked her lasgun, dropped to one knee and curved her body around the dumpster to take a shot. Something twinged in her shoulder but Callista ignored it. A pulled muscle, probably. Not important.

She squinted. A figure was jogging towards her, a shaggy outline that began with the blond mane spilling onto his shoulders and then continued with the rippling cloak he always wore. Throwing a quick look at her companions, Callista saw that they were aiming elsewhere.

Then she stared down at her body.

She'd fallen back on the pavement, hitting her head and knocking herself out. The cause was obvious — the smoking hole in the shoulder of her jacket.

'I'm unconscious,' she noted distantly. The blistering pain from the lasgun bolt came to her slowly, as though the signals from her nerve endings were moving through sludge. She saw her companions shouting, saw their weapons discharging, but silence blanketed everything.

Somehow this disconnect from her body didn't bother her as much as it should have. Callista rose to her feet and ghosted towards the man who often came to her in her dreams. It was so hard to stay asleep when she became aware of the fact that she was dreaming. She wouldn't waste a moment of this.

She stood before the dream man, hands on her hips, studying him. His slim form was familiar to her but the rest of his face was always a blur. Tonight, though, she saw his painfully blue eyes.

'I'm busy,' she told him.

'So I see,' he said.

She winced.

'Your shoulder?'

She nodded.

He pulled her into his chest and his hand fell over her shoulder; the pressure was painful at first, then his powers blasted through the limb and then all the way back to her heart. Callista burrowed against him, enjoying his warmth, knowing that he was healing her without even needing to ask. The energy emanating from him was brighter and more powerful than anything she'd felt in a Chipper. To her, he didn't buzz. He *glowed*.

'Why aren't you real?' she asked.

His chest vibrated with a chuckle. 'Why aren't you? I should like your name this time.'

'Nice try, dream man. Last time I tried to tell you my name I woke up. Perhaps we are not destined to meet.'

His fingers glided along her chin. Callista squinted to avoid the headache that came from trying to see past the fuzziness of his features.

'I can have a word with the one who controls destiny and make it so,' he said.

She snorted. 'You, on speaking terms with the Creator God? Not even the Chippers have managed that. Unless you mean one of the other sub-level gods, but I seriously doubt they have that much power.'

He wasn't smiling. 'You are afraid.'

'Of what?'

'That your dreams are only that — dreams. I know you would prefer to stay asleep. I confess I don't want this to end either. I never dreamed before you came along and I quite like dreaming.'

Callista had barely made the decision before violent winds began to tear her away from him. She shouted, 'Callista! My name is Callista!'

'Owww,' she said next, lifting her head from the cradle of someone's hand.

'You okay?' Matron asked.

Callista winced and sat up, finding herself surrounded by her clanspeople in a hovercar that was hopefully humming its way towards the Maria headquarters. She forced a smile. 'How lazy am I, falling asleep on the job?'

'Stark that — I thought you got shot!' Matron said. 'When

Subofficer Ala hears about this, she'll have you off the streets for weeks and — '

'I did get shot!' Callista exclaimed, suddenly remembering, and looked down at the hole in her jacket which sat right over her shoulder. Soft, unburned skin peeked through the gap. There was no evidence that a lasbolt had touched her.

Matron grabbed Callista's arm and pulled her down to inspect the area. Then the older woman withdrew, shaking her head. 'You're not really one of us, no matter how well you shoot — still living with your parents, still just a child...'

Callista bristled. 'My parents' connection to rich folk means I get into their houses and case them out for our smash and grabs, which Ala sure appreciates — and I do more than that! Ala wouldn't let me interrogate our prisoners if I wasn't any good at it. Now I'll be talking to her the moment we get — '

'Take Dancer home — we're hoofing it!' Matron called over to the driver and the hovercar slowed down just long enough for the clanspeople to throw their bodies into the darkness.

Callista blinked back furious tears. Some of them were younger than her, though a lot of them had been on the streets for years. They'd grown tough in alleys full of broken glass and shattered hopes. Callista knew how they saw her — the rich folk princess who they had to put up with because she helped them steal coin-chips and hovercars from her parents' friends. The very vehicle she was sitting in had come into Maria hands because of her.

'They're just jealous, mate,' the driver, Kick, said. He was in his sixties and was often relegated to driving. He seemed to enjoy it and claimed that carting around his clanspeople could be a lot more dangerous than actually entering a lasgun fight. 'If they had a warm bed with a giant vidscreen and all the food they could ever eat without so much as lifting a finger, they'd stay with the rich folk too.'

Rubbing her tired, flinching eyes, Callista crawled through the low cabin to plonk herself into the plush seat beside Kick. She watched the headlights chase away the night for a few long moments. 'I'm old enough to have qualifications, jobs, babies. And where am I? Still stuck with my parents.' Callista sighed. 'I'm not brave enough to ditch my comfortable fallback, Kick.'

Kick *hmmed* thoughtfully then patted her arm, his olive skin looking much healthier than her pale complexion. He yanked his hand back to turn one of the steering rods, barely managing to send the hovercar around a sharp bend in time. 'You just need a good reason, Dancer.'

Callista thought about the dream man. If he was real, she'd go with him anywhere. She argued in her mind that it was because he might tell her why she had these strange powers but if she was honest...her lips tilted upwards. She just wanted to be with him, feel him, smell him.

What if he was a cruel man? No, how could that be — she had dreamed him into being, so he must be perfect.

If he existed, that is.

CHAPTER TWO

The dunes were so still they could have been carved from stone. Enveloped in silence, the priest shed his cloak, the cold air biting into his skin and marking his flesh with goosebumps, then raised his hands, palms beseeching the stars. He was the last man standing tonight; the others lay in their floorless shelters, shoulders pressed against the sand that had supported them their whole lives but had lately become too soft, too tempting.

Battle awaited them at dawn. For now, the priest would try to raise their strongest defender. He turned deliberately from the faint glow of the campfire that warmed his tribe and became a black figure swallowed by a blacker night.

'My Lord Desine,' he whispered, keeping his voice low to avoid waking the others. They would have asked to join him, to draw comfort from the ritual. But tonight Head Priest Zron was worried that he would find no comfort for himself, much less any to share with the warriors who would risk their blood when the sun rose.

'My Lord Desine,' he tried again, desperately seeking the desert god. Of all the sub-level gods that existed beneath the Creator God, the Desine was only one that he served. 'I have not heard your Call. I have not felt your Smile. I do not know if we should fight. You...you have not told me...who is just, who is right, who will triumph, and who will turn in flight.'

More silence. It felt like insects were marching down his spine, eager to join the terror pooling low in his gut.

'*Desine*...you guide us,' he said, as much a plea as it was a reminder. 'Please. Should we fight or should we forgive the Kcazza tribe for insulting us? The Magic in me — it is weak, you know this. I...I am afraid their priests will destroy me.'

His fear did not wake the desert god, nor did the uncertain probe he sent with his powers. The Magic was a special gift that only men and women in the deserts were given. Jealous City Dwellers had put chips in their temples to seek another god; their powers were unnatural and weak. They surely did not have the love of *their* god.

The Desine loved his people. He was always there to guide them.

Zron fell to the ground and begged. But his god did not answer him.

***

Screams pierced his temples like nails. Sandsa batted the sounds away before his hand lazily moved to his mouth where it captured a yawn. A tendril of his shaggy blond hair curled onto his forehead. He ignored it. His hand fell to his side.

Standing atop the dune, he watched the destruction unfolding before him, blue eyes bright and framed by his tanned features. Down in the gully, nestled between the rock-studded dunes, warriors fired their lasguns and priests wielded their Magic, more devastating than any man-made weapon.

'But what does the Desine say?' the warriors shouted as the battle continued, wearing down their bodies and their hope.

No priest on either side heard an answer from their god, but still they said, 'Our cause is just! The Desine smiles! We win this day!'

The sun warmed Sandsa's back as he trudged away, wondering how to begin his task. He had searched his sprawling sands for anyone with her name and had failed...perhaps he would turn his eyes to the cities and the domains belonging to his brothers and sisters.

The taste of salt on his tongue gave him several seconds of warning before the Watine, the god of water, oozed into being.

'Pathetic mortals,' the Watine said in his low, sibilant voice. 'How they fall to pieces without us there to guide them through their wretched lives.'

Sandsa regarded his brother coolly and made no move to greet him. The Watine opened his tattered cloak and made a sarcastic gesture that could have been a wave or a threat. His hair, dripping with water and mucus, hung over his face; instead of hiding his permanently dour expression, the greasy strands enhanced it.

Sandsa held out his open hand. A whirling sphere of sand appeared on command, dancing above his palm; a not so subtle reminder for his brother not to test him. He allowed it to hover there for a moment, then extinguished it.

'Fayay,' he finally said, 'I have very little patience for your antics today.'

'You seem to have even less for the mortals,' Fayay noted. His cracked lips parted into a smile that revealed the fungus painting his chipped teeth. 'Are you punishing them? There are more delightful ways to do that. I can show you.'

Sandsa kept his face blank despite the disgust and anger he

felt. That Fayay thought Sandsa was falling into his sadistic ways was bad enough; Fayay offering to show him how best to torture mortals was beyond insulting.

'I am no longer their god,' Sandsa said and continued to amble away, allowing his beige cloak to fly up into the wind, exposing the simple threadbare clothes he wore beneath it.

A column of briny water exploded out of the dune in front of Sandsa, halting his path.

'What are you saying, *Desine?*' Fayay called.

Sandsa smiled grimly and turned back around to face his brother. 'You know what I mean. Oh, how could I forget. You don't.'

Fayay cursed. He lacked the mind-reading abilities that many of their brothers and sisters possessed and Sandsa had always made a point of reminding him of this inadequacy.

'We have lived for millennia, you and I,' Sandsa said, then patted four fingers to his mouth, as though smothering another yawn. 'And yet you do not understand. You never will.'

'You think you know more than me?' Fayay hissed. 'Do you perhaps presume to think you know more than *Father?*'

The laugh curdled in Sandsa's gut before it reached his lips. 'Father. Some father. The Ine is unfeeling. Uncaring. Their *Creator God.* He created this mess long ago. And now we must eternally clean up after him.'

Fayay's pale blue eyes narrowed. 'You are leaving the deserts to rot. What for? To live like some irresponsible mortal?'

'Ah, so you do not need to read minds to know my plans.' Sandsa clapped his palms together. 'You should congratulate yourself, Fayay.'

Fayay frowned in the direction of the two warring tribes as

they shouted and killed each other, all in the name of their god. 'Do you envy these maggots?'

Sandsa laughed darkly. 'Envy the mortals? Of course I do! Do you know what it is they have? We can guide them but it is up to them whether or not they listen. Free will, that's what the Ine gave them. Free will. They get to do whatever they want.'

'Listen to yourself. Mortals are foolish, pitiful creatures and —'

'Then why do you keep looking after them?' Sandsa demanded. 'The mortals — they're *his* creation. It's not our fault the humans poisoned their planet then spread so far throughout the galaxy that he lost control of them. He made us, his children, just so we'd take care of the ones he couldn't! And instead of one god meddling with their lives, there are now more than fifty!' Sandsa drew a breath. 'Now there will be one less. It is time I left my people to fend for themselves.'

Fayay's tongue danced over his bottom lip, like some sort of slimy creature sneaking out of a cave. 'I care as little for the mortals as you do, Sandsa. But it is our duty to maintain Father's grand design.'

'I...' Sandsa hesitated. 'I have my reasons.'

'Does your favourite, Kuja, know your reasons?'

Kuja, their youngest brother and god of the rainforests, was the only sibling Sandsa could stand, the only other god who had felt the loss when their mother had left their father to live as a mortal. But no, this wasn't something Sandsa could share with Kuja.

Kuja wouldn't understand. None of them would.

Sandsa spread his arms, deliberately providing a tempting

target to his brother. 'Admit it, Fayay. You despise being second best. If I leave, there will be no one to challenge you.'

The Watine's lips twisted. 'I will tell Father what you are doing. And he will punish you accordingly.'

'Hoping to impress him, are you?' Sandsa asked scornfully. 'Hoping he'll kill me because you never managed it? Do not bother, Fayay. He already knows. Don't you, Ine?'

Their father's presence bled into the landscape. Sandsa had the satisfaction of watching Fayay's already pallid face bleach even further. The Watine immediately exploded into wisps of water that evaporated in the arid climate as he teleported away.

Sandsa formed another sphere of sand in his palm and waited.

His father appeared in front of him. He was two heads taller than Sandsa and his body was so thin it was almost skeletal. His hair was a white crown, matched by a neatly trimmed beard, and his blue eyes were the twins of Sandsa's own. This was the Ine, the Creator God, the first deity that the humans had worshipped so many aeons ago, when they had been contained on one lonely planet, unaware that so many alien species shared the same god.

'We must talk, but not here,' the Ine said, his lips stretched into a genial smile.

His father touched his shoulder and the icy tendrils of a forced teleportation threatened to invade Sandsa's veins. He jerked away and threw the ball of sand he'd prepared; it shattered against his father's face. The Ine's apparent good will vanished. He clapped his hands and the rolling sand dunes around them disintegrated into blinding white walls and floors; with his love of the sun, Sandsa found this environment harsher and more cruel than any of his baked deserts. This realm, beyond the sight of mortals, was a boring cage, a palace of pain, not the home that the other gods seemed to think it was.

Standing there, on a walkway lined with pillars and his curious brothers and sisters, Sandsa howled a challenge then ran full tilt at the Ine. The columns of stone on both sides exploded into gritty tornadoes and twisted, spurred on by his fury. Balls of sand chased Sandsa, then overtook him. He threw everything he had at his father.

The Ine held up a hand. Sandsa froze in place and his control over the sands abruptly withered; his missiles dropped to the floor and the pillars became still and cold once more.

'Sandsa, my son,' his father began, 'you gave your people their own powers. You made them special compared to those that do not live in the deserts. That was no uncaring gesture.'

Sandsa pulled his lips back into a snarl. 'I only gave them power over the sand so they could protect themselves from the mortals who insist on inserting a chip into their flesh to talk to you!'

'Your people have "the Magic" so long as you are there for them. You are the source of their powers. What will protect them if you leave?'

'Nothing you say will keep me in your grasp,' Sandsa warned.

'If you abandon the deserts, my son, then you renounce your place among us.'

Sandsa felt the eyes of his siblings upon him and found himself unable to turn his head to regard them, to challenge them, to ask for their help. Kuja might try to intercede, but the young god would be too powerless to do anything. And Fayay...he would be loving this, anticipating the moment he became the most revered of all their siblings.

'One woman is not reason enough to turn away from your people,' the Ine told his eldest son.

Sandsa wet his lips. 'Father...'

'The woman in your dreams — do not let a reckless pursuit of her be your downfall.'

Sandsa's cheeks felt hot with anger and shame. So even his dreams were laid bare to the Ine. His father had watched them, had seen the woman that haunted him, called him, and offered so much more than anyone else could.

'I am a god, just as you are, Father,' Sandsa said lowly. 'But you forget. My mother was human, extended though her life was. You give the mortals the choice to obey or ignore us. Since part of me is human, I should be able to choose my fate. And I choose the woman in my dreams.'

'There is no choice to be made, Sandsa,' his father said. 'Do you not see this?'

Sandsa merely glared at him.

The Ine's expression remained infuriatingly calm. 'Then you will ignore me, the deserts and your duty, and place your focus entirely on this woman.' Not a question. An acceptance.

'Sandsa, no!' That was Kuja, the Rforine, tearing free from the line of silent gods to stand between Sandsa and the Ine. 'I lost Mum. Don't make me lose you too.'

The rainforest god was only seventy years old, practically a baby. And it showed. Green eyes growing moist, long copper fringe flying back over his head, face dotted with freckles, Kuja repeated his entreaty, anguished.

'Do not pretend you understand what is going on here,' the Ine told Kuja, his voice measured and unhurried despite the muttering that passed through those standing around them. 'You cannot help him.'

'I'm sorry,' Kuja whispered, turning to show his tears to Sandsa.

Sandsa shook his head. 'You've done nothing wrong. I know you can't escape him. Goodbye, Kuja.'

Stepping aside, hunched in defeat, the Rforine briefly squeezed his brother's shoulder before rejoining the ranks of those who would never dare raise their voices against their father. Another hand replaced Kuja's, one of iron and aeons, and the Ine pushed his eldest son backwards, saying, 'Desine, god of the deserts, you are hereby outcast from this realm, an immortal wanderer with no home. May you find what you seek.'

And Sandsa fell. But not to the floor, where the impact might have shaken the fear from him.

He passed through a white shroud that ripped when he touched it, he sailed down past stars and planets dancing in their ancient patterns and, as he continued to fall, he saw her face, a smile tweaking her lips. But then she was gone, unreachable in the blackness of infinity.

He hit the ground on a planet he'd never bothered to learn the name of and gripped sand between his fingers, cursing, using words invented by the mortals, then stood to stare around at the predictable blandness of one of his deserts. Nothing changed here beneath the sun — or suns, depending on where you were.

He knew every minuscule detail about his people, the nomads who had left the cities behind to seek his protection. Every speck of sand spoke to him constantly, nagging, telling him everything unbidden.

'I'm sick of it,' Sandsa said and his body collapsed into a sandy pile. He became a formless entity, searching...searching...

Eventually he arose somewhere else, surrounded by looming buildings peppered with lights. He stared up at the windows, feeling instead of seeing, and then he began to stride through the streets, lured forward by the promise of her.

'Callista,' he murmured over and over.

Of course she wasn't in the deserts; he would have found her sooner if that was the case. He could feel her somewhere here, just out of reach...

'Callista, Callista,' he chanted as he followed his dream.

***

Head Priest Zron wavered on his knees, unwilling to complete his fall to the killing grounds. He reached for the hazy horizon, begging for one last glimpse, one last touch, of the great Magic that the desert god had created for his people to tap into. He felt...nothing. He was not yet dead but the numbness in his limbs was spreading to his heart and would soon reach his eyes and his mind.

The Desine was gone.

'Abandoned,' Zron whispered in horror.

When at last he collapsed onto the sand, a darkness swallowed him, one that would soon swallow all the sands.

CHAPTER THREE

Callista would usually have slid in through one of the windows of her suite, but the grid of metal bars meant to keep her safe had recently been replaced with a laser variant. The thieves of Atsa City were growing ever more opportunistic after all, their brazenness fuelled by a lack of consequences because the Chippers remained in their stone outpost after sunset. They didn't do this because they acknowledged that the gangs ruled the nights instead of the governor who had invited them — no, they did it because GLEA refused to pay the medical bills of those who got involved with night-time activities on Yalsa 5. The expense would most likely outstrip the donations that the Agency received from those few grateful followers of the Creator God who lived on the planet.

Callista would rather have eased her way past bars instead of facing the echoing entrance hall that was formed by cold, unfeeling marble. Her keypass lay flat against her palm as the electronic door wheezed shut behind her, throwing out a puff of air which disturbed her dusty hair. It was already flinging around her chin again; she had pulled it back into yet another knot but none of the strands were long enough to stay in that position for more than a Yalsa 5 hour — which, conveniently, wasn't too far off the length of one Old Earth hour. The days were not dissimilar either so, unlike some other planets that kept to Old Earth time, night here generally tended to fall when it was supposed to.

Callista stopped dead when she realised she wasn't alone.

It was probably a good thing she'd remembered to stash her weapons under the front porch or she might have shot the two people waiting for her without realising who they were.

Eyes narrowed in defiance, she said, 'I am twenty-five. Old enough to retire if I was a miner on the asteroids. Old enough to go out and enjoy myself without coming back to this...this interrogation.'

Her parents were standing at the foot of a chipped grand staircase that was in danger of losing its rotted wooden railing. She could understand their desire for the coin-chips to fix it up, but she disliked them expecting her to help fund their lifestyle. As for the money she pocketed at night while working for the Maria, that was hers. Something they couldn't keep track of. She didn't touch the bank account they'd given her — not that it had much in it these days — because she preferred to keep her purchases a secret.

'What have you done?' her father demanded. 'See, your mother is so upset.'

'Isolde Israr asked you to marry him!' her mother cried, pacing on the first step as though afraid to fall to the floor, where her husband had planted himself.

Callista's father's loamy eyes lit with anger. 'You refused him?'

'You want me to marry a guy who whinges to you when his guards — no, *spies* — catch me eating a hamburger when he's decided I need to be on diet?' Callista asked, crossing her arms over her chest and causing her jacket, which was quite snug when she sealed it, to strain over the unfortunate assets that had made her the target of a millionaire friend of her parents.

Perhaps 'friend' was too generous. Accomplice, perhaps.

She'd had Kick drop her off three blocks from her parents' house so they wouldn't know that Isolde hadn't brought her home. Now she wondered why she'd bothered with the pretence; her parents obviously knew that she'd ditched Isolde at the restaurant. Clearly she would never make them happy unless she chained herself to some guy who wouldn't find her when she was in trouble and lay healing hands upon her...

'He's loaded!' her mother shrieked.

'So're the asteroid miners — and for some reason they got sent a bad reference after I applied so I can't be one of them,' Callista said, then shook her head, amazed. 'I can't believe I stayed here as long as I did. After tonight, I'm gone. You won't see me again.'

She slid her finger across the sensor that would automatically unzip her jacket. Her mother gasped when the leather parted, revealing what Callista was wearing beneath it. Callista smiled down at the black tank shirt which was emblazoned with the Maria logo. Hiding her gang affiliation beneath the jacket had been her way of feeling that she could, at any time, escape her parents' plans for her — not to mention the company of one Isolde Israr whose idea of taking a woman on a date was to abduct her at gunpoint.

Exposing the symbol now was a good way to show her parents what she thought of the tune they wanted her to dance to. She was terrible at dancing anyway. That particular flaw had earned her the ironic gang name 'Dancer' barely a month after signing in blood. It was really her parents' fault for letting her stay out so late, thinking she was looking for a suitor, hoping she'd been with Isolde, praying to any god that would listen that she'd been planning to drop some grandchildren for them.

Tonight Callista had actually spent some time with Isolde. But it hadn't been her choice.

The man had been waiting outside her parents' house with a hoverlimo and two heavily armed guards whose purpose probably wasn't to ward off gangs. No, they'd been there to ensure her compliance.

She'd been willing to play along, in the hopes that she would find out if he had any particular wealth stashed in an unprotected place so the Maria could raid it, but then Isolde had proposed, his mouth heavy not with food (he rarely ate more than a fistful of his plate) but a smug, certain grin. She had given him her answer in the form of kicking him beneath the table and then crawling through a window in the women's bathroom so that Isolde's henchmen wouldn't try to follow her for a few minutes. She still wasn't sure which had been worse — being trapped beneath his lewd gaze or being pinned under a hail of lasgun bolts barely an hour later.

Callista threw her keypass onto the floor. It skidded away.

'I could have fixed this starking house with money from the mines,' Callista ground out. 'But no, you had to go and tell the Galactic Mining Corp I was something lousy.'

When her application had been rejected by the corporation three years ago, she'd stormed off into the city and embraced Asta's night-life. The Maria were the best clanspeople she could have run into — they'd been lacking enough people that they'd stayed their lasguns and let her join.

'You could have just married him — it was easy!' her mother wailed.

Her father held out his hand, as if that gesture alone could convince Callista to stay.

Callista turned away from them, unable to douse the smile. The Maria didn't attack their own, so now that she was leaving, the safety her parents had unknowingly enjoyed would go with her.

The smile only grew as she neared the steel door barring her exit. How long would those fancy laser bars last when her parents ran out of the money to power them? She waved a few fingers over the sensor pad, but the door remained stubbornly closed. Above her, the lights dimmed. The mansion's failing power units were apparently starting to affect basic systems. Callista wasn't surprised.

'You can't leave,' her father said in his gentle baritone. 'It's not safe out there.'

As though to emphasise his point, the floor rocked beneath them, the accompanying explosion sounding much closer than usual. Her father's mind shivered with fear.

Callista laughed and reached for the emergency door release. 'I'll take my chances.'

Ala, the only subofficer in the Maria, would be very disappointed to hear that she could no longer use Callista's connections to the higher echelon to discover which rich family had what to steal or who had installed what security measures. But Callista wasn't worried. She contributed to her clan in other ways, whether it be with her lasgun or in the interrogation cells.

Callista heard her mother collapse to the ground with a sob of despair. She glanced over her shoulder. Her father was still standing, fists clenched, fury forcing his blood vessels to pop out.

'You need to marry and have children,' he said, his voice

increasing in volume. 'Callista! Please! You have to do this! For me!'

Callista stepped outside. The door closed behind her for the last time.

***

The humming baton swung around, sending sparks along the armour guard that ran the length of her assailant's neck. Callista offered a sweet smile as she returned the baton to her belt. 'Not doing your job if anyone can just waltz on in, are you?'

'Waltz? Good one, Dancer.' Bock chortled. 'And anyway, last I checked the palm print scanner was still workin'. No one but Maria can get through that door.' Noticing that Callista was glancing around the empty atrium of the Maria headquarters, he snapped his fingers in front of her face. 'Hey! Thought Kick dropped ya off at home or somethin'?'

'Oh, he tried...' Callista said with a wink.

Most of the gang was out marauding through the streets, though lately their numbers had thinned because their rivals, the Alcazaar, the ones currently acknowledged to rule the nights as they had the city's only Clan Leader, had started making examples of anyone who wasn't giving them enough respect.

If any other gang dared to use the title 'Clan Leader' or propped up an influential boss who could be deemed to be an imposter, they were headed for trouble. As a result, most clans did not have strong leadership. The Maria only did so well because they were under the watchful eye of Subofficer Ala. Subofficers were plentiful throughout the city — there were so many of them that all they did was squabble with each other, so no one gained enough power to challenge the Clan Leader. There was a good reason why Ala rarely promoted anyone else to subofficer in her gang.

The realisation that Bock was the only one available to guard the door drove a spike of worry into Callista's guts. He was a weedy doe-eyed teenager, his face smooth with youth and inexperience. He'd probably have switched to a better nickname if Ala had allowed him to; 'Bock' certainly didn't make him sound terrifying.

'Ala's here,' he said, ducking his head shyly.

'She's not going to notice you if you don't actually speak to her,' Callista told him.

He sighed. 'She's a *goddess*. How d'ya speak to a goddess?'

'Well, I seem to manage it on a daily basis,' Callista told him as she swung past. 'Just be your charming self, Bock.'

'Charming self,' Bock muttered. 'What a crock of shit.'

Callista killed the smile that would have hurt his feelings. Subofficer Ala was a good twenty years older than him and hardened from a lifetime of trying to push the Maria into glory. Her deep bronze skin was ravaged by fire and shrapnel, Ala's only reward for keeping the clan in line. She would have been their undisputed Clan Leader had they been allowed to openly declare themselves ruled by one. The Maria had lost that privilege fifty Old Earth years ago.

Ala was holed up in her study, a lasgun in one hand and a whisky in the other. Ice tinkled as the subofficer shot back the contents of her glass. Then she cocked her head to the side, her artificial eye whirring as it regarded Callista with a sharp red pinprick, so unlike the warm honey of her other eye. The dark stubble on her head meant that Ala hadn't managed to grab the time to shave it down in the past two days.

'Fifty years of Alcazaar fuckery,' Ala said and slammed her glass down so hard an ice cube leapt to freedom. She crushed the traitor beneath the pommel of her lasgun. 'Fifty years. They should've done us the courtesy of wiping us out when we lost the right to have a Clan Leader, hey? Save us this slow death.'

'I don't suppose this is a good time to mention I was proposed to this evening and then moved out of home?' Callista asked, reaching for the glass of amber liquid that Ala held out to her.

Ala raised the one dark eyebrow she had left. 'As your subofficer, that shit is not worth my time. I have a skirmish about to go down in Newheim South. As your friend, do go on. Proposed to, huh? This is the closest you've come to poppin' your cherry ever.'

Callista took one sip of her drink then wheezed. 'Doubtful, Ala.'

'It's unnatural, you being twenty-five and all pure. You do realise most of us get this over and done with by the time we hit sixteen, right?'

Callista fiddled with her hair until the knot holding it back from her face disintegrated. She sighed and tucked the useless elastic tie into her pocket. 'Believe me, I'd like to have managed that.'

Ala's eyebrow flattened over her eye. 'You can sleep with any of the Maria men. You'd just have to ask. You're pretty. You're not bad with a lasgun. So what's the big deal?'

'It doesn't mean anything, does it?' Callista asked, trying not to sound too desperate.

'What's this, Cals?' Ala asked, tapping her lasgun against the corner of her smile. 'Are you some delicate flower? Just get it over and done with so you won't be so freaked out about it. Now, I haven't been with one in a while but men, they like experienced gals, ya kno — oh, stark it.'

Ala's attention was now fully captured by the techpad on her desk.

'The skirmish?' Callista asked, dropping her train of thought — hard. There was no time for her personal problems when lives were at stake.

'Yep. It's goin' nova. We were meant to be taking out Subofficer Ranker, the douchenozzle from the Primus clan, 'cept looks like he got himself more firepower than we bargained for.'

Callista scooted onto the edge of her chair. 'We had a problem with the Primus tonight. We were supposed to just chase them off our patch, but Matron thought we should follow them into the No-Go Zone.'

'You didn't agree with her,' Ala stated, as though they had all the time in the galaxy to dissect one mission while another was falling to pieces.

Callista swallowed. 'She was in charge so I didn't argue. Anyway, no one listens to me, I'm just rich folk.'

'Don't have time for your sob story, Cals. Just spit out what you're thinking.'

'I think it was another gang, most likely the Alcazaar, that got the Primus to lure us there so they could jump us,' Callista rushed out.

She expected Ala to accuse her of coming up with a ridiculous theory, but the subofficer was frowning, her one good eye unfocused. Then Ala threw a hand across the table at Callista, almost knocking over her empty glass. 'I've been hearin' some rumours. Thought the Primus were too proud to be the lackies of the fuckers in charge. But we can't prove anything so none of the other clans'll gang up against the Alcazaar with us. Stark it. I can't send anyone over to Newheim South or I'll lose Market Street and...fuck. I'll have to go myself.'

'No!' Callista stood. 'We need you, Ala. They'll wipe us out for good if they get you. I'll go with Bock.'

There was a minute pause, much shorter than it took for a databyte to be sent across the Web. 'Go. Make sure you wear something better'n that.'

Ala indicated Callista's baton and the outmoded lasgun. As it was so sparse, new equipment was only doled out when absolutely necessary. Callista nodded and headed for the door.

'Cals?'

She turned.

Ala's expression was softer than Callista could ever remember it being. 'Come back alive.' Then that red eye blazed once more. 'Can't lose the best interrogator we've ever had, ya know.'

CHAPTER FOUR

Perched above the city on a crumbling building, chin turned down on the chaos in the streets below, Sandsa surveyed the only settlement on the surface of Yalsa 5 — Atsa City, yes, that was its name. It was surrounded by desert, its grimy walls now the only thing struggling to keep the encroaching sand out of the streets. Centuries ago, there had been a citywide shield, but it had since collapsed. There was no real need of it now — no desert tribes had attacked in generations. Those wars were long in the past.

Many of Sandsa's people were now within the walls of Atsa, eking out an existence while labouring for coin-chips, the currency of the cities. Sandsa did not blame them for seeking a life without him. What sane human would choose the sands, anyway? Bland, boring, no future, no hope, no *Callista*. He glanced down at his equally unexciting beige attire, frowned, then let his cloak billow away in the wind.

His attention was stolen by one particular fireball in the south. It blew up brilliantly in a burst of orange and red — so much brighter, so much more colourful and different and beautiful than anything in the plain white realm that he was now an outcast from.

Sandsa found he did not care much for what he had lost.

He was going to gain so much more.

Sandsa staggered, then fell to his knees. He pressed his palms to the rough concrete roof of whatever building he'd found himself on, blinking furiously as a vision, harder and faster than any tormenting dream, overcame him.

She was marching over broken glass, unafraid and determined, the heavy artillery weapon in her arms spurting an endless stream of lasbolts. Her face was blank, empty, hiding her true identity as always, but he caught a glimpse of the sleeveless tank shirt she wore beneath her jacket. It bore a strange symbol — a silver triangle guarding an eye speared with a drop of blood.

Beside her, a teenager batted away any stray bolts with a personal shielding device that wasn't even big enough to cover his own torso, let alone anyone else's. This boy flanked her, protecting her, but his efforts wouldn't be enough to save her. Ire rose within Sandsa. She was *his*. His dream, his salvation.

His Callista.

Sandsa's vision cleared. He was alone on the rooftop. Long ago he had wondered why he was the only one to have inherited the Ine's precognitive abilities. Now he didn't care, simply rejoiced that it could help him find her.

Sandsa exploded into particles of sand that disappeared then reformed near the fight that threatened her life.

***

'Bock, don't you dare drop dead!' Callista said aside to her companion as she jogged towards the Maria clanspeople sheltered behind a barricade made out of hovercar bodies.

Bock saluted her with his shielding device. Its hum paused ominously for a moment then continued on; the tech apparently wasn't ready to give out just yet. 'I wouldn't dare, Dancer! Least not until you don't need me no more.'

The line of Primus fighters that had been blocking the escape route of the Maria gang members had been punched through by Bock's enthusiastic driving. Callista's ears still rang from either the ensuing crash or his whoops of delight. She had been on the top of the vehicle, manning the lasgun turret and taking down anyone foolish enough to get in her way. It was lucky the Primus didn't seem to have the funds for hovercars — although, judging by the smoking ruin she and Bock had left behind them, Callista had to concede that the Maria were running through their own supply all too quickly.

'Report!' she shouted at her fellow clanspeople, hoping their leader was still alive to answer — and to make any hard decisions for her.

Several heads popped up. No one stepped forward. They all appeared to be low level 'grunts' (Ala had defended her use of the term, saying it made her people work harder to lose the label). Bock pointed down at one of the corpses nearby.

Callista recognised the body of a Maria clansperson she had once taken orders from and winced. She assessed the trembling troops. None of them seemed willing to stand, especially as a hailstorm of lasbolts started pelting at them from beyond the blockade. She looked helplessly at Bock who shrugged.

'Their rear line is down — we can retreat,' Callista said, pitching her voice low and forcing her audience to strain their ears. Hope lit their faces. But Callista shook her head. 'None of that. We can't let the Primus know we're weak. And even if we die, there are still plenty of Maria left in this city to avenge us — so let's do this!'

Callista blinked a few times, wasting precious seconds, but no vision arrived to help her out. Hoping her fear wasn't too obvious, she ordered her clanspeople to surge over the barricade, shields extended in one hand, lasguns in the other. The initial charge took down the Primus who had been creeping forward to test the Maria defences.

Callista sent some grunts down the sides, sneaking and skulking their way along while the main force acted as a distraction, yelling insults and running towards the Primus' opposing wall of scrap metal. Callista joined the last wave, trying to ignore the ache in her arms caused by carrying the heavier lasgun. When she first stumbled she stared down at the ground, unable to find what had tripped her. A moment later she toppled sideways and realised a bolt had caught her ankle. The scent of charred flesh assaulted her nose when she hit the ground. Furious that the injury would slow her down, Callista grabbed Bock — he had stayed by her side, swinging the shield over their heads — and used him to lever herself onto her feet.

'Sorry, Dancer!' Bock cried.

'Shut up — you're protecting far more important body parts than my ankle,' Callista said and hobbled back into the fray.

When she climbed over the Primus' first wall, she saw her people already dismantling part of a second one, making enough of a gap for them to tunnel through the piles of junk. Heat flared over her face and she became aware of Bock's hands curled into her jacket, having yanked her away from a near miss.

Callista shook her head when he told her to fall back and scurried forward again. She began shouting encouragement, but when her people touched one of the objects forming the barricade, there was a violent explosion.

The whole wall is rigged, she realised in the brief second before she was blown backwards. Her jacket protected her from the worst of it, though the skin on her face was grated raw by concrete. She couldn't remember screaming but her throat now rasped when she tried to call for help.

Callista stared unseeingly at the ground. Or was it the smoke-filled sky? She couldn't tell.

Anger invaded her thoughts. Why hadn't she had a vision that could have helped her? Why hadn't her dream man come? Should she just give up? Should she pray to the Creator God or the sub-level gods? Those newer gods were routinely looked down on, because it was the shared worship of a singular deity that had helped bind the galaxy together when humans had left Old Earth and started meeting other species. Even so, it was said that the Creator God looked after you no matter who you did or didn't worship.

Callista wondered if she would find proof of this after her death.

She felt her eyes threaten to close so she could seek out *him*, but she wasn't going to surrender that easily. She hadn't dropped her weapon and her legs weren't broken. She could still help the Maria.

She'd go down fighting.

***

Sandsa felt her lifesign flicker for just a moment. She was hurt, but not badly. Soon she would be taken hostage or killed or — no.

He rose from the tar, a human-shaped figure made of sand that shed grains and grit to reveal a man underneath. He stalked his way down the road, hot desert winds roaring ahead of him, sucking away oxygen and throwing sand over flames and into the eyes of those who might see his face. One particular gust of wind engulfed those who dared to aim their lasguns at him and ripped scratchy coughs out of their throats.

His opponents ran. Sandsa smiled. The winds dutifully retreated.

Dusting off his shirt, Sandsa glanced around and saw her, his dream woman, her lasgun slack in her hands as she stared at him.

'You can't be here, you're not real,' she whispered.

Sandsa held out his hand to her, trying to keep his fingers steady. 'I am real. And I am here. I've waited, Callista...'

'Don't wait — get me the stark out of here like you're meant to,' she said, her voice strengthening. She jerked away from him. 'Bock! Hotwire me a hovercar. We need to get gone.' She turned to Sandsa. 'Even if you're not who I think you are, you'll want to come with us. The Primus have some powerful friends who could be on us any minute now.'

He would have gone with her regardless of what she said to him.

Sandsa nodded, concealing his smile. 'Very well. I'm S —'

'No time for that,' she cut him off sharply. 'Let's go.'

CHAPTER FIVE

Sandsa left the hovercar the moment the packed vehicle drew to a halt inside the garage of a building that the gang members called their 'headquarters', then waited for Callista to join him before continuing any further. Barely a second after her fingers brushed his, a dark-skinned woman appeared in the doorway, thumbs hooked onto her belt as she surveyed everyone with two eyes, one real and one mechanised. Then she barked, 'How many of those Primus douchenozzles got away, huh?'

'Several, but they will think twice before coming after us again,' Sandsa answered, treading up the ramp towards her. 'I made sure of that.'

A lasgun appeared in the woman's hand quicker than the desert god could blink. A hush fell over the garage. Callista cleared her throat and stepped forward, drawing in line with Sandsa. 'He's with us, Ala.'

One dark eyebrow rose on Ala's face. Callista lifted her chin in response.

'Oh, sure, just bring anyone off the street into our headquarters — obviously you don't need my permission,' Ala said, her weapon unwavering. 'What gives? Does he even know what we are?'

Sandsa shrugged. 'I do not mind that you are a gang.'

'Are there any other gangs you *don't mind?*' Ala demanded of him.

'This is the first one I've come across,' he said, glancing aside sharply when cold steel snapped over his wrists, binding them together. Callista had surprised him with the cuffs. She was probably the only mortal who could, he reflected. 'And I don't think your people are unhappy that I intervened.'

The teenager from the battle, his shielding device still clenched in his sweaty hand, chortled. 'You can keep on intervenin' if you want. Hey, I don't see any lasgun on you. How'd ya do it?'

'Bock,' Ala warned then waited, as if she knew just how many seconds of silence would make him capitulate.

Bock jerked his head at Sandsa. 'Subofficer, he saved our arses. You've brought in others for less. You shoulda seen Dancer too, she came on in and...'

'Dancer, take him to a cell,' Ala said and turned, storming back into the upper levels of the building.

'So how'd ya do it?' Bock asked Sandsa keenly.

Callista slapped Bock's shoulder. 'Idiot. His weapon fried so he had to drop it. You'd better go clean up — I need to get some answers out of our friend here.'

'Fine,' the teenager grumbled.

***

The moment she opened the door Callista kicked the backs of his knees, forcing Sandsa to stagger over to the solitary chair. It was frigid against his skin, just like the room itself. No windows, no lamps, just whatever light managed to sneak in through the slightly ajar door. The cuffs cut into his wrists, an annoyance, but not one that he would have to put up with for long if he used his powers.

'What are you?' she asked, her eyes dark with suspicion.

'I am Sa —'

'No. No name. We both know what'll happen. I'll wake up and you'll be gone.'

Sandsa let his gaze travel to her wounds. She shook her head. 'And if you heal me I'll wake up without any proof that you exist.'

'Should I have let you die?'

'Might have saved you some trouble,' she said.

'I don't disagree.'

'You haven't answered the question. What are you?'

'Human?'

'Can humans command the sand where you're from?'

Sandsa kept his head very still. 'All who follow the Desine are given the Magic.'

'I've heard that about the desert god,' Callista said, frowning. 'But Magic? It's gotta be tech. I know Chippers get their abilities from the chips in their heads and, granted, I don't see any chips on the desert folk who keep saying they have their own god and magical powers and whatever. But it might not be so obvious as a chip.'

Pursing his lips, Sandsa said, 'Chippers. I know them, if not the word. You speak of GLEA, the ones with, ah, tech that enables them to access the powers my fat — the Creator God made available to them?'

Centuries ago, a human had somehow created a chip that, when inserted beneath one temple, gave them the ability to feel the energy of the universe around them — and the ability to manipulate it to some degree. Sandsa had once asked his father why he had allowed the mortals to achieve this; the Ine had then explained that his creation needed mortals as well as gods to look after them. Sandsa felt an old stirring of dislike for the Galactic Law Enforcement Agency. At least the mortals got to choose whether or not they wanted to become Chippers and run around looking after people they didn't care about.

'Yeah, who else would I mean?' Callista asked with a roll of her eyes. 'But enough. I have to know. What are you?'

'Why do you ask that so fervently?' Sandsa skirted his way towards her mind, not wanting to invade her thoughts but tempted to do so all the same. He was desperate to know more about her.

Callista's eyes flicked over to the doorway. No shadow fell there. She turned back to him, her lips warring with each other. 'Are you a dream made real? I've seen you every night, I've...'

She stopped speaking abruptly. Sandsa wondered why a pink tinge filled her cheeks and why her eyes darkened even further. Finally, he broke the silence. 'You have invaded my own dreams. Tell me, how is this so? You are just human.'

'Apparently so are you.'

Sandsa gave in and stabbed right through the outer layers of her mind. He blinked when he felt resistance against his probe, a clumsy attempt at deflection that could become so much more with training. After sifting through her memories and finding her most recent visions, he pulled back and gazed intently at her temple.

'You don't have a chip,' Sandsa said, even though that would not have explained everything; she had abilities that clearly didn't belong to GLEA.

Callista rubbed her forehead. 'Neither do you.' When she looked up, her face was full of hope. 'I thought I was the only one.'

'Only what?' Sandsa asked, wondering if his father had started giving mortals this natural ability just in case GLEA's chips stopped working.

'Were you born with it too?' she asked quietly. 'Is that why I can't read your thoughts?'

'I have learned to guard my thoughts. You haven't. I could clearly feel your fear during the battle. It's what led me to you — well, that and my vision.'

Callista's smile filled him with warmth quicker than any star's light. 'So you came for me. Finally.'

'Yes. I felt you for so long but I could never find you, and then last night...I wasn't just passing through, Callista.'

She shook her head. 'You'll need a better explanation than dreams and visions for interfering in our fight. If Ala believes you, she'll probably have you shot. If she doesn't...she'll ask me to press the truth from you.'

'Let me guess.' Sandsa gave her a smile of his own. 'You have never *pressed*. You find that sometimes you can simply read the information you need from the minds of your prisoners. Your superior doesn't know you don't use fists or threats to get what you want.'

'She can't know.'

'Why?'

Callista gave him an impassive stare.

'You are afraid she will think you're a Chipper and kill you,' Sandsa surmised.

'Worse. I'd have to defend myself and gun down anyone in my way...and I really don't want to do that. Not to my clan.'

Sandsa nodded. 'I see. So how can you help me?'

'I can give you a better story, one that Ala might just swallow. If you're lucky.'

***

'I interfered with the skirmish as a way of announcing my intentions to join the Maria clan,' Callista's dream man declared, staring up at Ala with as much dignity as the interrogation chair would allow.

Ala shone a lasgun sight directly into his eyes. He blinked.

'And not just 'cause you saw this pretty face?' Ala said.

'That too,' he said with a shrug.

Ala swung the sight onto Callista. 'I knew I should've slapped you on a recruitment poster. Alright. But you'll be the one to shoot him if he betrays us.'

Clamping down on her smile, Callista nodded.

Ala spun on her heel and was already in the corridor before she added, 'Praise the gods you might finally lose that troublesome purity of yours.'

'What does she mean?' the newcomer asked Callista.

Her cheeks flamed and she started limping towards him to unlock the cuffs. 'You'll have to swear in blood tomorrow. Ala'll put on a party for it and she'll ask you if you've picked a gang nickname yet. You should probably come up with one now otherwise you'll get stuck with something really — '

She stopped talking when he knelt before her, hands held over her wounded ankle. The white light emanating from his touch hypnotised her and she froze in place, fearing that this was a dream that would end all too abruptly. But he stayed.

His face drifted past hers again. Callista's lips tingled from the proximity of his mouth to hers, but she managed to remain still as he worked on the grazes on her face. When he was done, she snagged his hands in hers.

'You're not going to bolt, are you?' she asked. 'Because you owe me so many explanations. About what you are. About what I am.'

He smiled. 'Bolt? I wouldn't dare. Not when I've finally found you. *Callista*.'

'Bolt,' she echoed. 'That's it. I'm calling you Bolt.'

'Don't you want my real name? Haven't I proved I'm staying?'

Callista looked away. 'You've only proved that you're real, Bolt. Don't push it.'

Much to her relief, he nodded.

CHAPTER SIX

The Maria had two nightclubs in their thrall but the Bang Bang was their undisputed favourite. Anyone who entered wearing the wrong shirt would meet the bartender's faithful splatterlasgun, which spent most of its time proudly displayed behind him on the chrome piping that dominated the decorating scheme. The floor in the centre of the nightclub swarmed with legs, arms and even one set of tentacles. Bright lights strobed over the dancers, bathing them in red and silver, anointing them in the colours of their clan.

Sandsa stood awkwardly at the door, wearing his new Maria shirt that he'd acquired the previous day while being led around the clan's headquarters. He'd also been given a bed which consisted of a simple metal frame and a soft blanket that served as his mattress. The grey walls around the bed were bleak, making the tiny, narrow room seem much dimmer than it already was. But he loved it, because it was his.

Callista was fanning herself in one of the booths that ringed the dance floor, her hair pulled away from her face and exposing her bored expression. Sandsa watched her for a time, willing her to look his way. She did, briefly. Her uncertain smile shot something uncomfortably warm into his chest. He had not seen her since the night she'd named him, not even when Ala had called the clan into their large lounge room (the space must have had that function, because it had cushioned seats, entertainment systems and even a kitchenette in the corner) to draw some blood from him along with an oath that he would pay with more than blood should he betray them to the other clans, the most unfavourable of which was the Alcazaar.

Sandsa hadn't learned the majority of the names of the gangs yet, but he could know them all in moments if he used his powers. He found he didn't feel the need. But he did feel compelled to sit with Callista tonight. He was about to head towards her when Ala slid in beside Callista and began talking with a hand smothering her lips, clearly to obscure her words. Judging by the redness that spread over Callista's face, she was not comfortable with whatever her — subofficer, yes, that was the term — subofficer was saying. Sandsa eased a few grains of sands in that direction, ordering them to scuttle as close as possible. He was about to eavesdrop on the conversation when something hard and pointy jabbed his ribs — an elbow.

'Go over there, Bolt!' Bock said, a phial of ruby liquid swinging in his hand as he tried to righten himself.

'Are you old enough to consume that?' Sandsa asked, eyeing the drops that escaped Bock's drink to hang indecisively in the air before they obeyed gravity and hit the slick floor at their feet.

Bock chortled. 'I'll drink what I want, man! It's not like the Chippers are gonna bust me — they don't chase anyone who breaks the governor's laws after the sun's gone down. Now go get the girl! She's been eyein' you up all day.'

'Really?'

Bock's youthful forehead creased. 'You better watch it, though. Ala's mighty protective of her. Gotta make nice with the subofficer before she'll let you go after Dancer.'

'I believe Callista can make her own choices about who goes after her,' Sandsa said.

'Good luck, then,' Bock said then danced off.

Sandsa refocused on the booth on the other side of the dance floor and listened carefully to what the grains of sand were reporting back to him. His eyes never left the two women.

***

'Come on — there're plenty of douchenozzles here that'd want to dance with you,' Ala said, tapping the table with her stubby crimson nails. 'And I don't mean the one you insisted on inducting into our ways just so ya could bed him.'

'Bed...!' Callista cut herself off and hunkered down further in the seat. 'I can't dance, Ala. I'll look...foolish. Stupid. Idiotic.'

Ala snorted. 'I know how to use those dictionary apps, too, Cals. Coward. Virgin. Smitten. Anyhow, handsome one like him? He'll know how to treat a gal right. So don't worry. He'll make it nice for you.'

'What, the dancing?' Callista asked with a roll of her eyes.

'Dancing. Making love. Take your pick. As for me, I have a room of people to see.' Ala stood up and slapped the table, making Callista jump. 'Now dance!'

'No!'

'Might as well go back to your rich folk parents if you're gonna keep playin' it safe,' Ala said before disappearing into the throng.

Callista dropped her head into her hands. Her shoulders stiffened a moment later when she felt *his* presence draw near.

'Anyone sitting here?' Bolt asked, his soft words reaching her despite the heavy bass of the music pilfering everyone else's words from the air.

'Only dancephobes,' Callista said, watching as Bolt slid in beside her.

Their knees touched and she drew a startled breath. Then he leaned over, his blue gaze intense. Callista turned her cheek towards him, but he didn't try to kiss her. She felt oddly disappointed.

He smiled. 'Did you want me to kiss you?'

'You already saw into my thoughts, you should know,' she muttered.

'I do know. But I did not want to assume you were comfortable with it actually occurring.'

'This isn't fair,' Callista said after a moment. 'Why can't I see what you're thinking?'

'I shield myself well.' He pursed his lips. 'How much can you do with your powers?'

'We're really going to talk about this now?'

She heard a voice in her mind, one that unmistakably belonged to him. *We could dance instead.*

'Bolt, I look like an idiot on the dance floor. I don't dance for my clanspeople or for my subofficer — what makes you think I'll dance for you?'

Perhaps we can be idiots on the dance floor together? he suggested.

The inane laughter burst from her before she could stop it, but Callista saw his answering smirk and relaxed.

She held out her hand. He took it. They rose at the same time, their fingers linked, and entered the dance floor. Callista didn't even know what tempo was thrumming around them; she moved to the beating of her heart — and the beating of his. She skimmed her hand up into his mane of hair and tugged gently, eliciting a smile from him. When her other hand took residence on his cheek, he leaned into her touch like a cat, rubbing his face over her palm. Emboldened, she swiftly looped her arms around him, bringing him flush against her.

Those blue eyes widened and she felt his response — not in her mind, but lower down, pressing into her abdomen. She was surprised to see the ensuing confusion bleed into his eyes but said nothing, allowing him to ease her head onto his shoulder. Time blurred and slowed around them. She could have fallen asleep there, safe beneath his watchful gaze, encircled by his arms.

The song wound down. Callista tipped her head back as he stroked her hair, coaxing out the elastic tie and letting the brown strands fall over her face. Around them, people began to stomp and clap along to some popular tune. The tie dropped to the ground, forgotten.

'Aren't you going to kiss me?' she asked, trying to ignore the sly looks her fellow clanspeople were sending in her direction.

Bolt stared at her.

'Is that wise?' he fumbled.

Callista laughed and shook her head. But still she swooped in and planted her lips on his. It was a gentle and unassuming kiss but she felt the heat rapidly rising inside them both. She retreated, wet her lips, then dove in again. He acquiesced readily and she savoured the taste of him.

He drew back, frowning. 'Is it always so...so...?'

She hesitated. 'I don't know.'

'Do you want to get out of here?' he asked with a furtive look at the door.

She most definitely did. Callista snagged his hand and led

him outside onto the streets then through the city, until they found themselves on the outskirts of Atsa, the road so smeared by sand that it looked as though there were merely splashes of crumbling tar beneath the invading desert. Here the concrete wall that defended Atsa against the wild winds was almost completely gone, exposing the road to the endless dunes.

Callista watched Bolt, admiring the shadows playing over his handsome and very, very real features. His gaze was hot and desirous as he pulled her back into a kiss, their feet disturbing the sand — no, they were hovering above the ground and the sand was leaping up towards them, to bury them, to encompass them. Callista knew she should have been afraid, but he was with her, protecting her. She darted her tongue against his lips.

'Callista,' he gasped and their boots touched the ground.

She couldn't help the tremble in her voice. 'Bolt, do I...do I kiss better than anyone you've known?'

'You should know that I saved my first kiss for the woman who plagued my dreams,' he told her softly and she shivered when his warm hand strayed inside her jacket, his fingers brushing against the swell of her chest.

'Seriously?' she asked.

The corners of his lips dimpled slightly. 'Did you not also save your first kiss for me?'

Callista laughed. 'Of course I did. I don't know how long I waited, but I did. And now you're here.'

Bolt leaned in for another kiss but she planted her hands on his chest and pushed him away.

'I don't...really know you,' she reminded him.

He blinked. 'But we met before this, before our dreams were

made real. And the kissing...well, that's what we're meant to do now that we're together, is it not?'

Shaking her head, Callista took his fingertips to her temple. At her invitation, he delved into her mind, like the gentle drift of sand over time, and saw how absurd it all was through her eyes. That first kiss. Was it fate — or was it due to the pressure of her clan watching?

'I am equally unsure how to proceed,' he said at length, stroking her back. She had returned to his embrace and was now leaning her ear against his steadying heartbeat. 'I wish to see more of you, to get to know you. I...I assumed kissing was part of that.'

'It probably is,' Callista said and tightened her hold on him. 'But we'll take it slow. And I have conditions.'

Bolt glanced down at her. 'Conditions?'

She lifted her chin to meet his gaze. 'Yes. You're going to teach me everything about my powers. In return, I'll teach you what you need to know to survive on Atsa's streets. Anyone in this city is just as likely to get you as the Alcazaar and your fancy healing power doesn't work on yourself.'

'How did you know that?'

'I felt it.' She shrugged. 'So. Are we agreed, Bolt?'

The swirl of his thoughts went in a predictable direction.

Callista arched an eyebrow. 'No. I won't hear your name. That's not part of this deal.'

His mind was open, and hopeful.

'Maybe, one day,' she murmured and willed the night to last forever.

CHAPTER SEVEN

The lasgun blatted in her direction but Callista was already dodging the bolt before the owner of the weapon fired it. She expelled the air from her tight lungs and replaced it with a breath that fuelled the laugh she tossed towards her opposition. For a brief moment she went blind, then found herself watching the Primus gang member adjust their aim, their weapon moving sluggishly as though sliding through syrup — it was so easy now, to call down visions in the heat of the moment. Anticipating where he'd shoot next, she ducked, straightened, then blasted him straight in the gut.

Her shoulder ached as her arm suddenly shot out perpendicular to her torso. Callista flung her gaze down past her elbow and her eyes widened as she took in the lasbolt hovering in front of her palm. She slapped her hand down to the pavement; the bolt followed. Breathing hard, Callista wasted precious seconds staring. Chippers needed time to build up forcefields strong enough to move objects. All she'd done was think a split-second command at the lasbolt.

Not willing to trust her safety to a power she'd barely started learning how to use, she knelt to scoop up the personal shielding device she had dropped and glanced around at her fellow Maria as they fell into a protective ring with her at its centre. Rolling her eyes at their assumption that she was in any way important,

Callista forced her way to the edge of the ring just as the one surviving light in the alley weakened, then putted out.

Lasbolts thundered down the street, striking shields and concrete. Callista bellowed a challenge as she broke free from the group and surged forward. A foreign spike of worry suddenly stabbed at her and she hesitated for a costly moment, feeling Bolt slide along the edges of her mind.

Someone shouted.

Callista swung her small shield up and cursed, narrowly missing being shot in the head.

Quit distracting me! she sent to Bolt.

She sprang up and ran full tilt towards the barricade of smoking hovercars that the Primus had set up across the street. She did not need to look back to know she was being supported by her clan; she felt them, just as she felt her dream man. Bolt's presence was so strong it was as if he stood beside her, his hand on her shoulder.

Mere days ago it would have startled her to sense his energy this far across the city, right near the hoverbike bar that the Primus used as their headquarters, but now she found herself expecting it. Over the past fortnight, the happiest two weeks of her life, Callista had grown used to feeling him and speaking to him inside her mind. She and Bolt had spent their days almost exclusively together, trading knowledge and kisses.

But right now, as she barrelled through a gap between two trashed vehicles, following her shield and lasgun, she had no time for her memories or for him.

I could help... Bolt said.

Ala has barred you from any missions until you're ready — and you really shouldn't expose your powers just to bail me out of a small skirmish! she scolded him.

Outwardly, Callista was grinning. She'd just come across two startled Primus clanspeople.

The hot edge of her shield scored the chin of one; her lasgun drove a bolt through the other's skull. She then transferred her weapon to her left hand to finish off the first man as the Maria poured out from behind her. While her companions killed those remaining on the street, Callista stood in front of the bar, shaking her head. The dingy windows were boarded up with thin slabs of wood, a flimsy material that would never stand up to a barrage of lasgun bolts.

Their headquarters don't look particularly secure, Bolt commented.

'It'll be easy wipe them out,' Callista said and threw a look at Matron who was now beside her. 'You going to stop me or help me?'

Matron straightened, her lasgun resting on her hip like a tired child. 'Not gonna stop you. But I sure as stark won't be running in and getting us all killed. I'm the one in charge so I'm the one who gets the heat, you know.'

Callista gritted her teeth. She should listen to Matron, but here was a chance to eradicate an enemy for good.

'Fine, but you can't stop people coming in with me if they want to,' Callista said. Matron opened her mouth, but Callista was already bellowing to the others, 'We can destroy these fuckers right now — and we've got 'em cornered! So who's with me?'

The Maria cheered in response and followed her, lasguns held high. Callista didn't bother looking back to see if Matron was among them.

There was no resistance from the hoverbike racers in the bar. Unwilling to reach for their lasguns, they parked themselves beside tall glasses of something so vile and thick it might have been globbed into the drinking vessels instead of being poured. Some racers raised their hands in surrender; others pointed out Primus clanspeople hiding behind the tables. The Primus were then brought kicking and screaming into the centre of the bar, their death throes lit by ghoulish green lighting that made them appear to be the victims of some terrible ague.

Only when the bar was clear of Primus did Matron enter. Callista averted her eyes from the appointed leader of the mission and watched the bartender offer drinks to his new management. She was unable to shake off the unease tickling the hairs on the nape of her neck.

'The Alcazaar are going to want blood for this,' Callista muttered.

'You still on about the Alcazaar usin' them as muscle?' Matron asked, stalking over to hold out a glass to Callista. 'Give it a rest. If the Alcazaar really wanted us gone, they wouldn't bother wasting coin-chips to pay some other clan to fight us. They'd take us out from the inside. Much cheaper.'

Waving a hand to decline the drink, Callista kept her voice casual to avoid inciting an argument. 'Just trust me. I feel that I'm right.'

'I need more than feelings, Dancer. So does Ala.'

Callista winced. Was she now so used to someone finally understanding and accepting her that she was becoming careless? She settled for a shrug. 'I suppose we'll find out after the Alcazaar discover this mess.'

***

Sandsa knelt on the floor beside his bed and rested his elbows on the blanket, pressing his palms together as though in prayer, just as he had seen so many souls do in his deserts and in the domains of his brothers and sisters. He could have killed any of the Primus clanspeople who had threatened Callista's life, but she had sensed his desire to interfere and had talked him out of it. How could he continue to hide his abilities if it meant that she could get hurt?

He had enjoyed their days together but wondered how much patience he needed to burn through. He was acutely aware that while he had aeons to become an expert on Atsa's intricate gang politics, Callista had perhaps lived a fifth of her life already — could she really afford to waste her time like this? But he didn't push. He wanted her trust. He would need it for...for when he revealed his true identity. On the rare occasion that she thought about the gods, her mind was filled with a mixture of scorn and disbelief.

Last night he had woken in a panic, reaching for his mother as she succumbed to the ravages of time and crumbled to ash, murdered by her mortality. The images haunted him even now, searing across his vision until he was blind, his eyelids flapping uselessly. He could not call his mother's face to mind. All he saw was Callista, a mortal, withering away in his arms. He had to save her.

He collapsed into a puddle of sand that then disintegrated.

'Father!' Sandsa shouted at the edge of the desert, loath to venture further from Atsa City, his booted feet planted solidly on the last patch of concrete unsullied by sand. 'Father! I must ask something of you!'

He waited for over an hour, carefully keeping track of Callista to ensure that she did not return to find him missing. Eventually, the Ine arrived and offered to walk along the dunes with his son. Sandsa refused him, his fear tasting like bile on his tongue as he looked out at the desert.

'You are afraid that the moment you return to your domain, you will be forced to leave her behind,' his father said from several paces away, where his bare feet touched sand. 'That fear is nothing compared to what your people are feeling. They wait for you, they cry out for you, and they still try to bind themselves to each other in your name, though even their least gifted know you have abandoned them.'

'I wish to bind myself to a woman,' Sandsa said through his teeth. 'I deserve to have that option just as my people did.'

The binding process involved the mingling of spilled blood from two people, bringing them together forever; Sandsa had allowed his people to use the Magic they had within them to achieve it. After the ceremony, they carried identical scars on their palms for the rest of their lives, to show their loyalty to one another. It was how the Ine had bound himself to his human wife, so long ago. His immortal blood, after mixing with hers, had ensured her longevity. Of course, when the scars were taken from her, she had been condemned to death.

'I must ask you something,' Sandsa began, then hesitated, almost too afraid to know.

His father answered the question he had left unspoken. 'Yes. Your immortality would pass to her if you used the binding.' The Ine surged forward and grabbed Sandsa's shoulders. 'My son! Listen! You cannot cut yourself off from your people for too long or it will pain you in ways you cannot imagine —'

Sandsa clenched his fists. 'I don't want to be their god! And you made a mistake, telling me this. Now I know I will never lose her to death.'

He turned to go, but a whisper of hot wind, sent from the other side of the planet where the star still burned, touched his cheek. Sandsa drew in a breath. His heart ached. To roam the sands again, to guide his people, to whisper in their ears...

'I want nothing but her,' he said and retreated to the solace of his room. He lay on the bed, listening to the steady drip, drip, drip of a leak within the walls. His heartbeat evened out to this sound as he waited for Callista to return.

But still he heard the muted, desperate pleas from afar. His skin grew slick with sweat. Gasping, Sandsa threw himself out of his room and into the large shared bathroom, tearing off his clothes so he could sit in the corner of the showers, icy water streaming over his head, plugging his ears and washing away the creeping guilt that threatened to take hold of him.

***

Raucous cheering greeted the heroes of the night but Callista refused to be drawn into the revelry. Her eyes darted around the lounge room, scanning for one target. Finding him missing, she pinched the sleeve of Bock's jacket and asked, 'Did Ala forbid Bolt from joining the party tonight?'

The teenager would know. Bolt had been spending his idle hours in the armoury, where Bock seemed to live permanently. The pair were often caught discussing which weapon Ala would let Bolt use — if she ever granted him permission to carry a firearm.

'Nah, but I think he knows he's not her favourite clansman,' Bock replied, grinning. 'That's me, obviously, ain't it?'

Callista dropped his arm and ran up the stairs towards the sleeping quarters. When she cleared the last step, she slowed, blinking against the glare that assaulted her eyes. After a moment, her vision adjusted and she was confronted with the undulating rise and fall of barren sands that stretched into the horizon in front of her and — a panicked glance around confirmed her fears — behind her as well. The wind moaned, sounding deeper and more mournful than anything she'd ever heard in her life.

Tears leaked from her eyes but never made it to her desperate lips, now chapped from the heat. A cord wrapped around her heart, leading her forward. Her legs felt distant and wooden, like uncontrollable stilts, causing her to sway.

And then she found him, sheltered between two dunes. He was crushed, deflated, his body surrendered to the ravages of the desert. But when he looked up, his blue eyes were a bright oasis, lit with hope.

You found me...

The scene melted away. Callista started when she found herself in the male bathroom, an icy spray moistening her skin. She held out her hand to help Bolt up from the floor of the showers, then blushed when he accepted, his nakedness suddenly evident. Callista tossed a towel at him.

'Do you miss it?' she asked, turning her back in his direction.

'You mean the deserts?'

'What else?'

Bolt's hands curved over her shoulders and his lips grazed her neck on their journey over to one ear. Callista closed her eyes, trying — and failing — to stifle the ensuing shivers.

I would miss you more, he said. *And there was only torment in the deserts for me. Only torment — until you found me in my dreams.*

Callista arched backwards, moulding herself along his chest. *I would miss you if went back there.*

So I will not go, he said.

He moved her jacket aside to kiss the shoulder left bare by her tank top and then turned her around to capture her lips. His taste was so wonderful, so enticing, and she followed him into his room where she curled up beside him on the bed. They sat silently in the dark, absorbing the warmth of each other. After a while, Callista said, 'My powers are growing. Did you see what I did tonight?'

He nodded. 'I did. But I wonder if you can replicate that when adrenaline is not strengthening your focus. We will find out tomorrow.'

Eventually she grew tired and, waving off his offer of help, staggered into her own bed, divided from him by several walls. She sipped some coffein to keep awake, but soon found herself drifting into his subconscious. Bolt's mind was full of sand gently dancing against his skin.

It soothed him in a way she never could.

CHAPTER EIGHT

'The gangs are also known as clans,' Sandsa repeated, earning himself a kiss. 'Each clan has subofficers but only one clan is allowed a true leader — the Clan Leader. That does not seem fair. The desert tribes all have their own leaders to help them defend themselves. The gangs in Atsa are doomed to remain disorganised.'

'The system is meant to keep whoever's at the top, at the top,' Callista explained.

She was lying back against his pillow while he was seated at the very end of his bed. He found the view of her dark shirt creeping up her navel to be reward enough for losing most of the space to her. Her cotton pants hung low on her hips, but she seemed to be making sure that they gave no more ground in either direction. Sandsa regretted his own attire. His sleeveless shirt, which contained the Maria symbol, caused him no problems. But the leather pants Bock had pressured him into selecting from a storage closet full of stolen clothing were tight and pulled uncomfortably across a piece of his anatomy he had never considered an issue before.

'So if you do manage to knock out the reigning clan, you deserve to take over,' Callista went on. 'And why do you keep bringing up the deserts? I thought you said you'd given them up for something...better?'

She added a slow, salacious wink at the end of her sentence.

Sandsa wished he could have responded to her with something more comforting than a pained smile. He had felt her in his dreams again the night before; she had stood on the crest of a dune, watching and judging him as he walked in circles, never finding what he sought.

'What is it the Maria do, then, if they do not rule the streets?' Sandsa asked.

Callista snorted and started wriggling her feet against his side. 'Do you think we fight just for the glory of it?'

'Please do enlighten me,' he invited, capturing a foot with his hands and easing the boot off so that he could begin a teasing massage that deepened as her sighs became less indignant and more appreciative.

'The Alcazaar are the worst of the bunch,' Callista told him, her previous humour leaching from her beautiful features. 'If it wasn't for the unwritten rules — you know, don't kill civilians, no fighting in the No-Go Zone, stop fighting when it gets light — they'd hurt people. Innocent people. And one day they might be powerful enough to break those rules without fear of the governor or the Chippers.'

Sandsa pressed his lips together for a moment. 'You said the Alcazaar have been the reigning clan for fifty years, ever since they triumphed over the Maria. Is our clan only interested in regaining old prestige or do they actually intend to protect the people of Atsa?'

'Can't it be both?' she asked, jerking her foot out of his grasp.

'I suppose it can,' Sandsa conceded, stowing his hands on his lap. 'Alright. Why do the clans fight each other when they could band together to depose the Alcazaar?'

'Would you share that much power with someone else?'

He thought of standing on multiple dunes across the galaxy, his great tornadoes ripping sand from the ground and up towards the sky — and she would be beside him, her fingers wound around his, enjoying the magnificence of the deserts.

'Depends,' Sandsa said.

'The clans have fought each other for centuries; they're not going to stop and make nice now,' Callista said and pressed her lips to his.

He returned her kiss with fervour, exploring her mouth, indulging in her sweetness. Sandsa bucked when one of her hands delivered a sly slap to his backside.

'Taking liberties, are we?' Sandsa asked. He hiked her shirt over her stomach, raised one eyebrow and then dove in to deliver a raspberry to her bellybutton.

Callista tore away from him, shrieking with laughter. 'Enough! I surrender!'

'Hmm, so I have learned today, from my wise and learned teacher, that the Maria may be defeated entirely by the application of one's lips and breath upon their stomachs,' Sandsa said, tapping his chin with two fingers.

Callista snorted. 'Defeated? I think not!'

She tackled him back down onto the bed and straddled him. Sandsa had no wish to move or retaliate because he was enjoying the sparkle in her brown eyes and the rise of her breasts when she arched her back just so. He had seen much flesh as a god in the desert but it had never interested him. Now, though, he wanted to lift her shirt higher, to the globes that awaited his view, his hands...

Callista was kissing him again, her fingers pincered over his wrists, and he lost himself to the sensation of her hips grinding against his.

But then she suddenly stopped.

Sandsa made a noise of protest.

'Your turn to be the teacher,' Callista said, grinning as she retreated to the other side of the bed.

'I disagree — I don't think we're done,' Sandsa retorted.

She laughed. 'Oh, really?'

But Callista made no move to escape him when Sandsa crept up to her and delivered a deep, languid kiss. Her hand was cool against his skin as it slid along his bared stomach before raking over the dusting of hair on his chest. He had never given much thought to his nipples until they were tweaked and tickled in a fashion that seemed designed to drive him mad. He disposed of the shirt. It was a hindrance.

She bore him down and he fell backwards slowly, as though passing through sand, then surrendered to her. Her lips were now travelling down his jaw to plant open-mouthed kisses on his bare shoulder. Sandsa watched as her wet caresses dropped further still to touch a nipple.

'Callista,' he gasped.

Her teeth grazed the tender nub before she latched onto it. Desperate for something he couldn't define, he sat up and tugged her shirt over her head. The tie fell out of her hair and her brunette tresses sailed over her chin, briefly shielding the mischievous grin she threw at him. The tight grey band on her chest did nothing to hide the hardening peaks beneath the fabric. Sandsa caught her gaze and she froze, uncertainty gripping her thoughts.

Gently, he coaxed his way up her abdomen with soft, chaste

kisses, pausing only to dip his tongue into her navel. His lips reached the edge of the cloth that kept her breasts from his mouth.

'Sandsa,' she whispered.

She stood abruptly and yanked her shirt back on, expression stony. Without another word, Callista turned and stalked outside. Sandsa started to follow her but then winced at the tightness of his pants; he *had* wondered how manoeuvrable they would be in combat. Now he knew he needed something more flexible — especially if he intended to explore more of Callista.

Sandsa calmed his ragged breathing and hurried out of his room. She wasn't in the corridor. But Subofficer Ala was. The leader of the Maria leaned against the wall, one foot propped up behind her and a mug in her hand. Sandsa stilled. If Ala had been drinking spirits instead of coffein, he might have found her in a more pleasant mood.

'What happened?' she demanded.

Sandsa frowned. He had bared himself to Callista, his mind so terribly exposed that she could have glimpsed his origins. But she had only seen...

'She found out my name,' Sandsa realised.

Ala's one good eye narrowed. In her he read protectiveness for Callista and anyone else she deemed unable to defend themselves in war or in matters of the heart. Sandsa shrugged and added a small smile, hoping that would settle the matter.

'You've gotta be careful with her,' Ala told him. 'She's not been with a man yet. She'll be clingy enough without the sex.'

'I...I was not trying to...'

Sandsa wondered if his wrestling with Callista a few minutes beforehand had been a prelude to that. He hadn't been thinking about sex. He had merely wanted to divest Callista of those annoying clothes so that he could see all of her, touch all of her...

Ala snorted in a sceptical fashion. Sandsa was appalled to feel his cheeks grow hot. How could she read his thoughts, lacking any powers as she was?

'If you hurt her in any way, I'll put a bolt between your eyes, *Bolt*,' she cautioned him.

'I doubt you could kill me,' Sandsa remarked. 'But you needn't worry. Hurting Callista would only hurt me.'

'Alright,' Ala said, apparently reaching a decision. 'Report downstairs to the armoury. Keep Bock out of trouble and get a piece for yourself while you're there.'

Sandsa started moving past Ala, then paused to glance over his shoulder. 'I suppose you would not believe me if I said I was just as inexperienced in these matters as Callista.'

Ala's cheeks tightened. 'Right now I only care about your experience with shootin' things. Now go get a lasgun.'

***

Callista dodged the lasbolt an instant before it was fired right at the back of her neck. She dropped ahead of the one that would have hit much higher — and blown out a piece of her skull through her forehead had it been on a more potent setting. Whipping around, she lashed out with her hand. The third red bolt paused in front of her palm, as though considering its next course of action. Callista glowered at it, mentally threatening the lasbolt with a list of obscene words.

Then it hammered into her hand and she fell awkwardly onto her side, grunting as her joints connected with the hard floor of the training room. Ignoring the bruises and the pain accompanying them, Callista rolled over just in time to avoid another blast of energy.

She shot to her feet, eyeing the device as it hovered several paces away, readying its next low-powered shot. Callista closed her eyes, excluding herself from the stare down, and kept her arms pinned to her sides. The vision she summoned gave her three seconds to deflect the bolt with her powers. She only needed one.

She opened her eyes, taking in the scorch mark a full metre from her feet, and smiled, pleased that she could use her powers without lifting her hands like a Chipper.

And then she felt him.

Callista groaned and tapped the tiny communicator nestled in her right ear. 'Bock. Tell me Sa — Bolt isn't with you. I came down here to get away from him.'

'Hey, Ala sent him down — just bad timing, I guess,' Bock's voice chirped back at her. 'What'd ya do to my drone? I'm gettin' all sorts of weird error messages.'

'Maybe it glitched, Bock.'

'I only just stole it the other week!'

Another voice ghosted into her ear through the device. 'You are improving, Callista.'

Callista threw her earpiece to the floor, left the training room and walked over to the lasgun target range to see Bock tempting Sandsa with the higher powered (and much less precise) weapons that Maria boys seemed to enjoy using. Bock was wearing thick, dark sunglasses, no doubt a souvenir from the previous night when he had entered a battle he was always ill-prepared for: a drinking competition.

Sandsa's blue eyes were twinkling in her direction. Callista stifled her exasperated sigh.

Bock didn't seem to register the growing tension and kept prattling on. 'Now, you might want to get somethin' a little less showy, but I prefer the heavier stuff meself...'

'I think this weapon is more than adequate,' Sandsa said, indicating a small lasgun, much like the one Callista had selected as a replacement for herself a few days ago.

She smiled down at the floor.

'You any good with a lasgun?' Bock asked Sandsa.

'Never fired one,' Sandsa answered.

'Well, if you get the middle of this target first go, I'll shot meself,' Bock said, loading up an intermediate target.

Callista felt the ripples of power surrounding Sandsa as he strode up to the line marked on the floor. He lifted the weapon and loosed a lasbolt — off by a good three paces, but Sandsa used his powers to curve it towards the target until it punched a blistering hole into the centre. Child's play, Callista realised with unease. How long had he been using his gift? Who had taught him?

Bock lifted his sunglasses up onto his forehead, staring. 'Huh. And that's your first time?'

'Yes.'

'Try this one,' Bock said, arranging a much harder setting. This target sat behind bars of deflective lasers that weaved in multiple directions. 'I'll shoot meself for sure if you get it.'

Callista smothered a laugh. The kid — young man, she corrected herself — had no idea what he was getting into. As far as she knew, Bock had never honoured his bizarre bet. Sandsa lined up the shot. Took it. Got it.

'Holy Creator shit,' Bock breathed. 'Wanna try somethin' bigger?'

Whatever weapon Bock brought out for him, it took Sandsa barely a few tries to perfect it. This went on for a full hour until, finally, Bock stood back, admiring the belt he had strapped around Bolt. The thin strip of leather drooped under the weight of the various weapons Bock had given him. Callista suspected that Ala hadn't sanctioned quite so many.

'You're sure to be the next Clan Leader!' Bock declared.

'If someone else doesn't beat him to it,' Callista said and stormed away.

Simmering, she paced on the road outside the building, her eyes aching from the unexpected brightness of daylight. Water filled her vision which she told herself was from the glare. When Sandsa fell into step beside her, he said, 'I'm sorry. I feel...that it is something you wanted. To be Clan Leader. It's your dream.'

'No less stupid than my dream of leaving this rock to hit the asteroid mines,' Callista growled, turning around at one streetlight, far less mournful now than when it needed to chase the shadows of night away. 'I'm rich folk pretending to be a clansperson and they all know it. There's plenty here who are better than me. Even you — and you'll always be better than me at everything! These powers, these weapons...I just...I just wish I was at your level.' She sighed. 'I guess you've got a better chance at becoming Clan Leader.'

She stopped walking and buried her face in his chest, willing away her dark thoughts. Sandsa embraced her, saying softly, 'Not all dreams are stupid. And we don't need to stay in Atsa. We can go anywhere. Any planet.' He chuckled. 'Any asteroid. You name it.'

Callista said nothing, merely tightened her hold on him.

***

Now as silent as Callista, Sandsa took her hands in his, turning them over to study her bare palms. If he wanted to spend his life with her, he needed to mark her with the binding scars and soon. But how soon? Sandsa felt something for Callista, but he wasn't sure it was enough to last eternity or if she would ever return his feelings. He tried to peer ahead, to look into her future, and was disturbed to find he was unable to do so. His own future was similarly impossible to see.

Sandsa pressed his lips to her forehead, concealing his uncertain frown.

CHAPTER NINE

Deep, thrumming bass began at the pavement beneath his boots before filtering up through his bones. The sensation was not unlike what he felt when he activated his powers. Sandsa was no stranger to the sounds that belched from nightclubs now, having spent a night or two in the Bang Bang.

Though Subofficer Ala now allowed him the privilege of leaving headquarters unescorted, she had yet to assign him his first mission. So until then Sandsa roamed the nights alone, keeping his mind focused on Callista in case she encountered trouble. He was grateful for the separation for two reasons. Firstly, he had begun to feel a fierce, burning need to explore the skin beneath her clothes, which he supposed was a natural part of being a man in the presence of a beautiful woman, but it was distracting and disturbing by equal measure. There was much more to Callista than her tempting curves. Secondly, she had asked yet again why it was that he had both a Chipper's abilities and the desert Magic.

Sandsa paused in front of the set of steps that led down into a nightclub he had not yet encountered. The concrete forming the stairs resembled collapsed cakes, so broken apart by time and pressure that it was hardly a safe journey down them. Sliding a finger over the sensor at the edge of his leather jacket, Sandsa watched as the item responded to his touch and sealed itself over the telltale Maria shirt he was wearing. Given that he had not yet been taken down here by Bock, it was not somewhere he should assume was safe simply because he was a clansman — rather the opposite.

He negotiated his way down the steps, a hand grasping the fusty grey railing that ran along one side. When he reached the lower platform, he lifted his fingers in front of his face, studying the grime painted over the lines of his skin. Sandsa dusted the residue over his pants (more malleable denim this time — he had learnt his lesson), leaving a smudge on the black fabric.

Several strings of beads swayed in the doorway, shivering with each beat. Sandsa cut his way through them — and then he found yet more stairs, though these were smoother which made up for their lack of railing. He was led on by the distorted thuds of a song that seemed to be entirely made of bass, though as he neared the bottom of the steps a screeching melody became more obvious. The music brought to mind the distant howls of desert winds, so beautiful and resounding — his chest ached.

He distracted himself from his thoughts by looking around the nightclub. It was smaller than he had expected and filled with crisscrossing lights that seemed to be constantly at war with each other, fleeing and pursuing, clashing and disintegrating. The floor was like an Old Earth chessboard with its black and white squares, though the latter was lit up blue, and the clean, tight lines of the room were easily visible because it lacked bodies crammed into every space.

Once Sandsa's foot hit the floor, the music faded to nothing. The speakers grew still; no vibrations pounded out of them. After an excruciating silence, a mournful wailing dribbled out onto the floor, sending the couple who had been dancing straight for the bar.

'Stark that kid's playlist!' the bartender said. He leapt over the curved white counter and raced up to a machine perched on a platform above the dance floor, then fiddled with some knobs until the grinding, mindless rhythm returned.

The bartender lumbered back towards the bar, where his only two patrons had decided that a lack of service was the epitaph on the nightclub's gravestone. He watched them leave, his lips sealing together. Then he flashed a toothy grin at Sandsa and gestured to a stool. Sandsa sat with him for a time, watching the empty floor, before turning his attention to his companion. The bartender had dark, weathered skin, and the palm that scrubbed at his generous chin bore the scar of a man bound to his wife in the desert ways.

'Shouldn't've trusted my son with the playlist,' the bartender said, sounding rueful. 'He acts like carrying a lasgun means he can do anything! He's just too much like his city-born mother and he doesn't have a drop of the Magic in him. You know how it is, these people with their powerless ways.' He levelled his charcoal gaze at Sandsa. 'I can feel the Magic in you too.'

Sandsa started. He had reined in his Chipper-like powers to avoid detection from members of GLEA, because if they were able to sense other lifesigns and sometimes even his father, they would certainly be able to feel him. But it had not occurred to him that he would encounter his...his former people, nor that he would need to hide his identity from them.

'Warm greetings, brother of the sands,' Sandsa said, clasping the bartender's forearm as the custom dictated.

'Warm greetings, brother,' his companion returned.

That done, the bartender unhooked the strange padded orange vest he was wearing, revealing a grey shirt. Over the chest pocket a symbol of a spear was crudely drawn in black marker.

Catching Sandsa's gaze, the man patted his pocket. 'I'm Vom, from the Zatzat gang. There's a bunch of us desert folk from the Zatzat tribe — not from this planet, if you're wondering — who moved to this dust bowl so it seemed right to make our own clan. Where are you from?' He nodded at the lasgun on Sandsa's hip. 'Expensive piece.'

Sandsa could not recall Callista mentioning the Zatzat, nor indeed the names of any of the smaller clans. Her lessons seemed to be based exclusively on the Alcazaar. Sandsa shrugged. 'Bolt. I am sworn into the Maria, though I suppose I am not fully one of them until I undergo my first mission. Is this going to be a problem? I know so very little about other gangs.'

'Don't care, so long as you're not Alcazaar,' Vom replied. 'Do you want a job? I'm in need of a DJ, if you can't tell.'

Sandsa slipped his hands into his empty jacket pockets. 'Perhaps. I am not particularly busy. I do have a question, however.'

'Shoot. Well, not literally.'

Sandsa's laugh sounded alien to his own ears but mercifully the loud music swallowed it. 'Why is it you left the deserts?'

Vom leaned back onto the counter, his elbows supporting him. 'And miss out on all the money I make with this booming business of mine?' He chuckled. 'Look, I get that the Desine created me and gave me a little bit of the Magic so I can make grains of sand dance across the floor — watch — ' He demonstrated with a comically low-key display. 'I feel bad about leaving. A lot of us do. But it just wasn't...it wasn't our place. Our ancestors chose the desert god so he gave them the powers to survive the sands and get on with each other — well, they fight as much as they talk, but let's ignore that. Anyway, I didn't choose the god. I chose the cities.'

Sandsa nodded along with this tirade. 'There is nothing out there, nothing worth staying for.'

'The Magic causes me enough trouble here — might've avoided some awkward questions when the Chippers came by one night,' Vom said, his arms dropping to his sides. 'They're not so keen on sub-level gods and Desine-gifted powers, as you can imagine.'

'I thought GLEA's refusal to pay any medical bills for injuries incurred at night kept them unavoidably detained until daybreak?' Sandsa mused, remembering what Callista had told him.

Vom's expression was grim. 'Doesn't stop some of them. At least they pay for their drinks. Anyway, you want the job? All you have to do is see if the crowd is enjoying the tune and keep the jive going.'

'I am not sure I need money — I have all I want,' Sandsa said, thinking of Callista. He felt her mind reach out for his, her interest piqued by his strong feelings for her. *I am merely entranced by the thought of you — it may happen hourly, my Callista, so you can ignore it.*

I am not your anything, she responded, though her ensuing mental smirk eased the snap of her words. *Yet.*

A smile spread rapidly over Vom's face. 'Ah, in love are you? City girls aren't so keen on disfiguring themselves for marriage.' He raised his palms, exposing the binding scars fully. 'My wife didn't agree to go through with it until I gave her a ring with a rock.'

'And the rock made her want to marry you?' Sandsa pressed.

'Is that how one progresses in a relationship? Does the love follow?'

'What! You shouldn't bind yourself to a woman if you don't know if you love her!' Vom burst out laughing.

'I don't really have experience in these matters,' Sandsa muttered.

After slapping a hand on Sandsa's shoulder repeatedly, Vom calmed down enough to say with a straight face, 'Just because it feels like it's meant to be doesn't mean you can skip all the hard work of getting to know each other.'

'Are you only assisting me because we share desert powers?' Sandsa asked, frowning.

'We've got to stick together in this wretched place,' Vom said with a shrug, not denying it. 'Also it pays to have a friend in the Maria. They have the best chance of knocking out the Alcazaar and I wouldn't mind me some clout with your clan if that does happen!'

There was a sudden outpouring of thick steam from a machine in the corner. Sandsa glanced at Vom who waved a dismissive hand. 'Smoke machine. Dancers love it. It smells starking awful, by the Desine. Say, you can't get your Maria folk in here can you?'

'I know a few who might be interested.'

***

'Ala won't appreciate you doin' this,' Matron warned, flattening her back against the opposite wall of the lounge room as though to keep as far away as possible from Bock and his 'project'.

The teenager dug through the hole he'd blasted into the wall, pulling out a variety of cables. Calling for a technician was out of the question — Callista supposed they could have kidnapped one, but Bock had assured them he knew how to install their new acquisition. The vidscreen in question chose that moment to flicker into life. White noise buzzed its way through the room and pinpricks of white and black warred with each other on the surface of the device. The distortion reluctantly gave way to a map of the city after Bock thrust a data stick into the side of the vidscreen.

'Subofficer Ala should not have gone out with the rest of our clan tonight and left us here with nothing better to do,' Callista retorted, setting her cup of coffein on a nearby table.

Matron shook her head. 'Don't know why she left you in charge of headquarters instead of me. Misplaced trust, I reckon.'

'Ala knows I'm good for it,' Callista said, narrowing her eyes. She had liked Matron for years, though it seemed lately no matter what she did the clanswoman had nothing to offer but criticism. Callista focused back on the screen. 'Are you done yet, Bock?'

'You've been getting too big of a head ever since you left your parents' house,' Matron went on. 'We only got one subofficer left and I bet you're waiting for that promotion, grunt. Any day now, huh?'

Callista aimed a glare over her shoulder at the woman. 'Matron. If Ala thought I was subofficer material, why hasn't she said something?'

'Worried I'll beat you to it, are ya?' Matron asked with a grin. 'Don't bother yourself about it, Dancer. Not worth my time being a subofficer when we're losing anyway.'

'We are *not* losing. Once Ala sees how useful Bolt — '

'Ala don't trust Bolt yet,' Bock piped up. 'Says she'll kill him if he hurts you. Don't know why she hasn't taken his lasgun off him to stop him hurtin' you in the first place.'

Despite herself, Callista smiled. 'Bock, I don't think that's what she meant.'

'So why don't she trust him?' the boy asked and crossed his arms, the bright screen turning him into a dark silhouette.

'Dancer here might be so caught up in it all, this first love stuff, that she'll do anythin' that Bolt tells her to do,' Matron said with a sneer. 'Stuff like not interrogating him properly when he first joined us, or standing by and letting him kill our only subofficer. He could be a spy.'

Bock snorted. 'Bullshit. Bolt could kill Ala just fine even if Dancer tried to stop him. Have ya seen the man shoot?'

'He that good?' Matron asked, her forehead creasing.

The teenager used a few expletives to attest to Bolt's skill with a lasgun.

Matron shrugged. 'Could be Ala's jealous.'

'Of Bolt?' Callista asked, biting off a laugh.

Bock sounded dismayed. 'Nah, don't tell me Ala's into Callista. I've no chance if she don't like men.'

'You might still be in luck 'cause you're no man,' Matron jeered.

Rolling her eyes, Callista walked over to Bock and patted his shoulder. 'Ala likes women and men both, so you can relax. And she always speaks so candidly to me about her experiences that I doubt she sees me as anything more than a friend. Or a comrade.'

Matron opened her mouth but Callista held up her hand, forestalling further comment. 'That's enough. Or I'll tell Ala you think she's jealous. I'm sure she'll *love* hearing that.'

When Matron said nothing more, Callista poked a finger at

the map on the screen and drew a line along the street that led her to where she had fought the Primus during two separate skirmishes. One of the locations lay directly in the No-Go Zone; the other place, in Newheim South, was closer to Alcazaar territory than the old Primus headquarters. She drew a circle around the second location then dropped her hand from the screen. There was no way she could make any of the others believe her theory about the now defunct Primus working with the Alcazaar, especially with these red squiggly lines that were already descending into static. Did it even matter now anyway?

Bock's tongue slipped out of the corner of his mouth as he added in a few zigzags of his own, these ones worryingly close to the planet's only Chipper outpost. 'So this is where our lot went tonight.'

'Why didn't you go with them?' Callista asked, spinning around to address Matron. 'Ala told me it was you who figured out that the Miniatta were the clan the surviving Primus ran off to.'

'Wanted a break from the fightin',' Matron said, her gaze falling to the floor. 'It's hard counting all of you up and then counting fewer when ya get back in.'

Guilt lanced through Callista's heart. She had been with the gang for just three years; Matron had served much longer, and had seen many more of her clanspeople die. Callista would have let it go if she hadn't caught a flash of something in Matron's unguarded thoughts.

Callista nibbled the tip of her tongue. Before now, she would have assumed that what she'd felt from Matron was true concern for the safety of others. But Callista had recently learned how to use her powers with greater accuracy...and this concern was about something else.

Matron's hand lay over her lasgun and had for the past few minutes. The skin around her eyes crinkled gently, like always, but her cheeks were tight with tension. Callista tipped her head to the side, her vision growing dark as she delved deeper into the thoughts unravelling before her. In Matron's mind, the woman saw herself wearing a gang logo, but it wasn't the triangle of the Maria. Instead, Matron's shirt sported four blue dots in a line, a symbol that had been favoured by the...

'Primus,' Callista whispered.

'Yeah, we'll get the rest of 'em tonight,' Bock said, completely focused on the screen.

Callista swallowed. Matron was waiting for them to look away from her so she could shoot them without any resistance. Mentioning this out loud would yield no result, because Matron wouldn't dare try anything if they were ready for her. There would be no proof of the woman's intentions. But if Callista gave her an opening...

The hairs on the back of Callista's neck prickled as she deliberately turned away, exposing her back to a woman who had very conveniently positioned herself against a wall to ensure no one could get behind her.

Callista felt rather than heard Matron make her move. Whirling to face the threat, she sent out a hands-free blast with her powers and drew her lasgun at the same time. Matron's shot went wide, striking the wall beside her and gouging out plaster and concrete. Callista fired. Matron went down, grabbing her knee and howling, 'Stark you, Maria scum!'

'Holy Creator shit!' Bock exclaimed, spinning around. His eyes went wide.

'The Miniatta aren't sheltering the Primus, your real gang, are they?' Callista asked.

Matron scowled. 'You can't know that.'

'You're the last Primus,' Callista said, striding forward. She kicked the lasgun away from Matron's hand and pressed the butt of her own weapon against the woman's temple. 'Why be a subofficer for us losers when the Alcazaar have offered you the rank in return for taking us out from the inside?'

'Nice little story there, Dancer!' Matron said, the words hissing off her tongue like acid.

'The Alcazaar tried to *kill* you in the No-Go Zone!' Callista shot back at her. 'If I hadn't saved you, they'd have managed it. Why would you back them?'

Matron snorted. Though she said nothing, her thoughts were loud and clear to Callista. *They weren't aiming at me, you starking idiot. They knew I brought the Maria there for them.*

Callista considered arguing the point, but she didn't particularly want the woman to know about her powers. 'I trusted you, Matron. I thought you cared about us.'

'I'm gonna call Ala,' Bock said nervously. 'Don't want to be makin' enemies with the Miniatta for no reason.'

'Do it,' Callista said without taking her eyes off the traitor. 'So the counting. Was that to check our numbers so you could tell the Alcazaar how many of us were left each time?'

Matron stayed silent.

Callista bit into the side of her cheek, tasting blood. 'Your gang is gone. You should have just accepted the Maria as your own. What I don't get is why you tried to kill me of all people.'

'It's obvious,' Bock said.

'What?' Callista demanded.

The air beside her shifted as the teenager took up residence there. 'You're the next subofficer, if Ala has a thing or two to say about it.'

Callista took a moment to re-scour Matron's mind, then she jabbed the traitor with the toe of her boot. 'I'm the only chance the Maria would have to continue if Ala died — in your eyes anyway. I don't think Ala agrees or she'd have promoted me by now. You should be more worried about Bolt, you Primus piece of shit.'

'I'm saying nothin' more.' And with that Matron closed her eyes and tilted her head back, hands clasped on her ruined knee.

Callista pistol-whipped Matron, rendering the woman unconscious. She glanced up a moment later when she felt Bolt's presence, startled, because she wasn't sure how he'd managed to get back inside — the palm print reader on the front door still hadn't been taught his prints. And yet, there he was, standing in the doorway, unruffled by the frustration and hurt she poured back at him.

'So you couldn't let me handle this myself,' she accused him.

I was not responsible for deflecting that lasbolt and, poorly aimed as it was, I would only have needed to heal you to fix the matter, he said, his eyebrows lifting as he communicated silently with her. *And I have only just returned from my wanderings.*

Callista sighed and slid her arms around his waist, pressing her cheek to his shoulder.

Bock flew over to them. 'Ala's on her way back. No way are we hitting the Miniatta and starting somethin' with them for no reason. Holy Creator shit, Matron of all people!'

'The Alcazaar are feeling more and more threatened by us,' Callista said, extracting herself from Sandsa's embrace. 'We can't keep pretending they're just happy to sit there while we encroach on their territory.'

'And now they are using smaller gangs against you — do the Maria have the resources to fight several clans at once, the Miniatta included?' Sandsa asked.

Bock was already shaking his head. 'Come off it, you two. Matron was just a pissed off clanswoman who lost her mothership. Musta sucked to be spying all this time just to lose it all. Dunno why she didn't keep quiet and stay one of ours.'

'She attacked us because the Alcazaar asked her to,' Callista argued. 'Not because she'd lost her mind. Matron wasn't crazy.'

But Bock would have none of it and neither did Ala when she returned and brought the three of them into her study. Her red eye glowed in the dim light as she surveyed her clanspeople.

'I've heard the rumours, but we've been over this, Cals. There's no proof and we can't start suspectin' every clan on every corner — we can't fight all of 'em at once.' Ala rubbed her temples. 'And it doesn't matter anymore. Matron got a hold of a lasgun the moment I sent someone to check on her and shot herself. That's the end of our problems with the starking Primus.'

Callista crossed her arms. 'Fine. I have no proof. I still don't know why she thought I was important enough to take out.'

It never occurred to you to read Ala's thoughts the way you read Matron's? Sandsa asked. He was standing behind her chair, his hands on her shoulders.

Ala cleared her throat. 'You might have started out like rich folk but you have far more brain cells than the rest of my lot put together — even if you insist on throwing away good sense on this man.'

Callista felt Sandsa's amusement tweak her own lips.

'And if I'm honest, I should've done this earlier but I wasn't sure how dedicated you were gonna be when you were still living with those parents of yours,' Ala said, then paused to knock back her drink. She lifted her empty glass. 'Subofficer Dancer, how does that suit ya?'

'Oh, cool, we really need to celebrate,' Bock said, grinning.

Callista leaned over to push her young companion back into his chair before he could race off and start the party already brewing in his head. 'My first act as subofficer is to suggest that we send Bolt out on his first mission. He's good, Ala. Bock says he's the best shot he's ever seen. You've sent out plenty of douchenozzles before they were ready so don't you dare suggest I'm biased.'

The other woman rested her chin in her palm, assessing Callista with her natural eye. Then she nodded. 'Alright, Cals. Can't have a go at ya when I've given you the position. I also need to stop mollycoddlin' the ones I can't afford to lose. Now get out of here so I can drink in peace.'

As they left the room, Bock jabbed an elbow into Sandsa's side. 'She cares too much about me to lose me! Am I in with a chance or what?'

'You think far too highly of yourself!' Ala shouted after him.

Bock's smile melted away. Curiosity got the better of Callista; she reached back into the study with her powers, touching Ala's mind. The older subofficer felt the same level of protectiveness for Bock as she did for any other member of the Maria. And he really wasn't her type. Too young. Too fresh-faced. Too optimistic. Didn't he know there were plenty of other Maria women who would enjoy his company?

'Perhaps try your luck elsewhere?' was all Callista suggested, taken in by his downcast expression.

Bock threw his hands up. 'Luck! I don't have much of that. Hey, why are we wastin' time here — we got Bolt's first mission to plan!'

He skidded down the corridor, calling for his fellow clanspeople. Once he was gone, Callista hooked her fingers onto the collar of Sandsa's jacket and yanked him into a searing kiss. He responded eagerly, his tongue halting the progress of hers. Callista allowed him that victory, then pushed him against the wall, gasping when his knee slipped between her legs. But there was no retreating — his hand was on the small of her back, supporting her, warming her, and quelling the shivers that raced up from the base of her spine. Their lips parted for a moment, his breath playing over the moist residue of their passion. Then he lunged in for a longer, deeper kiss, one that would have lasted an eternity —

'Oh, get a room!' Ala said from her study.

Callista shielded her eyes from the vidcam that was pointing down the corridor. She'd forgotten that Ala had the feeds from various interior vidcams sent to her techpad so she could watch the comings and goings of her clan.

Sandsa swiftly stepped back, putting some distance between them.

'Where were you earlier?' Callista asked in an attempt to distract them both.

'I received an offer of employment which I accepted,' he said, his voice level. 'And I met a member of the Zatzat gang who seemed most keen on the idea of supplying night-time entertainment to interested Maria clanspeople.'

'Already bothering the newest subofficer with your suggestions, hmm?' she asked, smirking.

His handsome face lengthened into a laugh. 'Here is my next suggestion. You could visit me while I work and accept my invitation to dance.'

'Don't let my gang name fool you,' she warned. 'I'm not much of a dancer.'

'Perhaps we can be idiots on the dance floor together.'

She whacked his shoulder. 'Oh you.'

CHAPTER TEN

The Maria men crowed his name when Bolt emerged from within the Maria headquarters. Only one small lasgun rode the belt on his hip — Ala had ensured that he left the rest of Bock's suggested arsenal behind — and his palm was still warm from the door's security system being taught his prints. Sandsa had been concerned that he would have nothing for the locking mechanism to read, but it seemed his human form was no different from the flesh cladding his fellow clanspeople. This foray from headquarters would be his baptism of fire, though Sandsa supposed the phrase was ancient enough that none of his fellow clanspeople would know what it meant should he use it.

Sandsa slid over the bonnet of the hovercar, much to the delight of the men already seated inside. He wondered what they thought of his stretchy denim in comparison to their stiff leather pants. Perhaps they envied his practicality, he mused, smiling as he climbed over the opaque windows in the passenger compartment.

Sandsa knew he would need to keep his powers in check should he run into trouble, which his companions seemed keen on doing. They wanted to test him. He was still 'green', according to Bock. Sandsa preferred 'a blank techpad ready to be filled with databytes'.

'What are our plans for tonight?' he asked the man closest to him, a human so slim that his ribs were sharp, even through his shirt. This clansperson was known as Knives.

Knives laughed. 'We're gonna change that colour of yours, Green. And as a bonus we're gonna firebomb an Alcazaar hangout. Scared yet?'

'Hah! Bolt's so green he doesn't know what scared is!' another clansman chortled.

Sandsa shrugged. 'Scared or not, does it matter when a well-placed lasbolt catches me unawares?'

'Bolt's got a point,' Knives said.

And then they were off, tearing through the streets as dusk faded into dark night. Sandsa found himself grinning along with his companions' poor jokes, though he kept a careful eye on their lasguns. The weapons were permanently unholstered and their safeties were disabled.

I will return, he promised Callista.

You better or I'll kill you myself, she said.

***

Callista hovered by the window of Ala's study, despite it being shuttered with three laser-proof steel panels that blocked her view of the hovercar as it vanished around the corner in pursuit of fun and destruction. She suspected that no subofficer in the clan's history had dared to open the shutters, given the window's vulnerable position. This, along with the fact that the building's exterior vidcam had been recently destroyed during a strafing run, made it impossible to see the street outside. If they were Alcazaar, they could have replaced the vidcam already. It was not a matter of affording equipment — the Alcazaar did have more funds than most gangs, granted — rather, it was because suppliers dared not go around the reigning clan. It would mean a swift death.

'Sit down — you'll wear out the floor,' Ala said.

Callista obeyed, taking the seat across from her friend.

'So he's just like any of them boys looking to prove how big the lasguns in their pants are,' Ala said, reaching for the empty glass on the edge her desk, licked with grime though it was. 'Not this perfect man you've been bangin' on about without even bangin' him.'

Callista snagged the glass before Ala could get to it. Shaking her head, she reunited the item with its dirty siblings on the sinkplate in the corner of Ala's office, then hit a button which sent the mess away. She requested a clean glass that arrived within moments and took it back to Ala.

'We're taking things slow,' Callista said, pouring some whisky for her friend.

'Not surprising, given he also knows diddly squat about sex,' Ala said as Callista set the glass between them on the desk. 'Stark, you're as fussy about glasses as you are about who ya want to throw your virginity at.'

Callista eased back into her seat, staring at the surface of the desk. 'Do you really think he knows nothing? I mean, he said he saved his first kiss for me...I would rather be on an even playing field, so to speak.'

'He seemed not to know that when you get hot and heavy it can lead to other things,' Ala told her, then pulled out yet another dirty glass from somewhere and filled it, giving the cleaner vessel back to Callista while pouring herself a drink.

Callista accepted the gift and sipped it cautiously. Colder than coffein, it still managed to burn her tongue. 'He's very attractive, Ala. Of course I want the heavy petting to lead to other things.'

Ala spat stray drops of whisky as she laughed. 'Attractive! If you say so. Why haven't ya gone further yet?'

'It...it doesn't feel...it's not time,' Callista said, shrugging.

Taking advantage of the ensuing lull in conversation, Callista allowed her mind to skate away from Ala's study, soaring through the dark streets as she chased Sandsa and his companions. Down, down, she went, then tore ahead of them, slamming into the Dance Tower. The building, standing proudly on a roundabout, stretched up higher than the other skyscrapers surrounding it and throbbed with bass and stamping feet. The Alcazaar were here. And they knew the Maria were coming for them.

Then she felt the Chippers; they were a spreading stain on the street as they poured from their hiding place in a disused warehouse nearby. Armed with lasguns and their chips, they were preparing to go after the Maria. As Callista hovered there, watching them, one paused and turned towards her incorporeal form, his face lit by the glowing end of his weapon. He looked for her, curious and unafraid, his energy reminding her of an empty street — safe at first glance, but ringed by windows that could easily house a sniper.

He can feel me too, Callista realised in panic.

Callista twisted violently away from his gaze and flew back to Ala's study, where her body felt like a tight glove.

'Chippers — Alcazaar tower...!' Callista cried out before switching to mind-speech. *Sandsa! Chippers — they're coming for you! Run!*

Do you think I have not felt them? His words were calm, unbothered.

Callista gritted her teeth. *Stark it, Sandsa. If you don't run, I'll have to come after you.*

'Cals?'

Callista fell out of her chair, her knees slamming onto the floor tiles.

'Ala?' she said hoarsely.

'Are you having a fit or something? Look, it's a strong drop I gave ya, but even a lightweight like you ought to be able to handle it —'

'The Chippers and the Alcazaar are working together!' Callista used the desk to hoist herself up from the floor. 'The Alcazaar saw Bolt and the others coming just now and sent out Chippers — I don't know if the Chippers have joined the Alcazaar or if the clan's just paying them, but they're heading for the Dance Tower. We need to send more people. *Now.*'

Ala sipped from her glass for a few leisurely moments. Her artificial eye studied Callista's face, its advanced features no doubt registering her heightened temperature and her racing pulse.

Callista drew a breath and locked her shaking knees in place. 'I have powers but I'm not a Chipper. You checked me for chips yourself when I joined — and every year after that. The good news is I'm more powerful than them. But right now they're getting ready to pounce on our people down at the Dance Tower.'

'And this is why you've been botherin' us all with your wild theory about the Primus workin' with the Alcazaar — your powers told you about it?' Ala asked, her fingers straying to the button on her side of the desk, the one that would sound an alarm throughout the building and wake those not already engaged in fights across the city.

'Shoot me,' Callista said, slapping the table with both hands.

Ala opened her mouth.

'As your fellow subofficer, I am ordering you to shoot me!' Callista shouted.

The lasgun appeared swiftly — it was hard to tell where from — and Ala took the shot. Callista kept her arms completely still; Chippers had to channel their powers through their hands but she wasn't so restricted. And she needed Ala to see a difference between her and the enemy right now.

The lasbolt stopped dead between them.

After a charged heartbeat, it zinged away onto the metal plating over the window.

Ala's fingers hit the button on her desk then slapped her earpiece. 'All groups to the Dance Tower!'

Questions threatened to spew from Callista. Only two made it out. 'You're not pulling them away? Wouldn't that be safer?'

'Not lettin' those fucking Chippers know we're cowards,' Ala said, standing up, her drink forgotten.

'You believe me?'

'Believing is not that same thing as trustin',' Ala said.

Callista winced. 'Subofficer, can I join the others at the Dance Tower?'

Ala turned away to fiddle with her weapon. 'Why not? If you're more powerful than a Chipper, maybe we need ya down there to fight 'em off.'

Callista spun on her heel and ran.

***

The hovercar pulled up right outside the entrance to the Dance Tower, blocking a whole lane of traffic. Sandsa leapt out of the vehicle and straight onto the street, feeling his skin buzz with either excitement or the feeling of the Chippers closing in on them. The agents from the Galactic Law Enforcement Agency stood out like holes in a canvas, a violation on the landscape. They did not feel natural to him, not like Callista did.

'Alright, let's get this done — Ala says we got Chippers on our arse,' Knives said.

'Chippers? At night? Has Ala lost her head entirely?' a clansman exclaimed.

Sandsa turned to regard the speaker. 'Those are your subofficer's words. Do not question them.'

Knives distributed silver sphere-shaped objects among all the men. The seamless ball fit into one of Sandsa's hands and had a slight indention on one side — he made sure this was aimed outwards after he was told that this was where the weapon fired from. Someone offered Sandsa a personal shielding device but he shook his head; he would not need it. He lined up with his clanspeople, exchanged nods with them, then followed his companions into the tower.

They sprinted down through the red neon tubing that guided partygoers from the street into a den filled with half-dressed bodies. Thrumming, steady music filled the room, but no one was dancing. Even if some of them were missing articles of clothing, they weren't without lasguns.

They were ready and waiting.

'Don't let any of the Maria escape!' one of the Alcazaar shouted.

The Maria clansmen had no intention of escaping yet.

With each squeeze of the spheres in their hands, giant rings of fire burst free from the small indentations; the blasts then grew much larger than the unassuming balls projecting them. Sandsa was pleased when his shot hit the bar running the length of the back wall, causing phials and beaker-shaped glasses to explode, showering the Alzacaar in liquid fire. His victims started screaming.

Horror entered Sandsa's heart; it was a heavy, oppressive feeling that threatened to drop him to his knees. He faltered, but only for a moment — a new threat had arrived.

The Chippers slipped in from behind them, barring the exit. His adrenaline fanned by their presence, Sandsa turned away from his fellow Maria and marched towards GLEA's agents. The ball slid around in his sweaty grip. He might be a god, but the Ine had impressed upon his sons and daughters that the gift of eternal life did not necessarily come with invulnerability. Callista had sensed Sandsa's inability to heal himself; it had been a blessing at the time because she had assumed he was completely human. Now Sandsa felt fear.

He halted just before the invisible shield the Chippers had erected by combining their forcefields; it was a solid wall of air that threatened to push him out of the way. Sandsa shattered the barrier entirely with a simple smile. He then aimed his silver globe at the Chippers. Two of them diverted the fiery blast he sent with a smaller forcefield, their hands held up to channel their powers. Flames splattered the wall beside them. Sandsa could now sense the Alcazaar rallying against his companions, driving them back towards him.

They needed this exit. Sandsa intended to make sure it was clear.

A Chipper fired her lasgun at him; Sandsa sidestepped the ensuing bolt. He looked back at the woman, smirking, then waved his fingers in a parody of her gestures. She tumbled down, her hands slapping the ground to break her fall. Hair dropped away from her ear, exposing the ugly protrusion on her temple that housed her chip.

The rest of the Chippers opened fire on him but not a single bolt struck his flesh. Sandsa kept his arms loose by his sides, letting them see he did not need to use his hands. Several of the Chippers even took a step back at the sight of him effortlessly defending himself. Once more he fired his spherical weapon and watched the pack of them scatter in response. Laughing, he used his powers to split the shot into two balls of fire that chased them down. Sandsa watched the Chippers fall, screaming as they clutched their injuries. They would live. But they would be in excruciating pain until they were attended to.

Good, he thought and ran, his fellow Maria at his heels.

Ducking beneath the hailstorm of red lasbolts caused by both Alcazaar and Maria hands, Sandsa raced out onto the street. There Callista found him and took his hand, hoisting him up into a hovercar. He stole a brief, searing kiss, then they began to fire their lasguns in unison, their spare hands clenched between them. No stray or deliberate bolt struck them, instead bending around the invisible shield they had erected together.

Callista shuddered violently and he turned a concerned look onto her. She pointed at the fresh, uninjured Chippers now emerging from warehouse.

They were looking straight at Sandsa and Callista.

'Go, go!' Callista shouted at the driver and the hovercar bore them away over a sea of metal and glass.

The Maria surrounding them laughed and cheered as their convoy of vehicles made their retreat. Sandsa dismissed all of this from sight and from mind and slid his fingers beneath Callista's chin. She smiled up at him, a small gap forming between her lips, inviting another kiss; he gave it to her, his hands framing her face. When Sandsa pulled back, her eyes were bright and full of stars.

Then Callista clutched at his chest, her mind frantic.

'Callista?' he murmured, a thumb stroking her spine.

'Ala knows about my powers,' she whispered, her face tight with fear.

Sandsa frowned. *That is not the only thing troubling you.*

Her teeth gnawed on her bottom lip, drawing blood. *I have always been able to sense the Chippers.*

But...?

Tonight they felt me in return.

The only thing he could offer was an embrace. Words would not comfort her. He could not even hold her for long; soon they were taking hits as their convoy was chased through the city. Callista spent a few tense minutes shouting with a hand over the communicator in her ear, arguing with several drivers. She finally won the debate by saying, 'If we have to break the rules so we can live long enough to slam the Alcazaar for bringing the Chippers into this, then we'll do it!'

The hovercars soared into the No-Go Zone, bathed in the light shed from numerous, fully-functioning streetlights. The Maria's pursuers slowed, keeping to the shadows. It seemed even the Alcazaar were wary of tempting the ire of Governor Garnett's voters.

They probably preferred a governor they could pay off, after all.

***

'We lost ten,' was Ala's terse greeting. 'Would've lost more if you hadn't made everyone go through the No-Go Zone.'

Tension unwound inside her and Callista could breathe again, her lungs aching with the effort. Maria clanspeople poured in around them, headed for the bar in the lounge room. No one was willing to risk hitting the streets again tonight — not when the Alcazaar were prowling, baying for their blood. Callista looked longingly upstairs towards the sleeping quarters, but Ala wasn't done with her.

The older woman threw two fingers in their direction so Callista and Sandsa followed her into the study. Callista saw that several empty glasses were lined up along Ala's desk.

'Now I gotta know, what else are you keeping from me?' Ala asked once the door slid shut. She rarely closed it so Callista knew this was serious. 'Are you another Primus, tryin' to take us out?'

'No!' Callista said, resisting the urge to reach for Sandsa's hand. 'I am loyal to this clan!'

Ala's unblinking ruby eye fixed on them as she sat down and kicked her legs up onto the desk, her boots narrowly avoiding a fresh whisky bottle. Sandsa remained standing, his face smooth and devoid of any concern. Callista shot him an irritated glance. It did not matter to him if the Maria expelled him. He had only joined for her. If Ala cast her out, she would have nowhere to go.

'I'm sorry,' Callista murmured.

Ala shook her head. 'You're not sorry for hidin' this from me. I might only have one real eye but I can still see that, stark it.' The eye in question sized up Sandsa. 'You knew. She trusted you the moment ya dropped out of the sky.'

Sandsa slid his arm around Callista's waist. 'Yes. I imagine you know why.'

'You're like her,' Ala said, scowling at one of the loose straps on her boots for a moment. 'Chipper without a chip.'

Callista ripped her tongue away from the parched roof of her mouth. 'Ala. You know you can't shoot us. But you can bar us from headquarters with words alone. What's it to be?'

'I would've shot you if you'd told me about it when you first joined us,' Ala said frankly.

Callista met Ala's even stare with her own.

Ala sighed, her gaze moving to the wall behind them. 'You can stay. And I'll even let you keep the fancy rank, Cals. But you're not to go out with us at night for now — this means you too, Bolt. I have to think about what this means for us. Worse, though...' Ala visibly gritted her teeth, her lips curling back into a snarl. 'If there's evidence for the Creator God, you two're it. No chip. Imagine that.'

Ala's words continued to echo in Callista's ears even as she and Sandsa climbed up onto the landing that led to their rooms. When Sandsa made no move towards his door, she leaned against hers, pointedly keeping it shut. Though he maintained some distance between them, his eyes slid up one thigh.

Callista smiled, but only for a moment. 'Do you think the Creator God really exists, Sandsa?'

'Yes,' he said without hesitation.

'Why would he do this to us?' she asked. 'Make us this way? Was it to isolate us from the people around us?'

His mind darkened and Callista caught an image of Sandsa shouting, his feet braced on a road in Atsa's outskirts while his words tore across the desert. Sandsa gently guided her past the boundaries of his mind, the snatches of his memory vanishing along with the access she'd had to his thoughts. Callista supposed she should have felt offended. He was keeping something from her. But she sensed no malice in him. In fact, what she did sense was extremely strong...

'I wonder if the gods realise they are toying with people's feelings and lives,' Sandsa said, his eyes on the ceiling. 'But this I know. I am glad you have your powers, for they helped me find the woman I love.'

Callista felt her cheeks blanch. 'Sandsa...don't use that word.'

'Love?' He blinked once, twice, his blue gaze fixing back on her. 'Is that not what we have between us?'

Callista wondered what she was supposed to find in her heart. It was an organ that pumped blood, sustaining her body with every beat. That's all it did for her. Even so, she hesitantly focused on her chest region, waiting for an explosion of feeling that would surely announce her emotions. Her heartbeat was elevated, but that told her nothing.

Sandsa continued to stare at her, waiting for something she was not sure she could give him. She walked over, pecked his cheek, promised to see him in the morning and then retreated to her room. But if she could not hide from his presence anywhere in this city, how could she possibly hide from his feelings, separated by mere walls?

His mind was filled with sand again that night, though this time Callista was the one who walked over the dunes, searching for and never finding the treasure he had unearthed so easily.

CHAPTER ELEVEN

He felt as though he was submerged in sands warmed by stars when he woke. Sandsa lay there, unmoving, his smile fixed in place, even when the imagined blue sky faded into a grey ceiling stained with water.

'I love her,' he repeated the chant from his heart.

He had seen countless mortals across innumerous deserts toil under the fear of speaking that very word; some truly could not return the ardour of the one who had offered it, and others needed time to pry apart their own feelings. Sandsa, confident that he knew which was the case here, whistled some tune he had heard in the Dance Tower the night before and grabbed the grotty threadbare towel that had replaced the significantly cleaner one he'd thrown into the automated laundry system.

The piping hot water in the shower made him think of the deserts at first, but as the spray cooled his thoughts gave way to Callista. He could wait for her to solve the puzzle of her heart. He knew she must feel as he did, fumbling through new and mysterious territory.

He imagined the water falling over her, drenching her beautiful hair but never hiding the eyes that saw into him in a way his father could not seem to. Sandsa's mind did not stop there; soon he was imagining taking each article of clothing off her until she was wearing only droplets of moisture. Sandsa groaned and rested his forehead on the tiling. A certain part of his flesh and blood being had become insistent, demanding attention, and she filled his thoughts, worsening his situation. That troublesome organ was hard again and the veins along its shaft pulsed with each image of her that flashed before his eyes.

She was in the room with him, he realised.

'It is my understanding that the female bathroom is next door,' Sandsa said.

Callista lifted her arms, her hands disappearing to the back of her head where she twisted her hair into a stubby version of a ponytail. One corner of her lips deepened as she smirked, no doubt fully aware that the arch of her back had presented those pleasing mounds of flesh to him. Knowing that he was staring, Sandsa moved his eyes to no avail — the patch of curls at the apex of her legs was impossible to ignore.

'Never seen a naked woman before?' she asked with an even broader grin, slinking over to share the spray being jettisoned from the showerhead he was using.

'Yes, many,' Sandsa answered, then realised his mistake when she quickly crossed her arms over her breasts. 'Ah, that is to say...well. Yours is a flattering form and I have never been rendered so speechless.'

Nakedness was something that happened among his people, though mostly it occurred inside their private abodes with their intimate partners. Sandsa had smiled when he had sensed the love between consenting adults, but he had never been able to shake the envy, the need.

Callista's eyes dropped low, past his abdomen, and then the wicked smirk was back. Sandsa found himself grinning back at her, feeling no embarrassment or discomfort.

Stark, you're easy to look at, her voice ghosted into his mind. *But I really do need a wash after last night.*

Sandsa held up the soap. She took it. They washed together, slowly, eyes roaming over each other, hands never straying from their own bodies. To Sandsa's relief, his member softened by the end of the chore and he was able to assist in towelling her off without becoming too distracted.

Admiring her form as she hid it away again, Sandsa almost missed seeing that dreaded word he had used begin to form in her mind. Before he could comment on it, she blurted, 'Do you want to get out of here? Ala's forbidden us from going out on missions at night, but she laid no restrictions on cavorting with daylight — and I know a place or two that you might like.'

'Are you always so verbose when you are asking someone out on a date?' Sandsa asked, eyebrows raised.

'I rather thought we were past just...dating. Especially...' She paused. 'Especially,' she repeated, then lunged at him for a kiss.

He gathered her in his arms, pleased with the sensation of her shirt grazing his nipples. It was electric. After several delightful moments, Sandsa set her at arm's length, smiling. 'Let us cavort with daylight.'

'Put your shirt on,' she said, grinning as she tossed the item at him. 'I won't have anyone else catching a glimpse of the goods.'

He could still hear her laughing when she left the room.

***

Bleary-eyed Kick, having stumbled out of his nest of pillows in the garage, only needed a word or two from his newest subofficer before he relinquished control of a hovercar for the day. Callista ran a hand over the vehicle, noting that its angular lines had been in fashion well over ten years ago. It was hard to ignore that in the poor lighting of the garage, the maroon smeared on its knife-shaped body looked more like old blood than paint.

Sandsa, she noticed, had chosen to forgo his jacket. Callista couldn't blame him; it did get quite warm during the day in Atsa. She wasn't quite ready to shed the protective leather — she didn't have his confidence. He was so sure about everything, including his belief that she would return his feelings.

She settled into the driver's seat and, when he stared at her, said tartly, 'I've been driving since I was a girl. Have you seen any hovercars out there in your deserts?'

'Not everyone "out there" gives up tech,' Sandsa informed her. 'Some of my — some of the Desine's followers have permanent settlements as well as hovercars.'

Callista patted the passenger seat beside her. 'Sit. You can outshoot, out-power and out-talk me, but I'll be starked if I let you find out that you can out-drive me.'

She took the turn of his lips to mean that he accepted. When she reached for his thoughts, she found an excitable boy, one that bounced across the dunes in his mindscape, kicking up clomps of sand and running into the waiting arms of his — mother. His mind closed abruptly. Callista rested a hand on his knee and retreated back inside her own skull. His fingers wove through hers.

The garage blazed with light as the reinforced door between them and the road slid open. Smiling at Sandsa as he sat up expectantly in his seat, she guided their hovercar outside and almost immediately had to swerve around a smashed vehicle from the previous night, its ruins charred and robbed of anything salvageable.

Judging by his relaxed manner, Sandsa felt comfortable with her driving, though occasionally he would eye the steering wheel with something amounting to envy. Callista rubbed her thighs together, drawing his interest elsewhere. She grinned down the street.

They sailed into the No-Go Zone like any normal couple on a drive, unhindered by lasbolts or Chippers. Though it was early still, the star above them beat down onto the road, forming a shimmering haze above the surface of the tar. No one in this wealthy area would be heading off to work yet. They could afford to huddle inside their protective shells for a little while longer before they emerged, if at all, to tackle another day of trying to outclass their neighbours. Some of them might even consider abandoning their business ventures here on dusty Yalsa 5 and head for richer pastures.

Callista did not need to take Canat Road to reach her intended destination, but she took it anyway.

Lined with grand houses, their facades formed by stones that were meant to give them the appearance of class, this road had once been a daily route bringing her back to the mansion she had once called home. The fence enclosing the house and its immaculate garden was spiked and head-high, not much of a deterrent to the gangs but it probably made her parents feel safe. Callista noticed that the hedges inside the fence were still evenly trimmed. What had she expected — her old prison a derelict ruin after a single month?

It would serve them right, she thought.

Sandsa glanced at her. 'Callista?'

She blindly groped for her lasgun. The pocket holding it was designed for the larger, heavier artillery that other Maria favoured so she had to dig for a moment to retrieve her weapon. Once she was armed, Callista punched a button; the window slid down. Pinching the steering rods between her thumb and forefinger on one hand, she rested an elbow on the side of the hovercar, taking aim. The ensuing bolt slapped the gate, but then washed away harmlessly.

So. They had some defence against Atsa's night-life after all.

Callista dropped her lasgun and shook her head. She wasn't even sure if destroying the gate would have made her feel any better.

'My parents,' she explained.

'I understand,' he said.

Yalsa 5's closest star continued to dominate the sky as Callista drove, chasing away the coldest, darkest crannies surrounding them. She blinked; somehow she had forgotten how beautiful the city could look when it was not ruled by shadows and death. After passing more stately buildings, they arrived at Governor Park, its artificial lake an astonishing blue beside the pale green grasses that grew tiredly around it. No governor of Atsa City had bothered to spend any taxes on importing rich, foreign soils so any plants here were small and hardy or designed to love sandy ground. There had been attempts to generate interest in terraforming Yalsa 5 in the past, but it had always been deemed too expensive.

'Well, it's no beach, but it's not a bad place to relax,' Callista said, then saw the delight dancing in Sandsa's eyes as he vaulted out of the cockpit. 'Right. You don't care what it is, just that you're with me. Well, enjoy it while you can.'

Unease prickled along her scalp until she swatted at her hair, stamping out the feeling of...premonition? Callista closed her eyes for a moment and balled up her energy inside her, where it couldn't draw the attention of any passing Chipper.

I need to be careful when they're out and about, Callista thought. Her skin crawled as she watched Sandsa kneel at the side of the massive concrete container that was filled with sand and a parody of a sea. *But the Chippers are always out and about now. Even during the night. There's no escaping them.*

She shuddered.

Sandsa peered up at her. 'My love?'

The endearment was like a punch to the chest.

Callista looked away. 'Please...don't. Don't say that. Not yet.'

Not yet... The words bounced around his mind, infecting her own thoughts. *Not yet.*

***

'I love coming here,' Callista said. The bowl-shaped boat they had rented from one of the vendors on the edge of the lake coasted around the perimeter, guided by artificial currents instead of an engine. 'It's also the largest body of water in the city so expect some would-be athletes swimming around later.'

Sandsa scooped up some of the cool water from the lake, watching it trickle away between his fingers. He cupped yet more of it in his hands and tossed it onto his face. His eyes stung from the chemicals that kept the lake clean but he declined the cloth that Callista offered him, instead leaning over the edge of the boat to continue studying the surface of the liquid. He tossed a tendril of power into the shallow waves, tunnelling down for the sand beneath them, then felt his eyes widen as the water threw something back at him.

Impossible! Water is not in my domain! he thought.

Fingers clawed into the collar of his shirt, pulling him back into the boat. Callista patted his cheek. 'No, we're not here to get wet.'

'We're not?' Sandsa asked, his gaze finding the children treading along the edge of the lake in their colourful swimming costumes.

She laughed and shed her clothes. For a moment, Sandsa was confused, then saw that she was not entirely naked. She was now adorned in a small, two-piece swimsuit of her own. Once the outfit, mostly black with some silver swirls, was exposed, Callista leaned back against the cotton linen covering the seat that ran around the rim of the boat. She was sunbaking, Sandsa realised, bemused. It was not something his people did in the deserts — the sun was something to be avoided when it seared skin and stole a man's vital fluids. Some novices, in order to attain priesthood, ventured into the bare sands with only the Magic and a shred of fabric on their backs, embracing the delusions that came with dehydration, to better commune with their desert god.

Callista exposed her skin for the mere pleasure of it. Would she still want to do that when he took her into the deserts?

Sandsa shook his head. No, he was done with that life. In an attempt to distract himself from his thoughts, he cast his gaze around the boat and found a techpad that someone had left on the seat. Its screen lit up beneath his fingertips, revealing lines of text. He offered the device to Callista who laughed when she laid eyes on it.

'Someone was reading a romance novel on this techpad,

looks like,' she said, turning the device over in her hands. '*Seeking the Stars*. A classic by Atsa's own Julia Love — this one's old. Ala might make fun of my lack of experience, but women with more lovers than her still bawl their eyes out when reading this.'

'Is it a sad story then?' Sandsa asked, reaching for it.

Callista chortled, relinquishing the item. 'Oh, no. The lovers escape on a starship bound for Enoc — it's a planet some days from here — so that they can be together against their families' wishes.'

Sandsa turned his face up to the sky, peering through the atmosphere, to the stars and planets and other celestial bodies rotating in the grip of gravity or fleeing it with wild abandon. His companion brought him sharply back into his body when she said, 'I used to think these books were a load of nonsense.'

'And now?' Sandsa asked.

Callista smiled. 'I'm starting to think Julia undersold some parts.'

Her mind was suddenly filled with text that swiftly morphed into black and white sketches of two bodies merging into one silhouette. Sandsa added colour to the images and fleshed them out, literally in some cases, to illustrate what he knew of the act. Callista drew away from him.

'Will we find out if she undersold that?' Sandsa asked her with a grin.

'Maybe.' Callista gave him a sly sideways glance. 'If you're good.'

Sandsa chuckled and continued to page through the book, taping a finger on the edge of the screen to do so. He found himself entranced by the thoughts and sensations the characters experienced during intimate scenes. He knew his people in the deserts enjoyed sex, even when they did not wish to reproduce, but had long considered it beneath him. This book made it sound delightful. His palm skimmed a sensor on the bottom of the techpad, taking it back to the front of the book. The dedication sprang up on the next page.

To my eldest, for whom the sands rise and fall

To my youngest, for whom the trees bend and sway

To the one who scarred me, please set me free

Sandsa dropped the device. It struck the bottom of the boat with a muted clunk. He knew, he just knew. But still he asked, his voice rising in pitch, 'Who is this Julia Love? Is she...is she still here? Is she...'

Is she dead or is she alive, old and withered but still alive?

Callista blinked, the skin over her forehead creasing as she sensed the turmoil within him. 'That's a more interesting story than any of the tripe she wrote. It was just a pen-name — she used the sale of her books to bankroll the Maria so we could take over the city. I suppose even enemies of the Maria bought her work. I don't know of any other gangs who've used legitimate fundraising, though to be honest, no one knows all the clans that have existed over the centuries.'

'Go on, go on,' Sandsa pleaded.

'Julia Ine was our Clan Leader,' Callista said, sitting up to stare across at him.

Ine. She had used her former husband's name.

Sandsa nodded. 'And? What happened?'

'The Alcazaar killed her — that's how they ended up ruling Atsa,' Callista told him, her words hesitant and soft.

Sandsa coiled his grief back inside his gut. He stuffed every other feeling and exposed nerve in there with it, slamming his defences shut.

'Will you tell me why this hurts you so much?' Callista asked after several tense seconds of silence.

'She...meant something to me,' Sandsa said, his chest aching.

'No kidding. What else?'

But how could she understand? It had been more than fifty years since his mother had lost her binding scars and her former husband's immortality. She had then apparently come here, where violence had robbed her of her life before old age ever could. For him it was recent enough to still be raw, a blister that chafed against any dressing applied to it. To Callista, his mother's death was something that happened before she was born; it was a mere detail, a fact. And he was far too young to be Julia Ine's progeny in her eyes. Callista was openly derisive when it came to the gods. How would she look upon him when she knew what he was?

He had barely opened his mouth, still not sure what he could say, when a spray of water shot up from the surface of the lake and smacked across their faces. Callista was on her feet in an instant, her lasgun up and ready. Only after glancing around the boat did Sandsa recall that he had not brought his weapon. It was something he carried for show, so the Maria would not suspect he had something else in his 'personal arsenal' — a phrase he had picked up from Bock, though the teenager seemed to think his own particular arsenal contained abilities that could entice a woman into his bed.

'You filthy Alcazaar!' Callista shouted as the three hoverbikes responsible tore away, churning up water and sending children scrambling onto the prickly plants ringing the lake. 'Come back, cowards! Or are you afraid to face clanspeople who don't hide behind Chippers?'

The bike in the centre of the formation swung back around immediately, its flanking vehicles reacting a little slower. The leader of the trio was clearly the man on the largest machine. He was wearing a ridiculous neon blue top hat that was kept in place with a cotton strap and his clothes were colourful, trendy, and bore no apparent gang logos.

'Maria scum,' he said, tilting his head to one side to regard them with flinty eyes. 'You're the cowards! You ran from the fight last night and you didn't even offer me a dance, Dancer.'

Callista lifted her chin. 'I notice you're not denying that you're in with the Chippers, Cosmos. What did you offer them? Oh, I see.' Sandsa sensed Callista dart briefly into Cosmos' mind. 'You pay the medical bills for the injuries they sustain at night. And you pay them better than the Agency does. Interesting.'

Cosmos turned his leer onto Sandsa. 'You're the one the Maria trotted out last night, yeah?'

'Yes,' Sandsa answered.

'He's Bolt — could put one right between your eyes before you even blink,' Callista said, moving in front of Sandsa.

Cosmos smirked. 'What, without a lasgun?'

Callista threw an exasperated look at Sandsa. He would have offered a sheepish smile had he not sensed the true intent behind Cosmos' pursuit of them.

He knows, Sandsa told Callista. *He saw me deal with his clanspeople and the Chippers last night — that or someone informed him of my actions.*

You left witnesses? Her brown eyes were as narrow as the edge of a blade.

I...

Callista snapped off a shot with her weapon and burned a hole right through Cosmos' hat. The fabric smoked faintly for several moments. Callista grinned. 'Looks like my lasgun works just fine. What is it you want, Cosmos?'

Cosmos pulled off his hat to inspect it, scowling. Once he'd set the damaged object back onto his head, the man jabbed a finger into his own chest. 'Me? I can live without this guy joining our ranks. But my Clan Leader can't. He wants Bolt. He wants him by day's end. And he'll have him.'

'Your Clan Leader expects me to walk into Alcazaar headquarters and swear in blood to a gang I have no interest in joining?' Sandsa asked, reading Cosmos' feeble mind. 'I will not do that.'

'You can't refuse him,' Callista muttered out of the corner of her mouth.

'I can.'

'You'll plunge us into an all-out war!' She turned to him, her expression fierce. 'The Alcazaar will use this to end us!'

'They can try,' Sandsa said, lifting his hand the way a Chipper would.

Cosmos flinched and ducked. Sandsa smiled, dropped his arms to his sides and waited for the relief to cross the man's face — then threw a violent thought at him. The Alcazaar clansman tumbled into the water. After Cosmos started berating his cronies, they hauled him back onto his bike and fled. Callista's ensuing laugh was harsh and belied the fear Sandsa could feel coursing through her veins.

He wrapped her into an embrace and rested his chin on the top of her head, soothing her with his presence. She clung to him like a weed on a rock, desperate to remain anchored. After a while, he said, 'I came here for you. Not to involve myself in Atsa's gangs, not to destroy the life you have here — though I would not argue if you suggested we both disappear among the stars like the lovers in that book.'

'We wouldn't be in this mess if you'd killed everyone in the tower and covered your tracks,' she moaned into his shoulder.

'I wish I had killed them all,' Sandsa murmured. 'They deserve it, for what they did.'

The fury seeped from inside him, bathing his tongue in bile, coating his skin. He had stayed his hand last night. But no more. Not now he knew they had killed his mother, ended her life before he could touch her one last time.

Callista's palm grazed his cheek. 'Sandsa. I'm here for you. And I'm sorry. I've sensed how you feel about ending lives and I...I just said that.'

'A lot can change in a day,' he said distantly.

'Yes, it can.' She sighed. 'I really wanted to spend the day with you, showing you the places I loved in my childhood...now we'll have to return to headquarters and report on this.'

'This "all-out war" won't start until tonight, is that correct?' Sandsa pressed. 'We can surely enjoy ourselves for now — and we are both capable of defending ourselves.'

A wry smile twisted its way over Callista's face. 'You're a terrible influence on me.'

Despite agreeing to stay out in the sunshine with him, Callista remained tense as she drove. Her fears were not unfounded; it didn't take long for the vidscreen on the console to show the vehicles pursuing them.

'Looks like the Alcazaar want to get in early,' she said flatly.

Sandsa swung a look over his shoulder, spotting the hovercar that was chasing them — and the other two flanking it.

'Do we have enough weaponry to repel them?' he asked.

Callista snapped her teeth together. 'Are you kidding? They always get the best armaments. Still, Kick does tend to add a few modifications...' She punched a button. 'Kick, you there?'

'You're stuck with me,' Bock answered cheerfully.

'Bock, this is serious — we have three Alcazaar hovercars bearing down on us and I need to know what secret lasguns Kick may've stuck on this thing.'

'Holy Creator shit!' Bock exclaimed.

'Take the next right,' Sandsa instructed and, when Callista kicked up an eyebrow at him, he explained, 'A nightclub operated by the Zatzat clan is in this district. It is a good deal closer than our headquarters.'

'Zatzat?' Bock's voice echoed through the communications system. 'Them? They ain't gonna look twice at you, let alone blast some Alcazaar for ya.'

Callista slammed a hand on the console, narrowly missing a few buttons. 'Enough! I need to know about the weapons! I can start steering towards the nightclub but it's no good if we are blown to pieces before we get there.'

'I can protect us,' Sandsa told her.

She shot him a wild look as she pulled hard on the steering rods. The hovercar swerved violently as a large lasgun bolt sped past them, close enough to send the stench of scorched plastic through the cockpit. Leaving Callista in charge of avoiding any further blasts, Sandsa clambered into the rear of the hovercar, pressing his palms to the back window. There was no point in hiding what he could do, not anymore. He ground his teeth together until his jaw ached.

The next lasbolt was a direct hit — or would have been had it not bounced away, shattering the patch of tar it struck. By then Callista had located the weapons systems, though judging by the delicate coughing sounds the tiny lasguns made, they were not going to inflict much damage. Sandsa frowned and sent a larger, stronger burst of his powers.

One hovercar lifted, as though picked up by a giant hand, then listed lazily through the air before it smashed into the buildings on both sides of the road, again and again. It tumbled onto one of the other hovercars. Sandsa turned his attention to the last pursuant, only to see another three vehicles screech in from side streets, all of them mounted with much larger lasguns. These were manned by clanspeople who hung desperately onto the triggers so as to not be dislodged. Sandsa reached for his destructive powers — and stopped. He felt a petering lifesign in one of the ruined vehicles; someone was dying, because of what he'd done.

He hesitated.

But then he saw her.

A beautiful smile, a gentle hand brushing his cheek...it did not matter who it was, Callista or his mother, this was someone he had to protect. Sandsa heard the strangled cry and distantly noted that it was his own. Scattered grains of sand that had wended their way onto this road for centuries, ever since the forcefield protecting Atsa City from the elements had begun to fail, rose from the tar and merged. Angry, hungry for vengeance, a roaring tornado engulfed a hovercar and, moments later, spat out the vehicle's skeleton. Mindful that any of his followers in Atsa might see or feel this use of his powers, Sandsa swiftly let the tornado drop.

'What was *that*?' Callista said as she steered the hovercar closer to Vom's nightclub.

A line of Zatzat and other clanspeople were already stretched across the street outside, their hands held up to the sky. Sandsa started when he felt a thick rope lash around his heart, his soul, his being — then Vom threw up a wall of sand, aided by his brethren. The oncoming hovercars slowed, stopped, then started reversing.

'Sand fleas!' an Alcazaar hurled through the loudspeaker affixed to his cockpit. 'You won't be so lucky tonight when we send the Chippers after ya!'

As they soared away, their insults and hoots bounced back towards Vom who merely swatted at his face, as though dismissing an insect. Moments later, the wall of sand dropped.

Before Callista even began to steer the hovercar towards the gutter, Sandsa threw himself out of the cockpit to approach — *his people*. It was as though acid was filling his eyes, burning them, and he saw thousands of splintered images of these men and women — all of them starting their lives on the sands, all of them gifted. He knew each of them, knew their hearts...*my children*. They had called upon him to activate their Magic — and he had answered.

Sandsa nodded at Vom. 'Your interference is welcome and noted.'

'Rather generous of me, yes!' Vom's smile looked painful. 'You didn't turn up for your first shift last night, but the way I hear it, you've been too busy tangling with the Alcazaar. Starking *jenat* — fools mistaking your Magic for Chipper abilities are they? We heard the rumours.'

Sandsa supposed that it was going to come out at some point. He shook his head. 'They're not mistaking anything — I possess both sets of powers, though I have no chip.'

'Can all of you run around throwing tornadoes and sand walls at people?' Callista asked, marching to stand beside Sandsa. She eyed the Zatzat and their companions, her hand clenched on her lasgun.

Vom laughed. 'What? No! To accomplish such feats, you need at least twenty people behind you, as you see here.'

Callista glanced sharply at Sandsa. *I saw what you did back there. The tornado. You made it by yourself.*

Callista, my love, that was Vom and his people, not me, Sandsa told her but he kept his gaze on Vom, unable to look at her, in case she saw the lie in his eyes.

But she'd already read it from his mind.

You're lying to me, she said, frowning.

Sandsa grimaced. *I'm sorry.*

Her words became accusatory. *What are you hiding from me, Sandsa? What's so important that you can't tell the woman you supposedly love?*

She deserved an answer from him. He wasn't sure he could give her one.

CHAPTER TWELVE

Callista counted at least three different minor gangs among their rescuers, judging by the shirts and bandanas they were sporting. The weapons on their belts were not nearly so worrying as the powers they could wield. Still, if they were a potential enemy of the Maria, she needed to find out what she could about their deadly abilities.

So she accepted Vom's invitation to have a drink with him.

'In the deserts, we are born knowing we can touch the sands but it is only through asking for and gaining the Desine's permission that are we able to use the Magic,' Vom explained, raising his voice so that he could be heard over the noise belting out of the speakers. 'Some of the really powerful ones become priests and help their tribes in battle.'

Sandsa was flicking through various songs over at the DJ booth, pretending that he wasn't listening, but Callista was well aware of his focus on the conversation.

If you won't give me answers, I'll have to seek them elsewhere, she sent to him, not bothering to hide her annoyance.

'What sort of powers do you have?' Callista asked Vom.

Vom leaned across the counter to thrust his glass beneath a dispenser. 'We can make sand move, to trip our enemies, or to throw up a cloud of it to hide ourselves. Sometimes we don't even need to be near sand to call some of it into our hands.' He tossed back his drink, burped, then continued, 'And we can sense the Desine. All of our powers come from him. He's the source of them.'

An ache seeded itself within Callista's skull then spread outwards which each throb of the music's bass. 'The Chippers don't need to ask permission. Their powers — sensing lifesigns, making forcefields out of energy — come from their chip.'

'The chip just makes it possible for them to pull it from in here instead of from a god,' Vom told her, tapping his temple. 'The Chippers say they can feel the Creator God. I don't need fancy tech to feel the Desine.'

'What does he feel like?'

Vom rested his glass against his lips. 'Immense, raw power. Stark me, it's almost frightening. He suggests paths for us to walk and does not punish us for straying, unless it hurts folk — then he gets 'em good. Never kills them though, just makes 'em regret their actions.'

Callista leaned back on the bar, watching Sandsa as he shouted something at a Zatzat clansperson who had managed to climb up onto the booth to request a song. The beat became more hasty, more pounding. She closed her eyes, pushing away the distractions, focusing...feeling. There was nothing out there, no bright splotch on her mindscape. No god. She flicked a stray thought at the bar, then heard the crash of a glass and the surprised yelp of the person who had been holding it. The ripples of power flowed from within her.

So I'm like a Chipper, I pull it from inside myself, Callista thought, then frowned.

'You know Sandsa will be too busy to work here,' she said out loud. 'Most gangs usually operate at night. You might be better off turning this into a dayclub.'

'A dayclub.' Vom stroked his chin, looking thoughtful. 'Well, that's not a stupid idea, Dancer. Nowhere near as stupid as joining a gang that's so set on pissing off the Alcazaar.'

Callista reached for the warming glass of pink liquid on the counter and took a small sip. It was sweeter than coffein and not as strong as something Ala would have favoured. She swiftly knocked it back then wiped her hand over her mouth. 'The Alcazaar won't stop going after us. We have to retaliate.'

'They go after you because you're a threat,' Vom pointed out. 'The Zatzat and other clans like ours are not in it to take power from anyone. We do it for money, and to keep each other safe. The Chippers don't do a starking thing at night and the Alcazaar are more powerful than any one of our clans alone so we have to band together.'

Callista set her glass down and crossed her arms. 'Why did you help us? The Alcazaar will come after you now — them and their bought Chippers.'

'Bolt's a tribesman and we look out for our own,' Vom said. His face melted into a grin after she released an exasperated sigh. 'Alright, I'll speak the truth. There's no money to be made in working with the Alcazaar — we gave up trying once they nicked the hovercars we were going to sell cheap to them. Bolt's Maria. And he's attached to a Maria subofficer. Maybe your lot will be more profitable to deal with.'

'What do the Maria get out of this arrangement?' Callista asked.

Vom smirked. 'The codes that will shut down at least twenty of the Alcazaar vehicles.'

'With the war that's headed our way,' Callista said dryly, 'we'll need a lot more than that from you.'

***

'Should we return to headquarters and let our clan know what's going on?' Sandsa asked once they breached daylight upstairs.

'Are you that keen to avoid my questions?' Callista retorted.

He grimaced and looked away. 'I just thought that it might be wiser, not to mention safer, if we cut this day short.'

'I have a feeling I'm safest wherever you are, tornado-slinger,' Callista said. Her smile felt brittle. 'What need do you have for me if you're that powerful, huh?'

Sandsa bent down for a kiss that she kept chaste and brief by sealing her lips shut. 'Do not worry about that, my dear Callista. Your importance to me is not measured in what you can give me. But if you must hear it, you have given me understanding, patience and compassion when no one else ever has. You accept me and my powers...' He trailed off.

Callista sensed his discomfort and his fear, far more potent than his desire to share his secret.

What could possibly be worse than telling the truth? she thought.

Sandsa turned back to her, his expression haunted. 'I have been remiss in the truth with you because I am afraid of what you will think, though I begin to question my own caution because what should I fear? I need be no one but myself with you, Callista. I'll love you for an eternity. I am sure of that now.'

A tidal wave of warmth began at her toes and swept up through her body, threatening to dissolve all common sense. Callista cleared her throat. 'Nice speech. But when do we get to the part where you tell me the truth?'

Sandsa dropped his chin onto the top of her head. 'I'm not

sure. But I do know that I want to keep spending time with you today, outside of headquarters, here in the light. We won't be able to do this for a while, I can feel it. And surely if we are attacked, you, as a subofficer, can call for backup.'

'I can't bring our clan out here until sundown — there're rules about fighting during the day, Sandsa!' Callista reminded him sternly. 'We probably pissed the governor off last night by going through the No-Go Zone so I don't want to make things any worse by starting a fight when the star's still in the sky. But we don't really need backup, so we? I'm sure you could crush anyone who came after us, isn't that right?'

She left his side before he could answer and leapt back into their hovercar which, apart from a scorched line down one panel, seemed to be functioning.

Sandsa appeared on the other side of the plexiglass. 'If you do not feel safe here in Atsa...'

Callista gripped the steering rods. 'Get in. If these are the last few hours of daylight we can enjoy until we destroy the Alcazaar, I'm not going to waste them.'

Despite her nerves demanding haste, she took a more roundabout route to The Sample than necessary and even stopped to show Sandsa how to eat bright pink sugar floss that a vendor was selling out of his cart on the side of the road. Sandsa was still contemplating the unusual treat when they reached the opposite end of Atsa City. The moment they passed beneath the archway announcing their entry into the large dome, thick warm air clung to their clothes and skin. Sandsa sat up straight and peered around, a smile spreading across his face. The sticky remains of his sweet lay on the floor, forgotten.

School children on Yalsa 5 saw their first and only trees here, in a climate-controlled environment that was much easier to reach than what other planets had to offer. The Sample had been created back when there was talk of terraforming the planet; one hopeful company had erected the dome as an example of their work, but since no governor had ever been interested in paying for such a costly service, the dome was the only part of Asta City that didn't sit on sand.

Callista parked the vehicle and powered it down. Immediately the whir of the engine cut out. She missed the noisy children from years past and sat there in silence, taking in the abandoned rainforest habitat, her disappointment growing. Unchecked plants chocked the pathways and moss crept up onto the rocks that had been chiselled into and positioned as signs for different walks through the trees.

Desperate to reclaim the joy she had felt in The Sample as a girl, she snagged Sandsa's hand and led him down a path of concrete that was shattered with age and roots. With childlike glee, she danced between the worst of the cracks, making sure never to land on them. Callista glanced back at Sandsa when his fingers slid from hers. He was smiling, but it wasn't because of her. He was busy sensing something — *someone*, Callista realised.

'Warm greetings, brother,' Sandsa said softly. 'I'm glad you came to see me.'

Callista spun back around and caught sight of the stranger behind them. He looked to be only a couple of years younger than Sandsa but, unlike the Maria clansman, he could hardly have commanded attention anywhere outside a classroom. The newcomer's green eyes sparkled as he jammed a cap over his bright copper hair, somehow making it even messier.

'Brothers?' Callista asked, looking between them.

The man beamed. 'Yes. I am Kuja.'

'You don't look like you came in from the deserts,' she observed.

'Kuja is...he prefers rainforests,' Sandsa said hesitantly. 'And I need to speak with him privately. He would not disturb me unless it was important.'

Callista held nothing back, letting Sandsa feel her disappointment and distrust before she moved away to perch on a nearby boulder. Even though she couldn't hear them or see their guarded thoughts, she made sure to keep her eyes on both men. Sandsa looked more and more harried while Kuja waved his hands, pleading with his eyes as well as his words.

What could be that serious? Callista wondered.

***

'You need to come back, Sandsa,' Kuja said, plucking at the loose khaki shirt he wore.

'The Ine sent you,' Sandsa accused.

'No, no! It's nothing to do with him. It's just that I...I do not like the atmosphere in the Everything Portal,' the Rforine said, using his preferred name for the divine realm — it was a truthful label, Sandsa supposed, because every god brought their unique powers there. 'Fayay is just so...*triumphant*. And with you gone, he's decided he's in charge. He's punishing us for stepping out of line, for threatening Father's grand design, and he's told us that if we dare abandon our duties for even a single moment he will kill us! And he could do it!'

Sandsa snorted. 'Ridiculous. Fayay is not all powerful — he only commands water. And he can't even read minds.'

Kuja tore at his lip with his teeth. His tongue swiped the brutalised pieces inside his mouth. 'I can read minds, Sandsa, but that doesn't make me powerful. You know I lack telekinesis and I'm much younger than Fayay, much weaker. And what about your people? Don't you worry about them?'

'My people know when to leave the deserts in pursuit of better lives, if those I've met here are any indication,' Sandsa said with a shake of his head. 'And mortals kill each other all the time, even among your people. It's no concern of mine if the desert tribes destroy themselves.'

Kuja's eyes glistened. 'Your thoughts are so violent...you're planning to kill people.'

'If I kill them, they'll have deserved it, for what they did,' Sandsa said, expecting this to anger his brother but Kuja instead threw himself at Sandsa, wrapping him into a hug.

Extracting an arm to pat his brother on the back, Sandsa glanced over at Callista who blew out a breath, looking bored. He needed to finish this conversation, and soon. Again Kuja probed his mind; again Sandsa let him. Kuja moved back, frowning. 'Our mother died a long time ago, Sandsa. It does not matter how.'

'She could have lived long enough to — ' Sandsa broke off, not sure how to finish the sentence.

'I visited her, you know,' Kuja said. Sandsa shot him a startled look. 'I'm well aware that she lived here. You didn't — you didn't even look for her, to check if she was okay. I'm *afraid*, Sandsa. I'm afraid that you knew to come here anyway.'

Sandsa scowled. 'Callista is the reason I came, not Mother. I love this woman. Feel it. Know it.'

'I do know it. But what does it all mean?' Kuja asked, his eyes flicking from side to side, as though he feared they were being watched.

'Are you afraid that it means you can choose to live as a man, as I have?'

'I'm afraid these gangs will kill you!' Kuja cried. 'I won't go through this again!'

Hushing his brother, Sandsa curled an arm around Kuja's shoulders and angled him away from Callista. He lowered his voice. 'Kuja. I won't let any Alcazaar filth kill me. I'm having a bit of trouble seeing the future, but I don't need my powers to know I'm meant to stay with Callista.'

'You think it's a coincidence that she has strange powers and appeared in your dreams, luring you here?' Kuja demanded.

'Why would Father send me after her?'

Kuja hung his head. 'I don't know. I just don't.' Then he sighed. Leaves rustled around them. 'I'm jealous. We're all jealous of you, Sandsa.'

Sandsa gave him a piteous smile. 'There you have it. The Ine would never risk such widespread disgruntlement among all his children. It is not his doing. Tell Fayay he's the most powerful of us now, if he wants to hear it so badly. Farewell, Kuja.'

Kuja's expression remained pained as he sprinted away into the trees, his footfalls vanishing along with his form. Sandsa turned to Callista, noting the fire in her eyes and the stiffness in her posture. He loved her. He wanted her. But what would she hate more — the truth or a lie? He dragged his feet as walked over to her, his mind racing.

When he reached her, he knew what to do.

CHAPTER THIRTEEN

Callista matched his steps as they explored what The Sample had to offer, their fingers sometimes brushing against each other. He had promised to tell her everything, but after ten minutes of wandering they were still encased in silence. The muggy air threatened to drown her and she continued to swallow more and more of it until finally she turned to him and framed his face with her hands. 'Just tell me. Whatever you're hiding, it's torturing you.'

'I can't...' he whispered.

Callista held his eyes. 'Sandsa. I feel like you've done something pretty huge to be with me. But I can't say that magic word back to you if I don't know who you are.'

'Perhaps you should sit down,' he suggested and she did, on a bench that was so weathered and chipped it was a miracle she didn't fall through the rotted wood.

Sandsa knelt before her, trembling. His fear was so palpable that Callista felt her eyes sting with tears.

'There are many sub-level gods,' he began. 'The desert god is one, the water god is another...these gods exist beneath the Creator God. But you know all this.'

'Are you giving me a lesson on how the universe works?' she asked wryly.

Sandsa stared down at her knees. She could feel him withdrawing into his mind so she cupped his chin with one hand

and guided him into the chair with the other. He smiled gratefully and leaned into her touch. 'Callista. I am very powerful. No one in the deserts could match me. My...chipless powers are part of that, not separate from it.'

'I suspected as much.'

'This is because...I am the desert god.' He paused, then rushed on when she said nothing, 'I am the Desine made flesh and blood. I command the deserts and Kuja commands the rainforests — that's why he vanished so quickly, if you were wondering. And our father...'

'Stop talking,' Callista said.

He did.

She drew a breath. 'You're a god?'

'Yes.'

Callista closed her eyes for a moment. He was telling the truth. And he was deeply afraid that she would reject him because of it.

'This doesn't change anything,' she told him. 'I still love you.'

His smile threatened to become infectious. 'You love me?'

'Sandsa!' she cried, her thumbs dipping into the corners of his lips and setting them at a flat line. 'With this lack of focus, how am I supposed to believe you're a god capable of omniscience?'

'Perhaps it is difficult to focus when you are so close to me?' he mused.

The laugh burst free from Callista before she could stop it. 'Sandsa. Get on with it.'

Sandsa pursed his lips. 'What do you know about desert powers and their limitations?'

'Only what Vom has told me,' she answered. 'I know they have to ask for permission to use the Magic and then they're restricted to minor displays of power. You don't have that problem.'

'No. I don't.'

Callista opened her mouth but her next words were lost in the ensuing scream of tortured wind. A tornado made of sand tore up around their feet, encasing them, tugging them away from the seat. She clung to Sandsa's shoulders as they hurtled into the sky and buried her face into his chest, reaching into his core to feel the immense power he was wielding.

He was a chasm; she fell into him.

When the wind stilled, Callista pushed him away to stare around at the endless desert and its seamless horizon. Her eyes ached from the glare and her tongue withered inside her mouth as the dry air began to rob her of precious moisture. Odd that she would feel moist in another place right now, but he was a god and he desired *her*.

She turned back and kissed him, then pulled him down to the sand with her. His mouth moved, drawing a hot, wet line from her lips to her earlobe. He'd barely grazed it before she gasped and leaned into him, inviting the kisses that spilled down her throat. Callista gazed up at the sky until spots danced in front of her eyes then dove into the shelter his neck provided, puckering his skin between her teeth. Moans escaped the lips travelling onto her shoulder, where he could proceed no further because of her jacket. He removed and discarded the item then slid the strap of her shirt down her arm.

Callista hesitated for a moment, then tossed her anxiety down the nearest dune, enjoying the unfettered slide of lips from shoulder to bicep. She offered no resistance when he pulled the shirt over her head, nor when he began tugging at her bra band so that he could expose her. His eyes darkened as she retreated to lie down in front of him. The sand was surprisingly soft against her back — she realised she could feel it moving beneath her, delivering a gentle massage that set the nerves of her skin on fire. It should have felt unusual. It didn't.

Sandsa came to her and kissed one pert breast, sending shivers cascading throughout her entire body. She watched as he swirled his tongue around her nipple, avoiding it, teasing her, never quite giving her what she wanted. He started to detach his lips from her skin but Callista slid her hand to the back of his head, threading fingers through his hair, guiding him lower, closer, *closer*. His mouth sealed over her breast and she arched her back, moaning as he obeyed her mental wish and moved over the sweat-slicked crevice between her mounds of flesh to find purchase on the other breast. She fed his mind with the intense bursts of warmth emanating from within her.

Sandsa...let me explore you, she said.

Please do, he responded.

Callista sat up and reefed his shirt up off his chest. She trapped his arms above his head in the tangles of the fabric, snickering until something audibly tore. Throwing the offending item away, Callista devoured his skin, trailing her taste buds over each and every micrometre of his chest. She drank in the groans that reverberated low on his body and followed them to the source, kissing his hair-dusted abdomen.

She lost herself in inflicting pleasure on him and in the pleasure he gave her, though they made the unspoken agreement to go no further than the edges of their pants. It was a tantalising barrier to dance across, for fingers to tease along — the boundary made the sensations even more intense. At last she lay beside him, her cheek against his chest. She did not question the shade at first, lulled into a doze by the beat of his heart and the fingertips etching heated lines over her back. But when Callista finally turned her head she stared up in amazement at the wave of sand cresting above them, the countless grains restless as they maintained the shape.

'Desert god, huh,' she said drowsily. 'You could destroy the Alcazaar in a heartbeat.'

Sandsa abruptly stiffened. The wave disintegrated, showering Callista with grit. She spluttered for a long minute, then wheezed, 'Sandsa, what's wrong?'

'Can't you hear them?' he asked, sitting upright and flinging his wild gaze around the dunes.

'I...I can't hear anything.'

'*Listen,*' he insisted, grabbing her hand, pulling her into chest

—

— and then she listened.

There were thousands, *millions*, of them begging, demanding, pleading for their god. Their words were like claws, digging into him, tearing his very being, hurting him in ways a lasgun never could. He had abandoned them. And now they had come to claim him.

You must not keep him from us! the voices cried.

Callista looked up at Sandsa. His blue eyes were vacant.

She was losing him.

'Sandsa!' Her hands found his shoulders and shook him. 'We need to get out of here! Take us back to Atsa!'

I can't... he said weakly.

'Take us back to Atsa *now!*'

Another wave of sand rose, then fell. Callista closed her eyes as it smothered her, then opened them again to see buildings she had known all her life. They were just inside Atsa City, right on the edge of it, where the ruined roads had not seen maintenance in centuries. She spun around and saw Sandsa flat on his back, gasping. She scuttled over to him and pillowed a hand beneath his head.

'What happened?' she asked.

'I used too much of my powers and they found me,' he said softly. 'It was hard enough to ignore them after a handful of weeks. How will I cope after months, years, *decades*?'

Callista pressed her lips against his forehead. *No one can force you to abandon me, Sandsa. No one. I can feel how powerful you are.*

'Powerful,' he repeated scornfully. 'I can't call upon the sands, even to destroy the Alcazaar, because the deserts and my people will feel me and demand my presence, and they might win. So now I am restricted to the sandless, chipless powers that we share.'

Callista helped him sit up. She hated to say it, but she had to. 'If you stop letting Vom and the others source their powers from you, they'll be helpless. I had a look at their weapons and, I'll be honest, they haven't got the firepower to defend themselves.'

Sandsa grimaced. 'They must learn to live without me. Without the powers. Because I am never going back. I *can't*. I can't be the god anymore.'

'Why?' she asked, brushing sand off his shirt.

Sandsa reached for her hand. She gave it. Together they descended into his mind, into the memories strewn with the cobwebs of time and buried beneath layers of hurt.

***

A boy in his mother's arms, laughing as sand skids over his fingers. A single clap of his hands smashes the small eddies and he turns a grin up at her, a beautiful woman with stunning aquiline features. Her eyes hold warmth in their hazel depths.

She loves him. His mother loves him. And that's all that matters.

He grows and grows until his cheeks are lined with a gentle blond fuzz that irritates him so much that he forbids any hair to breach his face. Soon he becomes old enough to do his father's bidding. He must become the deserts so he does — and he forgets what he is, what he was, and he roams the sands endlessly. He looks after those who have left the cities behind, gifting them with abilities, guiding them. He loses himself and becomes the god.

It takes years, but his mother finds him and pulls him back. The light hurts his eyes when he retakes human form and he's confused by the starkness of the deserts. They were beautiful before. Now he can't trust them. How did they make him forget who he was? How did he forget her?

He pummels the sand beneath his fists. She lets him. And then she hugs him like he's a little boy again. But his father — the Creator God, that spiteful Ine — has no mercy to give. Sandsa is not allowed to know the happiness the mortals enjoy. And he must not see his mother so often. He must stay in the deserts and return only to discuss important matters with the Ine.

The affection he sees between lovers makes no sense to him. He never sees it between his own parents. He never feels it himself. He even fears he does not love his mother — is he merely attached to her because she is the first face he saw?

Sometimes he takes a human form that lasts for several minutes so he can stand atop the dunes, staring down at the campsites belonging to this or that tribe. He could be among them. He could be one of them.

But he's not. He has to guide them. It is a hopeless existence but he accepts it. Century in and century out, he does what he is created to do. Eventually brothers and sisters arrive. Some of them he gets along with. But he has little time for them, besieged as he is by his duties in the desert.

He can't be sure, but he thinks more than three millennia might have passed since his creation. Does time pass when you go nowhere? He feels nothing. And his existence has no meaning.

Until...Kuja. When Sandsa visits home — or the white expanse that everyone else calls home — he sees his mother holding the baby and his life changes. He loves this boy, this rainforest god. He later takes him on adventures; a man and his kid brother, running wild over planets, dodging through whirling portals made of turbulent sand or fluttering leaves. They chase each other like mortal children do and steal a ball from one family, bouncing the rubbery toy between them, laughing and playing and using their powers for themselves, not just others.

Kuja grows up and the Ine can't make him to go to his rainforests. Kuja wants to stay with his brother so it's Sandsa who is sternly told by the Creator God that he must cut off ties with his favourite sibling for the good of the galaxy.

Sandsa refuses. His mother backs him up. But the Ine will not have it.

She has the binding scars that the Ine gave her, and the immortality that came with them. But now she has caused two sons to reject their destinies and their duties.

And she will not apologise.

Sandsa witnesses the stripping of her scars. He is confused — why is she not angry? Why is she not screaming, hitting, spitting? So he does those things for her. But she tells him not to, it's okay, she's a human, she never belonged here.

'But you made me feel!' he shouts.

'Be there for Kuja,' is all she says before she leaves, condemned to her short mortal life.

Sandsa knows he cannot fight his father. The Ine is the greatest, oldest power in the universe. Losing is a certainty and so hot, human anger rages inside the desert god. He finds that it causes wild sandstorms that threaten his people. It will be his fault if they suffer.

So Sandsa goes back to them and saves them. He casts away his anger but with it goes the joy he knew so briefly.

Over the decades, such terrifyingly short decades, he visits Kuja in secret — but are his activities really shielded from the Ine? How can he know? Soon he stops seeing his brother because he fears that the Ine will punish them both. Sandsa's life fades to nothing for a third time. He no longer cares about his own people. He doesn't even care if his guidance hinders more than it helps. He knows he should feel guilty about that. But he doesn't.

And then the woman comes to him in his dreams, far more beautiful than anyone he's ever seen, including his mother. He belongs with the dream woman. He is meant to be like her, made of flesh and blood and desires.

She is his lifeline. And he must leave this numb existence to find her.

The price he pays is worth it.

His powers, though useful, would only pull him away from her, back to the deserts and the people there. The god could overthrow the Alcazaar in a heartbeat, but the god is not allowed to feel, to love.

He just wants to be a man.

A man in love with a woman.

***

When Sandsa came to himself, he saw the tears glistening in

139

Callista's brown eyes and felt the warmth of her palm against his cheek. He kissed the pads of her fingers, one by one, then clasped her hand to his chest. Her gaze held his for a long time, her eyelashes flickering beneath the star's fading light. Releasing a breath that felt as though it had been trapped inside his lungs forever, Sandsa said, 'I aspire to be as human as you, Callista.'

'You would give up being a god for me?' she asked, her voice shaking.

Sandsa smiled. 'I already did.'

'It's a good thing that no one could match the powerful chipless man you make anyway,' she said, a grin now curling her lips.

Her mind was brimming with images of his past and he could not recoil from his memories now that she had them. But Callista embraced it, all of it, and then she skidded towards the future her visions were showing her — countless days fighting beside him, risking her life with him —

'You're immortal,' she murmured.

Sandsa nodded. 'Yes, but I am not invulnerable. A stray lasgun bolt could very well kill me.' Before she could voice her next thought, he powered on, 'Do not worry. Our binding scars will ensure your immortality. I do not intend to lose you.'

'Easy there, you,' Callista said, lightly tapping his cheek. 'I might be entertaining the love notion but I won't be...*binding* myself to you until I'm ready. If I ever am,' she added.

'If?' Sandsa repeated, smirking.

'If I did not love you, I would slap that look off your face.'

'I love you too, Callista.'

Then he kissed her. And time vanished.

CHAPTER FOURTEEN

The layer beneath the tree canopy was dark when they returned, risking one last burst of Sandsa's powers to teleport them back to the hovercar. The moist air inside The Sample murmured along Callista's skin, smothering the blush that had begun on a completely different side of the city. She leaned into Sandsa, enjoying his warmth, still amazed by how much he had gone through, how much he'd given up. For her.

Callista felt the strings tying him to the deserts strain and fray, but not snap entirely, not yet. Telling her his secret had just been the beginning, she knew, but already his shoulders stood higher, and his smile was fuller than it had ever been. His frequent kisses were ridiculously innocent considering what they had done. And what they would do...

Her thighs clenched. His eyes darkened when he caught the traitorous thought.

Callista rolled her eyes. 'I'm human. I can't help having those thoughts about you.' She paused. 'My love.'

'My love,' he repeated.

They resumed their positions in the hovercar, though not without Sandsa viewing the driver's seat with a hunger akin to what he felt for her. Callista hoped to distract him by leaning forward, pressing her chest against the steering rods and forming a deeper dip between her breasts than usual. She felt a spike of interest from him. But then it was buried beneath his concern.

The falling night was nearly upon them.

As she drove Callista's eyes chased passing shadows and her heart began to slam into her ribs more rapidly. Sensing her tension, Sandsa rested a hand over one of hers. What would it be like, she wondered, living when all of her friends had died, when Atsa City itself had finally been reclaimed by the wild desert?

She pictured herself standing in these very streets, surrounded by ruins, her voice the only sound in a desolate place. And then she glanced at Sandsa, understanding the loneliness he had suffered. It was beyond bearing.

Callista turned onto the road leading to their headquarters and immediately tapped the brake. The hovercar slowed, its engine purring a soft challenge. The blockade ahead was formed by four large vehicles, four bulky metal boxes packed with an array of lasguns and lascannons, though Callista had yet to see the reputed flamethrowers — why would the Chippers want to get that close to their victims anyway?

The Chipper tanks were painted a deep indigo, making them hard to see in the fading light. Dashed down two sides of each vehicle were the standard five gold strokes that GLEA used to advertise their presence. Callista had seen this symbol on enough Webcasts from enough planets to know who it belonged to.

'It is tempting to resort to my godly powers,' Sandsa murmured.

Callista firmed her lips into one tight line. 'I bet it is.'

He cupped her cheek, his gaze boring into her. 'The thought of having to leave you will curb that temptation. Now. I have already shown my powers to them — you have not.' Sandsa moved his hand to her shoulder and squeezed. 'You do not need to risk exposure.'

Callista shrugged him off. 'Can't stop me backing you up with a lasgun.'

'I wouldn't dare,' Sandsa said, leaping out onto the pavement in one swift movement.

She tapped her lasgun against her thigh as she followed him down the road. She was impressed that Sandsa felt confident enough in his abilities to face the Chippers alone, but if he was clamping down on his powers the way he had promised her, then he was definitely going to need a subofficer at his back. The view wasn't so bad either.

She admired his tight backside in the practical denim he'd swapped the leather for. The fabric, though more flexible, definitely still clung in the right places. His walk was different and his knees were slightly bent these days, no doubt from learning to keep his stance low during his training with Bock in the armoury. Even though he lacked a weapon this night, his hips still favoured one side as he sauntered forward to meet the Chippers. Callista remained a few paces behind him — she wasn't crazy enough to put herself right in the firing line when he had used his powers for much longer than she had been alive.

'It is almost too dark for you,' Sandsa told the woman who stepped out to meet him.

This Chipper was not entirely human. The spray of purple freckles over her features was too delicate to be viral in nature — that and her scalp was covered with tiny tentacles that looked more like stubby toes than hair. Standing out on her temple, beneath a patch of stretched skin, was the chip that allowed her to touch and warp the universe's energy.

'Did you waste most of the day looking for us?' Callista called over Sandsa's shoulder. 'Well, if the Alcazaar *are* footing your medical bills and paying you better, I suppose it's worth braving the chill of night.'

The woman fiddled with the zipper of her purple jumpsuit. Callista supposed it must be a uniform because the other Chippers were also wearing them, though this woman's jumpsuit bore enough gold strokes on the shoulders to indicate that she had a special rank.

The Chipper dropped her hand from the zipper to her holstered lasgun. 'I'm Colonel Jeras Nerani and I don't work with any starking gangs. The ones behind me don't either.'

'So there are renegade Chippers who have had enough of doing the bidding of the Creator God, how surprising,' Sandsa said blandly. 'You cut into your skin to insert those chips and yet he rarely talks to you. Clearly he is not worth the effort. It's likely your traitorous comrades have worked this out for themselves.'

'We do not use the chips solely to reach our Creator,' Jeras said, murmurs sounding behind her as the other Chippers echoed their agreement. 'To serve the galaxy, to protect those who need it, to uphold the laws of each planet's governing body...those are the Agency's goals.'

Sandsa lifted one eyebrow. 'You threaten us with your tanks merely for a philosophical debate?'

'We're not all sellouts!' the colonel said, her very human green eyes darting between the two clanspeople. 'So what are you, Bolt? Desert magician? Or is your chip hidden?'

'He can't move sand and he doesn't have a chip,' Callista said, answering for Sandsa. 'I've seen him use his powers. He's not limited like you or the desert people.'

'I can demonstrate, if you like,' Sandsa offered.

Jeras snapped her head from side to side. 'No! I do not want to die at dusk, thank you. The Agency may argue the point. I'm here for your help.'

'You want him to deal with the Chippers who're working for the Alcazaar,' Callista guessed. 'You're not powerful enough to take out the clans or your renegades, are you?'

'It's just the one gang I want gone,' the Chipper said, visibly grinding her teeth. 'I understand how this city works. This day/night agreement between the governor and the gangs has worked long enough that it's practically official — so that's not my issue. No. There's too many of my own people involved.'

'So ask the regional commander of this solar system for reinforcements!' Callista snapped.

Colonel Nerani cast her eyes down at the road — and her disappearing shadow. 'One of them is the regional commander. His words mean more than mine to our superiors.'

'You fools actually expect me to side with you?' Sandsa said with a twist to his lips. 'If your *Creator God* will not help you, then I certainly won't do it in his place.'

Jeras retreated a pace, scowling. 'Some of our agents are hurting innocent people. And so too are those Alcazaar you're fighting against. You're worth twenty of us, being the way you are, and I don't care how you got your powers. I only care how you use them.'

'Rather dark out, isn't it?' Callista said, waving a hand up at the pinpricks of light arrayed across the night sky.

'Yes, it is,' Jeras agreed and sought the safety of a tank.

The Chippers soared away, presumably to the outpost housing those of them who had not sold out to the Alcazaar. Sandsa turned to Callista and pulled her into a deep, lasting kiss.

When he released her, she said, 'Colonel Nerani really needs our help, I could feel it.'

'I know. But that does not mean I should assist her.'

Callista released a hiss of air. 'We're going to have to fight her renegades either way. And I'm scared they'll overpower us. We're not gods, neither of us. Not anymore.'

'I won't let them hurt you,' Sandsa told her in a low voice.

They kissed again, hands wandering and diving beneath clothes, sliding along bare skin, testing the boundaries they had shied from earlier. The kiss took everything from Callista but she gave more, hungered for more.

You are my future, he whispered. *Only you.*

Callista kept her tone playful. *We'll see. Ala says no one ends up with their first.*

Their first what? he asked, confusion seeping into his thoughts.

Callista began to laugh, but it was short-lived.

The war had already begun.

CHAPTER FIFTEEN

Midnight blue and studded with broken lights, the hovercar was almost invisible on the nightscape of Atsa City. It was filled to the brim with Maria packing lasguns, and there was no possible way for it to have left headquarters after the fall of dusk. Sandsa had distantly noted its arrival, gleaning from the minds of his clanspeople the orders that had brought them out this early. The governor had forbidden the clans from venturing into daylight and his threat of sending GLEA after them had kept everyone in line until now. But since the Chippers were already attacking the Maria in the darkest hours, it seemed Ala had decided that she was done playing by the rules.

The hovercar careened into view, much too fast, and went wide. A large lasbolt struck the tar beside the driver's side of the vehicle, a lucky miss, because the driver had not yet noticed he was being followed. He was simply enjoying his ride. But when hot tar splattered the door and sloshed up over the opaque windows, the driver lost his ignorance and gained panic in its place. He began zigzagging down the road.

'Chipcopter with infra-red vidcams!' Callista snarled, pointing. 'Governor Garnett banned them from bringing those here to Yalsa 5. And Colonel Nerani wants us to help her when she's obviously had these in storage? The Alcazaar's Chippers had to get them from somewhere!'

While the hovercar continued to swerve alarmingly, she

ducked inside their headquarters, presumably to rouse some reinforcements. But what could the Maria do? Sandsa's clan had neither the galactic connections nor the permission of the Alcazaar to import anti-air lasguns, the artillery required to face off against a knife-sharp 'copter. Its windows were as dark and smooth as black ice and the four hoverpads spaced evenly underneath the craft where whisper silent. No wonder the clanspeople in the hovercar hadn't noticed they were being pursued.

The 'copter continued to strafe the road, its bolts skirting the perimeter of the vehicle, toying with the occupants. Sandsa started sprinting down the road, uncoiling the power within, preparing to take the 'copter out —

Something exploded behind him. Sandsa tossed a look over his shoulder and saw that the front of the Maria headquarters had been scoured clean by a large blast sent from a lascannon. A second Chipcopter had arrived — and it was a lot better armed than its companion, Sandsa noted grimly. Callista's lifesign was a steady thrum behind the blast-proof shutters so he need not worry about her, but still he reached for her mind, a glancing touch that she blocked —

This time the fireball came from in front of him. Sandsa shouted in anguish. How could he have let himself be distracted like some...*like some mortal!* The hovercar now lay on its side, its wounds glowing and belching smoke into the night.

Sandsa glared up at the 'copters as they drew in line with each other. All it took was a single thought from him and the flying machines collided, flattening together like pressed paper. They flamed briefly then hit ground, blackened and unidentifiable as anything that had ever broken free from the grip of gravity.

Sandsa gritted his teeth as he approached the unbearable heat exiting the wreckage of the hovercar. Bodies spilled from inside the vehicle, scattered like the toys of a petulant child.

They can't die because of my lapse in concentration! Sandsa thought, calling on swirls of sand to swarm around the bodies in preparation for teleporting them away.

Sandsa, no! Callista's voice cried

Sandsa blew out a breath. She was right. He couldn't risk it. Already he heard the voices, gentle whispers for now, but if he activated the Desine's powers they would rise into a howl of despair. He gnawed on the inside of his cheek, welcoming the coppery blood into his mouth, the reminder of what he was. A man. A mere man. He would have to rely on this fleshy vessel and its limited powers from now on.

Sandsa stepped no further towards the ruined hovercar, intending on using his telekinesis to bring out the bodies in one go, but he found his ability to use it stunted. He frowned. *Of course. The god was more powerful than me. But that does not mean I am helpless.*

One body rose from the ground, hovered, then drifted to safety.

One clansperson saved.

But there were still many more people in there, people who would not survive if he kept removing them at this frustratingly glacial rate. They needed him. They needed him *now*.

Sandsa entered the wreckage and knelt beside the person closest to him. The skin of his fingers blackened and bubbled when he slid them between tar and victim. Flinching from the pain, Sandsa scooped the fragile body into his arms and carried his fellow Maria clansperson away from the flames and the chemical fuel tank that could explode at any moment.

Callista was suddenly there to take his burden. Releasing the man into her care, Sandsa returned to the inferno and retrieved another. And another. Still more bodies coasted away, as though held by invisible hands.

On the sixth trip, he saw Ala shouting at him, her mouth oscillating furiously even though no sound seemed to escape her. Sandsa squinted, trying to read the words from her lips.

'She keeps saying you'll die if ya keep this up!' Ala roared, suddenly audible.

'It would make matters less complicated for you if I did,' Sandsa said, swinging around, uncaring that he could no longer feel his fingers, his palms, his wrists.

Ala grabbed his shoulder, pinning him at her side. 'I'm never gonna think you're good enough for her but you are Maria and, stark it, I will not lose any more tonight!'

'So let me finish my job.'

Sandsa walked back into the flames. Just one clansperson left now. Just one. He stumbled over rubble and hit the ground. The sound heralding the fuel tank's death seemed to come at him from all sides, as though several people stood around him, hissing through their teeth. As he crawled towards his goal, the knees of his pants disintegrated, giving way to roughened road that rubbed his skin raw. His vision swam; his arms were reduced to stumps — no, they were burned and bleeding but still intact. He distantly regretted not wearing his jacket.

Sandsa reached the last victim. They did not appear to be injured — but then he turned them over. Half the woman's face was a mess of blood and ichor. Trying not to retch, he held his mangled hand over her face, forcing weak streams of white light to pour from his fingers. Relieved that he still had this power, reduced in potency as it was, he watched the healthy pink spread slowly from her jaw to her temple.

He knew he should have waited until they were both outside to heal the woman, but he wanted to keep this particular power secret. His clan would constantly demand it of him and he wasn't sure he could recover quickly enough to perform on command. His powers were now greedily eating through his energy reserves faster than they ever had before. He had to force himself to yank his hand away from his fellow clansperson's face when the healing began to take too much from him.

Sandsa looped his arms around the woman's torso and hips, gathered her against his chest, and tried to stand. His aching legs refused. He swore at them, using many choice words that Callista had insisted were part of the local vernacular. His thighs, seared with heat, trembled. Eventually, one knee obeyed, rising unsteadily through the smoke. Sandsa coughed. His eyes watered. And then his precious cargo fell onto a bed of ash and distorted metal. A tortured rasp peeled over his lips as he bent over to retrieve her. But he was too weak.

He toppled over the woman, his chin striking the blazingly hot tar. Sandsa's eyelids sealed; prying them apart was a mammoth task, made more difficult by the junk that tried to glue his eyelashes together. Defeated, he allowed one last gasp of air to escape and submitted his body to the road that had become his final resting place.

Two boots appeared beside him. He tipped his head to the side and studied them; the soles were worn and melted and the hardy hide was interrupted by holes that spewed blackened blood.

As he watched, the boots grew, lengthening into legs that were translucent and ethereal. A torso, arms and head followed, until she existed in all her glory.

The spectre crouched beside him, her face savaged by her manner of death. 'No, my son. You cannot share this grave with me.'

'Mother?' he croaked.

She was still so beautiful, even with the burns cascading down her face, even with a hole in her throat oozing gunk and one of her arms hanging at an odd angle. Seemingly unaware of these injuries, she reached for his hands, hauling him up from the road; he nearly tripped over the Maria clanswoman lying beneath him in the process. Sandsa crouched down to touch her, but his fingers sailed through skin and bone and even tar, invisible to the world. He staggered back up onto his feet again and looked over to find his physical form splayed out on the road. His shirt was in tatters, torn away from burns and cuts. Mercifully, he felt nothing.

'You died here,' he said, focusing on his mother rather than his discarded body.

She nodded once. 'Yes. This very road. This very way. The Alcazaar are not very imaginative in their attacks.'

'How are you...?'

'Enough.' Icy fingers lay across his lips. 'You live still.'

'How...?'

Her smile was as brilliant as it had been when she still lived despite her cheek being torn open, her teeth in plain view. 'I can't tell you, Sandsa. It's not my place. Go back to her. Go back to Callista.'

Sandsa captured her hand and tightened his grip. 'But Mother, I...I've missed...'

'I'll always be here, watching over you,' she said, her voice becoming an echo, her face dissolving. 'Go back to her...go back to her *now!*'

He floated for a moment, free of feeling, but then he fell back into a vessel of agony. The nearby tank screamed into his ear, an explosion imminent. He grabbed the Maria clanswoman and shot to his feet.

Callista, I need your help! he sent.

He cried out, then telekinetically hurled the body he'd been carrying through the air. He couldn't see Callista catch the woman with her own powers, but he trusted her, knew she could do it. He stumbled, then burst into a wonky run. He nearly fell several times but he kept going, desperate to reach the mortal woman whose body was hot with passion for him, whose mind was warm with thoughts of the future.

Sandsa found himself face down on the road again, tasting blood. His tongue had been caught between his teeth when he'd hit the ground and his nose had taken a battering of its own. Flames danced over him, taunting his exposed skin, but then they receded, the fuel that had given them life now covered in the dry foam being blasted from nozzles on deep purple tanks.

Nerani's Chippers? Sandsa thought. *But it's night-time!*

Callista was near him, a ball of emotion — anger and relief. Her focus was entirely on him; the woman Callista had caught was being carried away by another Maria clansperson, one who seemed surprised to find her in such good health. Sandsa leaned heavily onto Callista and could not stifle the smile that slipped onto his lips. He felt anaesthetised by her very presence.

With her help, Sandsa managed to turn around and face the

lifesigns he could sense nearby. He shouted at them, his throat crackling, 'Come out, you filthy Alcazaar! You murderers!'

The nearby Alcazaar force appeared from behind a corner two blocks away, then began advancing. Those who weren't passengers aboard the heavily armed hovercars marched on foot, their weapons at the ready. Within moments a pack of Maria clanspeople had poured out from their headquarters and sprung up defensively around Sandsa, lasguns out and charged.

Ala drew in line with Sandsa and nodded at him, her face grim. She felt ready for a fight — and so did her people. This barricade made out of Maria bodies was far longer than any line-up of the Creator God's sons and daughters. The willingness of these people to stand up for a stranger who hadn't been one of their own for very long was both touching and confusing.

Guarding their backs were the Chippers he had spoken to earlier, though there were markedly fewer of them than the Chippers on the side of the Alcazaar. Sandsa's eyes found Colonel Jeras Nerani. He was astonished by the determination that fanned each breath and cranked each beat of her heart. She was standing by them at the risk of angering her regional commander. She could lose her rank and her life. But she didn't care. Because protecting the people of Atsa City was more important to her.

Sandsa felt Callista stiffen in response to the growing number of Chipper lifesigns. She withdrew into herself, hiding her presence. There was no point in Sandsa doing the same. Everyone here had seen or heard about what he could do.

The oldest of the Alcazaar held his fists above his head. His clansmen dutifully fell back, allowing their Clan Leader to stand out. He looked about seventy, his white hair styled into a high starched apex which resembled a single frozen flame. His sun-spotted skin was now also riddled with red dots thrown by the sights of Maria weapons. He seemed unbothered by his peril and continued forward, leisurely tapping his cane on the road. As he drew nearer the Maria line, it became apparent that he was much shorter than any of them, but he was just as lean as a still-fighting Clan Leader should be.

He stopped mere paces away and levelled his gaze at Sandsa. 'Bolt. I am CL. You refused a request from your Clan Leader to join the Alcazaar. Will you walk this way now, before any more blood is shed on your account? I will spare most of the Maria this night if you do.'

The man had apparently changed his street name to the initials of his position. It was a presumptuous move, even if he had earned the right to make it.

'I am having enough difficulty standing,' Sandsa said. He was still relying on Callista to remain upright and knew she couldn't support his weight for long. 'But even if I could walk over there, I wouldn't.'

CL raised his cane. Several of the Maria ducked, but Ala, who was on the receiving end of the cane's capped base, didn't so much as flinch. A long, sharp blade, so basic it didn't even thrum backwards and forwards like those favoured by many of Sandsa's clanspeople, shot forward, halting a whisker from Ala's nose.

'Only your subofficers can make this decision for you, Bolt,' CL said with a sad shake of his head, as though he was disappointed in Sandsa. 'You are their responsibility...for the moment.'

Sandsa felt his lips rear back from his teeth. 'You killed my mother. My subofficers would understand my need to seek vengeance.'

'Is this true, about his mother?' Ala muttered out of the corner of her mouth.

'Yes,' Callista answered shortly.

'Can't blame him then,' Ala said.

CL fluttered his hand in front of his face, as if fanning himself. 'I do not recall your mother. But there have been many innocents killed in the crossfire. Unfortunate. But this is Atsa City. Such things happen.'

Sandsa, you are too young to be Julia's son! Callista reminded him.

Sandsa's fingers curled into claws. 'You can't offer me anything that will make me forget my thirst for your blood, CL.'

'There are many things a man might thirst for,' CL told him. The blade slipped back inside the cane. 'I can promote you to subofficer.'

'Bolt is already a subofficer,' Ala said.

Several pairs of eyes swung to her.

'Made him one last night,' she continued, her snarl victorious. 'You can see why, right? Him being better than the Chippers.'

'You knew about his abilities?' CL asked her, frowning.

Ala chortled and the rest of the Maria echoed her. ''Course. Why do you think I didn't kill him when he turned up lookin' for trouble? But here's the thing, CL, he's not the only one I have.'

Callista's nails dug through a hole in Sandsa's shirt and found flesh. He hissed. She whispered an apology and loosened her grip. Sandsa wanted to comfort her, but a potent exhaustion was beginning to creep in from his fingers and toes. Either the spotlights on the Alzacaar hovercar's were dimming or he was fighting impending unconsciousness. He suspected the latter.

CL clicked his fingers. One of his Chippers strode forward and declared, 'Any of your clanspeople who have chipless powers must be handed over to the Galactic Law Enforcement Agency.'

'They're not your starkin' property!' Ala said, slapping a lasgun against her thigh. 'My clanspeople don't have chips or any tech that's yours so they don't owe you Chippers a single starking thing.'

'And the Agency *should* respect the free will granted to us all by the Creator God,' Colonel Nerani spoke up from beside Ala.

'And what're you gonna do about this, Colonel?' the opposing Chipper said scornfully. He had many more gold strokes on the shoulders of his uniform than Nerani did. Clearly he was the regional commander.

Nerani's smile was full of teeth. 'Our superiors are not likely to believe any report I file if you write a contradictory one. But not to worry, the more you lot get up to, the more proof I'll have to get you thrown out of the Agency.'

'What's it to be, Subofficer Bolt?' CL asked loudly, so that all those gathered could hear him. 'Surely you don't want all these people to die because of you?'

Sandsa blinked, though the action seemed to take centuries because his eyelids felt so sluggish. 'I will not be an Alcazaar or a Chipper. No, CL...I intend to *become you.*'

CL snarled and turned his back on the Maria. Once he was safely inside an armoured hovercar, the Alcazaar retreated. Sandsa took one step forward to follow them but tripped — and fell into darkness.

***

'Colonel Nerani!' Callista called from the ground, cradling Sandsa's head in her lap and ignoring the feet slapping the tar around her as the Maria mobilised to chase the Alcazaar down. 'I need your help.'

'In a moment,' promised the colonel before rapidly exchanging words with Ala. They were trying to reach an agreement on where to launch their biggest attack.

'I need your help, stark your Creator God!' Callista snapped.

Ala's heavy boots clomped over to her. 'Cals, this isn't about you and your lover boy anymore. Get him inside — Bock can look after him. I need you on the streets.'

Callista raised her glistening eyes. 'Ala, I think can heal him. *But I don't know how.*'

'You chipless?' Jeras asked, the tiny tentacles on her head swinging to one side as she moved her head to regard Callista.

Callista nodded.

'Lieutenant Bartan!' the woman bellowed and another Chipper appeared. 'Look, we can't heal or do anything fancy like that, but Bartan here has a knack for finding what needs fixing in people, thanks to the same glitch in his chip that weakens his forcefields. He can't just sense lifesigns, he can pinpoint bad energy right up to the cellular level, see where something's gone wrong. If you really can heal, which I'd not be shocked to hear at this point, then maybe he can help.'

Callista nodded once at Nerani, then transferred her fierce gaze to Ala. 'As your fellow subofficer, I am ordering you to fuck up the Alcazaar's night for them!'

'As if I would do anything else!' Ala said, rolling her good eye. The mechanical one remained fixed in place. 'When you get him sorted out I want you with me, Subofficer Dancer. You gotta help me set an example — I don't want all these subofficers I'm about to promote to think it's okay to sit down and catch a breath when there's fightin' to be done.'

'Are you sure you want to share the clan with that many subofficers?' Callista asked, smiling.

A dark cast fell over Ala's face. 'Honestly, Cals, I don't expect most of them to survive the night. So make sure you do.'

The undisputed leader of the Maria and Colonel Nerani both headed towards one of the purple tanks belonging to the Chippers. Callista stood to wave off her clanspeople as they hurried into the night, wishing she was heading out with them.

'Can't fucking believe it,' Bartan growled beside her. 'Working with the likes of you.'

Callista frowned at the lieutenant, taking in his bulky form and the thick neck that ended with a round, squashed face. 'This man is your colonel's only chance of putting down the Alcazaar.'

Bartan grumbled something under his breath then grabbed Sandsa, lifted him bodily over one shoulder, and stomped over to the Maria headquarters where a skeleton crew was stationed. Callista could feel the restless energy of Bock in there; Ala had ordered him to stay behind. The teenager was understandably unhappy about this.

Callista followed Bartan, stepping carefully over scarred concrete. The damage was mostly cosmetic, thanks to how the building had been constructed, and since cleaning was a costly expense it would probably become a permanent alteration.

Callista pressed her palm to the print reader. A small beep confirmed her identity and the door slid open. Once they were both safely inside, they moved upstairs and into the lounge room where Bartan cleared a table before lying Sandsa atop it with surprising gentleness. He then balled up Sandsa's ruined shirt into a makeshift pillow.

Callista hovered nearby, hands dangling uselessly by her sides. She wasn't sure if she could actually heal Sandsa, because they hadn't reached that stage in her lessons — and because she'd never attempted to do it. What if she tried now only to fail? Biting her lip, she watched the uneven rise and fall of Sandsa's chest. His breaths were so short, so shallow. She wanted to run her fingers over his skin, to reassure him that she was there, but there were so many burns.

'Can he heal?' Bartan asked, jerking his head at Sandsa's supine form.

Callista nodded.

'How's he do it?'

'He holds his hand over the injury...' Callista trailed off as Bartan came over to her. He seized her wrist and positioned her hand above Sandsa's body.

'That'll be step one then,' Bartan said, letting go of her arm and taking up a position at her shoulder. The chip beneath the skin on his temple seemed to be pulsing in time with a heartbeat. 'I'm told you can sense stuff. I guess we'll find out. First you gotta link up with me, like...a passenger. Then we'll go inside him and find each little teensy dot of bad energy. These dots, they'll correspond with a physical bit of him, so I guess that's what you'll have to fix.'

Callista nodded but the moment she reached for Bartan's mind she hit a wall of static that buzzed angrily at her. She recoiled, then reminded herself that she didn't need to hide from the Chippers, or that sensation, anymore.

She loosened the muscles in her shoulders and arms, her

posture slumping, and tried again. The link between them vibrated uncertainly, then finally settled.

Bartan was a hulking mass filling both the room and her mind, but now that she was connected to him and could see his good nature, she thought of him as an oversized teddy bear. She spent some time studying each facet of his lifesign, marvelling at how limited his powers were, then let him feel her apology when impatience flooded his energy.

'Let's get this over with,' Bartan muttered from somewhere far away.

And then he yanked her down into the body of the man she loved.

Blood roared and whooshed disconcertingly around them. Callista's brief panic faded into curiosity as Bartan began to indicate the damaged areas to her. She wasn't sure how he managed to do this, given that neither of them had hands in this...form. But it worked — where he saw pockets of bad energy, she saw something that needed healing.

Shoving aside her fears, Callista moved through blackened, blistered cells that shook at her presence. She commanded them, coaxed them, and badgered them until they stirred back into life. Each ropey edge of the cells blazed with light, new and healed, but she didn't stop to celebrate the discovery of her new power. There was too much to do.

Bartan's presence now felt distant, weak. He was struggling to catch up to her, lagging three or four paces for every one of hers. But she didn't go back for him — she no longer needed his help. Injured cells were now calling out to her, showing her how to find them.

Emboldened, Callista skipped even further ahead, finding a

rhythm in Sandsa's steadying heartbeat. Soon phantom hands were gliding along hers and fingers filled the spaces between her own, drawing her further into the dance. Two spirits circled each other, recognising, laughing, loving. Somehow they were both there, as real as they were in the life beyond Sandsa's body.

You figured out how to heal me, Sandsa said, looking around at her handiwork. *Clever.*

Only returning the favour, she responded with a grin.

Sandsa's tone became sharp. *Who is that?*

A Chipper. I needed his help.

His sensing abilities are exceptional, for a Chipper, Sandsa noted. *You won't need his help next time. And hopefully with enough practice you will be able to heal me fully.*

Callista brushed her lips over his cheek. *I have to go. Our clan needs me.*

She peeled open the dry, gritty eyes that belonged to her physical form and leaned forward, anchoring the heels of her palms on the table and fighting the dizziness that spiralled down from her skull and into her bent knees. When she refocused, she saw that Sandsa's skin was now bright red and shiny, not fully healed but no longer black like overdone meat. She pushed herself away from the table and spun towards the exit, then immediately regretted it when her head started pounding.

Warm hands led her away from the door and pressed her into a chair. Callista watched dully as the table approached her, then realised the high pitched squeal was not caused by her headache, but by the chair beneath her as it was being forced across the floor in Bartan's strong grip. The Chipper knelt at her side, saying, 'I can feel in your energy that you've exhausted yourself. Relax. It'll pass. Give it time. Nice work, by the way. Nerani'd welcome you into the Chippers anytime.'

'I'm stronger than anyone with the chip, aren't I?' Callista mused.

Bartan nodded. 'Loads more. Makes you wonder if the Creator God has heard our pleas for help in fighting the galaxy's evils and is giving us his answer. In you.'

The snort of disdain was ripped from her nostrils, causing her head to ache more fiercely. 'I doubt it. These powers are the reason Sandsa found me and left his home behind. The Creator God can't be happy about that.'

Bartan stared at her, confusion creasing his forehead. 'What the stark are you talking about?'

'Go,' Callista told him instead of explaining. She suspected he wouldn't believe her anyway. 'Go help your colonel. And tell Subofficer Ala I'll be along when I can.'

Bartan nodded then left without further comment.

Once he was gone, Callista eased further back into her chair, willing her strength to return. The Maria needed her — and her lasgun. She couldn't let them down.

One long hour later, she was ready.

CHAPTER SIXTEEN

Several explosions rocked the city all at once, briefly turning night into day. One of the blasts blew heat right into her face but Callista pressed on. Her jacket was scorched in places and her boots were caked with the fire-resistant foam that the Chippers had spewed across the road, dousing the walls of flames the Alcazaar had erected to keep their pursuers at bay.

The string of lights in this pleasant neighbourhood were now lifeless and stood watch over handfuls of shattered glass. Some windows in the nearby buildings had followed suit, though others were protected from harm by humming shields. Callista sensed the fear of the people trapped inside their residential prisons and felt no sympathy for them; they had been content to live in a city with a gang problem so long as they didn't have to see or hear any evidence of it for themselves.

Callista skidded and swore. The foam was slippery and the vision that sprang up to blind her didn't help matters; she nearly missed seeing the potentially fatal steam of lasbolts in real time as it thundered down the middle of the road towards her. Callista held up her shielding device and gritted her teeth, painfully aware that she was the sole person in the group with defensive tech. The people behind her only carried lasguns and the small shield she was carrying would barely protect her, let alone them.

Her head throbbed in protest as she reached for her overtaxed powers once more.

Sparks showered around her in a V-shape, colourful and deadly, but none of the Maria fell. Callista had ordered her clanspeople to follow several paces behind her and was glad they'd obeyed her. But she wasn't sure how much longer she could lead them. Her arms ached from holding her lasgun and the shielding device for hours, her eyes burned from the heat of too many too-near lasbolts, her telekinetic forcefield trembled and thinned — and then something inhuman tore its way out of her throat, a tortured shriek that even made the Alcazaar pause.

The stream of lasbolts abruptly petered out.

'Come on, keep at it!' Callista shouted. 'Let's get that Alcazaar scum!'

'They're behind us!' someone screamed in response.

Callista flicked a look over her shoulder and counted two hovercars bearing down on their position. 'Bock! Try the codes!'

Without checking to see if they were lucky enough to immobilise any of the hovercars with the codes Vom had given them, Callista dropped her hold on her powers and moved forward, relying on the shielding device instead. She knew her limits — and she wasn't stupid enough to think she was invincible, not like some of the younger members of the Maria who had fallen across her feet during the night. Her fingers had itched to heal them, but each injury was an hour she could not afford to waste.

A cheer went up behind her — the hovercars must have stalled. The ensuing cracks of windshields splitting open spoke of doomed Alcazaar falling into the hands of her clanspeople. Still more Maria followed Callista; she relished hearing their footfalls and drew strength from their presence, even as the red forcefield filling the oval frame she carried spluttered out and groaned back into life. The device was failing. It was probably only good for one more lasbolt.

The street almost disappeared beneath a swarm of lasgun bolts when they reached the bowl-shaped cul-de-sac where the Alcazaar were waiting for them. The wealthy denizens here always kept their vehicles hidden away in subterranean garages so there was no barricade of hovercars. No, here there were streetlights knocked over, gutters and piping ripped down from roofs and discarded armaments that had failed their owners. Littered among the debris were hundreds of flesh-rending tacks.

Callista hissed when one punctured the side of her boot, biting into her skin. With each step a lance of pain shot through her ankle, tensing her calf muscle, but she did not dare bend over and remove it. One second of lost concentration could cost her. The Maria supporting her fanned out to either side of the cul-de-sac, undaunted by the lasbolts that continued to rain down on them.

Callista strode through it all, trusting her clanspeople to cover her. She was their subofficer, their superior, and they would defend her until her last breath — and then someone else would step up and enjoy the protection granted by their sacrifices. Right now they were helping her reach the lowest lying balcony, the first tier of Alcazaar defences that spread up the front-facing sides of the buildings.

Callista's shield winged away the shot aimed at her head and her lasgun took down the clansman who'd been waiting for her. She spent some time studying the tank-sized lascannon he'd left behind. The controls were easy enough and, better still, the flexible mount allowed her to aim it at a steep angle. She smiled and slid into the seat, caressing the trigger for a long moment.

Then she began to strafe the balconies above her, screaming with triumph as lasbolts tore through metal and flesh like an electroknife through butter. Around her bodies fell from the sky.

'Subofficer!' a Maria clansman called up at her. 'Subofficer — there's no one left up there!'

She swung the heavy, rounded butt of the weapon towards the ground. 'Anyone down here?'

'We've won, Subofficer Dancer!'

Callista blinked and took in the destruction around her. Three houses had lost their top stories entirely and multiple balconies had broken apart on the road below. She scanned the area with her powers and found no innocent lives lost, only frightened souls hunkering down in the lower levels of the buildings.

Who says rich folk don't have any sense of self preservation? she thought. Then she remembered that once she had been one of them and laughed. She was now a subofficer and ruled the streets while they hid like cowards.

She descended into the cul-de-sac and wrinkled her nose. It reeked of smoke and scalded flesh. Chunks of tar and pavement had been uplifted — the road was ruined, and so too was the decades-long peace of the No-Go Zone. But no one dared come out to challenge what was happening and what would continue to happen until either the Maria or the Alcazaar were wiped completely from the sandy surface of Yalsa 5.

Callista counted her companions. Eight out of ten left was a roaring success. She had lost seven out of twelve on a previous charge only half an hour ago. She smiled vacantly at her clanspeople, preparing a rousing speech for them, but then her knees gave out and brought her to the ground.

Callista groaned. 'I just want to sleep.'

'I feel that,' Bock said, crouched nearby and grinning fiercely, a cracked tooth peeking over his lip. Callista had used her rank to countermand Ala's orders and get him out onto the streets. She hadn't done it out of pity — a vision had shown her how many lives he could save if she brought him along. She didn't regret it.

A bolt had scored Bock's cheek, leaving a burn that was angled up from his jaw to his temple. Some of his hair was gone too. The acne that had plagued the teenager now seemed obscenely unimportant. He was a man now, one who wore his torn shirt and sole-stripped boots with pride. His belt, too, spoke of his bravery — it was warped from a close blast that had mercifully left flesh and vital organs alone.

Callista assessed her own injuries as sunlight poured into Atsa City for the first time since the war had begun. The mark on her arm was new, both a lasbolt wound and a sign that she had fought and been injured just like the rest of them. Her fellow clanspeople grinned at her as they passed, beginning the journey that would take them back to headquarters.

They were almost on Canat Road when a tank with wheezing hoverpads intercepted them. The vehicle's purple paint was more obvious now that the shadows of night had receded. Despite the tenuous alliance that existed between them and the Chippers, the Maria baulked and drew up their weapons until Bartan emerged from the top hatch, arms spread to show he was unarmed.

'Your Subofficer Ala wants you at the Agency's outpost!' he called down at Callista. When she hesitated, he added, 'It's just two blocks away. And I could kill you right now if I wanted.'

Callista gave Bartan a nod, waved off her companion's

concerns, then turned to Bock. 'I think Bolt's waking up. Go get him for me.'

'You can tell that from here?' Bock asked, his eyes gleaming. 'Cool.'

'Yes, cool,' Callista said, smiling when she felt nothing but admiration from him.

'I bet if I had them fancy powers Ala would notice me,' Bock grumbled.

Laughing, Callista slapped his shoulder then climbed up the ladder set into the side of the tank. Bartan was there to help her through the hatch. Once she found a place to stand inside the passenger compartment she noticed that the décor was at odds with the colourful exterior and the uniforms of those who owned the tank. Everything was utilitarian, with sharp, grey edges. Even the seats looked like they would be more at home in a hovercar mechanic's garage. The driver, who was crammed into the cockpit, could apparently see through the tinting that seemed so uniformly purple on the outside because she whipped the tank around a corner so fast that some of the Chippers were thrown to one side. A few of them had managed to hook their hands into various notches on the wall in time. Being one of the latter, Bartan kept Callista upright, grinning at her discomfort.

By the time they reached the steps of the outpost, Callista felt wired, as though someone had pumped her veins full of coffein instead of blood. Dizzy, she paused on her way out of the hatch, her elbows braced on either side of the opening, breathing deeply. Shaking her head at Bartan when he offered her assistance, she half-slid, half-fell onto the footpath, wobbled on her feet for a moment, then followed the lieutenant up the stairs. The outpost's ornate masonry revealed it as Chipper in make — its white marble would have been imported from Gerasnin, the world that housed the Agency's headquarters.

The large archway that formed the entrance was filled in with what appeared to be two pieces of ancient wood, but though they opened outward in an old-fashioned style, they gave a metallic screech as they did so. Callista squared her shoulders as she passed the Chippers guarding the door and made her way into the entrance hall. This was as far as she got into the building, because the room was filled with Maria clanspeople.

'We bloodied and bruised them last night!' Ala crowed and her people writhed with delight. Most of the Chippers present remained resolutely still at the perimeter of the room, but Colonel Nerani was standing beside Ala on the steps of a grand staircase that snaked out of sight.

'But that's not good enough!' Ala said sternly.

The room hushed, but not in anticipation of her next words. All pairs of eyes were now fixed on Callista who straightened out of the limp the tack from the cul-de-sac battle had given her, determined not to show how awkward she felt. She had preferred being invisible among the Maria, just another grunt obeying orders. Now she was a subofficer and they expected her to *give* those orders. Callista brushed her hair behind her ears, displaying her unblemished temples, then adjusted her jacket to make sure it revealed the uncreased Maria logo on her shirt.

'They'll lick their wounds this day,' Ala said, catching Callista's eye and jerking her head in an unmistakeable 'come here' gesture. 'But they'll keep on fightin'. And we can't let them get what they want.'

Callista made sure she positioned herself on a step lower than where her fellow subofficer was standing and bowed her head, waiting for permission to speak to her clan. Ala was still the leader of the Maria, powers or not. Once Ala nodded at her, Callista said to the assembled masses, 'The Alcazaar only want me and Bolt because they're afraid — they know that we can beat them.'

'I've been thinking about that,' Nerani spoke up, expression distant. 'Seems to me the Creator God made you both the way you are so that you could help us protect his mortal children.'

Callista sliced her hand through the air, silencing the colonel. 'No. Whatever the Creator God's purpose was in making me, it certainly wasn't that. *But...*' She turned to her fellow clanspeople. 'I have free will and I choose Maria! Maria!'

'Maria! Maria! Maria!' came the shout.

'So what's next?' Callista asked her friend.

Ala grinned down at all those awaiting her orders. 'Oh, so none of you caught a good night's sleep and you're still rearin' to go?'

They cheered in response.

'Well, tough, you need some sleep, you crazy douchenozzles!' Ala said and they laughed.

Callista smiled along with them but found her gaze drawn to the doors. They parted slowly, reluctantly, admitting the intruder. His skin bore the healing outlines of his wounds and he was still without a lasgun, but it was clear he was ready for a fight. Callista saw that his hair was pulled back into a stubby ponytail and decided the look suited him.

Subofficer Bolt cleared his throat. 'Some of us have had enough sleep and would like to enter the fray, regrettably late though we might be.'

***

Sandsa woke to a swell of fear and triumph smothering Atsa City. He accepted Bock's assistance out onto the street and continued to lean on the teenager until they reached the Chipper outpost. When he saw that Sandsa was able to climb the stairs unaided, Bock wished him luck before heading back to the Maria headquarters, in case Ala rebuked him for abandoning his post.

Sandsa eyed the Chippers on guard outside the doors. He was tempted to use the god's powers to teleport into the building to avoid passing them but quickly stifled the urge. He had to make an impression, something to make people look twice, but not something that exposed what he was — what he had been. So before the doors opened he used one of Callista's elastic ties to pull his hair back to the nape of his neck.

Callista's joy at his arrival filtered through him. Sandsa favoured her with a smile, then went to stand beside Ala; the subofficer immediately took his hand and held it high over their heads. He noticed that she kept the chant to 'Maria!' instead of 'Bolt!'.

'So while we're sleeping in our beds, you'll what?' Ala demanded.

Sandsa, we might be the same rank as her but she's still our leader, Callista cautioned him. He didn't need the warning; he knew Ala wouldn't hesitate to show her displeasure if he circumvented any of her orders.

Sandsa performed a shrug. 'Whatever you deem wisest, Subofficer Ala. But might I suggest a daylight attack on the Dance Tower — nothing serious, just something to keep them quaking in their beds, wondering when we'll next attack.'

'Make it serious, Bolt,' Ala told him. 'They'll laugh you out of there if ya do anything less. The rest of you? Get some starking sleep!'

Sandsa turned to admire Callista, intending to remain a respectful pace from his fellow subofficer, but she grabbed the fresh undamaged shirt he was wearing and yanked him into a hot, hard kiss. Around them, Maria clanspeople were beginning to break away, smothering yawns with trembling fingers. Others made a show of staying on that little bit longer, to prove how tough they were, but Ala would have none of it. She told them that any Maria who was caught napping that night would be forced to stay at headquarters, doomed to share none of the impending glory.

Callista relaxed against Sandsa, her cheek sinking into his shoulder and her beatific smile dimming. Tired though she was, she let him know that a delicious ball of warmth seemed to have taken up residence low in her abdomen. Sandsa gently pried her away and rested one hand over the burn on her arm. When he lifted his fingers, the skin was healed. He then knelt to deal with the tack in her foot.

'Cals,' Ala said, stomping back over to them, flanked by Nerani. 'You're takin' a nap back at headquarters. Don't argue. Now, Bolt. I know you're good but even you'll need some help with this attack.'

Sandsa rose to his feet. 'Who am I taking with me?'

Nerani was the one who answered. 'I'll be sending a whole bunch of mine with you while your clan rests in preparation for tonight's festivities.'

'Won't that leave Atsa City unguarded, if your agents are not performing their daytime duties?' Callista asked, though the twist of her lips suggested she was not all that bothered by that thought.

Nerani rubbed her eyes. 'The decent folk should know what we do for them. If we're missing for a day then they might realise we need a bit more funding and donate to the Agency, don't you think?'

GLEA relied heavily on the donations of worshippers of the Creator God to continue their services, though Callista had told Sandsa she was sure they must have another source of funding. Their expenses verged on astronomical and not everyone shared their god.

While Nerani sped off to recruit some Chippers for their mission, Sandsa led Callista out onto the porch which had been smoothed by hundreds of feet passing over it every sunrise and sunset. He cupped Callista's chin with both hands, delivering a kiss that barely disturbed the moist seam of her lips, and felt her weariness began to ebb, replaced by a spike of desire that forced her eyes open. Callista slid her palm under his shirt, skimming it up over his navel with a higher destination in mind, but he rested a hand over the five distinct rises her fingers formed beneath the fabric, halting her progress.

'I promise there will be time for this later,' he told her in a low voice.

Callista cast her frown at the ground. 'This line between not using your godly powers and staying alive...it is terrible of me to even think this, but I want to command you to survive at any cost.'

Sandsa leaned his forehead against hers. 'I will not need to become the god, I promise you. I have plenty of other powers to draw on.'

'But what if using *those* powers is the path to making more concessions, like drawing on the deserts and becoming a god again?' she asked, biting her lip. 'What if you can't control it, like when Vom and his lot called on you for the Magic?'

'Then you may punish me however you see fit.'

Sandsa supposed he should not have added the wink, for he already felt her exasperation at the frankly lewd images in his mind. Callista rolled her eyes and kissed him. 'I love you. Don't die.'

'I shall endeavour not to.' He lifted her palm to his lips, then whispered against her skin, 'I am a man, not a god. The only things that are required of me are love and humanity and I have a very compelling reason to supply those.'

***

The three moons danced among the stars, glowing with delight at their freedom, never coming close enough to be captured from their orbit around a nearby planet. Kuin of the Bretani had stood beneath the moons since night had fallen, her lasgun limp in her hand as she weaved unsteadily on the feet that threatened to give out on her. The leathers of a warrior adorned her form and the lasgun added to her fierce image, but she was no fighter. Her Magic was useful in other ways. Sometimes she could feel when the deserts were about to birth a terrifying but magnificent sandstorm, the type that could strip skin from bone and tents from their pegs. She had saved her tribe by predicting such storms in the past.

Kuin now needed to save them from worse than a storm. The Bretani had never been violent in her childhood, but lately they had been ignoring the will of the Desine and making war with the neighbouring tribes. At first she had blamed the advice given to her brother, the chief of the tribe, by the priests and priestesses. They were the voice of the desert god, the voice that guided them into prosperity. Surely the Bretani would be the better for their wisdom. But when Kuin had spoken to them, their eyes had been wide with fear. They had heard nothing, so there was nothing for them to give.

Just as Kuin had feared, her brother was entirely responsible for his ill deeds.

He was eighteen, old enough to replace their mother, the former chief. She had fallen to the sand, the foam of poison atop her lips. Kuin had watched her brother since then with narrowed eyes as still more bodies appeared, all belonging to those who had dared to oppose his plans. He had stopped sending enough warriors to protect the edges of their territory, instead planning to use every last able-bodied man and woman to claim land that did not belong to them.

The Bretani would need more warriors than they had to secure the larger territory if they even managed to acquire it; she had told her brother this only to feel the sting of his lasgun slapped across her cheek. Her people were restless and unhappy and there was but one way to save them.

'My Lord Desine,' she said hoarsely. 'Desine, please, my lord. I know I am the youngest and cannot inherit the chiefhood, I know that. But my people...is it best for my tribe that he rules them, or is it best that I kill him and take his place?'

The cold night air burrowed into her chest and surrounded her heart. Still no answer came to her. She stretched out an arm to trace the darkening horizon with her fingers, unfurling her small powers to search for any sign of the god who had cared for her from the moment she had been planted in her mother's womb.

An hour later, her knees succumbed to the sand and she cried, releasing the precious moisture from her body into the desert.

The Desine had not answered. Her powers had felt nothing, found nothing. He was meant to be all around them, all the time, always listening. If he did not deign to speak to her, then that meant she did not deserve to hear anything but silence.

You are unworthy, she imagined the Desine thinking as he regarded this small girl fouling up his beautiful deserts. *You plot murder against your brother. He is the chief of your tribe. You are nothing.*

'I'm sorry, my Lord Desine, forgive me,' she whispered, the words lost to the mournful wind. 'You are my god and see all, know all. But I cannot stay in the tribe of my mother. I can't. I can't watch him destroy us.'

Kuin of the Bretani turned and walked away from her tribe, her guilt and despair leading her into desolation. Standing on a nearby dune was the physical form of the Ine, his brow furrowed like any human's did when something of concern had been presented before them.

My son, the true chief of the Bretani leaves this night, her people doomed to languish beneath the heel of her brother, he sent to Sandsa. *Learn your lesson quickly, because the deserts need you.*

His eldest son did not respond.

CHAPTER SEVENTEEN

A haze hung over the street leading to the Dance Tower. This part of the city was by no means unique; every micrometre of Atsa seemed to be obscured with the smoke left behind by a night of desperate fighting. An unwelcome desert wind reached Sandsa, its wispy voice assuring him that it could make short work of the haze. He shook his head, ignoring it, and focused on his current situation. He and a large group of GLEA agents were about to approach the tower and storm their way into it. The Chippers had already raised their hands and erected a chain of forcefields that coalesced into a long, uninterrupted wall which fell to their feet and rose higher than the tallest agent's head. It was invisible to the naked eye, but Sandsa could sense it, almost even taste it.

'Stark, they've got a shield generator covering the lower floors,' a Chipper beside Sandsa sighed. 'If that wasn't there, we coulda shot through those levels and toppled the whole starking tower without even getting near it.'

'That must be a new feature; they did not have it when last I attacked them here,' Sandsa said, a hand gripping the inferior lasgun that the Chippers had given him. 'No matter. I'll find the generator and destroy it for you.'

His companion laughed. 'Make sure you leave some of the action for me, clansman! But, if you don't mind,' he said, suddenly serious, 'don't do it until they raise the alarm. There's a fair few innocent folk who live and work in that building and I'm kind of paid to make sure they don't get hurt.'

'It might also help if the people of this city see the Maria trying to save lives instead of viewing us as the head merely replacing the one we lop from the shoulders of the Alcazaar,' Sandsa noted.

The Chippers began to march their shield wall forward. Their tanks coasted after them, their weapons silent, waiting for a command from Major Injii, the woman in charge. Sandsa stayed in the space between these two lines, watching his purple-clad companions. He missed his clan's symbol and their favoured black — and he missed one person in particular, missed her so much all he wanted to do was lie beside her, savouring every micrometre of her quivering, creamy skin...

He shook his head and exhaled. Callista had done her duty, so now he must do his.

'Incoming!' Major Injii bellowed. She was standing up through the hatch of her chosen tank.

Lasbolts hit the shield wall like a torrential downpour on a small puddle and ozone filled the air, an acrid taste underpinned with a deadly sweetness. This was apparently enough provocation for the Chippers to respond in kind.

The tanks' lascannons, perched over the top of the shield wall, swung around and took aim. Their low setting caused a slim, non-fatal blast to erupt from the weapons, forcing Alcazaar clanspeople to duck from the upper windows of the tower, where the building's shield did not extend. Major Injii swore when a returning shot, much wider and thicker and sourer on the tongue, gouged through the air beside her. The Alcazaar weren't trying to minimise casualties; rather the opposite.

'They're using full power in their weapons so watch it!' Injii warned.

Their march had now brought them barely a block from the tower. Sandsa felt it moments before his companions did — the swarm of Alcazaar-paid Chippers squatting nearby. They were a cold void and a magnet all in one, threatening to pull him down into their depths. He stilled and stared at the flat chrome building that housed them, waiting for the Chippers around him to react.

'Oh shit,' an agent in front of Sandsa said.

'Major Injii!' Sandsa called up to the woman. 'Split your forces. If you keep your renegades busy here then some of us can make it to the Dance Tower.'

'Sounds good to me!' was Injii's answer.

Half the line of agents peeled away, taking their forcefields with them; the invisible wall snapped into two directions, like a rubber band stretched to breaking point. A hot, heavy blast left the tower and screamed towards the gap forming between the two groups, heading for an exposed tank. At the last moment, it obeyed Sandsa's mental command and veered off, shredding the road and causing a hovercar parked nearby to explode.

One Chipper whistled loudly. 'You make it look so easy, clansman!'

'His name is Bolt, is it any wonder?' another shouted, laughter chasing his words.

'Eyes ahead, mouths shut — lives are at stake!' Injii snapped at them and they silenced, hunkering down behind the dramatically reduced shield.

Some of them were gnawing into their lips as they concentrated, funnelling energy through their hands and into the linked forcefields. More and more lasbolts thundered in their direction, threatening the integrity of the shield, so Sandsa diverted what he could. These blasts warped away from them, as though pulled by gravity towards the sides of the street. Sandsa shot a look back at the people they had left behind, watching bodies fly through the air to meet stone and steel. But he could not watch the Chippers suffer, not when there was so much to be done.

Sandsa touched the minds of the agents walking in front of him. They were all linked in a honeycomb effect that strengthened the shield, making it stronger than any individual forcefield alone. They trusted each other implicitly, because they were united by their purpose: to bring peace and safety to Atsa City. Sandsa tested the wall's strength, momentarily unnerved by the buzzing sensation that came off the Chippers, then tensed when he realised they were feeling him out in return. Almost immediately they accepted him as part of the link and he was overwhelmed with an incredible sense of belonging. Cheeks damp, lips pulled into a smile, he lengthened his stride to match theirs. Within a minute, they were at the base of the Dance Tower. Their shield was a quiet transparent shroud compared to the noisy crimson one that rose six storeys above them, protecting the lower levels of the building.

Arrayed around the entrance were Alcazaar using bodies and debris to conceal themselves while they fired lasbolts at the Chippers. One of the clan's large mounted lascannons had already fallen over, its electronic innards spewed all over the road, but there was no celebrating, not yet. Some of the Chippers disengaged from the shield and raised their clenched fists, redirecting lasbolts back to each turret, turning them to slag. But the clanspeople on the road weren't the only threats; marksmen higher up on the building, able to aim over the wall of linked forcefields, shot at the tanks, obliterating one and the Chippers inside it.

Anger seared Sandsa's heart just as fire had seared his skin the night before. Power burst free from him, knocking every last remaining Alcazaar to the ground. He ran at the shield wall, passed through it with little effort, and snatched an abandoned lasgun from the ground. It was heavier than he'd have liked and needed two hands to carry it, but the lasbolts it loosed made quick and brutal work of the clanspeople before him. Their lifesigns faded and disintegrated, but Sandsa kept firing, wanting to utterly destroy the bodies of his enemies. The Chippers recoiled at first, then two of them grabbed his arms and a third confiscated the lasgun.

'It's done, they're dead!' Major Injii told him, disgust bleeding into her words.

Sandsa's lip twisted. 'You think they deserve any less? For what they took from me?'

She shouldered past him. 'We don't have time for overkill; it'll only slow us down!'

After a shouted order from her, the shield wall fractured and the Chippers filed through the narrow entranceway, lasguns and hands extended. Some of them even dropped their shields entirely and sliced their hands through the air, diverting bolts with small forcefields before they even came close. Sandsa flanked them, darting to the sides to deal with any Alcazaar who were using holes in the walls to fire from adjacent rooms. He barrelled through one such hole and found himself in a chamber full of enemy combatants. First he felt the heat of their gazes — then came the heat of their weapons.

The deadly lasbolts turned back on those who had delivered them. Not just one bolt per clansperson — no, he returned every single blast. The Alcazaar's heads exploded, their chests grew gaping holes and some lost their legs entirely below the knees. Sandsa snatched a lasgun from a limp hand — the weapon's enlarged barrel promised sufficient destruction — and strafed the room until not a single exhale belonged to anyone but himself. He stood, chest heaving, until a Chipper ran in and shouted muted words at him while pointing up a stairwell. Supposing it was safer than the hoverlifts which could be shut off at any moment, Sandsa chased after his companion.

The next two levels passed in the same way, with Alcazaar pouring down the stairs or out of a maze of rooms and tunnels. By the time Sandsa and the Chippers hit the third level, the floor shook beneath them as an alarm chimed from somewhere within the building. They stepped aside to let people flee, clutching their possessions — some wore Alcazaar colours but carried no weapons so they let them pass. Sandsa didn't protest this decision. He knew he needed to save his powers for those more willing to offer a fight.

On level five, the Chippers attempted to learn the location of the shield generator protecting the building by asking the Alcazaar they came across, but most of these clanspeople had neither the knowledge nor the rank to know anything useful. One of them, however, did know something — Sandsa read this from the man's mind and mentioned it to Major Injii. On her order the Chippers brought their lasguns to bear on the clansman, but he stared back in silent defiance, his back arched by the tight bindings that kept his hands pinned behind him. He didn't believe the Chippers would carry out their threat. And Sandsa had seen and heard enough to know that this belief was not unfounded.

'This is wasting time!' Sandsa snapped, moving forward to crush his newly acquired lasgun against the man's throat. The reproach of the Chippers behind him was palpable but Sandsa didn't care what they thought. 'Where is the generator?'

The Alcazaar wheezed breathlessly for a moment, then managed to work a glob of saliva down his chin. Even if he had not managed to launch it at Sandsa, the insult was evident. Sandsa plunged into the man's mind, stabbing through milky layers of arrogance and fear until he found the information he wanted. He threw the man against the wall with a careless thought then turned and marched around a corner to the door he knew to look for. The locking mechanism flashed red when he slapped the button beside it so he used his powers to rip the metal panel filling the doorway aside. The room he exposed was filled with soft blinking lights and the cool air that rushed across his face alerted Sandsa to the importance of the electronic circuits within.

Standing back, he lifted his lasgun and blasted the entire system. This must have killed the building's shield because moments later his companions started shouting for a retreat. Sandsa left the ruined generator, ignored the Alcazaar clansman slumped against the wall, and descended the steps. He did not care if the man escaped or found his grave in the building, though he suspected the Chippers would evacuate him.

Once Sandsa emerged from the Dance Tower he joined the agents sprinting towards the fight they had lost half their forces to earlier. Flying debris encased in forcefields was being launched from both factions of the Chippers, some finding their marks, others swinging wide and hitting nearby buildings. Major Injii unhooked a large, outdated communicator from her belt, yelled an order into it, and then two tanks broke away from the assault on the Alcazaar's Chippers. The vehicles shot down the road, their lascannons screaming with each large blast that escaped them.

The tower fell with a fearsome crash. The shockwave hit Sandsa only a second later — he was flung forward, but cushioned himself with his powers. The agents around him were doing the same thing with their forcefields. He expanded his control and caught an unconscious Chipper before she snapped her neck on the ground. Around Sandsa agents began scrambling to their feet and legging it over to the tanks which were taking heavy fire from the other Chippers. He jogged after them, but slowed when they disappeared into the vehicles, unsure if he should follow.

Major Injii didn't bother telling him it was fine to join them. She just grabbed hold of Sandsa's shirt and pulled him into a tank. He stood through the open hatch, torso and head exposed as he watched the plume of dust and smoke rise from the tower's remains. Spitting grit from his mouth, he sent a blast of power outwards, causing a large portion of a nearby building to collapse onto the remaining Chippers and Alcazaar who'd started to run down the street towards the retreating tanks. When Sandsa dropped back inside, he smiled around at his companions, waiting for the cheers of victory. They didn't come.

'I confess I do not understand your people's aversion to killing your enemies,' Sandsa said aside to the major.

Injii glared at him. 'You chipless people'll keep me up for nights to come. At least those of ours who go bad can have the tech ripped from their skin, cutting them off from the Creator

God. People like you...how are we supposed to catch you, let alone contain you?'

'And what does sparing your enemies have to do with that?' Sandsa asked, wincing when he felt an unchecked wave of fury emanate from the major.

'Revenge is not justice,' Injii said, her orange eyes like twin drops of vivid poison. 'If a criminal can be convicted of it, then we should not do it ourselves. It's hypocritical. When my superiors ask me to kill, then I must follow those orders, but it is always a last resort.'

Sandsa snorted. 'So you would prefer to risk your life to incarcerate someone instead of just killing them.'

'Yes!' Injii growled.

'You think I'm dangerous,' Sandsa noted. 'But the Alcazaar needed to be punished for killing my mother. Destroying them saves innocent lives.'

Injii shook her head. 'There's no reasoning with you.'

'You wouldn't go after those who hurt the ones you love?' Sandsa asked, peering around at the Chippers. None of them flinched away from his gaze. He turned back to Injii. 'Not even for the wife you keep in your thoughts? Would she want you to sit by and do nothing to avenge her?'

'She's an agent of GLEA just as I am; she understands this,' Injii said, scowling. 'Those who do not abide by our rules are struck out of the Agency and I have put too much time and effort into my career to risk losing it.'

'You are going to have difficulty ensuring everyone follows those rules, I imagine, if more people like myself and Dancer appear,' Sandsa commented. 'What will you do then? Hope they are benign and don't come after you?'

Injii swallowed. 'You are just two people.'

'So far,' muttered one of the other Chippers.

Sandsa asked to be dropped off on the side of the road, nowhere near the Maria headquarters. He did not specify the reason.

CHAPTER EIGHTEEN

Sandsa jogged through the smoke curling its way up from the road and cast a quick look around. Balconies hung alarmingly off the sides of buildings and many windows were so warped it was hard to tell if the glass had fallen from the misshapen frames or if it had first been shattered by lasgun bolts. Sandsa slowed his pace often to check the cockpits of abandoned hovercars, but soon found that a vivid yellow X painted on a vehicle meant that he would find no one inside. He sensed the energy of people nearby, though he wasn't sure if they belonged to the Zatzat. He only needed to use a tiny, inconsequential nudge to feel out their powers, but even that minor action filled his stomach with a burbling guilt that threatened to leap up his throat and choke him.

When will I stop acting so thoughtlessly? he wondered. *I can't keep putting myself in a position where my people or the sands can hear me. They could very well steal me back with their pleas, their cries, their unrelenting demands.*

The man's reflection he saw in the rare intact glass he passed was not that of the Desine, god of the desert. A fine, light stubble was spreading over his face, refusing to slow; he could not remember the last time he'd needed to shave. The blond hair that had spent millennia never reaching his shoulders was now tied into an ever-lengthening ponytail that lashed his back as he walked. The god was someone else, someone who lurked at the edges of his mind, trying — and failing — to lure him away from Callista.

'Vom?' he called. 'How are you faring after last night?'

The nightclub owner, shirtless and limping, emerged from the stairwell that was sheltering far more people than Sandsa knew were in the Zatzat gang. Vom winced and slung a hand over to his shoulder, massaging what was presumably a sore and abused muscle. 'Warm greetings, Subofficer Bolt.'

'What happened?' Sandsa asked, frowning as more injured clanspeople followed Vom out onto the street.

'The Alcazaar figured out where your Dancer got the codes to the hovercars, not that we made it hard for 'em,' Vom said, hissing when Sandsa pressed fingers to the uneven lines that lasbolts had gouged into his back. Sandsa eased a few dribbles of his power down into the clansman, just enough to speed his body's natural healing on its way, but not so much that it would reveal the Desine's presence. Vom kept talking. 'They sent more than we could handle.'

Sandsa indicated the growing crowd behind Vom. 'But you asked the other minor clans for help. Did not enough people come?'

'*Tsi*, yes, just enough,' Vom said and then sighed, scrubbing a hand over the bristles on his chin. 'But we could not defend ourselves. We met a challenge that cannot be overcome.'

'Chippers?'

'Worse,' Vom said grimly.

Sandsa waited for him to continue, but it was a lanky woman with much lighter skin than Vom who diverged from the pack to explain. 'We called upon the Desine. He did not answer.'

Panic drove Sandsa into his mind, into his memories, but he

saw only the faces of the Alcazaar he had killed. Hovering a hand over his heart, Sandsa felt...nothing. There was a cold, empty spot inside him where he should have felt the call of his people, so close by. He had heard voices from across the galaxy mere weeks ago.

'Perhaps...' Sandsa hesitated. 'Perhaps the Desine knew that you would not need his assistance.'

Vom's expression remained stony. 'It's more than that, Bolt. More tribesmen and women keep pouring in from the sands — from other planets, too. They say the Desine abandoned them weeks ago, but we felt him yesterday.'

'If this is where he was last felt, wouldn't you come here, Vom?' the woman beside Vom asked, her crystal-like eyes glittering in the light shed from the star overhead. 'Subofficer Bolt — that is your rank now, isn't it? — can you use your powers? Can you feel our god?'

Sandsa withdrew from Vom. Words piled onto his tongue only to be swallowed back to his tonsils. He wasn't the Desine anymore. He was Subofficer Bolt of the Maria, future lover of Subofficer Dancer. Many of his people, including Vom, had made their choice first, heading for the cities even before their god had ever left them.

And what of those that arrived only after you, my son, abandoned them? His father's voice flew in from the deserts, more pungent than anything the hot winds could have brought. *Will you not return now before more of them come looking for you?*

'No,' Sandsa said out loud, answering all questions.

'A dark day indeed,' Vom murmured. 'Don't know how we'll make it through this war.'

'A war that should only be between the Alcazaar and the

Maria!' the woman exclaimed, then shot an unrepentant glare at Sandsa.

Sandsa averted his eyes from hers. 'It was my fault. They wanted me and I said no.'

'What, you'll fight to stay where you are?' she asked, surprising him with a laugh. 'I'm Diamond and you're mad, giving up that platinum opportunity — you could've climbed your way up to Clan Leader in there.'

Sandsa raised his eyebrows. 'Who says I can't be Clan Leader through other means?'

A dangerous hush fell over the gathered clanspeople. The smoke began to clear, revealing more of the wounded among their number. Sandsa forced himself not to look at them.

I am a man. For Callista. I cannot be anything else.

Diamond stared at him. Then she snickered. 'Sure, go ahead. If you do manage it, I'll get you a ring for the woman Vom's told me all about. No charge.'

'Don't suppose a Clan Leader has any time to be a DJ,' Vom said, shaking his head.

Sandsa smiled. 'I'll still need a good place to celebrate — the Alcazaar took out the Maria nightclubs last night. But that's not what I came here to discuss.'

'What are you here for then?' someone asked from the rear of the twitchy, nervous pack.

Sandsa took a deep breath, inhaling the scent of destruction. Around him, pressing against his skin, were the fears of those trying to make a living for themselves in a city fraught with peril. The Chippers could be seen moving around in their tanks but it was obvious they were not focused on keeping the streets safe.

Sandsa wondered just how many people had realised that the Chippers were actually assisting the gangs.

'How many non-Alcazaar and non-Maria clanspeople do you suppose there are?' Sandsa asked, directing his question at the nightclub owner. 'They would be a significant addition to a war, wouldn't you say?'

Vom's lips curved into a grin.

Once they were done talking, Sandsa reached out and clasped Vom's forearm. The other man's reciprocal grip was much tighter.

'Take care with our lives, Bolt,' Vom cautioned him. 'Without the Desine on our side, we have only you to look after us.'

Sandsa bowed his head, his arm limp in Vom's hand. 'I will not abandon you the way...the way he did.'

*****

His kisses began gently, as though they were pressed to a layer of cotton wool dividing him from her skin. But then his lips touched hers and his tongue claimed her mouth, drawing her from the comfort of sleep into the much more welcome sensations of loving and being loved. Callista smiled into his kiss and tugged at his shirt. It wasn't until he had discarded it and was working on her own — along with the bra band — that she realised she was indeed awake and that the aches she had earned during the night were beginning to grow, though they seemed a lot less important than the fingers ghosting over her breasts.

Callista pulled him down for another kiss but his mouth evaded hers, travelling down her throat and evoking goosebumps as it went. Grinning up at her, he darted down to press his lips to a nipple, then engulfed more of her flesh in one swift motion. She gasped. His tongue swirled around the hardened nub while he suckled, causing restless heat to fill her abdomen and her hips to rise impatiently towards him.

Callista smiled at the ceiling as he transferred his mouth to the other breast. He kept two fingers rolling the first nipple between them as sparks shot down to the throbbing core between her legs. She knew he sensed her need because his hand crept down her stomach, caressing it briefly, and then slipped beneath both her pants and underwear in one easy glide.

Callista stiffened. He paused.

'My love?' he asked breathlessly.

She simply nodded.

He cupped his hand to her moist mound for a delicious moment, then his fingers began to search through the top of her folds for her sweet spot while the heel of his palm ground slowly into her weeping entrance. Callista moaned and felt her body sink further into the bed. She touched his mind, wondering how it was that he was so good at this, and read from him that he had known about sex for millennia and now wanted to bring that kind of pleasure to her.

Callista threaded her fingers through the ones he had left on her hip, squeezing his hand each time she pulsed for him. But his touch was still too gentle, too unsure, and though his ministrations continued for several long, torturous minutes, Callista found her hips heaving towards him, trying to force his fingers into a different rhythm.

'Sandsa, wait, I need to show you how I like it,' she whispered.

His blue eyes were soft and vulnerable as he gazed at her. 'This is not pleasing you?'

'It is,' Callista assured him, resting a hand against his cheek. 'But I know my body. I've touched myself there so I know what I...what I like. It took me a bit of time to learn how my body works so I can't expect you to get it right on your first go.'

'You have touched yourself?' he asked lowly.

She nodded, then grinned when she felt the desire spark inside him. He quickly lay on his side, moulding himself along her form, and awaited her instruction. Callista took his hand in hers and pinched his index finger, then used it to draw a slick line over her hip and down to the crease formed by her thigh. She positioned him on her desperate, engorged bud then started moving his finger in a slow, circular motion. His breaths echoed hers, becoming faster and shallower as she continued to guide him. The first twinges came sooner than she expected, but she supposed it was because she was sharing this intimate act with him.

One twinge in particular plateaued and her clitoris thrummed with pleasure, sending warm waves cascading all through her body and down to her knees, making them feel weak and incapable of ever supporting her again. Just when she thought it would end, his finger pressed more urgently against her and she cried out before batting his hand away and slumping back against the pillows.

Smiling beatifically at the ceiling, Callista almost didn't register him pulling her pants over her hips or briefly easing her upright to drop her shirt over her head. He then embraced her from behind, his chest warm through the fabric covering her back. She wondered why he'd bothered dressing her at all, because his fingers slipped beneath her shirt and drew nonsensical patterns on her stomach. Callista let her eyes drift shut.

His thoughts began churning.

Callista roused herself. *Sandsa? What is it?* She paused. *Vom and the others. Sandsa...are you sure you don't want to go back to them?*

I love you, Callista. You mean more to me than countless, nameless others.

Callista dawdled through his recent memories. She saw him fight, saw him avoid using the god's powers, and saw him survive. And then there were his attempts to broker alliances with the minor clans...but there would be time to discuss that later. She smiled and reached back to stroke his check but touched his lips instead. His tongue darted out to capture a digit and he suckled on her finger in a way that made her thighs tighten and her clitoris swell with returning interest. He released her finger when she squirmed and groaned, his hardness pressing into the small of her back.

Callista hesitated. 'Sandsa, do you want...um...do you want me to...?'

She knew better than to hope she had shielded her anxiety from him. His hands grazed her thighs as he murmured, 'I am satisfied with your pleasure this night, my Callista. There will be time enough for you to explore me with your fingers...with your mouth...because we have eternity. For now, I would simply like to hold you.'

Callista relaxed against him. 'I love that we can sense each other this way. I never need to worry about what...what's inside my mind. You accept all of me. But,' she grinned, 'easy with that eternity talk, okay?'

'Okay...for now,' he said, a smile tainting his words.

'Are you always so sure you'll get what you want?'

Sandsa's hold on her tightened. 'I would like to know that you will stand beside me centuries from now.'

'And what happens to our life here?' she asked, watching the afternoon shadows stretch their way across the floor. 'We can't stay on Yalsa 5. People would start to wonder why we don't age.'

'We can always go somewhere else.'

'But how can I leave what I've made here?'

Sandsa pressed his lips to her shoulder. 'There is no hurry. And my home is you, Callista, no matter where you are.'

You've given up so much for me, she thought, troubled. *I should be able to give up one small life for countless lives with you.*

Thankfully, it wasn't long before sleep claimed her once more. She had never felt this warm, this relaxed, this safe — and all because he was holding her, protecting her from the galaxy.

***

In her dreams, she saw a man, a stranger, and went to him.

He turned to her, revealing eyes bluer than the sky curving above him. His face was youthful, despite the lines that pain and experience had written over him, and his brown hair was streaked with dust. The lasgun on his hip was larger than Callista would ever have chosen but it suited him. He followed her gaze with his own and laughed.

'I know you think it's overkill, but you haven't seen what I've had to face,' he said, taking her hand and leading her down Canat Road which was constantly shifting between old and new, destroyed and rebuilt. 'And I don't particularly want to draw attention to myself by relying on my powers. I've got enough eyes on me as it is.'

Callista squeezed his hand, feeling his fingers contort beneath her grip. 'Are you real? My son?'

'Ouch,' he said with a smile, flexing his hand. 'I'm sorry I can't linger — I need to get back to my wife.'

She turned their hands over. Four palms offered to the sky. Four palms slashed with the marks of a binding, one that transferred blood and immortality. This was her future, she realised, a time after she had accepted Sandsa's gift.

'Your wife...' Callista murmured, feeling warmth flood her veins.

Overhead, the clouds groaned and grumbled with the presence of an oncoming storm. Callista glanced around, watching the buildings bow and wave like trees. When she looked back at her son, she saw that he was wearing a purple uniform, one that Callista was now far too familiar with. She lunged at him but he began to fade.

'Why are you wearing that?' she demanded.

'Don't you know?' he asked, his words snatched away by the howl of a tortured wind.

The plea tore from her throat. 'Don't go! Stay *here*! Stay with me!'

Callista closed her eyes to avoid watching his body disintegrate completely — and then woke, Sandsa curled up behind her. It took a long time for her breathing to even out, and even longer still to lapse back into a doze.

CHAPTER NINETEEN

'So you just went and made this decision without talking to any other subofficers,' Ala said, pacing along the pavement outside headquarters and occasionally pausing to step over debris. 'Might've told me. Not like I kept us together for the past two decades or anything!'

Sandsa looked at Callista who merely raised an eyebrow. She remained by Ala's side while the horde of non-Maria clanspeople continued to show up en masse, all packing weaponry. Several Maria subofficers were also in attendance, including the newly promoted Knives. Mindful that he owed Ala an explanation, Sandsa said, 'These clans do not wish to rule the city and so have agreed to help the Maria defeat the Alcazaar.'

'What happens when the lyin' scum stab us in the back, though?' Knives asked. Ala's mechanical eye swung over to Knives and he held up a hand, his tone growing defensive. 'Hey now, if one subofficer can get away with makin' peace with a bunch of other clans without your say-so, then this subofficer can speak out of turn.'

'See what you've done, Bolt?' Ala growled.

'Ala, it was not done to supplant you,' Callista assured her.

'No? You think I'm stupid enough not to see what he wants?'

Vom's large figure cut a path through the gathering crowd and the stirrings on both sides ceased, allowing the man to speak unhindered. 'Bolt can see we have greater numbers than the

Alcazaar if we join together. If what the man wants is to rid us of the Alcazaar, then my people are happy to help him. And it's not like your leadership has done the Maria any favours, Subofficer Ala.'

'Ala kept us together,' Callista said firmly, 'and made sure we remained a viable threat to the Alcazaar. But that's not the point. We want to win this. Ala, Vom gave me the codes we've been using to neutralise their hovercars.'

'Why?' Ala asked, suspicion heavy on her brow.

'Seemed like a good idea to make nice with a powerful clan,' Vom said, drawing laughs.

A clanswoman interrupted the confrontation with a shout, announcing the arrival of four Chipper tanks. Several eyes lifted to take them in, then rose much higher to the Chipcopter flying behind the tanks. This caused more than a few people to mutter among themselves.

Sandsa swallowed, mentally preparing to take on the Chipcopter if need be. 'My friends. Subofficers. The Zatzat and the other gangs here were formed out of necessity by people who wished to protect themselves and their families from the violence of Atsa. They know that the best chance to achieve this is to support us in our fight.'

Ala's red eye selected several new faces to scan. 'Alright. But, Vom, you gotta understand what you're getting into. If you start fighting the Alcazaar, your people will die. I mean it. If we lose, all of you will die.'

'Then we die,' Vom said simply.

'Easy for you to say, Vom!' someone chortled. 'I got my mother-in-law's mortgage on another planet to pay off. She'll never let me hear the end of it if I get myself killed!'

Sandsa stepped forward before the spreading laughter could detract from the seriousness of the situation. 'Clanspeople, do you agree to take the orders of Subofficer Ala during this war, without any attempt to take the mantle of Clan Leader for yourselves?'

'Yes!' Vom boomed and the chorus followed. 'Yes, yes, yes!'

Callista left Ala's side and came towards Sandsa. He caught her in his arms and they kissed, surrounded by those who had joined them in fighting this war. While the 'copter hovered overhead, the tanks began to disgorge armed passengers in purple jumpsuits and Vom had to quickly quieten scores of uncertain clanspeople who were not aware of the truce between the Maria and the Chippers.

'Do you think this will lead to a good outcome for Atsa?' Sandsa asked Callista in a low voice. 'I can't...I can't see if banding together will lead to the end of the Alcazaar.' He decided not to mention that his ability to peer into the future, which had already been difficult to use for the past few weeks, was now severely hampered by ignoring the god's powers.

Callista smiled at him. 'I think that this home, while we have it, deserves every attempt to make it something better.'

'While we have it,' he repeated, nipping her earlobe. Then he turned to the nearby Chipper who had just finished clearing her throat noisily. 'Colonel Jeras Nerani. I take it this particular Chipcopter belongs to you.'

The woman nodded. The tiny periwinkle tentacles on her scalp shivered in response. 'Until my superiors find out what I'm doing with it, that is. Tonight it's your chauffeur service. Governor Garnett wants a word with the two of you.'

'You will have to ask Subofficer Ala if that is agreeable,' Sandsa told her, offering a polite nod to Ala.

'Why bother askin' me anything?' Ala asked sourly.

Sleep was the order she had given her people, but she hadn't obeyed it herself. Sandsa felt the darkness encroaching on her consciousness and burrowing into her thinking processes. Sandsa held both her eyes, real and artificial, and said, 'Because this might be a trap and you care about the safety of your people, even the one who has stolen the admiration of your peers.'

Ala's laugh sounded like metal grinding over pavement. 'The colonel here might be a Chipper but she's not scum. I trust her. And I like Cals far too much to send ya off to certain death. She'd probably take issue with it — worse, I think she might even love you.'

'I do love him,' Callista said.

Ala flapped a hand at her. 'Cool it. You just met him. You can't know that already.'

'I do know.'

'As for takin' all my respect and power...' Ala went on.

Sandsa tensed.

'...my job was to protect my people, like Vom did for his lot,' she finished, smiling sadly. 'Your job's somethin' else, evidently. Take good care of her — you owe me that much, Bolt.'

He nodded once then strode towards the 'copter, Callista at his side. The airborne vehicle lost height so rapidly it looked as though it was about to crash, but then it drew up short, staying low only long enough for them to board. Within moments, Ala and Nerani became tiny objects, like expendable pieces on an ancient chess board. Next to shrink were the buildings and the explosions that were cropping up all over the city; the latter now resembled colourful splashes on a pond.

'I will not do all the talking, I promise you!' Sandsa shouted over the whistling wind so that Callista, who was searching for the button that activated the automated restraints, could hear him.

'Talking seems to do a lot for you,' she said, glancing up. 'You managed to unite a plethora of clans *and* make nice with your girlfriend's best friend all in one night!'

'Girlfriend?' he echoed.

Callista retreated into mind-speech as a particularly strong gust of wind jolted the 'copter. *Well, I can't call you 'lover' yet.*

Why not?

It's just how things progress, I guess, she said, physically shrugging. *Girlfriend is lower down on the scale. Then lover. Then other labels turn up.*

And is 'wife' one of those labels? he asked.

Callista did not respond, though he noticed that her hand shook when it reached for his.

The 'copter pilot did not spare them a single glance during the entire journey, nor when she set them down on the largest building in the city. The governor's base of operations was sleek, silver and graceful, almost like one of the sea creatures that Sandsa knew his brother Fayay, the god of water, dealt with. The chrome on the building's exterior might have been painted at some point over the centuries, but now its bare surface gleamed, a beacon above the chaos down below. It would be so easy to see the people streaming over the distant paths and roads as insignificant nuisances, Sandsa mused. He was disturbed that this thought reminded him of how he'd viewed the mortals in his deserts.

He climbed out onto the flat square that marked the top of the building and turned to Callista, holding out his hand. Tossing him a mischievous grin, she refused his help and leapt past him, landing steadily on her feet.

'I love you, but sometimes you've got to remember I can handle myself,' she told him when he joined her beside the section of the roof that was sinking to form stairs.

You are a very capable individual, but together we are greater than anything we could ever be apart, he said, his fingers grazing her cheek.

She gave him a smile, but it was brief, uncertain. *I'd still like to be great on my own, Sandsa.*

They descended the steps as one.

***

Unsurprisingly, there were guards at the entrance to the governor's study. They remained unmoving, even when the wooden door between them swung out in the same archaic style that the Chippers favoured. Callista would have scoffed at this had she not heard a hidden metal panel retract before the door opened. If the governor needed to seal himself inside his study, he would have two layers of protection.

Governor Garnett stood when they entered. The only furniture in the room consisted of a cluster of chairs and an ornate circular table that played host to a silver bottle with a tall, elegant neck. Wine from another planet, Callista noted, an expensive brand that her parents had foisted on her over the years. She hated its cloying taste but had learned how to smile and pretend it was the best thing she'd ever tarred her tongue with.

The governor reached for the bottle and began pouring its contents into three tumblers.

Only once his visitors were seated did he lower himself into a chair. Shorter than Callista remembered and now bearing as many individual threads of silver in his hair as her father did, he still maintained the bulk of someone who could best a clansperson in a physical fight. His genial smile painted him as paternal, but his pale eyes were flinty.

Callista leaned back in her chair and slung a leg over her knee, making sure she earned his disapproving look. The governor quickly reactivated the smile and extended a tumbler to Sandsa who shook his head. Callista copied the gesture.

'I believe I have the both of you to blame for the recent turmoil in this city,' Governor Jon Garnett remarked. 'The current Clan Leader and I have spoken on this matter.'

Callista threw a worried look at Sandsa. *He's not lying; he has to speak to the reigning Clan Leader to keep Atsa running. I've only been in the Maria for three years — you even less. Do we have a right to upend the entire city?*

But Sandsa was smiling. 'Governor Garnett, I propose that the current method used to police Atsa City is flawed.'

'Enlighten me,' Garnett said, bending his fingers at the knuckles as he pressed them together.

Callista cleared her throat. 'Families are forced to form their own clans simply to survive the night. Not everyone can afford the safety of the No-Go Zone.'

'The very zone that your gang now stages battles in?' Garnett mused.

Sandsa's chair creaked as he shifted forward. 'Governor. Do

you want these conflicts to continue to endanger the innocents of your city?'

'I imagine he only cares about how they vote,' Callista said, rolling her eyes. 'And I suspect he makes a lot of money out of levying taxes on imported weapons and equipment. The more the Alcazaar bring in, the better it is for him.' She cut herself off to give the governor a significant look. He shrugged unapologetically then retreated from the table when the wine in the bottle began to slosh around angrily.

Callista drew in a steadying breath. The alcohol stilled.

Garnett eyed the bottle for a moment, then said, 'Callista Krendasta. What makes a woman born into wealth and presented with an even wealthier husband choose the streets? She turned down Isolde Israr, Subofficer Bolt. You must be something special.'

Callista ground her teeth together, trying not to let the man get to her. 'Israr is only interested in looking out for himself. He'd rather sit around counting his coin-chips than try to fix this city.'

'Or perhaps Bolt has powers which can influence your perception — Israr would be most upset if I mentioned this to him,' Garnett said with almost believable concern.

'If you're so worried about Bolt messing with your thoughts, then why meet us?' Callista snorted. 'Neither of us have the ability to make you think something you don't want to. And we're not here to dance to your tune. I don't know why Colonel Nerani thought this would be a good idea.'

The governor's lips flattened into two straight lines. 'I met with both of you because undoubtedly one of you will survive the upcoming conflict and I wanted to get a measure of the next person I will have to deal with.' He spread his hands, a gesture that emphasised his lack of weapon. 'CL may not see it, but I do. You are a real threat and I want to impress upon you the need for my continued existence — leave me alive and I will make you my partners in ruling Yalsa 5. I can make the gangs and their night-time leaders officially part of our constitution. GLEA can't touch you then. They don't make a habit of overturning a planet's governing body, no matter how it is formed or what activities it conducts.'

Callista laughed and shook her head. So he didn't care about the people of Atsa — he was just making sure he was immune.

'You understand that our discussions will be very different from CL's,' Sandsa told Garnett.

'We *will* change things,' Callista added.

The governor sealed his palms back together and tapped his fingers against his lips. 'If I continue to benefit, I do not see any issue with new leadership. I shall let you go now as I imagine you will be very busy tonight. Die well, if you do.'

Sandsa and Callista stood in one motion. The wine bottle lifted from the table at the same time and the tumblers rose to lazily circle it, as though they were orbiting a star. Governor Garnett's eyes narrowed but he made no further comment. Callista smirked, saying nothing and letting the governor wonder just which one of them was responsible for the casual display of chipless powers.

Holding hands, the Maria subofficers left the room and returned to the roof where the Chipcopter awaited them.

CHAPTER TWENTY

Two nights later, Callista crossed her arms and kept the growl from clawing out of her throat. 'Ala, stark it, you know I'm good in a fight. Don't sideline me.'

'Tough, Cals, you're a subofficer, not a grunt — you need to be directing your people, not duckin' lasbolts,' Ala said, slicing the edge of her hand through the cooling air, cutting off all dissent. Dusk was deepening into night. 'You can probably throw some of your fancy moves from up on that balcony anyway. Bock'll be with you to make sure ya don't do something stupid, like run into the fight instead of winnin' it.'

'I get why you wouldn't want him on the street — '

Ala shook her head. 'No. No, you don't. The boy's smart like you, haven't ya noticed? I want him to learn off you. He worships the ground ya walk on.'

'Bock would lick the ground *you* walk on.'

Ala's forehead creased. 'Not sure that's any worse than him droolin' whenever he sees me.'

Hiding her smile, Callista took the overgrown garden path leading to the abandoned mansion that was to be her tomb for the evening. When no patter of feet immediately followed her, she turned to watch Bock scuttle up to Ala just as the subofficer was about to hoist herself into a waiting hovercar. Bock's hands twisted in front of his chest. His lips trembled. Callista winced, feeling the ardent emotions swirling around inside him and escaping through his mouth. He was declaring his feelings, baring it all.

Ala shook her head and ruffled his hair as though he was a child. Waving him off, she vanished inside the darkened cockpit and was borne away to another imminent battle. Bock stood there for several long moments, his shoulders sagging. Then his spine lurched upright and he bounded over to Callista with a wild grin.

'Let's do this!' Bock said, his excitement not quite wiping away the melancholy Callista could sense nibbling at the edges if his mind. 'I'm gonna earn myself a subofficer rank, you just watch.'

'Can you still take orders from your current subofficer?' Callista asked mock-sternly.

'So long as you don't order me to stop lookin' at Ala,' he answered, grin still growing.

Callista rolled her eyes and headed for the mansion. 'Follow me, you douchenozzle.'

'That order I'll take!' he said and hurried after her.

***

Tired, bruised and running, Sandsa barely had time to wonder where his latest lasgun had fallen and who the last remaining man of his group was. Their feet fell together in a steady rhythm as they chased the Alcazaar clanspeople who had attacked them. Sandsa's companion might have been from a minor clan but he wasn't helpless; he still had his weapon and was using it to fire a steady stream of lasbolts that became an unbroken line to follow. His aim was impressive, especially given that his dominant arm was flinging uselessly along beside him.

'I won't insult you by warning you to duck!' the man shouted.

'Wise choice!' Sandsa yelled back and used his powers to project a shield in front of them, a semi-sphere that absorbed the return fire then flung the lasbolts back towards their origin, cutting the men and women down as they fled.

'Fuck!' the other man said and dropped his lasgun. 'That's hot! And I'm out of charge!'

'We have no immediate enemies,' Sandsa said, patting the man's shoulder in what he hoped was a reassuring way.

He withdrew his touch almost immediately, but the thousands of tiny pinpricks that had punctured his skin were still working their way up his fingers. There was something familiar about this man, with his eyes as dark and mysterious as a desert night. He did not belong here — he should be wielding the awesome power of the deserts —

'Pagnus of Vieta,' Sandsa whispered.

His companion sent him a startled glance. 'What?'

'Your name.'

'Nah, my name is Josh Freeman,' the man said with a shake of his head. 'And it's been that since...since,' he finished softly.

Sandsa closed his eyes, only for a moment —

***

— and he returned to a time when he had been sand scattered over the surface of countless planets. Pieces of his being were swirling around a boy who had strayed too far from his tribe, the Vieta. The skin-stripping sandstorm bore down on the child but he defiantly roared back, the picture of a tribesman who wasn't afraid of death.

But he was.

His roar disintegrated into a plea. 'Lord Desine, help! I'm not as good as my brother!'

His lack of confidence will kill him and it will be no one's fault but his own, the Desine thought. Yet, though this boy looked nothing like a certain sibling called Kuja, there was something about him that reminded the Desine of his brother, that same uncertainty that the rainforest god always carried. And so the Desine stayed with the young tribesman, telling him, *You can survive this. You can survive anything.*

The fringes of the burnt orange storm engulfed the boy, tearing at his clothes, buffeting his hair, threatening to wear him down to the bone. But Pagnus of Vieta met the challenge, hands held high above his head as he called upon his powers, and the sand obeyed him, cocooning him instead of swarming him, thinning the air instead of stealing it. When the boy faltered, he called upon the Desine again — and his god answered him, bolstering him, keeping him on his feet.

After an hour, the sandstorm dropped away to a dirty smudge on the horizon, leaving Pagnus to collapse onto the sand, his energy spent. He was barely ten and untrained in his wild powers, but he would have become a revered priest in his tribe — if there had been anyone close enough to rescue him, to give him water and to shelter him from the blistering heat.

The Desine rose above the sprawling sands, shed his need for atmosphere in a way his siblings never could, then soared above the reaches of gravity, observing the planet as it shrank before him. Moments later, the starship whose occupants he had sensed the energy of tore through his insubstantial form on its way to a small settlement on the surface below to refuel. The god coasted through the corridors of the vessel, noting that the men and women aboard were slavers. It would be a hard life for the boy if he was taken by such people, but Pagnus would overcome it.

Sandsa planted the idea in the captain's thoughts and as he'd hoped the ship changed course. The captain called to her crew, 'This rock has some of those sand fleas! Them tribes don't register their kids on the Galactic Database so no one'll notice if we grab one or two.'

The ship's sensors found the barely flickering lifesign that belonged to Pagnus of Vieta and guided its captain towards it. The slavers descended the ship's ramp the second it hit the sand, found the boy and then took him aboard, his body limp in the arms of his captors. The Desine injected one last spike of confidence into Pagnus, knowing the boy would need it to escape and return to his people, wiser in the ways of the galaxy. The tribes on this planet knew very little of what lay beyond their atmosphere and were vulnerable to exploitation from others.

Pagnus would learn, then he would pass on that knowledge. It was a good plan. It would help so many people.

Just not Pagnus.

***

Pagnus — Josh — waved a hand in front of Sandsa's face. 'You okay, Subofficer Bolt?'

Sandsa waited until he trusted himself not to blurt out an apology before he met the intense gaze of the man he had wronged. 'We lack a vehicle.'

'Walking's good for you, man,' Josh told him with a wink.

'But I only have one good hand and no shield or working lasgun to put into it. Suggestions?'

Sandsa cast his eyes around for a weapon for — *Josh*, he reminded himself. One of the fallen Alcazaar was clutching something that might do. Kneeling and standing back up in one smooth motion, Sandsa acquired the lasgun and presented it to his companion. Josh accepted the weapon and looked it over for a couple of moments before throwing in an appreciative whistle. Now armed, he cheerfully fell into step beside Sandsa, making the occasional comment about the lack of public transportation in Atsa City. Eventually Josh conceded, without any interference from his listener, that it would be far too dangerous for anyone to stand out on the street at night and wait for some government-funded hovercar to show up.

'How is it you became a Freed clansperson?' Sandsa asked as they continued to troop down the darkened road, hopefully heading towards a Maria-held site.

'Oh, membership's easy,' Josh said with an abrupt, biting laugh. 'You just have to be a former slave. I was stolen off Ilbb then wound up on Yalsa 5 after I escaped. We got ourselves enough people with enough lasguns to repel any slavers who come lookin' for any of us.'

Sandsa kept his eyes on the road. 'You come from Ilbb, known for its worldwide worship of the Desine — does that mean you were a tribesman once?'

'It's possible,' Josh answered after a lengthy pause. 'Vom said he could feel the Magic in me but I can't, man. It's also considered bad form to jump clans, so I fully support your refusal to do. And anyway, if I was stolen out of the deserts, what does it mean now?

I can't change what happened. Even if I was a tribesman, I'm not one of them. Not anymore.'

Sandsa spent several minutes plodding along the pavement on the side of the road in silence, his anger festering in his gut before spreading to infect his heart, his mind. What kind of man — what kind of *god* did that to someone?

Why did I ruin his life? Why didn't I just teleport him home? Sandsa thought, kicking a loose chunk of concrete that had fallen away from the footpath, causing it to hurtle across the road. *I forced him from the deserts, into the life of an exile...for what, some plan I concocted to teach him something I could have just told his people?*

Josh drew up short, his breath rattling in his chest. 'Ow. Can I rest for. a minute?'

'May I see your arm, Josh?' Sandsa asked, concern overriding his guilt.

The other man shrugged. 'Sure, if you tell me your real name — I never understood the gang name thing.'

Sandsa moved around behind Josh to his injured side and ran his fingers over the tattered teal cloth of the Freed clansman's shirt. The insignia of Josh's clan seemed to be two simple lines on the cuffs of both long sleeves, though on this side the symbol had been scorched through by a stray lasgun bolt. As he began to discreetly heal Josh, Sandsa told the man his name, then added, 'I was a desert man myself and I...I can feel that you have great power.'

'I don't *feel* it and I don't want to.' Josh flinched. 'Ow. Stop poking so hard.'

Sandsa lifted his hand and let it hover instead. 'My apologies. Are you angry that you never had the choice to stay in the deserts? Do you remember anything from that time?'

'Are the questions supposed to distract me or are you just this curious?' Josh asked, shooting a look over his shoulder. 'Wow. If I didn't know better, I'd say you had the healing touch. But no one can do that, right? Not even the Chippers.'

The air around them grew wet and heavy, crawling into Sandsa's limbs and weighing him down. He glanced up.

You could heal him completely if you used your full powers. This was not his father's voice; these were the oily tones belonging to Fayay. Sandsa hadn't seen or sensed his brother for weeks.

Sandsa stiffened. His patient started to turn around but Sandsa pressed down on Josh's shoulders, keeping him still. Scanning the nearby streets and failing to find the god of water's human form anywhere in sight, Sandsa curled his lip. *Fayay. You make a habit of lurking — is it because you are too afraid to face me?*

'Do I remember...I remember being surrounded by sand,' Josh said slowly. 'I used to have nightmares about it. My owners beat me until I stopped crying out in my sleep. I had to...erase it from my mind to survive. As for the choice? Doesn't matter now.' Josh stretched out his good arm, the lasgun steady in his grip as he indicated the buildings standing over them. 'I can choose where I land so I picked here. Not sure why, but I did.'

Sandsa drew back, frowning. He was still rattled by Fayay's presence and it bothered him that so many of his people had come to Atsa City recently. It was hard to forget them when he saw them everywhere. Shutting himself off from them kept him sane, kept him human — and he planned to keep doing it. The damage was already done to Pagnus; what more could Sandsa do about it now?

'All done, Pagnus,' Sandsa said, retracting his touch.

The man blinked. 'Josh, I told you it's Josh.' His gaze roamed to where his injury had been. 'And wow, I really didn't hurt myself as much as I thought I did.'

Sandsa stowed his hands in his pockets, furious with himself. He had used too much of his powers to heal Josh and now the winds were whispering again. A hot, uncomfortable pressure arose somewhere below his sternum, threatening to crawl up into his throat.

Sandsa swallowed. 'What causes you to reject your origins now, when no one can stop you returning to your tribe?'

'You need to know that badly?'

'Yes.'

'I'm afraid I'll want that life,' Josh said, his gaze falling to the concrete beneath his feet. 'And that I've wasted my time in not chasing it. If I accept that it's part of me and that it's something I want to *make* part of me, then what the fuck have I been doing this entire time?'

Sandsa stowed his uneasiness and began walking briskly down the road again, Josh at his heels. He let his companion think it was because he was in a hurry to assist the Maria, not to escape any lingering humidity.

Fayay, stark you, why are you here? he snapped.

The Watine didn't answer.

Around the next corner Sandsa and Josh ran into a fresh battle, luck seeing them behind the Maria line. Without a word to each other, both men entered the fight. But no matter how many lasbolts demanded his attention, it was impossible for Sandsa to forget what he had done to his companion.

***

Callista crossed her arms, scowling down at the battle below them.

'Aw, she'll come 'round,' Bock said, shifting from foot to foot and glancing furtively at the street, also clearly desperate to join the action.

Callista clenched the chrome railing that ran around the perimeter of the mansion's balcony to keep from giving in to temptation. She had chosen this building because it had been left empty for some time by friends of her parents, though if she'd had her way she wouldn't have had to find somewhere to direct the battle from in the first place. Annoyed, she stabbed the heel of her boot onto a faded tile, cracking it.

'The same way she came around when you declared your true feelings just now?' Callista snorted. 'Forget about it, Bock.'

Lasgun fire erupted below. Callista tapped her earpiece and instructions fled her mouth before she even knew what she'd planned to say. The tiny insect-like figures she was directing moved at her command, changing the outcome of the battle — or so she hoped. When one Alcazaar started gunning down more clanspeople than she could spare, she seized him with her powers and hurled him against a thick wall that smashed his head open.

'Hey, at least I tried,' Bock muttered.

Callista flung a severe look at him. 'Can't you see I'm busy right now?'

'I know you wanna be down there,' Bock said and slung his elbows on the railing, staring down at the carnage from his new position beside her. 'I do too. S'no reason to get nasty.'

She winced. 'Bock, I'm sorry, I didn't — '

'Chipcopter comin' in from the south,' Bock interrupted.

'I see it.'

The ominously silent 'copter swooped down low over the road, its guns aimed directly at their balcony. Callista narrowed her eyes and threw a deadly thought at the 'copter. It wobbled, then shook violently. She gasped, overcome with the terror filling the minds inside the airborne vehicle, and staggered back from the railing. She had nearly regained her footing when Bock tackled her to the floor, covering her body with his. Dazed, Callista tried to rise from the tiles but Bock immediately flattened her again. The strafing began.

'Subofficer Dancer, do something!' Bock shouted into her face, his spit striking her cheeks.

Callista forced herself to concentrate. The invisible shield her powers generated lit up with a volley of fire. Bock rolled off her and seized the large splatterlasgun he had leaned against the wall earlier. He leapt back up and pumped it rapidly, screaming at the top of his lungs. The ensuing bolts sailed through Callista's shield and peppered the 'copter until it dropped out of view. Callista used the railing to get to her feet and managed it just in time to witness the 'copter hitting the ground. The accelerant in its tanks exploded.

She nodded at her companion. 'Thanks for the save.'

'Back at ya,' Bock said, breathing heavily. 'Holy Creator shit, I wish we had Bolt here.'

'Me too. But I think we can make do with me.'

Callista gnawed on the inside of her cheek when someone fell to a stray lasbolt that she did not predict — and, admittedly, could not even deflect. Exhaustion was winning. Her heart was shuddering against her ribs, banging on bone, and her vision was beginning to shimmer. She leaned her forehead against the parallel lines formed by her thumb and index finger.

Bock released a hiss of air. 'We're starked, aren't we?'

'Maybe not,' Callista said, her lips curving. 'Bolt just arrived.'

Bock immediately turned to look for Sandsa, giving Callista time to hack up what felt like a lung over the side of the balcony. She was relieved to find only saliva dripping from her lips. For now the smoke shed by burning wreckage and glowing lasbolts was a nuisance, but if it got any worse it might become a fatal distraction.

Callista latched onto Sandsa's mind and sent him her orders. He acknowledged them immediately and got his companion to lay down fire while the massive shield created by a former desert god allowed the Maria line to move forward. Callista bit her lip, envying the display.

She started when Bock's grip landed on her shoulder. When had he grown so tall, she wondered, that he could meet her eye to eye?

'You can still love the guy even if he's better at this one thing,' Bock told her, his manic grin returning. 'You're great at organisin' shit and he's not.'

'When did you become so wise, Bock?'

'Dunno, but it works for me, right?'

Callista laughed. 'Absolutely. Now shut up and find something to shoot.'

The battle now required her full attention. So she gave it.

***

'Do you ever wonder if the Alcazaar can spawn from a handful of dirt?' Callista asked, stepping over a body. She paused to kick the man's head to one side, exposing his glassy eyes.

'No, because it is impossible,' Sandsa replied. His eyes grew distant. 'Even I cannot...could not create people with a handful of sand.'

'You know what I mean.'

Sandsa pulled her into his chest and pressed his lips to her forehead. 'I do. This war feels never-ending and it has been but a fortnight. Eventually the numbers opposing us will dwindle.'

'Our numbers aren't as exhaustive as theirs,' Callista said, her sigh ghosting over the nipple hidden beneath his clothes.

He twitched in response. 'Ah. Yes. There needs to be one decisive encounter then.'

She breathed against his chest again. The nipple hardened, pushing against his shirt.

'Callista...'

'Mmm?'

After darting a quick look around at the nearby clanspeople, who were dusting themselves off and heading for the safety of whichever headquarters they had originated from, Callista slid her hand under Sandsa's shirt and rested it against his abdomen. The blond hairs on his stomach shivered as she followed their trail down to the belt that kept her from venturing further. Then she struck, cupping the interested bulge at the front of his pants. Sandsa cursed.

'Where did you learn those words?' she asked with a smirk.

'I hardly think that matters right now!'

Callista would not have described her response as a giggle, but anyone listening might have mistaken it as one. She took his hand and led him into the empty mansion where she threw him against a couch she had passed on her way back down from the balcony earlier. They entwined and she lost herself in the hot, wet kisses that followed, in the confusion of skin on skin, never knowing which part was touching where. His pants had been wriggled to his knees at some point.

'Please,' he whispered, no words or thoughts stretching the sentence further.

Callista's fingers danced over him, moving lower and lower. When she finished tracing a line down his soft skin to the crease of his leg, his cock twitched towards her palm and she shot him a look. 'Are you doing that on purpose?'

'No...' His eyes closed. '*Callista...*'

Her clitoris throbbed impatiently in response and Callista held in the moan. Carefully balancing herself on his thighs, she teased her fingers along his hardening shaft. He hissed when she reached the tip, where a bead of moisture was slowly forming. On impulse, Callista bent over and captured the drop with her lips. It was salty and thicker than water and somehow not as disgusting as she'd imagined. Sandsa's hips rose. She kissed him again, then slid her tongue over the area, wetting it, drawing desperate sounds from him —

The communicator in her ear buzzed.

Sandsa groaned.

Callista grabbed her earpiece and yanked it out, tempted to hurl the device against the wall. She glanced down at the veined member that still stood to attention, distracted, wanting to continue tasting it. Sandsa's eyes were now open, wide and desperate.

Callista cleared her throat and activated the earpiece now cradled in her palm. 'Yes?'

'Thought you two could sense this kinda disturbance with your powers?' Ala's voice asked.

Callista sighed, her spare hand still casually exploring Sandsa. He had been rising from the couch to join the conversation but flopped backwards and laced his fingers over his face, muttering something under his breath.

'Ala, I'm a little preoccupied at the moment — ' Callista began.

'I bet you are.'

'Ala! Just tell me what I need to know.'

Armed with the knowledge of an attack directed at the Zatzat headquarters, Callista nipped Sandsa's lips then leapt off his lap. He followed her, belting his pants back on, and looped his arms around her waist. Callista found herself pulled back into the curve formed by his chest as he lay sweet little kisses along one side of her neck. She drank in his attention for a moment more, then tore away from his embrace.

'We can finish that conversation another time,' she said, winking.

'I anticipate that conclusion with every breath.' Sandsa's mournful expression dissolved. 'Now. What do you need me to do?'

CHAPTER
TWENTY-ONE

As dusk descended on Atsa yet again the craters inflicted on the cityscape revealed that they had been dormant cauldrons waiting to be stirred back into life to spew blood, flames and screams. With each night the Alcazaar dared to come that much closer to the heart of Maria territory. Since Ala suspected it wouldn't be long before they hit her headquarters, she asked the other clans to assist with ringing the area.

'I hope the Desine bothers to show up tonight,' Vom said as he loped past Sandsa. 'The Alcazaar and Chippers get us good when we're powerless.'

Sandsa's throat tightened. Callista must have sensed his discomfort because her fingers quickly wove through his. *Sandsa. He won't turn up. He can't.*

The Desine could stop all this nonsense in a single heartbeat.

Are you only saying that because we haven't managed to finish our titillating conversation? she asked, arching an eyebrow.

Sandsa decided not to answer that, because she already knew she was right, and his eyes instead found Josh Freeman who was part of a group that was about to head down Canat Road to the position Ala had ordered them to take. Josh was cracking jokes to anyone who would listen, but his own smile was weary and forced. Guilt threatened to choke Sandsa, but then Callista distracted him, her palms on his cheeks, her lips on his own. He allowed her gentle kiss to erase his memories briefly, so briefly, then pulled back to say, 'What I did to him, Callista…'

'No, what the desert god did to him,' she cut in.

Sandsa grimaced. 'It is not so easy for me to distance myself from my own past.'

'Sometimes I want our first day together to be the first day of your life because it'd be a lot simpler,' Callista told him, then stole another kiss. 'And I feel like…I shouldn't be suppressing who you are, just so I can have you at my side.'

'I am the one who is suppressing myself.'

'But for who, Sandsa? Please don't make it my fault. Please.'

Sandsa curved his hand around the back of her neck. 'I did it for me. I have never been freer. I have never been happier. I owe fealty to no one but my clan and the woman I intend to marry.'

'For *that* comment, I'm sending your group to the opposite end of Canat Road,' she said tartly, but she was grinning as she turned to go.

He kept hold of her hand and used it to tug her back to him. 'Callista. What if…what if to save lives and end this war, I should be what I was, and allow people like Pagnus and Vom to use the powers I gave them?'

'But you'd give yourself to them and never stop — I can feel it, I know you wouldn't be able to stop once you started,' she whispered. 'They'd take you from me and you'd let them — and I…I don't think that's what you want.'

'It's not,' he insisted. 'Because I want you.'

Callista snatched her hand back from him and hurried away.

***

226

The battle raged on but oddly there were no Chippers to be found, not even Nerani's folk. This caused a rash of rumours to spread amongst the Maria and the other clans, their discontent growing louder with each passing minute. Ala eventually took it upon herself to bellow into multiple communicators, ordering everyone to stop wasting their time on gossip so they could spend more of it raining fire on the Alcazaar. Curious, Sandsa stretched out his senses and felt all the Chippers clustered in one section of the city. Their energy was filled with indecision and turbulence.

No 'copters swooped in from above. But it was dangerous enough without them.

Sandsa felt a violent tug on his heart when he collided with Vom while sprinting towards a line of Maria who needed his help. Clutching his chest, winded, Sandsa willed himself to stay within his flesh, his powers curled up inside him like a serpent.

Vom grabbed his shoulders. 'Sandsa! We need your help in raising the Desine!'

'He has abandoned you — why do you continue to place faith in him?' Sandsa asked, snapping any tendrils seeking him in half.

'It's the only weapon we've got left.'

Sandsa's eyes found the Zatzat clanspeople gathered behind Vom. Most of them held lasguns that were warped beyond recognition by heat from repeated firing. Some had even been reduced to fighting with their bare hands.

Sandsa waved one of his clansmen over. 'Subofficer Knives. Lasguns and shielding devices for our allies.'

'What, don't they got their own?' asked Knives as he trotted up to Sandsa.

'Direct my request to Bock,' Sandsa instructed the man.

Knives raced off, but his disapproval trailed after him.

Vom was now staring at Sandsa in disbelief. 'Sandsa, no lasgun can make me feel useful. Losing my powers…it's like losing a limb. You don't feel this — you still have your chipless powers to fall back on.'

'You do not need some invisible deity to make your decisions,' Sandsa said flatly. 'And I wonder if perhaps the Desine wishes to pursue a life unbothered by people constantly demanding things of him and never giving anything in return!'

'But you are thinking like a man — the Desine is not one of us,' Vom reminded him.

Sandsa met his intense gaze without flinching. 'I would not begrudge the Desine for thinking like one of us, wanting to be like one of us. He owes you nothing, Vom.'

'I have a son, Sandsa. Should I ignore my responsibility as a parent because some days I am tired of looking after him?'

The road shook beneath his feet. Sandsa slumped sideways but Vom caught him before he hit the ground. Something pounded against Sandsa's temples, something important, something demanding attention — Callista. He wrapped the cord of her presence around his wrist, tightening the knot so hard that if it had been a tangible connection it might have cut off the circulation in his hand. Sandsa staggered the first few paces towards where Callista's plea originated, supported by his friend.

Friend? Sandsa considered the word as he straightened and shook off the man's help. He was surprised that when he tore down the road Vom followed him. *I was missing out on more than I realised. But to keep this friend, I must abandon him…*

He listened for Callista's voice, but her silence stretched on and on. His heart, trapped beneath his ribs, pounded unsteadily.

Losing her would hurt more than being caught in another hovercar fire.

'I have disobeyed Subofficer Ala,' Sandsa realised, slowing as he remembered the clanspeople he had left behind, the ones he was supposed to lead.

Vom grabbed his arm. 'I'll take your place. It's Dancer, isn't it? She in trouble?'

Sandsa cursed and tapped a finger to the communicator sitting inside his ear. 'Subofficer Dancer — Callista? *Callista?* Why did I not think to try this earlier?' he asked his companion. 'Am I that reliant on my powers?'

There was no answer from the device or from Vom who touched his shoulder briefly before hurtling over to those Sandsa had abandoned, bellowing orders in his stead. Sandsa ran in the opposite direction, trying not to trip on strewn and shattered bodies.

He was soon confronted with the sight of Alcazaar clanspeople pouring through the gaps between the smoking shells of overturned hovercars. Their charge was held at bay by a weak smattering of lasgun fire from a group of Maria led by Bock, whose face sported more cuts and grazes than Sandsa could count in one glance. The young man stood tall and proud and was barely covered by the faltering shields that two of his companions held up for him.

'Where is she?' Sandsa shouted. 'She was meant to be directing her group from here!'

'We're a little overrun, Bolt!' Bock roared back at him.

Sandsa stormed past Bock, clipping the clansman's shoulder as he went, and exposed himself to the Alcazaar. He smiled, daring his opponents to take a shot at him, then struck. Metal debris slammed into the Alcazaar, pinning them against the road and shredding their flesh. He found Callista curled up nearby, her body lifeless and her mind unresponsive. Sandsa hurried over to her and arrived just in time to see her eyes flutter open.

She wasn't hurt, just stunned, but she needed him. The battle was no longer important.

Something hot seared across his shoulder. Sandsa hissed. 'I will be back in a moment, Callista.'

He rose and began marching towards the person who had fired the lasgun bolt. The Alcazaar clansman responsible swore, dropped his weapon, and bolted before Sandsa could retaliate.

'Nice work,' Ala piped up from his communicator.

'The Alcazaar have fallen back already?' Sandsa asked, a hand covering the earpiece.

'Yeah, I know, way too easy. Probably 'cause the Chippers haven't showed up.'

'Why haven't they?' he asked, moving over to help Callista stand.

Ala's voice was cool, but her thoughts were laced with concern. 'Internal strife. A general from another system showed up and decided to punish both factions. Can't blame 'em, really.'

Callista's communicator must have also been receiving the subofficer because she frowned and joined the conversation. 'We've lost the Chippers?'

'Dunno yet, but it can't be good if Nerani's not answering me,' Ala said dryly.

Callista adjusted her jacket but Sandsa could see that the tears and holes it had gained over the past few nights didn't offer much protection against the chilly night air. 'Don't they care about saving lives?'

'More lives have been lost in this past month than in many years, I feel,' Sandsa murmured. 'The Chippers cannot keep adding to the deaths. Their superiors would disapprove.'

'What Bolt said.' Ala offered no more.

Sandsa curled an arm around Callista's waist and began leading her back to headquarters. But she wasn't done. 'This is ridiculous! We have been fighting for the good of Atsa.'

'We fought to keep one man beside the woman he loves,' Sandsa remarked.

'That was just an excuse,' Callista said, shaking her head. 'This war has been brewing since your mother died, Sandsa. We deserve to live without fear of the Alcazaar.'

'More people will be hurt if this continues.'

'I know, I just...' Callista closed her eyes. 'I wish it was over.'

'As do I.'

***

It was early still, far before dawn, but the Alcazaar tide had receded for the night. The unease of the Maria and their allies hung over Canat Road, causing arguments and even one person to brandish a lasgun. Subofficer Ala took to patrolling the street, a weapon tucked into each hand, snapping at anyone who spoke too loudly.

Inside the Maria headquarters, Sandsa guided Callista into her room, stripping the shredded jacket and the layers beneath it from her body before laying her down on top of her bed. He shed his own shirt and kicked it aside, then came to kneel beside her.

She reached for the burn on his shoulder. 'You should let me deal with this.'

'I will be fine, so long as I know that you are,' he said softly.

'You've fixed me up heaps of times, let me return the favour,' she protested, but did not complain when he pulled her pants off, his eyes and fingers roving over her skin as he examined her. His touch drew a gasp from her lips and an insistent throb from between her legs.

'Doesn't seem fair for you to keep yours on,' she told him.

He laughed. His pants soon joined hers on the floor and Callista stared unabashedly at the firm, lengthening organ that was now free of any restrictions. Sandsa arched his eyebrow at her. Grinning, Callista wriggled out of her grey underwear and squeezed her thighs together, enjoying the liquid heat that was pooling deep inside her. She shivered pleasantly as he rolled her onto her side and spooned her from behind, his chest warming her back.

The sheet glided gently over her breasts when Sandsa heaved more of it over them. She smiled as she felt him shift behind her, his hardness revealing the reason for his discomfort. A thrill shot through her, reawakening her fading adrenaline.

Outside, the city smouldered. It was hard to care about this as his fingers circled her bellybutton. She wanted his touch to dip much, much lower.

'I had a dream that we were married,' she said after several long moments.

Sandsa nuzzled the side of her neck. 'So did I.'

'And we had a son,' Callista went on.

'Blue eyes like mine, fiery spirit like yours...'

She hesitated. 'Did you see what he was wearing?'

'No, the dream wasn't that detailed,' Sandsa answered, a smile lingering in his voice.

She decided not to chase the issue. Instead, she asked, 'Do you think it's inevitable, then, that we will marry and all that?'

'Do you not like the idea of being married to me, Callista?' His breathing hitched.

Callista curled her hand around his. 'Of course I do, my love.'

They lay there together for a time, silent and content. She muttered a protest when he suddenly slipped away, removing the support of his body and causing her to drop onto her back. But then he was straddling her, his eyes somehow darker than the night. Callista wet her lips as he pulled the sheet away, exposing her hardened nipples. He immediately gave them attention.

Callista moaned. 'Aren't you going to ask me?'

'I am done waiting for an answer I know I will receive,' he whispered against her heart, pressing his obvious desire against her hip.

Callista's heart skipped a beat. 'You should still ask. It's only polite, Sandsa dear.'

'And then I assume, once I have done so, once I have your answer...' His voice dropped lower, into a growl. '...we will do exactly what your mind has been Webcasting for weeks?'

Callista writhed when his tongue swept around one nipple, not quite touching it, driving her mad. His fingers skimmed through the curls below her abdomen, sliding into the moist dip that welcomed him further and further —

'Ah,' she gasped.

He withdrew. 'Did I hurt you?'

'No, but...' She found herself blushing. 'Sandsa. I...I'm scared.'

'Me too,' he said, lying beside her, his hand on her abdomen.

Callista gripped his index finger and led it to her clitoris, preparing to guide him again, but his hand wriggled free. She tilted her head back as he began to show her what he had learned.

'*Wife*,' he murmured.

'Not yet,' she reproached and he continued his ministrations, bolder and firmer than before.

'Callista...' A deep, desperate note escaped him.

He was in her mind, feeling what she felt, which only made the sensations more intense. Sandsa's touch left her swollen bud but she did not have time to protest. His finger entered her and Callista stilled, eyes wide as he dipped further inside, up to the first knuckle.

'Oh, alright!' she said, caving. 'I'll marry you.'

Sandsa paused. 'Are you...'

'Yes, I'm sure! Now stop stalling.'

Electricity shot through her when she faced him, her hand glancing over his hip before gliding south. His balls were soft to her touch, the hair dusting them as blond and gentle as it was on the top of his head. She clasped her fingers around his hardness then gently lifted them to the tip that leaked desire over her knuckles.

While she was distracted with exploring his body, Sandsa reached down between her legs, his finger taking up the circular motion she had taught him. Callista squirmed away from him. 'That's not fair. Why don't...why can't I feel how you like to be touched?'

'I never tried,' he admitted.

Callista smiled, her palm brushing his cheek, then darted down to tease him with her lips. Enjoying the desire in his eyes and the sharp gasps he made, she wrapped her mouth around his shaft and slipped down a little way, stopping when it became uncomfortable. She didn't think she could swallow any more of him — how would she fit all of him inside her?

Callista dropped back down onto the bed, hands resting on her stomach. 'Okay. I'm ready. Are you?'

'Yes, wife,' he said and knelt over her, his member proud and hard, a string of lazy precum wending its way onto the hairs below, knitting them together.

Callista mewled in surprise when he suddenly kissed her weeping entrance — it was a moist, open kiss that he seemed to enjoy, for his eyes were closed when she looked down at him. She did not get to admire this sight for long because soon she was clutching his scalp, digging through the knots in his hair. Slick and sure, his tongue followed his finger's earlier path into her, evoking gasps —

'Stop!' she exclaimed.

When he looked up at her in concern, his mouth was soaked with her juices; an arousing sight that made it all the more difficult to restrain herself. He smiled. 'You are close, aren't you?'

Callista answered by thrusting her peaked nipples into the air.

Kissing her forehead, Sandsa nudged her legs further apart with his knee. With one hand resting on her hip to comfort her, he leaned heavily onto the other, fingers dipping into the sheets. She tensed when his hardness first grazed her. Carefully, he eased into her moist heat and slowed when he met resistance. He was gentle and cautious as he slid further inside her but she felt his mind beginning to unravel, his carefully manicured thoughts crumbling as he was overtaken by hot, demanding passion. She dug her nails into his backside as a warning when he jolted forward a little too fast.

Breathing raggedly, Sandsa began to work himself in and out of her. The feeling of being stretched was uncomfortable for several moments, but then Callista spasmed impatiently around around him and her nails carved more deeply into his flesh. Finally, with one long, seamless glide, he sheathed himself entirely within her and stopped, his chest heaving. Callista watched her own nipples rise and fall with each trembling breath she drew. Catching her gaze, Sandsa smiled and clasped his mouth over one of her breasts. Tingles that began there rapidly spread down to between her legs.

Sandsa... she sent to him, unable to articulate her wants, her needs.

She drove her knees into his sides, urging him on. Sandsa groaned and reared back, his stiff member retreating just enough for Callista to see her liquid desire coating him. And then he was thrusting slowly into her, sweat slipping along his brow. His arms shook with the effort of both holding himself up and keeping himself from ravishing her.

'Please,' she whispered. '*Please.*'

His pace quickened. Each time he borrowed within her, a stab of pleasure surged through her body, causing Callista to moan inarticulate sounds instead of his name. His chest, damp with sweat, slicked her breasts, moistening them, making it easier for their skin to slide together. Her mouth found purchase on his shoulder, suckling to anchor herself as much as to excite him. Then her folds clenched around him, stealing every last drop of thought, until Callista went rigid, her vision tunnelling.

Sandsa cried out into the pillow beside her head. A hot burst filled her but it wasn't enough so Callista rocked up against him, forcing his pelvis to dance with hers, and then her mouth dropped open soundlessly as the pleasure hit a crescendo. This sweet release continued for several long thuds of her heart. When Callista finally came to herself, she found Sandsa collapsed on top of her, panting, his thoughts scattered and incomprehensible.

'Wow,' she breathed.

Sandsa heaved himself to the side then propped his head up with an arm, regarding her with half-closed eyes. A pleased smile tugged on his lips. 'Oh, my love. That was wonderful.'

'And messy,' she said, cupping her trembling core and feeling the mingled fluids from their lovemaking dampen her hand. 'What — Sandsa...!'

He took her hand in his and guided her fingers between his lips, one at a time, his tongue caressing each line and knuckle. Callista sighed and surrendered to him again, lapping up his attention as he moved his mouth over her body, evoking a warm cascade of shudders. When he dipped lower and cleaned her with his tongue, she enjoyed a smaller climax.

Callista loved the smug expression marking his features, one that made him even more handsome. Returning her smile, he moved her onto her stomach. A knot in the sheets pressed against her still damp mons, causing her to groan. She continued to lie there as his hands started working over her shoulders and lower back, removing the last of her tension.

Her pillow was so soft against her cheek and it smelled of both of them, of sweat and sex and belonging. Watched over by the man she was going to marry, she allowed herself to drift away.

CHAPTER TWENTY-TWO

Sandsa watched her slip into slumber, her mind clouded with exhaustion, then leaned over and used his fingers to swipe away the hair that covered her neck, exposing her skin for him to kiss. He then crept over to his shirt and pulled on the damp cloth, wrinkling his nose at its stench. But her smell was on him too; a heady perfume that followed him even after he left the room. He met Bock on the stairs where the younger man sized him up.

'*Nice*,' Bock began but cut himself off when Sandsa shot him a dirty look.

'I would rather you didn't say — or think — such things about my future wife,' Sandsa told him. 'Now. Did Kick make a vehicle available for me like I requested?'

Bock sighed deeply. 'Yeah. Had to promise to clean the garage later. Doin' you a big favour, ya know, so you're gonna let me drive. Where we headed?'

'Alcazaar headquarters,' Sandsa answered. Though his companion's face immediately blanched, Sandsa went on, 'I have business there. And while I could discreetly make my way into the study of the Clan Leader and sling a few drops of poison into his glass of wine or whatever it is he drinks, I need to make an entrance so I can take credit for his death.'

'You're going to — *kill* the Clan Leader?' Bock stared at him.

Sandsa marched him down the stairs one step at a time until the younger man regained his senses enough to wriggle away from Sandsa's grip, his eyes wide. Sandsa did not stop walking. Once he heard Bock following him, he said, 'If the best way to protect the Maria and the woman I love is to take stewardship of this city, then I will do it. By any means necessary.'

'Callista's gonna kill you,' Bock warned him.

'I know,' Sandsa said, pained.

The moment their boots hit the ramp in the garage, Bock rushed ahead to the passenger side of the hovercar parked directly in front of the exit. He popped open a door which fell from the chrome frame and converted into three short steps. The newly opened gap in the vehicle's body revealed burgundy leather seats, a vidscreen and a drinks cabinet. Sandsa tipped his head to one side, impressed, then climbed in. It was obviously Kick's best and most impressive beast and looked as though it had rarely seen action.

'Oh, it's kitted out right,' Bock assured his passenger as he slid into the front seat, pausing to add a ridiculous padded hat to his head, the sort of one professional chauffeurs wore on certain wealthy planets. 'The lasproofing isn't half bad. S'even got a lascannon stowed underneath. Right kind of pimped vessel for a Clan Leader.'

'Clan *Leaders*,' Sandsa corrected.

Bock tossed a grin back at him. 'That won't stop her getting mad at you, Bolt.'

***

The roads Bock chose were clear and undamaged, though Sandsa caught a whiff of acrid smoke in the air when he lowered the window beside him. He leaned back to enjoy the breeze only to start when the window slid shut. Bock gave him a reproving look. 'Lasproofing only works when you keep the windows up. A Clan Leader's gotta get used to recycled air.'

'And suppose I fail this morning?' Sandsa asked, quirking his lips into a smile.

'I'll just say the hovercar's a gift when CL asks why I'm in his driveway.'

Sandsa laughed. Bock's gaze remained on the road, his eyelids fluttering against the invading sunlight — when was the last time Bock had been out during the day? His face was pallid and his knuckles were even whiter on the steering wheel. Shadows of doubt crept through the young man's mind, but he was distracting himself with thoughts of Ala.

Sandsa saw various vendors emerging from the safety of their homes to set up their stalls for another day of enticing customers. Only a handful of locals were brave enough to hit the streets, usually those whose livelihoods relied on them selling as many wares as possible. Sandsa wondered if they ever hoped for tourists — but who would visit a city torn apart by gangs?

The hovercar slowed in front of a grand house with an expansive porch framed by four large pillars that resembled slumped bloated men. Multiple Alcazaar guards stood either side of the small ramp that led from the tapered driveway up to the porch's shattered tiling. The heavy steel door of the building, designed to withstand bombardments, would have once been smooth and seamless; now it was chipped and cracked. The lasguns mounted on the front of the building had taken a pummelling as well, many of them now reduced to blackened craters. There were two of them still swinging around, the tortured whirring of their movements loud enough that Sandsa could hear them from the road, even with his window securely shut.

His blood pumped faster as he sent his consciousness further and further out into the desert. The wild sands answered, crying out to him, promising to obey him if only he returned — he should have squashed this connection, but he embraced it, drawing on the powers of a god. A twinge beneath his ribs warned him that his people would sense him soon. Sandsa ignored the pain, instead focusing on what he needed to do. He leaned over. to swipe his thumb on the sensor on the handle but Bock was quicker — the teenager sprang out and hurried over, opening the door for him.

Sandsa then ambled up the ramp and nodded at the guards. They eyed him warily.

'I have come to kill your Clan Leader,' Sandsa said and dodged the ensuing lasbolts.

His own weapon remained on his belt as he lashed out with the Desine's might. A savage gust of sand-laden wind knocked his opponents over. Sandsa casually strolled over to the unmoving Alcazaar and killed each of them with their own lasguns. He erected a shield half a second before the artillery on the wall exploded into life, their slow reaction time revealing that they had been in manual mode all along.

He spared a look down at the road and saw that Bock was back inside the hovercar, apparently reading a book on a small techpad, though he was tapping the screen with his finger a little too frequently to be spending enough time on any of the pages.

Sandsa allowed this lapse in concentration. He was a god; nothing could come close to harming him now.

The mounted lasguns dropped to the porch, a pile of snapped arms and wiring. Sandsa approached the unguarded door and pressed a finger to the centre of it. Cracks multiplied on the panel until it fell inwards and broke apart on the smooth metallic floor.

Sandsa took his time in ascending the main staircase, torrents of sand scouring skin from bone and weapons from hidden locations behind and around him. He walked through the storm, smiling, not bothering to move any faster to reach his destination. Some of the Alcazaar dropped to their knees, hands pulling their heads to the ground in surrender. He let them live. The Maria would need new grunts to carry out their legwork when they became the ruling clan in Atsa City. As he drew closer to the lifesign that represented the Clan Leader, one woman knelt with her hands raised to the air, revealing the binding scars on each of her palms.

'My Lord Desine,' she whispered.

Though her Magic was not particularly strong, even she could sense her god brandishing his full powers. Sandsa felt her, saw the destiny the Desine had once written for her, but he sidestepped that part of his past as easily as he sidestepped her. The Clan Leader met him further along in the corridor, waving off the guards who clamoured to take the hits for him. Sandsa and CL regarded each other for what probably felt like an eternity to the Alcazaar leader. Time ticked away.

'So you have come to seize what is mine with the powers of a Chipper instead of allowing me a fair fight,' CL said distastefully. Since the Alcazaar leader would have done the same thing in his place, Sandsa knew the man was just stalling.

He threw a laugh in CL's face. 'No. I came with the powers of the desert god, because I am he, and I am sick of this fighting that keeps me from the woman I love.'

To his credit, the leader of the Alcazaar did not flinch or back away. CL merely stood there, accepting the end of his reign, submitting himself to the tornado that encased his body. When the sand cascaded into a puddle on the floor, it was stained red, forming a soiled bed for the bleached bones that fell upon it. There was silence but for Sandsa's ragged breathing as he fought the urge to flee into the deserts and become one with them —

He bit down on his lip and tasted the blood of a mortal.

'I am your Clan Leader now,' Sandsa declared.

No one dissented. They stayed on the floor, trembling before him.

'Your clan is no more,' Sandsa continued, surveying each bowed head. 'You are now Maria.'

Their angry muttering was muted, distant, fearful. Sandsa stomped a foot and the building groaned and cracked around him, sand burrowing into its foundations.

'This war is over,' he said.

Sandsa paused by a rose bush in a neighbouring yard on his way out. He ripped a flower free from the bush and snapped each thorn off its stem as he approached the hovercar. Behind him, Alzacaar spilled out of their disintegrating headquarters, fleeing into the city. He supposed some of them would not stay on Yalsa 5, afraid of his vengeance. Others would report to the Maria later, hungry for the wealth and power that surrounded a Clan Leader.

Bock opened the passenger door for him and Sandsa slid inside, nursing the flower. At first, all Bock could do was stare unseeingly at the road, then he exploded, 'Holy Creator shit!

We're back in the game now!' He indicated the flower, chuckling. 'Think that'll make her forgive you, Clan Leader?'

Sandsa curled his fingers around the perfect bud. 'She feels exceptionally angry right this moment.'

Bock chuckled. 'Don't blame her.'

***

She ran.

Sand swallowed her heels with each step until it became almost too hard to keep going. She fell, but then she pressed on, her knees sloughing through the soft ground. When she finally reached the top of the dune, she tried to get up only to rock back on her haunches, staring down in horror at the bodies stretching out before her.

For each one he kills in your city, a voice said, resonating deep within her, *countless more die in the deserts, unguided by his hand.*

Callista looked over at the man who now sat beside her, his legs crossed beneath him and his sharp elbows resting on his knees. He had the same startling blue eyes as Sandsa but his face was longer and leaner and his hair was white, though she sensed it was more for aesthetic purposes than to betray his age. He was ancient. She felt it. Her powers rose to greet him, giddy and shy. This was the one who the Chippers claimed their tech could reach. Any number of them would have begged to trade places with her. She would have accepted in a heartbeat.

'Creator God.' Her mouth was so dry her tongue momentarily stuck to her teeth. 'The Ine. Sandsa's father. Father of all the gods.'

Granter of your own powers, added the being, his smile sending a traitorous wave of warmth through her.

'I never asked you to.'

This was all planned long ago.

Callista snorted. 'You mean you planned to lure your son out of the sands with dreams about me? That's your own fault, Ine. If you'd not made me, made him sense me and vice versa — he'd still be doing his duty. Oh, but you see everything, past and present. I suppose this all makes some sort of fucked up sense to you.'

The Ine peered down at the carnage that reached into the horizon. *This is his doing. The tribes fight each other out of fear. Some claim that they still hear the Desine. Others slaughter these boastful tribes, upset that they have been abandoned, angry that others would lie.*

'You have a slew of sons — pick another one,' Callista said, leaning forward onto shaking hands to lever herself off the ground.

Is a god supposed to interfere with an insignificant city's gangs? the Ine asked, remaining seated and in no way diminished even when she stood above him.

Callista shook her head. 'Sandsa's not a god. He's a man. He's mine.'

You think he can simply deny what he is?

'Free will is supposed to be your slogan. You figure it out.'

The Ine's gaze rested on her for an uncomfortable stretch of time. He then spoke aloud, using the voice box of his fleshy form. He sounded weary, like a man who had lost something, though Callista refused to let herself feel any pity. 'He promised to fight this war as a mortal, because if he uses the powers of a god, his deserts and his people may steal him away from you. Shall I show you what he is doing while you sleep peacefully?'

'"Peacefully" is an exaggeration, I think,' Callista said with a snort.

His chuckle sounded like one of Sandsa's own, but older, more practiced, as though he had laughed at many insignificant creatures before her. Callista suspected few mortals had ever seen him, let alone conversed with him. It occurred to her that she should make use of this opportunity so she asked, 'What's the deal with me and the Chippers anyway? They look after us mortals in return for the fancy powers, but what am I supposed to do?'

'You will either bear an important lesson or the salvation of the sands — that choice belongs to you,' the Ine told her, rising to his feet. 'Enough of this. You must see what he is doing.'

He waved a hand. The desert scenery faded into a seamless white expanse. In front of them a rectangle hovered, like a vidscreen, but completely lacking any three-dimensional features. It merely existed, a hole in the universe, showing Callista her lover as he killed the Alcazaar and brought them to heel. A dark film spread over the screen as Sandsa approached CL, hiding both men from view, and she started shouting, screaming, pleading him not to do it —

He can't hear you. Not from here. A dry laugh. *But he can hear the voices. He can hear the deserts. How long do you think he can resist them?*

Callista whirled around, baring her teeth. 'Take me to him.'

It is too late. The Ine began to retreat from her, gliding smoothly away as his form faded. *He is a Clan Leader now. Is this what you wanted?*

'Yes,' she answered softly. 'But not like this. No man can do that.'

A god can.

'He's still adjusting to the ways of mortals — my way!' she cried.

The words echoed now, taking their time to reach her. *The longer he denies his godhood, the more painful it will be for him when he returns.*

'He won't go back,' Callista snapped.

He will be eternally tormented if you force him to choose between you and the deserts. Is that what you want for your son, the one you are destined to bear from this very night?

By now the Ine was a distant speck, barely visible against the colourless surroundings. Callista tried to run after him, but her feet refused to move. She shouted, 'My son is not yours! He's *ours!*'

She woke alone in her room. The pillow beside her, where Sandsa's head had lain, was cold and bare. Seething, she rolled off the bed, yanked on her clothes and tried not to trip on her way over to her boots. After all they had been through...after what he had promised...her anger seeped out across the city, as potent as her love for Sandsa. She made him feel it.

Despite this, a seed of excitement threatened to outgrow the walls she had erected to contain it. Callista dared to delve inside herself for a moment and felt the tiny spark that announced her son's presence. Trembling hands clipped her lasgun to her belt. There was so much to plan, to worry about, to look forward to.

But right now you and I need to talk about what you've done! she said.

I am on my way, Sandsa responded.

Callista's heart froze. For a moment, he had sounded just like...the Ine, his voice underscored by raw power.

CHAPTER TWENTY-THREE

The garage door stood brazenly open when they returned. Kick waved them inside, shaking his head in disbelief. Bock jumped out of the vehicle as soon as it came to a stop but Sandsa planted his feet on the oil-stained floor before the younger man could open the door for him. Seeing this, Bock gave him a grin then scrambled out of sight, shouting to all who dared to slumber when their victory was at hand.

'The Alcazaar are finished,' Sandsa informed his remaining companion.

Kick's eyes roved up and down Sandsa's filthy but unmarked clothes. 'Don't you dare give me any false hope, mate.'

'You can believe me now, or when the last dregs of the Alcazaar start dripping their way in here,' Sandsa said as he brushed past the clansman.

The crowded lounge room upstairs rocked with applause and cheers when Sandsa entered behind Bock. Someone forced a drink into Sandsa's hand. He stared at it, shrugged, then belted it down his throat. The sounds of triumph swelled around him — and abruptly ceased.

Subofficer Ala walked into the room, frowning when people did not part before her. Her artificial eye zeroed in on Sandsa.

'Rumours are flyin' around. And here you are, alive and well, so they must be true.'

'Oh, it's true,' someone said acidly.

Callista appeared in the doorway, hair mussed up wildly behind her and one strap of her shirt hanging dangerously low on her shoulder. Even while furious she was beautiful. Sandsa guiltily stoppered that thought but knew she had already caught it.

'You exhausted me, made love to me, simply so you could run off and steal the title of Clan Leader while everyone was in bed!' Callista said, stamping the floor with her boots and forcing out vicious thuds.

A clansman burst out laughing. His peers glared at him until he quietened.

Callista marched forward, her lips forming distinctly different shapes as she seemed to war between fitting more words into her mouth or sticking her tongue into Sandsa's. When she did kiss him, she nipped his bottom lip between her teeth, drawing blood, then retreated a pace to righten her clothes. Sandsa held out the flower he had picked for her; Callista accepted it only to crush it inside her fist. She discarded the remains of his gift on the floor.

Subofficer Ala was the next woman to advance on him. 'Did you do this?'

'Yes, the Alcazaar are no longer — ' Sandsa began, then stopped. 'Oh.'

'Oh!' Ala repeated. 'You waited until my Cals was asleep so you could go and do somethin' ya knew she wouldn't like. What kind of boyfriend are you?'

Callista cleared her throat. 'He asked me to marry him, Ala.'

The room exploded into celebration once more. But Ala was having none of it. Her lip curled. 'Got you when you were weak, did he?'

'Did you honestly think I could have ever become Clan Leader?' Callista asked, rubbing her temples with one hand. 'Do you think any of us could have done it? No one else can abuse his powers but him.'

Sandsa shot her sharp glance. She sent him her memories in return — crawling through sand, watching the destruction in the deserts, meeting his father. He flinched.

'How will we ever know if we could've won on our own now?' Ala demanded.

Sandsa slipped his arm around Callista's stiff form. 'The Alcazaar deserved to be toppled. And power like that should not lie in one set of hands. Today I took the title and today I tell you this — the Maria have not one Clan Leader but two.'

Callista shook her head, eyes on the floor. 'Sandsa...I don't deserve this and neither do you.'

'Nonsense,' he said, then raised his voice again. 'I have brought down the Alcazaar — the city is ours! But listen — beside me I place Clan Leader Dancer, someone you have known far longer than me —'

'And prettier to boot!' Knives said.

'Much prettier,' Sandsa agreed. 'So what do you think, my fellow Maria? Two Clan Leaders to ensure our continued victory?'

'YES!' the Maria answered.

Callista seized his arm as the jubilant shouting continued, steering Sandsa downstairs and into the abandoned armoury. Lasguns and other pieces of equipment hung on the walls, untouched and unneeded. That fight was over, but another was just beginning.

'Are you a human or a god?' she demanded.

Sandsa said nothing. Instead he knelt before her, pillowing his cheek against her abdomen while his mind twisted with uncertainty and fear. He could sense that she knew how close he'd come to leaving for the deserts. How could he keep resisting the voices if they were that loud?

'I did it for you,' he finally whispered.

Callista closed her eyes briefly, accepting his words. 'I understand. But my husband will be a man, a mere man. I won't marry a god who could abandon me at any moment.'

'I won't do it again,' he vowed.

'You had better not,' she said, pinching his earlobe and sending a shock of pleasure racing through him. 'Or our son might get the wrong idea and start slinging sand around in front of his playmates.'

'Our son.' A statement. A fact. Sandsa smiled into her shirt. 'I can feel...I can feel the seed of him, but I cannot communicate with him yet. When he is developed enough, I will.'

Callista shivered. 'Your father...said that I'm to bear a lesson or the salvation of the sands. What could that mean?'

A drop of icy fear trickled down his back. *He always has plans...*

'It doesn't matter what he says,' Sandsa said, forcing a smile. 'Because I am staying here with you.'

'As a man.'

'As a man,' he agreed, tugging gently on her hands until she too was on her knees.

Her scowl subsided into a wobbly smile. 'Ala is not as

concerned for me as she is angry that this opportunity was taken from her.'

'She knew she could never accomplish it the way things were,' he told her.

Callista sighed and eased her chin onto his shoulder. 'That's true. But you can understand her disappointment. Ala spent her life working towards this. And some outsider turns up and does it in a matter of weeks?'

'We have won, it does not matter how,' Sandsa said, stroking her cheek.

Her voice turned wry. 'We've won. But we've still got lots of work to do.'

'What should we do now?' he asked her.

Callista bit her lip. 'Sandsa, I want to get married.'

'I believe we already established that.'

'You know what I mean.'

He did.

'You think it will be a much needed symbol for the gangs,' he stated. 'A sign of peace. A step towards stability in this city.'

Callista burrowed into his chest. 'Yes. And we should invite all the clans and the Chippers to the wedding. If we can spend half an hour not ripping into each other's throats, then that will be something.'

'We managed to fight together for the past few nights,' Sandsa pointed out.

'That's when we had a common enemy in the Alcazaar. And I'm not sure if you've noticed, but we haven't heard from our Chippers in a while.'

He pursed his lips. 'Ala may not understand what we hope to achieve.'

'She's only known one system — fight until you're on the top,' Callista reminded him. 'No one has ever told the clans that there's another way.'

'Can it be done?'

'Can't you look into the future and see for yourself?' she asked with a playful smile.

I stopped seeing that far ahead when I met you, he thought, shielding the words and his concern from her.

'I don't need to,' he said out loud and drew her into a kiss.

CHAPTER TWENTY-FOUR

'Sandsa! Stop pandering to your fans and get over here.'

After making his apologies to the small circle of clanspeople he had been conversing with, Sandsa moved through the throng of bodies swaying to music pumped out by Vom's most reliable DJ in weeks, then dropped into the plush seating that ran around the rim of the nightclub. The intelligent fibres in the cushions immediately swarmed into the position they deemed most comfortable for him. Sitting either side of Sandsa were Vom and Diamond, a grin shared between their faces.

Sandsa nodded towards the dance floor. 'I see business is booming, Vom.'

'I've now got the patronage of every clan in the city,' Vom said, looking pleased. 'Peace is profitable, it seems!'

Taking a moment to scan the crowd, Sandsa saw the riotous mix of gang colours and symbols. Some dancers even wore casual clothes bereft of markings and could easily have wandered in from any of the residences nearby. Ever since Governor Garnett had proclaimed that he was dealing with two new Clan Leaders and that both of them were working to instil peace in the city, the people of Atsa had emerged from their hiding places. Sandsa had to admit that a month of clear skies and quiet streets might have been the real incentive.

'What is it you wish to discuss with me?' Sandsa asked, directing his question at Diamond.

The clanswoman held out a small wooden box with a dirty bronze hinge. Sandsa accepted the item and opened it to reveal the ring inside. A wiry silver band wound twice around before diverting to support a small purple stone that would sit just below the first knuckle. Sandsa set the ring in his palm, studying it from different angles by tipping his hand from side to side.

'It looks expensive,' he said at last.

'Just what a Clan Leader deserves!' Diamond told him with a grin. 'And she'll recognise it.'

Vom chuckled. 'Anyone who's watched a vid in the past two years will recognise it. This ring used to be lent out to the big vidstars to wear on screen. They were trying to sell it to the highest bidder when it disappeared.'

Sandsa dropped the ring back inside the box. 'Then it is stolen property.'

'Like your title isn't?' Diamond said with a snort.

'But will she like it?' Sandsa asked the man on his left.

Vom rested a heavy hand on his shoulder. 'Women like wearing pretty trinkets. Well, except Diamond here who just steals them.'

'I can wear the starking thing myself if it'll make you feel better, Bolt,' Diamond offered.

Vom waved his fingers over at the DJ. The music segued into something slower and Sandsa's thoughts fled to Callista who was busy elsewhere.

What are you hiding? she asked.

Something I am told you will like.

Ooh, intrigue. Tell me later.

Sandsa met Diamond's gaze. 'I'll take it.'

'Lucky Dancer,' Vom said, shaking his head. 'Don't tell my wife about your services.'

Diamond lifted an eyebrow. 'But you'll soon be able to afford a better rock for her ring.'

'Rocks don't a good marriage make!' Vom insisted.

***

The lasbolts pelted towards her, all released within microseconds of each other. Callista laughed as she weaved around them. The wild bolts missed her completely and shot past her to pepper over Jeras Nerani's face. The mounted lasguns fell silent at the colonel's command and the red forcefield humming between them disintegrated. Nerani tipped her head towards the shield generator installed on the floor. 'Glad I had that put in.'

'I wouldn't have sent them your way if the shield hadn't been there, you know that, Jeras.' Callista rolled her shoulders to loosen the tension gathering in them. Even during the war she had not tested herself like this. 'I hear the governor asked GLEA to let you stay on Yalsa 5.'

It was the first time Callista had dared to bring up the planned removal of all GLEA agents from Atsa City. She would have mentioned it sooner had she not been desperately trying to convince the clans they could work together. And then there were the hours spent worrying about a child whose heartbeat was still barely detectable by doctors relying on devices instead of powers.

Jeras sighed. 'Fat lot of good it'll do. We're gone in a few weeks.'

'But why?' Callista asked, retrieving her lasgun from Jeras' outstretched hand. She clipped it onto her belt. 'Is it because we finally have a peaceful system governing Atsa at night and GLEA is no longer needed?'

Jeras' lips twitched. 'Sure, a peaceful system whose leaders weren't elected, just thrust on everyone.'

'No one elected the Alcazaar's Clan Leader either. And I think we're the better option.'

The Chipper stroked the tiny tentacles on her scalp, looking agitated. 'The blame doesn't lie solely with you. We should never have got involved — on either side.'

'But it was for the good of the people you were protecting...' Callista trailed off when she felt the shame twisting inside the Chipper like a knife in her guts.

Jeras waved a hand at the ceiling. 'Yeah, but the Agency isn't so keen on leaving any of us behind when no one worships the Creator God here. Atsa doesn't even have an altar for him, let alone a temple. This isn't the first time we've packed up and left worlds because of that.'

'You don't agree with your superiors,' Callista stated, reading the woman's thoughts. 'You think GLEA should protect people regardless of what they believe in.'

Jeras' gaze fell to the floor. 'Look, I can't say anything or I'll lose my job. And I like my job. For the most part. But I'm not gonna worry too much about Atsa — I think you'n Bolt have got this city covered.'

The ensuing silence grew steadily more uncomfortable. Finally, Callista cleared her throat. 'Do you want lunch? I might as well pay you back in some small way for helping us. You'll be punished for your part in the war, won't you?'

Jeras grimaced. 'Yes. I'm being demoted. And I'm starking glad, because that means I'll avoid the worst punishment.'

'Which is?'

'Having my chip taken from me.'

Later, when they were sitting down in a nearby restaurant that only had two of its glass windows boarded up, Callista watched Jeras over the edge of the large pink menu. The Chipper seemed to be seriously considering the wine list. Sighing, Jeras set the list down. 'Well, I can't imbibe, because it'll mess up my chip, but at least I can live vicariously through you.'

Callista smiled, keeping her fingers locked on the menu to keep them from drifting to her abdomen. She planned to announce her pregnancy soon, but she wanted Ala to be the first of her friends to know. And Jeras...Callista wasn't sure she could trust someone who would do anything the Creator God asked of her.

'I might abstain this time,' Callista said lightly. 'I need to keep my mind clear these days, what with ensuring that the clans work together.'

'So how do you keep the peace anyway?'

Callista grinned. 'Mostly by reminding everyone that we're in charge and can flatten them like we did the Alcazaar.'

Jeras snorted.

They spent the rest of their time chatting about the different planets that Nerani might be posted to next. When the Chipper left to use the bathroom, Callista dropped her smile and fought the nausea that was threatening to transform into something more physical. She rested her elbows on the table and moaned. *I am not ready for this. I can't deal with two gods, especially if one of them is inside me.*

When Nerani returned, Callista announced that she had business to attend to and stood. She started to count out the necessary amount of coin-chips, then remembered that the restaurant was run by one of the minor clans. No one here would accept her money.

Jeras' eyes remained on the table. 'Huh, didn't notice that earlier.'

Callista looked down at where her elbows had rested and saw that two small piles of sand had been left behind. She slapped her arms, but no more grains fell from her.

Nerani chuckled. 'You'll live. Sand gets into Atsa all the time, especially with that citywide shield missing. You'n Bolt better get that fixed up.'

'Sometimes I wonder if I shouldn't keep the sand at bay,' Callista murmured.

After they left the restaurant, Callista waved until the Chipper vanished around a corner. There were no promises to keep in touch. They had never truly been on the same side.

When Nerani was gone, she held out her palm and watched sand trickle through her fingers. The pavement around her began to swim as she blinked back tears. *Please, my son. Don't. Please. You can't be this.*

'You cannot change what he is,' her new companion said.

Callista closed her eyes. 'I choose not to see you.'

'Regardless, I am here. How long will it be before Sandsa neglects his promise to you?'

'He won't do it again,' she said firmly.

'Because you, Callista Krendasta, have decided it?'

She unsealed her eyelids and glowered at the Creator God. He had a lasgun on his hip and was even wearing a faded Maria shirt, as if he had the right. Callista curled her top lip. 'It's not about what I want. It's about what Sandsa wants. Do you honestly think that him dreaming about me made him wriggle out of your grip? I was just that extra grain of sand that tipped the balance!'

'I did not realise you were so astute in the ways of immortal beings,' the Ine said, one eyebrow creeping up his forehead — a very deliberate gesture, Callista thought, given how rarely he took human form.

'He won't go back to you, not now,' she warned.

'His people suffer without him, just as he suffers without the deserts. He cannot ignore them.'

'Maybe his people shouldn't rely on some invisible best friend to tell them what to do with their lives!' Callista snapped then turned on her heel, putting him behind her.

Already waiting for her on the curb was a black Maria hovercar with barely any lines visible on it. Still shaking from her encounter, Callista dropped into a seat and stared out the window at the empty pavement for several moments. Then she realised that the driver looked very familiar.

'Subofficer Ala.' Callista leaned forward to give Ala's shoulder a brief squeeze. 'Shouldn't you be keeping the Maria in line?'

'Is that what I'm doin' these days?' Ala asked with a snort. 'Never heard of a Clan Leader leaving someone else in charge of their own clan.'

Callista climbed over into the front passenger seat, grinning. 'Ala, I'm running a city. I don't have time to run a clan. And besides, you're the best subofficer the Maria have ever had.'

Ala chortled. 'Oh, I starking know that, you douchenozzle. But it's too quiet in this city now. I don't trust it.'

'Are our newer, ah, friends from the Alcazaar giving you any trouble?' Callista asked.

Ala stabbed the ignition sensor and the vehicle shot off down the road. Callista saw that they weren't going directly back to headquarters and made no comment, waiting her friend out. Once the hovercar had turned several corners, Ala answered, 'Nah. Most of them wanted out so I bought their one way tickets off this rock. But this quiet won't last long, Cals. It just can't.'

'Why not? The other clans seem amenable to not fighting each other and they've all agreed to patrol the streets at night so Atsa stays safe.'

Ala pulled the vehicle over to the side of the road and turned in her seat to look at Callista. 'Oh, great, so we're like Chippers now, lookin' after everyone. What happens when you and Bolt get yourselves killed, huh? What happens then? Who gets to be in charge?'

'In that unlikely event, I guess my son can look after Atsa for us,' Callista said, touching her abdomen and smiling.

'Stark it, Cals, they've got implants for that!'

Callista sighed. 'Yes, well, I didn't think. Neither did Sandsa. But it is something we want and we have...ample time to come to terms with it.'

Eternity, she thought. *Eternity...oh, Sandsa, I don't think I can do it.*

'You need to get hitched — soon,' Ala advised her.

Callista rolled her eyes. 'Since when were you so traditional? We've been so busy fixing up the mess we made that I haven't had time to plan anything.'

Ala grunted.

'You really could have done it, you know, become Clan Leader,' Callista said softly.

A weak laugh escaped Ala. 'No, Cals. I never could've done it. But that won't stop me givin' my Clan Leader advice, so don't think you're in the clear.'

Callista leaned in, preparing to hug her. 'I'd never want you to stop giving me advice.'

Ala scuttled back, moving out of Callista's reach, and only stopped when she hit the door on her side. She was scowling. 'None of that mushy shit. I gotta get my Clan Leader back to safety. Unless you're talking to the governor today? Can't say that's safety.'

'No, Garnett would rather not see us,' Callista said, smiling. 'It helps him pretend that he's the only one in charge, even if he did consult us when he started putting those ads out on the Web.'

'Ads? What ads?'

'Oh, you know, ads showing Yalsa 5's best features. For potential tourists.'

'Tourists! Is he mad?'

***

'Should I discuss pertinent work matters as requested or is my nudity enough to sway you from that for at least an hour?'

Sandsa lifted his gaze from his techpad. He had been reading about various offers involving trade and real estate ventures from companies keen to deal with Atsa's new Clan Leaders. He supposed he should look into some of them to help fund the night-time protection the city needed, but right now he only had eyes for the bold, and very naked, woman leaning against the doorway of their penthouse in the Maria headquarters. Ala had handed the whole top level over to them despite their protests. The subofficer had even had it renovated for them.

Sandsa stretched in his chair, emphasising the tenting of his pants, and waited for Callista to come to him. Her hips swayed as she approached, brown eyes lit with mischief and hands gliding down her thighs. He could already smell her, a sweet, promising tang. It was intoxicating. He reached for her but Callista smacked his hand away and tsked. A grin sliced across her face.

Then she began dancing before him, turning to fill the space between his two gaping legs with her invitingly curved posterior. Sandsa had his hands on his knees, but it was taking more and more effort to keep them there. In a matter of moments, he couldn't remember why he was trying to restrain himself and reefed off his shirt. Sandsa offered her an innocent expression when Callista glanced over her bare shoulder at him.

'Don't stop on my account,' she said with a smirk.

Sandsa dispensed with his pants and was very glad he did for she engulfed him almost immediately. The slick movements of her tongue drove him further from coherent thought. Her fingers then glanced below the swell of his manhood to graze his balls, massaging them with a firmness that only stirred him further. She kissed his thigh, licked her way up his shaft — and then her mouth was on his. She tasted of musk and desire.

He gave no resistance when she took his hand and led him into the bedroom. They made love all over the bed, kicking the sheets away and laughing when Sandsa's knee collided with the headboard. Later, after Callista had flopped against the pillows, he crept back into the other room to find his pants and dug through one of the pockets. Ring in hand, he returned and knelt on the floor beside the bed, holding the item up for her inspection.

Callista's eyes widened and she scrambled over to him. 'Sandsa, I know this ring. *Every* rich folk knows this ring. How did...how did you even get it?'

'Diamond impressed upon me the importance of pretty rocks,' Sandsa replied, smiling as she slipped it onto her finger. It fit perfectly.

'I don't need a ring or pretty rocks to know you love me.' Callista grinned and pulled him into a kiss. 'But they definitely don't hurt.'

Her laugh warmed him and then her body set him aflame once more.

CHAPTER
TWENTY-FIVE

Sunlight was stealing its away across the surface of Yalsa 5 but it had yet to breach the darkness thrown across Atsa, and for now the city slumbered, lit by tiny streetlights instead of explosions. Viewed from up here on the roof of the Maria headquarters, Atsa reminded Sandsa of the deserts at night, when the campfires of his tribes dotted the dunes.

A tornado of leaves, vines and branches appeared beside him, right on time. Sandsa waited out his brother's embellished arrival then unleashed a hug onto Kuja. That done, he retreated a few paces and smiled down at the Rforine who had no smile to offer in return.

Kuja's sea-green eyes were filled with fear. 'Sandsa, they know. Everyone knows. About Callista.'

'Did you tell them?' Sandsa demanded, surging forward again.

Kuja held up a hand. Two small trees sprouted from the flat roof, breaking apart concrete to stand either side of Sandsa and snagging his hands with twisted branches. Sandsa made no move to shrug off his bonds but he gritted his teeth when he felt his forbidden powers rise inside him.

'No way, never!' Kuja exclaimed. 'But you can understand

why everyone is watching you. No one has ever abandoned their duties before. We don't even know if we're allowed to marry.'

'Or procreate,' Sandsa added.

He heard lightning crack over the deserts behind him. The dunes in the distance groaned in distress, but he refused to turn his head, afraid that if he looked at them they would find some way to lure him away from the city.

Kuja looked aghast. 'Oh no, Sandsa. A son?'

'You used to ask my permission before you dug into my mind, Kuja.'

The Rforine sighed. 'Sandsa...I want you to be happy. You deserve it. But this is going to complicate things.'

The laugh that escaped Sandsa was dry and threatened to crack his lips. 'No, it only complicates my return. It's less likely I'll leave a family than one woman. And Father needs to stop bothering Callista. If he thinks he can bully her into leaving me...'

'He talks to her?' Kuja asked, eyes wide.

'Yes,' Sandsa said flatly. 'Possibly because I refuse to listen to him.'

'He doesn't speak to just any mortal, Sandsa.' Kuja frowned. 'He must have a plan.'

The sky was now infused with pale orange but dawn failed to erase Sandsa's unease as easily as it did the shadows of night. He had woken earlier from a nightmare to see sand flying around the room and dancing over Callista's sleeping features. The tiny form growing inside her had thrummed with raw power.

Sandsa held this image in his mind for his brother. 'He's *strong*, Kuja. Stronger than me.'

Kuja's pale complexion somehow had more colour to lose. He grabbed Sandsa's shoulders. 'Listen, Fayay hates you and if he finds out, he'll come for your son and take him and teach him to fight against you — if your son is that powerful, he might win!'

Sandsa snorted. 'Fayay wouldn't dare.'

'If you insist on abandoning your powers he can dare to do anything!'

Sandsa gripped his brother's fingers and pulled them off one at a time. 'Fayay should no longer feel threatened by me. He's the most powerful of us now. As for my powers, if I use them I could not...'

'Not what?' Kuja challenged. 'Not be with the woman who loves you? I don't understand why you can't just take her into the deserts!'

'I promised her that I would remain a man,' Sandsa told him.

Kuja's voice dropped in volume and pitch. 'Does she know how close you are to giving in to the deserts?'

'I promised her,' Sandsa repeated.

'Does she know how powerful your son is already?'

'It doesn't matter. He does not need to know the true extent of his powers.'

But Kuja was shaking his head. 'That's just it, Sandsa. He might never know it, but everyone else will.'

'Is Fayay planning to come after me?' Sandsa growled.

Kuja shrugged helplessly. 'I don't know! But he's been talking to our brothers and our sisters, and he seems to have half of them convinced that your leaving has ruined Father's grand design.' The rainforest god drew a breath. 'Some of them are even saying that if you won't return to the deserts then they will *make* you do it. And I don't think they meant just talking to you. Sandsa...they might try to hurt Callista.'

Sandsa crushed his fists onto the ledge that ran around the

building's roof. When the wall stayed firm, he stabbed his awareness into it, feeling for the sand in its concrete mixture. He was poised to shatter the ledge, but then the whispers started, begging him to do it, begging him to unleash himself and return to them. Sandsa hastily withdrew.

'Can't you see anything in the future?' Kuja asked him.

Sandsa sighed. 'No. Not more than a few minutes. Even before I reined in my powers my ability to peer further ahead was becoming unreliable. I can't see if Fayay comes after me but...will you fight with me if he does?'

Kuja's head snapped up. 'Of course I will!'

'Then no one can hurt my wife or your nephew.'

'Nephew?' Kuja echoed, a delighted smile spreading over his face.

Sandsa nodded, grinning. 'You are his favourite uncle, or will be.'

The glow that had been filling Kuja's eyes died. 'I'd love to be an uncle, Sandsa. But we mustn't forget the situation. I'll speak to our siblings and see if some of them will side with us.'

They embraced again, this time in farewell, then the rainforest god turned away and jumped up onto the ledge. Vines began creeping out of Kuja's sleeves and he grabbed hold of them, about to catapult himself into the aether, but at the last moment he tossed a look over his shoulder. 'Sandsa, it's one thing to keep your son from the deserts — he will not miss what he has never had — but it's another thing entirely to deny yourself something that's been a part of you for so many centuries.'

The Rforine hurtled forward, exploded into green wisps — and then he was gone.

Sandsa peered down at the lines on his palms as they slowly

filled in with tiny flecks of sand. He shook out the traitorous grains and stomped down below, to where the woman he loved was slowly rousing. The woman he had given an unbreakable promise.

***

'But I'm afraid,' the boy said.

Sandsa, standing several heads above him, guided his brother out of the shadows and into the light. Even in this temperate rainforest the air was wet and oppressive and the desert god despised it, but he knew it felt different to Kuja. Gliding towards the Rforine's mind, he gleaned from it the sensations the young god was experiencing — to Kuja, the humidity was a soothing bath of encompassing warmth. The trees, the creatures, every decomposing leaf — they all loved the nine-year-old boy whose hands could weave them together.

'Afraid of hurting them?' Sandsa asked, indicating the trees.

Kuja nodded. 'I'm no good at this. I'm not old like you.'

'Old! What does that mean to us gods?' Sandsa laughed. 'Listen, Kuja, feel it...your domain, the rainforests, work for you. They speak to you and listen to you, just as the sands do for me. With their help, you can make the mortals do your bidding.'

'Don't push him if he's not ready, Sandsa,' their mother's voice said. She appeared out of thin air, walking towards them and pulling her cream-coloured cardigan further around her. 'And you know you should gently guide the mortals towards their destiny, not force your will upon them. If you cared for them the way you do your brother, you would understand this.'

Kuja ran for the hug that his mother gave. The boy turned a pout onto Sandsa. 'You should go play with the others.'

'But they...' Sandsa paused. 'I care even less about them than I do the mortals.'

His mother's eyes remained on Sandsa, letting him hear the thoughts that she so easily guarded from a boy who had not yet realised he could use his mind-reading abilities to permanently eavesdrop. Sandsa, you are allowed to love as mortals do. You are my son too, don't forget that.

She waited him out while dusting imaginary specks of dust from Kuja's shoulders. The boy made a fuss but didn't try to wriggle out of her grip.

Kuja is no different from the rest of them, *Sandsa told his mother.* I would spend time with my other siblings if they wanted me to.

Even Fayay? *she asked, smiling.*

***

Callista sat up slowly, drawing her index fingers along the edges of her eyelids until they hit her cheekbones. She leaned forward and began sifting through the images fading from her mind. Needing more, wanting more, she latched onto the source of the vision and traced it, expecting to find her lover's mind — but then she hit a white wall of static.

You needed to see what he was, before you helped him to become something more, whispered the voice of the Ine.

Yes, I helped him become more, not you, Callista responded, gritting her teeth.

The Creator God's presence ebbed, then vanished.

Somehow she knew she'd be seeing him again. And soon.

Callista glanced up as Sandsa entered the bedroom. His smile was bright, but the corners of his lips worried away into his cheeks. She opened her mouth, then swallowed when nothing emerged. Finally, she managed, 'Sandsa, were you talking to your brother?'

'He is pleased at the prospect of becoming an uncle,' Sandsa replied, pressing a knee onto the bed and levering himself over to kiss her. 'I was remiss in that I forgot to ask him to attend our wedding, though he may prefer to witness the binding only.'

'You want to do the binding right after the wedding?'

'I need to pass my immortality onto you as soon as possible.'

'You're asking more than you realise,' Callista told him.

'Do you not want to marry me?' Sandsa asked, his eyebrows scrunching down his forehead.

Holding up her hand to expose the ring that had not left her finger since the night he had given it to her, Callista said, 'Of course I do. I love you and would happily grow old with you. That's how mortals do it, Sandsa. You're asking me to not grow old.'

'I will not insult you by reminding you that our son would suffer your death.'

'And yet you just did.'

'I do not want to argue about this now,' he said and attempted to steal another kiss.

Callista turned her head. His lips touched her shoulder.

'It's just...I need time,' she whispered.

Sandsa released a long, low breath. 'You have it.'

She cupped his face and did her best to distract him from his impatient thoughts with the swirl of her tongue. Eventually Sandsa excused himself to shower in preparation for their visit to the governor later in the day. Callista remained on the bed, sheets wrapped around her shoulders.

Why had the Creator God sent her that vision of the past? She had not seen anything in it that would convince her to leave Sandsa; in fact, she felt pleased that she was the reason that Sandsa now cared about mortals like Bock, Vom and Ala. Perhaps the Ine had meant the vision as a gift, an apology, or even encouragement. Callista found herself thinking about her own parents. She could hear their voices so clearly it was as if they were in the room with her.

You should find out who you are, make your own decisions…now why don't you stop scowling and do as you're told? You owe us. We made you.

Callista studied the walls enclosing her. They were mostly decorated with dark, sombre colours. It was tempting to let her mood slide the same way. But then she thought of Sandsa, of his handsome smile when he woke, a sight she would never grow tired of seeing.

Callista left the lonely bed behind her and joined him in the shower.

CHAPTER TWENTY-SIX

'I don't want no starking Miniatta near our headquarters!'

Many subofficers from multiple clans were seated around the round table in the conference room, a large frosted chandelier watching over them. Months ago, Callista might have visited a place like this with her parents and then hidden in some corner while the rich folk of Atsa idly spent their evening. Renting this room would put most people in Asta into debt for ten years, but it had been graciously loaned to her for that afternoon's session. Callista hoped the venue's owner had done it out of respect for what she and Sandsa had achieved and not because he had been afraid the gangs would destroy his decadent hotel if he refused to let them use it.

'Oh, come on, it's not like we're gonna attack you,' a Miniatta suboffier chortled, leaning over the table to grin at the opposing clansperson. Her sleeves slopped into several bowls of bright red dip, part of the spread of complimentary food that had been provided for them. 'Clan Leader Bolt will waste us if we go against the rules. 'Sides, we get paid to make sure you sleep soundly in your beds!'

It had been a big ask to get the city's suboffiers here the first few times. The clans had spent centuries distrusting each other and spilling blood over territory and hovercars so it wasn't at all surprising that they still squabbled and kept their hands on their lasguns. But they had been quick to realise that if they kept the streets safe and quiet at night, they were rewarded with coin-chips and more patrols. Anyone caught causing a disturbance was punished with the loss of these privileges. Greed and the fear of Sandsa ripping them to pieces the way he had the Alcazaar was enough to keep them from going at each other — for now.

Vom cleared his throat. 'Well, I speak for my lot when I say that we're not in it for the coin-chips.'

'You just want us to stop fighting so no one blows up your nightclub!' someone shouted. 'Creator God knows your shitty playlist is reason enough to go to war.'

Even Callista smiled along with the ensuing laughter.

Vom leaned back in his seat, looking about fifty times more relaxed than Callista felt. 'I will remind you that I have a DJ now. And I'm making a tidy profit 'cause I'm open all day, all night. I've even got some of the civilians wandering in.'

'Perhaps they don't know what to do with themselves now that they don't have to keep repairing the things we destroyed?' Callista suggested, earning herself a few chuckles.

The only one who didn't seem amused was Vom. 'Just saying, it's starking nice not to worry that my son's going to die every time the star falls out of the sky.'

The room quietened.

'Maybe I can deal with one or two Miniatta outside our place at night,' the clansperson who had started the ruckus said. 'No more'n that, okay. They stink up the place.'

Callista ended the meeting after going over how many clanspeople needed remuneration for the previous week's patrols. She asked Vom if he wanted to stay and renegotiate the payment for the Zatzat, but he said he had something more pressing to deal with.

When at last there was silence, Callista tucked her techpad into its case and released a lengthy sigh. She then looked up, frowning. There was one person left at the opposite end of the table, divided from her by a selection of food and discarded drinks. This woman's face was hard to read and her stance was casually confident. Her shirt marked her out as a Maria, but the steel armband she wore, a practice instituted by Ala, revealed that she came from a dead clan.

Callista's hand strayed to her lasgun. 'You used to be Alcazaar.'

'And the other Clan Leader used to be a god, so what?' the woman retorted.

'What are you talking about?' Callista demanded.

The former Alcazaar clanswoman held out her hands in a placating gesture. 'I'm Maria now, through and through, I swear. Didn't know I was fighting against my god now, did I? Would've changed sides earlier if I'd known. Name's Assila.'

Callista stood and slid the techpad case along the table as she made her way towards the woman, ready to defend herself if she had to, though Assila shouldn't have access to any desert powers without Sandsa acting as a source.

'Is it a shorter patrol you want? More coin-chips?' Callista asked, probing Assila's mind. Resentment simmered constantly in the woman's thoughts. 'Ah. You want a better position in the clan. Ala is the one to talk to about that. Bolt and I are not involved in the day-to-day running of the Maria.'

Assila tucked her hands beneath her belt. 'Tried that. Ala don't trust me.'

'She didn't trust me either, at first,' Callista said, picking up her techpad and holding it in front of her stomach like a shield. 'She'll come around.'

'If I just had my powers, I could show her how good I am...'

Callista stiffened. 'There is no desert god. Not anymore. Your powers are gone. Do you understand me, Assila?'

'You gotta wonder how long the peace'll last if Vom and his lot find out that one of their Clan Leaders is the god that abandoned them,' Assila said, her smile showing teeth. 'Think the Zatzat can cause enough damage to set off another war?'

'I'll speak to Ala for you,' Callista bit out.

'Good.' Assila started heading for the door, but then she paused. 'Makes you wonder, don't it? The Creator God giving you these powers? It helped you grab the Desine's attention.'

'Believe me, that is not what the Creator God intended. Now.' Callista pointed at the door. 'Get out of my sight before I crush your skull simply by thinking about it.'

Only after Assila had been gone for a full minute did Callista sink into a chair, shaking, and cover her face with her hands.

Why did you give me these powers? she asked.

Silence. Callista rose from the chair and took slow steps towards the exit, dreading to find Assila outside. The antechamber was mercifully empty. Callista closed her eyes in relief. *I know you can hear me, Ine. Did you give me these powers so Sandsa would notice me?*

His words trickled into her mind. *Yes. So that a lesson could be learned. Or so that salvation could be brought to the sands. Which will it be?*

Callista gripped the doorframe, fury tightening her knuckles.

Will you ever tell me what the stark that means? she demanded of the Ine.

He did not answer.

CHAPTER TWENTY-SEVEN

His people called for him just as the sky was darkening into deep, royal blue. Sandsa was standing on top of the Maria headquarters, as he frequently did while waiting for Callista, his earpiece switched on in case anyone needed to speak with him. But this form of contact was more like a hook around his ribs, tugging and trying to topple him over the ledge. Sandsa bit his tongue, hoping the pain would help him fight the urge to succumb, but he knew he was losing.

He ripped out his earpiece and threw it onto the concrete where he crushed the device beneath a boot. Stamping his way back inside, he passed various Maria clanspeople who tried to catch his attention and ignored them, feeling glad that Callista was busy. He could not let her doubt him when she was so close to admitting out loud that she was ready to accept his immortality.

When he barrelled through the large doorway leading into the garage, he was met not by sycophants encouraging him to take this or that hovercar, but a road that was half buried by the invading desert. He realised he was somewhere on the edge of Atsa City — his domain had brought him here against his will, outside of his control.

He kicked the sand off his boots and shook out his arms, spraying the ground with the hateful specks. This done, he stormed past a decayed generator that would have contributed power to the shield that had kept Atsa safe centuries ago, and headed towards the nearby cluster of Zatzat clanspeople, all of them standing in a circle with their forearms clasped. Josh Freeman was the epicentre of this activity, but his indifferent expression was at odds with the intent ones surrounding him.

'What are you doing?' Sandsa demanded, grabbing Vom's arm and tearing the large man away from the group.

'You came!' Vom said, his stunted powers a cord that lashed out wildly, seeking their source. 'We are trying to contact the Desine! Will you join us?'

I wish you had not succeeded, Sandsa thought, wincing.

'I am sorry but I cannot,' he answered quietly.

Vom stared at him for a long moment then nodded, accepting his decision, and turned back to the circle. None of the other clanspeople spoke, but their combined efforts were a constant weight on Sandsa's mind. They weren't even doing it for themselves — they were doing it for Pagnus of Vieta, to help him reconnect with his past.

Sandsa took a step back, towards the road, but he had lingered too long. Sand exploded up from the ground like a geyser and fell over his arm, rotating around the limb again and again, begging him for instructions.

Come back to us, come back, the sands whispered. *And tell us what to do.*

For a moment, he could think of no reason to deny them.

Callista, Callista, he mentally chanted until it was all he could hear.

The Zatzat clanspeople continued to pour more will into their summoning. Why couldn't they accept that he had abandoned them, just as they had abandoned the deserts? Why couldn't they leave him alone?

He wanted to look away but his eyelids were frozen open, forcing him to watch.

Sandsa!

One blink. Two blinks. *Callista. I won't. I won't do this.*

I'm coming. Don't listen, don't let them sense you. And don't make Vom or any of the others angry with you. We still need their support.

Sandsa released a laboured breath. She was right. He forced himself backwards — it was more of a stagger than a retreat. When his boots finally touched the road, his lungs expanded, free of grit and pressure. He even laughed. Sand skittered away from him, confused, fearful.

Then he caught a whiff of rotting seaweed.

Fayay, he said, letting the loathing lather each syllable.

Look at what you did to this man, the god of water said and tsked. *And for what? So he could learn about the dangers of the galaxy and report back to his tribe? You never let him choose. You forced him off his planet and into slavery. And you think I am cruel?*

Sandsa clenched his fists. 'No. You cannot know this. You can't read minds. Who told you?'

Who have you told, brother? Think hard.

Sandsa shook his head fiercely. *Kuja would not betray me.*

Fayay said nothing and let the silence grow. Growling, Sandsa stabbed deep into the Watine's mind — and reared back. *Father? Father told you? Why?*

Perhaps he wants me to repair his grand design for him, Fayay remarked.

'I will never go back!' Sandsa spat.

The Watine's laughter swelled in the horizon before it swept in past the oblivious mortals and slammed into Sandsa. He spat out a mouthful of freezing water, his eyes stinging with salt.

Fayay, show yourself! Or are you too afraid of me? he roared.

Afraid of a mere man? mocked Fayay from somewhere just out of sight. *Next time they call for you I will answer. Then I shall whisper into their ears and punish those that refuse to obey me.*

Sandsa snarled. *Don't you dare go near my people!*

Are they still your people if you abandoned them?

Fine, Sandsa said, gritting his teeth. *They're yours. Now leave me alone!*

Should I leave your son alone as well?

GO AWAY!

Sandsa wrenched back the hand that he had clamped over Callista's arm. The angry red slashes his fingers had formed on her pale skin caused horror to flood through his veins. He jerked away, ashamed, but she caught his wrists and pulled him into her embrace. Sandsa breathed heavily into her neck, closing his eyes as her fingers massaged their way up onto his scalp. His shaking slowly eased under her caresses, both physical and mental. When he lifted his head, he saw that the clanspeople were milling around, their circle broken.

Vom was murmuring into Josh's ear, a hand on the other man's shoulder. When Josh failed to respond, Vom's gestures became more exaggerated.

Sandsa looked back at Callista, stricken. 'I hurt you. I can't possibly ask you to undergo the binding when the process will also cause you pain.'

She reached up and curved her palm around his cheek. 'A little pain is nothing compared to the joy of waking up beside you every morning until the end of time.' Her kiss was cool against his flushed skin. Then she pulled away, creases forming on her forehead. 'Another brother? He didn't feel as amiable as Kuja.'

'The Ine told Fayay about our son, which I can only imagine was meant to make me angry enough to use my powers,' Sandsa said, aiming a sneer towards the dark horizon. He could still sense Fayay out there, lurking, thickening the air with moisture.

'Can Vom and the others call you like this again?' Callista asked.

'They may try, because they felt me respond — I did not mean to!' Sandsa drove his fist into his thigh. 'I cannot fathom why these people, who deliberately left me before I left them, would even...it must be Fayay's doing.'

He shot her a look when she laughed.

'Sandsa, my love, do you realise what you inspire in our people — the people of Atsa?' Callista clarified. 'Ala never thought the Maria could take control of the city. It was impossible. You changed that.'

'*We* changed it, my dear.'

'Yes,' she said, nicking his lips with her own. 'If one man can destroy the Alcazaar, and bring peace to the city, can you imagine how possible everything looks to people now? They're *dreaming*. Can't you feel it? I do, at night — I feel their minds, full of hope. And that's why Vom attempted to bring his god back, even though he knew it wouldn't work.'

Sandsa sighed. 'I almost wish I had answered them. The things I did to Josh...'

'Does Josh want the Desine back in his life?' Callista asked him.

'I thought not...'

'Go talk to him. It might make you feel better.'

'Callista...'

She pressed a finger to his lips. 'If you do it right now, you will have the pleasure of returning to someone who wishes to bind herself to you for eternity. I think you can manage a short separation, don't you?'

Sandsa seized her in a brief kiss before jogging over to Josh and Vom.

Josh tossed up a hand in greeting. 'Sandsa. I'm glad someone has a lick of sense of around here. Don't know why I let Vom talk me into this.'

'You do not...begrudge me standing aside when I could have joined in and helped?' Sandsa asked, startled.

Josh shook his head. 'No way, man. I've been remembering bits and pieces here and there since we last spoke. I was going to *die* in the desert before the slavers found me. The Desine must've made sure they did. And I'm grateful for that. I think I even felt his presence. But that's over, done with, and I don't want to return to the deserts and live a life that sounds, frankly, horrible. I didn't get a choice back then, but the Desine's letting me make one now. I respect that.'

Vom glanced towards the dunes in the desert, hidden from view now that night had fallen. 'It's not as bad as it sounds.'

'Would you go back?' Sandsa asked him.

'No,' Vom admitted, but then his expression hardened. 'The Desine is missing, Josh. That's why he has not come to guide you.'

Sandsa cleared his throat. 'Perhaps it is time for the Desine's people to move forward without him. They no longer need to bow to his demands.'

'A father has no right to make sure his children are on the correct path?' Vom demanded.

'Kids've gotta grow up sometime,' Josh said, shrugging. 'Besides, not sure you lot deserve the Desine if you only call him when you want something.'

Sandsa swung a severe look at him. 'It is not like that at all.'

'Isn't it? Seems to me the Desine might have a reason to stop talking to us.'

'The Desine means something different to all of you,' Callista said, descending the eroding sandbank and coming towards them, a hand on her visibly swelling stomach. 'This should be discussed when tempers are not running so high.'

'Nice words, Clan Leader Dancer,' Vom said with a shake of his large head. 'But that is exactly when men speak the truth, with the fires of anger lit beneath them!'

But Callista was not looking at him. The object of her gaze stepped forward.

'Well, how 'bout you shut up and let the women deal with things more rationally,' Diamond said, smirking. 'Dancer's right. Plus I got a thirst comin' on and I mean to spend money quenching it in your club.'

Sandsa planted a mental kiss in his lover's mind; Callista brushed it off, keeping an eye on the clanspeople as they filed away to their vehicles. No one offered a ride to Josh and nor did he chase any of those who had been so keen to help him out only an hour beforehand. One empty hovercar remained, its neon yellow paint announcing its presence far out into the desert night. Sandsa recognised it as one that Kick refused to lend to anyone except his Clan Leaders.

'Can I ask why you took part in this if that is how you feel about the Desine?' Sandsa quietly asked Josh.

The man sighed and scuffed the toe of his boot through the

sand. 'Ever since I ran into you, Bolt, I've been having weird...weird dreams. I remember the desert. My own clan's getting sick of all my rambling so I thought I'd try out Vom's lot.'

'And you've just realised that your views are not compatible with theirs either,' Callista said, her hand finding Sandsa's and her fingers twining through his.

A cool pinprick touched the back of Sandsa's hand. The drops of moisture were intermittent at first, spitting here, spitting there, but then they began falling at an increasing rate. Rain on Yalsa 5 was rare enough that Josh and Callista both peered up at the sky, startled.

Fayay. Sandsa kept his growl silent. *Will you not go somewhere you're wanted?*

The answer come in the form of frigid water trickling down his spine. He grimaced.

'Vom seems to think the Desine should follow us every second of every day, but having a god telling you what to do doesn't really prepare you for the big bad galaxy,' Josh said, pulling a hood over his hair to keep it from getting damp. 'The Desine saved me. Awesome. But at what point do I become responsible for my own life?'

Sandsa nodded briskly. 'You make an excellent point, Josh. We should not expect all the hard work to be done for us. The Desine would feel that the way you are conducting your life is payment enough for saving you all those years ago.'

I'm coming, Sandsa, taunted Fayay. *Will you be able to defend yourself, hobbled as you are?*

Callista flinched. 'Sandsa...'

'Would you like to join the Maria?' Sandsa asked Josh, touching the man's elbow and steering him towards the remaining hovercar. Callista stayed behind, a hand wrapped around her lasgun.

'I thought all clans were pretty much the same unit these days,' Josh said with a snort, though a good-natured one. 'Gotta say, some people don't particularly like being told what to do by Clan Leaders instead of their own subofficers.'

Sandsa winced. 'I thought this was what people wanted. Cohesion instead of factions. Peace instead of war.'

'There's less dying, so that's something.'

'I think I did it to make her happy,' Sandsa admitted.

Josh paused beside the hovercar and studied him for a moment. 'There're worse reasons to kill for.'

Sandsa punched his code into the keypad on vehicle and watched the door drop open. He indicated the driver's seat. 'I take it you know where our headquarters are?'

'Really, you'd let me touch this? Drive it?' Josh's voice rose several notches.

'They say that when men and women fight together a bond forms between them,' Sandsa said, thinking of the tribes and the sayings he had given them.

They obeyed every one of your demands, because you were their god, Fayay sneered.

Sandsa gritted his teeth. 'Josh, you should leave. Callista and I will be able to find our own transportation.'

Kuja, he sent. *I need you.*

Already on my way. Callista called me.

'Goodbye, Pagnus of Vieta,' Sandsa said softly. 'You are Josh Freeman now and forever.'

Josh hesitated. Sandsa fought the urge to shove him bodily into the rounded compartment. Finally, the new Maria clansman asked, 'So how come you know that name? I...I don't know if it's stuck with me because you called me that during the war, but I think it *was* my name.'

'I still sense the Desine,' Sandsa told him. 'Though I try not to.'

Josh slid into the seat, but continued to hold Sandsa's eyes. 'I see. Good luck getting a taxicar out this far.' His face became clouded. 'I can sense you. A little. Let's not tell Vom we can still do this 'cause he'd never leave us alone if he knew. Goodbye, Sandsa.'

The moment the hovercar careened around the corner, Sandsa ran back to Callista. He threw his body over hers, shielding her just as a jet of water thundered up behind him, bowing his back with the force of an irrepressible tide. As they toppled to the ground, Sandsa shouted, 'Kuja!'

His brother helped them up, then all three of them stood together, united in a wall of flesh and power. What Sandsa sensed inside Callista frightened him. He watched as her teeth tore a fleck of skin from her lip, blood beading there as she tried to temper their unborn child's powers.

A cascade of briny water hit the tar, scouring away any specks of sand that were clinging to the road. The torrent curled into a sodden seaweed cloak which Fayay then lowered from his face.

Ocean spray hissed from the gap between his lips. 'Good evening, brothers.'

'It is an evening, though I would argue it is not a good one,' Sandsa retorted.

'I see that living among mortals has provided you with wit and...' Fayay's pale tongue darted out of his mouth. '...an incubator.'

Fayay suddenly staggered to the side. When he whipped his head back around, he glowered at Callista who had sent a telekinetic blast his way.

'Call me an incubator again, water god,' she said with a very unpleasant smile.

The Watine stamped one foot. Jets of water tore apart the road, heading straight for her. Callista danced aside at the last moment and threw a laugh at him. 'It must really gall you that he gave up the power you thought you wanted only for him to get what you actually want.'

'I want nothing like you!' Fayay spat.

'You're jealous, we can see it in your thoughts!' Kuja said, curling his hands towards his wrists. Vines sped out of the ground at Fayay's feet, encircling his ankles and rising up his calves. 'And you cannot beat us, Fayay. You are just one god.'

Fayay's pale eyes glinted. 'For now. But I do not need help to beat one pathetic mortal.'

His next attack came hard and fast. Sandsa did not even allow himself time to blink. He threw himself in front of Callista, prepared to take the brunt of the blast, but it didn't come. He stared up in disbelief.

The water Fayay had hurled at them could have been an icicle, had it not been sloshing and rotating in front of Sandsa's chest, seemingly unable to complete its journey. At first Sandsa could not think of anything to say or do. Then a surge of anger belted through him and he diverted the wet missile to the ground just as he had done with so many countless lasgun bolts. The water exploded over the sand but shied from his boots, as though afraid to come near him.

'Father has lied to all of us!' Sandsa shouted into the stunned silence, though he knew they all heard the quaver in his voice. 'Our domains do not need a specific sibling. If I can command water, then you can command sand, Fayay. You're so worried about the deserts needing a god? Then fill my boots. If you can.'

The water deity shrank back, hooking his cape up over his face and using the gesture to disintegrate into a puddle. Sandsa blew out a breath and sagged. Kuja stared at him with wide eyes and asked, 'Sandsa, have you always commanded both water and sand?'

'Is this the first time?' was Callista's question.

Sandsa swallowed. 'I was using my chipless powers to deflect the blast. That is all.'

'I felt...' Kuja hesitated. 'I felt the water move in you, brother. Don't deny it.'

Sandsa shoved his hands into his pockets. 'Why would I be able to use both? And if we can all do this, then why has Father not told us?'

'He doesn't want us to know we can be replaced,' Kuja whispered. 'That we can be killed with no negative impact to our people.'

Callista surprised Sandsa by moving over to the Rforine and resting a hand on his shoulder. 'You are *not* replaceable to your brother. I've seen what you mean to him in my visions.' Her smile lit the night. 'Sandsa, this means you don't have to feel guilty about leaving your people. One of your brothers can take over the deserts.'

'There is so much we do not know and we...we are supposed to be gods!' Kuja said and burbled with laughter. 'Maybe *I* can replace you, brother.'

Sandsa reached over to cuff his brother on the head. 'Don't

get any ideas. Will you stay for the wedding? It's in two weeks if you want to attend.'

'I will even officiate your binding afterwards,' Kuja said with a grin, but then his lips drooped. 'What am I supposed to do at the mortal ceremony?'

Callista tugged the rainforest god aside and began to explain the custom of standing up beside the groom, something Sandsa had only heard about from Bock the day before. Nodding, Kuja repeated, 'Best man. I think Mum would have agreed that I am the best of us two, brother.'

'You behave very poorly for a seventy-year-old,' Sandsa told him.

Kuja grinned. 'You still behave poorly! Should I tell Callista just how old you are?'

'No!' Callista and Sandsa said as one.

CHAPTER TWENTY-EIGHT

'Impressive,' Governor Jon Garnett commented, hovering a palm in front of the enormous semi-spherical shield that now covered the entire city. 'Even with my resources, I never could get a citywide shield running. I was told the one we had was too ancient to fix. And stark it if the new generators didn't cost several times our GPP.'

Uninterested in delving back into their previous discussion regarding Yalsa 5's Gross Planetary Product, Sandsa smiled and waved a hand, indicating the desert beyond. 'I find the sand in our streets distracting. And spending money on infrastructure goes a long way to keeping people happy.'

The governor chuckled. 'I wonder if they're happy about the amount of coin-chips you and Clan Leader Dancer are throwing around the place for your wedding. I hear this evening's festivities cost almost as much as getting this thing working again.'

'Will you be attending?' Sandsa asked.

Garnett retracted his fingers from the humming forcefield and tapped his lips. 'I have yet to decide. I only received an invitation because of what my presence can offer.'

Sandsa smiled, shaking his head. 'Do you still think we need you to improve our image?'

'Well, with the decent folk, yes,' the governor said, linking his arms behind his back as he leaned forward to inspect the shield more closely.

'I rather thought the clans were now synonymous with peace — and surely people are enjoying the provision of services that this city has long lacked.' Sandsa nudged his elbow against the shield for emphasis, fighting a flinch when a bolt of energy hammered through his bones.

Garnett's head bobbed back up. He was frowning. 'I kept the city safe during the day by asking GLEA to send us agents, agents who are no longer with us thanks to your actions. Now I have to pay security forces to replace what was previously a complimentary service.' He held up a hand, forestalling comment. 'But I'm happy to go to your wedding if it means everyone thinks I helped you out with the shield.'

Sandsa let his smile stretch over his cheeks. 'Of course.'

The governor fell into step beside him as they left the edge of the city and headed towards two separate hovercars purring in wait on the side of the road. The sleeker, shinier one belonged to the Maria and Kick, the driver, could be seen sharpening a blade through an open window.

Garnett paused, half-turned towards his hovercar. 'Tell me, Bolt, why is it you placed this shield high on your priorities?

'I really cannot stand sand,' Sandsa replied.

Garnett's eyes narrowed. 'Really.'

Raising his eyes to the forcefield that painted the sky with a faint orange hue, Sandsa felt a wave of despair wash over him. 'I thought the voices would be quieter if I fixed the shield. It appears I was wrong.' He blinked. 'Farewell, Governor. I will see you this evening.'

Sandsa slid into the back of his hovercar and closed his eyes.

Even as Kick drove him further and further inside the city, he could still hear the ever-increasing whispers. The sands continued to call for him and pester him, even when his people had given up.

And all he could do was cover his ears.

***

Her reflection lifted trembling fingers to her hair, brushing stray brunette strands off her face. The ring on her left hand briefly caught on the earring dangling from her ear, an impractical adornment that would probably have gotten her killed a few months ago. Callista lowered her hand and gave herself a wobbly smile. Her queasiness had driven her from the knot of women outside and into the bathroom. Now they kept calling through the door, wanting to know when she'd come back out. Ignoring them, Callista bent over the sink to scoop water into her mouth, scrubbing away the bitter taste of vomit, then caressed her stomach, using gentle thoughts to soothe her son. He seemed restless, but she supposed her morning sickness could be blamed for that.

Callista glanced up at the mirror and gasped.

A girl on the verge of adulthood was staring back at her. The teenager's young face was battered by sun and wind and her grey eyes were surrounded by taut lines. One hand held an antiquated lasgun and the other was cupped to the sky, sand trickling away between her trembling fingers. In the distance, beyond her small, insignificant figure, dunes rose and fell like waves. Callista felt her son's thoughts abruptly grow turbulent. He lashed out — and the mirror cracked.

Callista stepped back, breathing hard.

She saw her own face now, but behind her stood the grandfather of her child.

She refused to turn around.

'Why do you keep showing me that girl?' she asked the Ine.

His expression remained as smooth as marble. 'She is Kuin of the Bretani, the true chief that her people need. Her powers are lost to her and so she cannot claim her tribe from the brother that is leading them to ruin.'

Callista glowered. 'So get Fayay to fix it. You know he wants Sandsa's domain.'

'Each of my children has a specific place. I will not allow Fayay to rule the deserts.'

'So have another child. You don't need Julia Ine. Any woman will do.'

Something flashed in his blue eyes. Was it pain?

Callista doubted it.

He pressed his hands together, carefully lining up each and every finger. 'I have a grand design for the universe. Everything occurs as it is meant to. You drew Sandsa here so he could learn how to care for the mortals and guide them properly, not force his will on them.'

'The lesson I bore...' Callista murmured. Fear needled her heart but she wasn't sure why.

The Ine dipped his head into a nod. 'Now that you have taught him this lesson, he must return or the salvation must come in his place — Sandsa cannot be replaced by any of his siblings. He can wield the powers of many domains. They cannot.'

Callista swallowed the jagged rock that seemed to be pressing against her windpipe. 'I knew it. I knew he was more powerful. He must be like that for a reason. Why?'

'His destiny is not for you or anyone else to know yet,' the Ine said lightly. 'But enough of that. My son is a god. You deny a part of him that cannot be changed. Or resisted.'

'He chose me over the deserts!' she cried, hands fisting at her sides. 'Don't you get that?'

'And do you understand that everything happens as it is meant to?'

Callista shook her head. 'You are repeating yourself, old man. Don't come to my wedding. Parents who want to control their children should have no part in their happiness. I never want to see you again.'

'You know what I will say and it frightens you,' he said, his voice softening.

'No,' she whispered, closing her eyes.

'You can feel it, can't you. Sandsa never needed to abandon the deserts.'

'That's not true! You pushed him away. You told him he had to choose.'

'I never told him that,' the Ine corrected her. 'My son can have his deserts and he can have you. But you won't tell him that. Because, Callista Krendasta, you are afraid. You are afraid of what it will mean to be the wife of a god.'

When she opened her eyes, she saw only her frightened face in the mirror. More and more cracks began to spider over her reflection, forming shards that then broke apart and cascaded into the sink. Her tears poured over her cheeks to join them.

Could it be true? Could Sandsa have both her and the deserts? Could Kuin and all those poor people out there have their god while Callista had her husband? She buried her fearful thoughts deep inside her and locked them down so tightly that even Sandsa would have trouble finding them.

She forced a smile onto her face and left the bathroom, emerging into the penthouse bedroom where Ala and a group of clanswomen were already waiting for her. Her wedding dress was carefully arranged on the bed but Callista made no move towards it.

Ala slung an arm over her shoulders. 'You alright, Cals? Thought I heard somethin' break.'

'Only a thousand hearts across the city,' Diamond said, grinning, a stimstick balanced between two fingers. 'Bolt's starking fine and he'll be off the market by tonight.'

Callista pulled a face. 'I'd rather not think of my husband as something that can be bought.'

Or replaced, she added silently.

As they fluttered around her, burying her in heavy cloth and heavier makeup, Callista could not help but think about what the Ine had said. If Sandsa was told he could have her and the deserts, he would leave Yalsa 5 in a heartbeat and drag her with him. She knew that without even seeking his mind across the city.

The Ine had to be lying. He would say anything to make Sandsa return to him.

Callista continued to laugh along with her friends.

But the Creator God's words were like poison, eating at her from the inside.

***

Kuja looked bemused as he raked his eyes over the expansive

room where his brother would undergo the mortal ceremony. Many of Sandsa's fellow clanspeople had been suspicious of this brother who had appeared out of nowhere, especially when he had baulked upon being given formal attire, but Bock had taken to Kuja immediately. Right now Bock was off to the side, discussing the event's security with guards from multiple clans who were there to ensure the wedding went ahead as scheduled. While his new friend was busy, Kuja tugged the sleeve of Sandsa's suit and asked, 'How long must I stand here? Bindings only take a few minutes. This seems more elaborate.'

Sandsa chuckled. 'I am sorry to inform you that I require your presence for a lot longer than a few minutes.'

'You would think that with their limited lifespans they would opt for something a bit less time-consuming,' Kuja muttered. Then he brightened. 'Callista has agreed to the binding and the immortality that comes with it?'

'She has.'

Kuja sighed wistfully. 'She must really love you, brother. I envy you.' He hesitated. 'Sandsa, what is it like to...?' The young god broke off, his lips oscillating soundlessly.

He was saved by the arrival of Bock who inserted himself between the brothers. Bock nudged Sandsa's side. 'The woman doing the flowers is starkin' fine. Do you think I should ask her out?'

Sandsa raised his eyebrows. 'But what of your affections for Ala?'

'Might as well get some practice so Ala finds me more desirable,' Bock said with a wink. He turned his attention to Kuja. 'So, did you come for just the wedding or do ya want to join the Maria?'

Kuja's cheeks paled behind his freckles. 'Just the wedding, thank you. I must return to my...job when all this is over.' He pursed his lips. 'Tell me, has this love of my brother's worsened or bettered the city?'

'Kuja!' Sandsa said, shaking his head in annoyance.

Bock chuckled. 'Bettered. Never been able to make eyes at the pretty girls who only show up in daylight before now, have I?'

'I see,' Kuja said and turned away.

Sandsa frowned at his brother's back. He wished Bock had said something about the peace in Atsa, but it didn't matter because the thoughts in Kuja's mind were already tangled on another issue. Sandsa sent Bock over to check on the ushers responsible for the hundreds of guests then turned to his brother.

'Do you think it would be wrong to...practice?' Kuja asked in a strained voice.

'You speak of intercourse. It is not something I considered until Callista and I...grew closer.'

'Surely you were my age once, Sandsa,' Kuja grumbled.

Sandsa laughed. He remembered the strange, urgent sensations of his youth and how he had dismissed them, disappearing into his duty. Now, though...Kuja would be unable to ignore something he saw his brother acting on daily.

'Kuja, using the word "practice" suggests you wish to move further down that path. Do you...' Sandsa hesitated. 'Do you think you could abandon your people for love?'

Kuja lifted glistening eyes. 'This is tearing you apart, Sandsa. I hate to see you in pain.'

'That is not an answer.'

'I could never leave my people,' Kuja said, frowning. 'But even if I did find love...it must be daunting to a woman to shed her mortal life and friends. And what if we grew tired of each other?'

Sandsa stepped back, disturbed. 'I will never grow tired of her, Kuja.'

'I did not mean —'

'I will not lose her!'

Something cracked overhead. Sandsa looked up, expecting to catch a mouthful of dust from the ceiling, but it remained intact and smooth. Instead, gentle specks of sand rained gently over them, uninvited and unwanted.

He refused to hold his brother's knowing gaze for long.

***

Callista curled her hands over her knees to avoid looking at the palms that would soon bear scars. She chose to keep her eyes on Ala who had draped herself over two seats in the long, luxurious cabin of a vehicle that may or may not have been stolen from rich folk before the clans turned honest. The blue dress Ala was wearing seemed out of place, as though someone had forcibly wrapped it around her rather than her choosing to shimmy into it. Her newly-shaved scalp gleamed.

'Didn't get ya a gift or anything,' Ala said, peering through the shadows closing in on the windows. Dusk was chasing them across the city. 'Figured letting you take over the city was enough.'

Callista forced her eyes wide, hoping they would dry before any of the gathering tears could fall. 'Ala, being your friend has been the greatest gift. You trusted me when you really shouldn't have.'

'Got that right,' Ala said. She slapped Callista's thigh and scooted back when the other women in attendance batted her away to smooth the dress over Callista's legs. 'Stop lookin' like we're going to some funeral. It's your wedding, you douchenozzle. I'll see you happy or I will punch Bolt, powers or not.'

Callista's smile had started to hurt her cheeks by the time they arrived at the venue. She stayed in the vehicle as her helpers poured out onto the pavement and ducked her head, hiding her face from the vidcams hovering nearby. Tonight she would lose her mortality. Sandsa was used to watching people die then fade to dust. She wasn't. She hoped she would never become used to it.

Callista bit her lip and grimaced when she tasted a smear of lipstick on her teeth. She sucked it away — after all, she had to look good for the local vidscreens which would be filled with footage from the wedding. Those images of her would last forever, a reflection of her unchanging face.

Ala stuck her head back into the cabin. 'Come on, Cals. You're not gettin' any younger in there and I'm not exactly fresh either. Let's get this over with.'

Callista wondered if she was walking or actually floating when she left the safety of the hovercar. Smiles swirled dizzyingly around her and the beat of her heart seemed a distant echo in her ears. She felt nothing, not even the chill of evening on her cheeks.

Flanked by Ala and Diamond, she walked into the building and into her future.

***

People frantically clambered over each other beneath the high-vaulted ceiling, like ants spilling towards a prized morsel. The din

304

was overwhelming so Sandsa focused on the long runway leading up to the large, ornate doors that kept his bride from him.

'Stark me, half the city must have turned out!' Bock said, waving towards the seething crowd. He shot Sandsa a quick look, grinned, then dropped his hand onto Sandsa's shoulder. 'Hey, the bride's supposed to be late. It's tradition.'

'It is?' Sandsa wet his lips and glanced down at his palms. He had Callista's promise. But her thoughts, now closer than they had been all day, were taut — and some were buried completely.

Kuja smiled, no longer fidgeting. It seemed he was now content to wait for the proceedings to begin. 'Be happy, Sandsa. Mum would be.'

Something knotted itself around Sandsa's gut. 'Do you think so?'

'I...I am sorry for what I said before,' Kuja said so quietly that Sandsa had to lean in to hear him. 'If living as a mortal makes you happy, then it is all I want for you, brother.'

Silence fell as the doors split apart to reveal Callista and two women in shimmering blue dresses — Ala and Diamond. The silhouette of a dagger on Ala's thigh served as a warning that Callista was still under her protection. The heavily armed audience dutifully kept their weapons pointed at the ground.

Wearing white and a radiant smile, the bride began to descend the sloping floor at a crisp pace. Sandsa smiled when saw the black boots beneath her dress. Her eyes caught his across the room and he felt his insides fill with warmth.

Bock drew in a sharp breath beside him. 'Ala is beautiful. Scratch me eyes out if I ever look at another in my life.'

Kuja blinked. 'I thought you said you needed to practice.'

'Don't remind me how I strayed!' Bock sighed.

It felt like an eternity had passed before Callista clomped up onto the platform and was finally there with Sandsa. Kuja and the others faded away. Even the celebrant who led them to the centre of the platform became an unimportant part of the background. Sandsa took Callista's hands in his and stroked her knuckles, reassuring her, bathing her in his love. Soon he felt his lips form the words required by the planet's laws. Her mouth echoed his. He only knew that everything was over when he heard the raucous cheering of the crowd — some of them were even firing lasguns at the floral arrangements, much to the dismay of the decorators. Sandsa gathered his wife in his arms and kissed her. Her laugh slid over his lips like warm honey.

Sandsa broke away and led her up towards the doors, where they escaped into the night. Once inside the waiting hovercar, sharing smiles and tender thoughts, they let their hands roam, the darkened windows protecting them from the prying eyes of the crowd.

Kuja plopped himself into the driver's seat. 'Bock is standing very close to that Ala woman. He informed me that such events are emotional and he might have a chance with her later.'

Callista peeled her lips away from Sandsa's. 'I didn't know you could drive, Kuja.'

The rainforest god grinned. 'Sandsa isn't the only one who hangs out with mortals.'

As he revved the engine, Callista looked outside, at the horde of people behind the lasproof plexiglass. Her cheeks blanched, causing her skin to look as pale as the dress she wore. Sandsa followed her gaze.

Vom was there, waving them off, and beside him Diamond was doing the same. But there was another woman with them, a former tribesperson if her companions were anything to go by, and her eyes were trained right through the window as though she could see them. She seemed familiar, but Sandsa supposed that once all of his people had been familiar to him. The woman turned and touched Vom's arm.

Callista stiffened.

But then Kuja sent the vehicle swooping across the road and they were thrown back into their seats. Callista laughed and scolded the Rforine as they careened their way towards their destination.

***

The trees inside The Sample bowed overhead, shielding them from the evidence that they were inside a man-made dome. Callista kicked the hem of her dress, uncaring that twigs were catching on and ruining the fabric. Kuja stood before them, his arms stretched out as he soaked up the adoration of the minuscule rainforest that surrounded him. Leaves detached themselves from the trees to dance over his face, caressing his cheeks, then quietly dropped to his feet.

Callista watched this display of power, then looked at Sandsa. His hand squeezed hers.

You are worth more to me than what I lost, he said, his eyes sparkling. *Having command over the deserts is not payment enough for an eternity of loneliness.*

Sandsa...

She thought of telling him about Assila, who had been standing beside Vom after the wedding, and the woman's ability to reveal the Desine's true identity. At that very moment the

Zatzat could be planning to move against the Maria. But she didn't want to worry about this, not now, not on her wedding day, when everything was meant to be perfect. Callista stomped down on her thoughts but she could tell by the lift of Sandsa's eyebrows that he had sensed her anxiety.

Kuja was now kneeling on the ground, cupping his hand over his lips as he whispered something to the plants that shivered around him.

Callista swallowed. *Sandsa. I'm scared. I'm scared of losing Ala, losing Bock, losing all my friends. And what if we hate each other? What if we fight? What if...*

What if we touch a happiness neither of us has ever been allowed to know? he asked.

Callista closed her eyes and called up images of her son. The blue eyes of his father, the gentle nose that neither sloped down sharply like Sandsa's nor curled up prematurely like hers, the patient smile that could see out a million years. Her son would fall in love, she recalled. She would live to see him marry. And she would do everything in her power to make sure he never donned a purple Chipper jumpsuit. She peeled her eyelids apart and kissed her husband.

She would regret it later, if ever.

Sandsa cleared his throat. 'Kuja. We are ready.'

'Yes, we are,' Callista said, smiling at him.

Kuja rose to his feet and advanced on them. Callista held out her hands, palms facing the tree canopy, just as Sandsa was doing. The rainforest god looked between them. 'Sandsa, do you want me to just do the binding or do you want me to recite the words they say in the deserts?'

'Recite the words,' Callista said, then glanced at Sandsa when she felt his surprise. 'It's still part of you, Sandsa. I would not deny you this.'

Sandsa bowed his head. In his mind she saw the memories of him standing invisible behind countless couples in the deserts as they bound themselves together before a priest or priestess. He had blessed each union but had watched with growing envy. Now he was finally experiencing it for himself.

'Seems a little redundant, but alright,' Kuja said with an amused twist to his lips. 'Tonight we witness the binding of Sandsa Desine and Callista Krendasta.'

Callista's palms warmed despite the breeze that had kicked up beneath the trees. The Sample's climate control could have been responsible but she suspected it was due to Kuja's powers. Drawing deep breaths, she turned to face Sandsa and clasped his hands, pressing her skin to his. Kuja said something Callista couldn't catch and then she gasped as light erupted between Sandsa's fingers and her own. The pain came before she was ready for it, a stinging slice down each palm. It continued to irritate and burn for several long moments before the sensation slowly faded.

'You have her blood as she has yours,' Kuja said in a low voice. 'You are bound and that cannot be easily broken.'

Callista withdrew from her husband and studied her hands, expecting blood but seeing faded scars instead, as though she had been bound to Sandsa for years.

Kuja coughed into his hand, sounding embarrassed. 'May the Desine smile on your binding.'

Callista managed to stifle the giggle. Sandsa took her fingers to his lips and kissed them. Then he said softly, 'He smiles.'

'Have you ever not smiled on a binding?' Kuja asked him.

Sandsa's blue eyes grew distant. 'This is the last one I shall smile upon. Now I would like to have my wife to myself. Thank you, brother.'

Callista recalled Ala's confusion when her Clan Leaders had said that their honeymoon would be spent on Yalsa 5, as if nothing had happened. Callista knew she would have to give up Atsa City one day, when she failed to age, but until then she intended not to miss a single moment of her life here.

Kuja stepped away, toward the trees. 'I will return when your son is born. You will need me then.'

Fayay... Callista wasn't sure if she thought the name or if she had pulled it from Sandsa's mind. But then they were alone in the tiny rainforest, where once she had laughed and played as a child. Just this one night, there would be no thinking, no worries. Only pleasure.

He came to her and she lost herself in him.

Later, they curled up together on the ground, their skin glistening with sweat and the spray of moist air from hidden vents. Unable to follow him into sleep, Callista skated through his dreams instead. The deserts were beautiful to him, but each sunset with their broad strokes of oranges and pinks had failed to move him the way she did. He loved her smile, the hidden curves of her skin — and the boots. He definitely loved the boots.

Callista half-closed her eyes, finally tired, but then she caught sight of a translucent woman standing beside a tree. She wasn't afraid of the ghost. She was afraid of what it meant to see her.

'Julia Ine,' Callista whispered.

'The being that was my husband will ensure there is a god of the sands, and soon,' the woman cautioned, her voice carrying across the clearing. 'Be careful. Sandsa might not have a choice, but you do. So choose wisely, Callista, or you will lose both my son and yours.'

Callista shook her head fiercely. 'No. All three of us will be together for eternity. The Ine can't separate us now.'

Julia's expression remained grave. 'But you will separate my son from the deserts. When you do not need to.'

Sandsa stirred. The spectre abruptly vanished.

'My love?' her husband questioned.

Callista tickled his brow with her kisses. 'Shh. I am here.'

CHAPTER TWENTY-NINE

Callista watched her face ripple in the surface of the water beneath her and heaved again. A single line of bitter bile crawled over her lips. Grimacing, she spat it away then slumped backwards into the arms of her husband. He wiped her mouth with a towel and made awkward assurances while she lifted one of her palms before her eyes and studied the scar.

'Don't even try to talk me out of this meeting,' she warned him.

Sandsa kissed her cheek. 'I only ask that you go with caution and call me when you are in danger. The governor will not be upset if I leave him early.'

'I can handle myself.' Callista fought the urge to roll her eyes at his protectiveness. 'And there hasn't been a disagreement since the Spinners threatened to blow themselves up over that territory dispute three months back. They were quick to realise how stupid that sounded.'

'I did not mean the...I did not mean mortal threats,' Sandsa clarified.

'I would rather worry about a stray lasgun bolt than Fayay swooping down on us.'

'Callista, my love...'

'Look, I know he's a danger to us, but I'd rather...' Callista closed her eyes briefly. 'I'd rather worry about the enemies I know how to fight. The ones I *know* we can fight.'

We can deal with Fayay, he said.

We're just chipless humans with a long lifespan, Sandsa — he's a god!

If I must use the powers of a god to protect you and our son, then I will, he vowed.

Callista swiped a finger beneath each eye, catching the moisture that had gathered on her lower lashes. 'I know. But if you do, you might not come back.'

She blocked him from her thoughts and stood to escape the confines of the bathroom.

***

Barely an hour later, Callista was perched on the edge of a plush seat, feeling the fibres beneath her constantly rearrange themselves to accommodate her tension. Either side of her, immovable masses of muscle fidgeted with their lasguns, giving her sideways looks as if they couldn't quite believe the trouble she had given them. She continued to stare right ahead, ignoring them. They were nothing; she could kill them with thoughts alone.

It seemed Sandsa's fears for her safety had not been entirely unfounded. A hovercar had torn up tar on its way towards her outside the hotel, where she had been about to meet with the city's subofficers, its lasguns aimed right for her. She would have destroyed the guards had they not insisted that they would take her to her parents. Callista had paused then, surprised that she had not thought of her mother or her father in so many months.

Let them see how well I am doing without them, she had thought.

Then she had entered the armoured hovercar of her own free will.

The hovercar's driver suddenly turned onto a road she was not expecting him to take. If she asked why her parents had moved to a different house the guards would probably not even answer her if they knew. She had suspected that her parents' dwindling coin-chips would force them to find more affordable accommodation, but as the hovercar approached a tall ivory fence that looked like a line of grim spears jutting out from the earth, Callista wondered if they were imprisoned in this looming mansion instead.

Callista scowled. She was familiar with Isolde Israr's residence, having spent an evening or two there herself, always in the company of her parents who would deliver a stern look or a kick beneath the dining table should she not behave. They had always been so anxious when they'd sent their daughter out alone with Israr, though not because they had been worried about her. No, they had been more afraid of her doing something sensible, like turning down an unwanted proposal. Callista smiled for a moment, remembering. She had met Sandsa that night.

The hovercar approached the fence at full tilt and Callista gripped her knees as they moved closer. At the last moment, a part of the road slid away to reveal a ramp and they followed it down into a concrete box that served as a garage, the hatch clanging shut above them. Callista climbed through the window before her guards could unlock the doors and glared at them when they hurried out after her. 'Just where exactly do you suppose I'll run off to in here? Israr would have made sure that the doors are locked to anyone without the right palm print.'

'My dear Callista is right as always!' Isolde boomed from the entrance of the garage. Though he had his hands held high, the ludicrously long sleeves of his bright azure cloak fell lower than his waist.

Callista crossed her arms. 'Where are my parents? I was meant to be visiting them.'

A smile bloomed over his features. 'They are my honoured guests.'

'Honoured guests or reluctant hostages?' Callista asked, adjusting her shirt so that the Maria symbol was more obvious. She hoped Israr would realise she was involved with gangs, even if he could not identify the clan.

Isolde frowned. 'That shirt is not fashionable, not at all, and you will need to stop wearing it now that you are no longer in a gang. Now come! Food awaits.' He eyed her. 'Although it seems you have gained weight since my eyes last beheld you. No matter. I can arrange a smaller portion for your plate.'

Callista felt her son's presence unfurl within her, offering her unimaginable powers so that she could escape. She tore a large chunk off her tongue and hacked it between her teeth before swallowing what remained.

We cannot use those powers — you are not a god, she told her son.

His reluctance to obey came in the form of a roiling inside her gut. She winced and forced her stomach to settle. Her son was a wild spirit inside her sometimes, so much like his father...well, what Sandsa had been like when he'd appeared that night to come to her aid. Callista sighed. How could she teach her son to abandon the powers that could save him from situations like this?

Callista followed Isolde up narrow wooden steps that creaked beneath their feet and into the foyer. It had possessed a grand entranceway once, but the front doors had since been removed and the gap was now blocked in with dirty beige stone which did not match the gentle grey marble of the room. Callista almost laughed. He still feared the clans if he was hiding behind that.

'Callista! Oh, Callista, we feared the worst!' her mother bawled, flying down a twisting staircase to inflict a hug on Callista.

'Isolde told us that he spotted you running with a gang, that they had surely abducted you against your will,' his father said, incorporating himself into her mother's unwavering embrace. 'He concocted this plan to rescue you days ago and enacted it with much danger to himself.'

Callista pried herself away. 'Sure. Huge, massive danger, sending his big burly bodyguards.'

'Don't be ungrateful!' her mother scolded. 'You should be pleased that he went to so much trouble to ensure his beloved was safe — though you have clearly had more than enough to eat!'

Callista waited for her father to join in with some comment about her weight but he simply looked down at her stomach and smiled. Bewildered, but touched that he had guessed and was happy about her pregnancy, she managed to flip a smile of her own at him.

'Is he going to propose again?' Callista asked her mother, looking around for a seat to sink into but finding none. Her feet continued to ache.

Isolde clapped his hands together once. 'Why, yes! I have always loved your shrewdness.'

'As I have always loathed your inability to grasp the simple concept that your interest has never been reciprocated,' she fired back. 'Did my parents play you false, Mr Israr? Or did you harbour your own delusions?'

'Stop insulting the poor man,' her father said with a shake of his head. 'You have made your feelings clear. I will not make you marry Israr — there is clearly no need for it.'

'What!' her mother exclaimed, furious.

Callista looked between her parents, mouth slightly open, then sealed it up again when she felt her husband, his presence zigzagging through the city like a snake searching the dunes. She assured him that she was in no immediate danger but his awareness continued towards her anyway and her retinas itched as he saw through her eyes, taking stock of the situation.

I will end them, he growled.

Who says I need your help? Callista demanded.

This man has kidnapped a Clan Leader, my wife, the mother of my child...

Callista refocused on her mother's entreaties for her to apologise to Isolde.

She cleared her throat. 'Mr Israr.'

'Isolde, my dear, you will need to get used to calling me that,' he corrected, smiling.

Callista snorted. 'Mr Israr. I feel it's only fair that I tell you that you've endangered your life by kidnapping me. Yes, kidnapping. Not rescuing.'

His lips shivered. 'Oh?'

'*Oh,*' she mocked. 'You have committed a hostile act against Clan Leader Dancer from the Maria clan.'

Israr blanched. 'But that's...impossible.'

'What is she going on about?' her mother hissed.

'Surely you remember that when she left us she was already

wearing that gang shirt of hers,' her father said and swiftly grabbed his wife's arm, keeping her palm from connecting with Callista's face (Callista had erected a shield already, having known the slap was coming).

'I thought it was just bad fashion sense!' Callista's mother snapped, struggling against her husband's grip.

Callista rolled her eyes away from them and over to Isolde just in time to see his cheer crumble into uncertainty. 'I joined the Maria gang of my own free will when the Galactic Mining Corp wouldn't have me. So I'm curious, rich folk. Do you know how Atsa City is really run?'

Israr bowed his head. 'It is not something that is spoken of in polite society.'

'Fuck that shit,' Callista said. 'There, I'm not polite society. Go on.'

Surprisingly, it was her father who responded. 'The nights belong to the gangs. We know the Clan Leader — Garnett says it is plural now? — well, the Clan Leaders are the governors of the night. But...'

'It's unbearable to speak of such things!' her mother cried.

Isolde's smile had returned now, much to Callista's dismay. 'Oh! But this is excellent news. My associates will be so impressed. A Clan Leader for a wife!'

'Two more things,' Callista said, grinning as she reached for Sandsa. *Actually, my love, could you do a small favour for me...*

His mental laugh was answer enough for her.

Callista's mother frantically fanned herself. 'Can it get any worse?'

'I'm married to Clan Leader Bolt and we are having your grandson,' Callista said, smiling.

Isolde swung an accusing look at her parents. 'She's married! I cannot enter a poly marriage — my associates are *very* traditional! Can we arrange a divorce?'

The floor shook. Callista idly inspected a fingernail.

'What was that?' her mother asked.

The wall filling the doorframe exploded inwards and sent a hail of stones flying towards them. Callista drew a breath and shouted, 'Stop!'

It was if as someone had hit the pause button on a vidscreen. Her parents and Isolde were already half-turned from the shrapnel, hands rising to cover their faces. When nothing struck them, they peered through their fingers at the chunks of stone suspended in midair, eyes and mouths wide. Callista waved a hand at the daylight streaming through the gap in the wall. 'My husband has just blasted you a new door, Mr Israr. Nice of him.'

'Yes, yes, very nice of him,' Isolde said, nodding.

'Lucky for you, I have some very useful powers,' she said conversationally. 'I could kill you in any number of ways, but I'm not in the mood for it today.'

The debris abruptly scuttled to the sides, clearing the way for the man who had taken a city — and her heart. Sandsa strode through the billowing dust, wearing the suit she had helped him into that morning for his conference with the governor. Callista smirked at the thought of him sitting in a high-backed chair, discussing important details with a man her parents had been so desperate to invite to all of their excessive parties. She remembered an intricate ice sculpture at one particular event — it had melted when their climate control system, ageing and decrepit, had conked out.

Isolde dropped to his knees. 'Clan Leader Bolt, accept my deepest apologies! I was deceived!'

'Forget that!' her mother bawled. 'Those powers — she's gone and joined the Chippers!'

Her father cleared his throat. 'Actually, she was born with them. She had no choice in the matter so I'd rather you didn't hold her to account for them.'

Callista stared at him, mouth agape, then hesitantly tried something she had never thought to do. Her first feather-light touch on his mind went unnoticed, but then his chin shot up and his eyes narrowed. His core of power was weak, minimal, but it was there — and had been there all his life. Not only that, he had been aware of her powers too and had feared that she might expose hers to society.

'Why didn't you just tell me?' She did not need to elaborate. He knew.

'It is something that was given to me,' he said, studying the wall to his left intently. 'Not who I am.'

Callista rested a hand on his shoulder. 'Dad. You chose to bury it. I chose something else.'

'I had to bury it...I *had* to...'

The pain hammered into her forehead and she accepted his memories as he held them up to her, unfiltered and sharp. His powers had manifested early — his parents had thought they could beat it from him and he had let them think they had. He had buried his powers to survive, first from his family, then from a society that would never understand him.

Blinking furiously, Callista wrapped her arms around her father. 'I am so sorry. I didn't know. How could I?'

'What is she going on about?' a shrill voice demanded.

No need to check who said that, Callista thought. Her father's mind glowed with agreement.

'I wanted to take you with me to the Chippers, where our powers would have been normal instead of embarrassing,' he moaned. 'But *he* told me the chips would nullify our powers. You had to be found. The powers had to stay so someone could find you.'

'Who told you this?' she asked, her mouth dry.

He straightened out of her embrace. 'The Creator God came to me. He chose me. He said he would take the powers away once I had achieved my destiny.'

'What destiny?' Sandsa demanded, stalking over to stand beside Callista.

'You have to understand. I did it so I could be free.'

'*What destiny?*' Sandsa repeated.

'I had to keep her here, near the deserts,' her father bleated. 'I had to. So I told the Galactic Mining Corp not to take her. And I had to make sure she provided what the Creator God required. I thought pushing her to marry Israr would help speed up the process...'

Callista gritted her teeth. 'What did the Creator God require?'

'A grandson,' he whispered.

She threw herself in front of her father. He struggled behind her on the floor, his mind scrambled and confused. Shielding him from Sandsa's next blast of telekinetic power, Callista snapped, 'No! It's not his fault. He was used!'

Salvation of the deserts. The words rolled through her head, over and over, then over again. *His siblings can't replace him. But his son could. The child I bear. The salvation of the deserts.*

'Does anyone mind if I...make myself scarce?' Isolde asked in a high-pitched voice.

'Take me with you!' Callista's mother screeched.

Callista didn't bother to watch the two schemers scurry out the new entrance that a lascannon had gouged into the mansion. She kept her eyes on the two remaining men. 'Dad, is all this true?'

Her father nodded. 'I have only done what the Creator God asked of me.'

'*Ine*,' Sandsa spat.

Callista wound an arm around her husband. 'He is nothing to you anymore. You have free will and the choice to do whatever the fuck you want.'

Sandsa's blue eyes shimmered with tears. 'But if we only met because of his will...if you only carry our child because...'

'Then maybe he wanted you to leave and find happiness all along?' Callista suggested, a little more flippantly than she intended. She felt the doubt manifest inside him and retreated back into her mind so he wouldn't see the truth in her thoughts. *A lesson or a replacement...*

Callista looked at her father who was now hunched over on the floor. 'I feel sorry for you, Father. You had no way of knowing that you could have ignored the Creator God and lived your own life. So get out of here. Find a new planet. And never contact me again.'

'I...do not know what I should do, now that my purpose is achieved,' her father murmured.

Callista fought the swell of pity and didn't quite succeed. 'I'll have funds shifted into your account. Just know that if you're still in Atsa by next week, I'll let my husband do exactly what he wants to you.'

She and Sandsa turned and left her father there, knowing he had nothing, not even regrets. Her unease followed Callista all the way back to the Maria headquarters and into their spacious penthouse. She remained as still as a statue while her amorous husband stripped her of her clothes. But then his mouth enveloped a breast and she cupped the back of his head with her hands, surrendering to the mindless delights that he could bring her.

***

He watched her sleep after they made love. The sheet was tangled around her naked limbs and one fold of black silk was creeping up her thigh like an insidious trickle of darkness. Splayed out on her left side, hand digging beneath the pillow that supported her tired head, Callista looked untouched by fear or uncertainty. But even though Sandsa's intense delivery of pleasure had relaxed her, he had still been unable to puncture the shield around her thoughts.

Sandsa kissed her brow then let Kuja know he was ready to be teleported away from Yalsa 5. In moments, Sandsa's body collapsed, showering the floor with vines and greenery that vanished once their deed was done. He rose as a man among the trees on the planet Bagaran, light straining through the leaves to touch him. Kuja dropped down from the branch where he had been crouching.

'Kuja, what did you need to speak to me about?' Sandsa asked.

'They'll come for you, they'll come when he's born,' Kuja whispered, unable to meet his brother's gaze.

Sandsa let his voice drop into a growl. 'It is not enough for

Fayay to take my place in the deserts — he must come after my family too?'

Kuja's shoulders sagged. 'He has tried to use your powers. But he can't. Fayay says there must be a god in the deserts and I suppose he thinks he can replace you with your son if you don't agree to come back.'

'We'll stop him,' Sandsa vowed.

'So many of the others are joining him. They think he is right — the Desine must return. The grand design must be maintained.'

Sandsa drew a shaky breath. 'Are we alone against them all?'

Kuja named the siblings who did not wish to involve themselves in the fight. Sandsa waited to hear more, for Kuja to list more of them, but his brother stopped there, wringing his hands. Kuja's rounded cheeks dimpled with distress. 'Sandsa, it's worse than that.'

'Worse than the three of us against practically an entire pantheon of our brothers and sisters?' Sandsa asked disbelievingly.

Kuja's expression was twisted with anxiety; his mind fared little better. 'Yes! Nothing you've done was a surprise to Father. I think you were meant to have a son.'

'I do not know why that was in the Ine's plan. It worries me.'

'He must have foreseen your disobedience,' Kuja said, nodding vigorously. 'He must have! He knew you would have no intention of returning — he must have seen this years ago — so he set his plan into motion.'

Fury blinded Sandsa and he spun away. 'So he engineered this. All of it. He made Callista and Atsa my downfall. Before I even made the choice to leave. The mortals call this entrapment, Kuja! Why, a Chipper would lose their job for doing it! But not

Father. Not him. Not the *Creator God*,' he finished with a sarcastic bite to his voice.

'But if he knew you would leave...' Kuja hesitated. 'I think Callista was chosen to provide a replacement. A new god of the desert, carrying your blood and the blood of a chipless human...he's more powerful than you, Sandsa. Our own mother had nothing like what Callista has. If Fayay gets his hands on him...'

'He will not have him!' Sandsa snarled.

'We're just three people,' Kuja pointed out, sounding crestfallen.

Sandsa paced, his nails digging into his palms. He knew the glance he shot Kuja must have looked wild. 'What kind of father does this?'

'He is the Ine, not a father,' Kuja said. It was the first time Sandsa had felt any overt anger within his younger brother and he blinked at the rainforest god. Kuja bowed his head. 'I never had the strength to stand up to him. Not like you.'

'Your new resolve will not save us,' Sandsa told him, sinking his knees into the filthy leaf litter beneath him, uncaring that it smeared his pants. 'This is mad, you helping me.'

'I am not refuting that. I just want to hear your endgame, brother.'

'I will trade my life for his if need be,' Sandsa vowed. 'He still has a chance to be human. I am not sure I ever truly had that opportunity.'

The stillness of the rainforest abruptly gave way to a screaming gale. Trees splintered and leaves tore, their fragments scattered over the two gods.

'I did not know you felt so strongly about this,' Sandsa commented, glancing around.

Kuja also stared. 'It wasn't me. I felt it come from you.'

Sandsa threw his frown up at the tree canopy. 'Perhaps all Fayay needs is some time to learn my powers. I seem to be able to use yours now.'

'I do not think we have the luxury of time, brother,' Kuja warned him.

***

'What are we meant to do?' Sandsa asked his wife when she woke.

Callista blinked once, read everything he presented to her on the surface of his mind, then leaned against the headboard, fingers laced over her swollen stomach. Weariness was like gravity on her and her lips were dry and cracked from the recycled air.

'Sandsa...' She hesitated, as if considering whether or not to continue. 'Fayay can't master the deserts.'

'We do not know this for sure.'

Callista shuddered. 'Regardless, we need to leave this planet.'

'You want to leave?' he asked.

Pain drew hard, straight lines across her forehead. 'No. We've done so much to help Atsa. But it's extremely irresponsible to stage a war between gods in a city full of innocent people.'

Hidden away in the dim bedroom, his bare skin pressed to hers as they huddled together, Sandsa allowed himself the delusion of safety. Her desperate kisses were a lure into further distraction and he could see no reason to resist.

'The deserts can't have either of you,' Callista whispered fiercely.

'But the deserts aren't the ones coming to attack us...' Sandsa trailed off, silenced by the determination he could feel inside her.

'We'll manage,' was all she said before they both surrendered to the need of becoming one.

CHAPTER THIRTY

Callista tried not to fall asleep but she was exhausted. So incredibly exhausted.

Her eyes slid shut. And then the visions came for her.

***

The Desine returned to the deserts alone, so that his son could live as a man, raised by a woman.

Kuin of the Bretani, so long abandoned, raised her hands to the sky and called upon her god. The cold night air drifted over her skin, but she refused to shiver, to let it distract her.

And then, a minute later — she felt him.

'Desine,' she murmured. 'You have seen what my brother does to our tribe. I have no right to fight him. I know. I know this. But...'

It is not wrong to look after your people, Chief Kuin.

Kuin fell to her knees and sobbed as the desert god swirled around her in his insubstantial form. He had returned to guide her. And yet...she heard a mournful note on the winds. The Desine had returned to his deserts, but he was missing some vital part of himself.

She dared not ask.

***

When the Desine's son was a baby, they came for him. The gods laid waste to Atsa City, its smoking ruins a reminder that no one, not even a desert god, could forget his past. Fayay defeated all those who stood in his path, then took the child and raised him with hate in his heart.

Kuin of the Bretani, now so much older, trundled over the dunes, seeking water. Pausing to rest and lifting her hood, Kuin squinted at the sky. She regretted coming here now that the suns had chased away the shadows of night and any remnants of the promise her god had given her. It had been so long since she had thought of her brother, of the people dying beneath him. But she had seen him in a dream last night, older and meaner, beating his fists into flesh.

She stopped on the dune where her god had asked to meet her, nervous, fearful. He was not like his father. He was untested.

The Desine's son came to her.

He walked up the dune like a man, shedding his own hood and waving up at her as though he was greeting a friend. The dark shadows in his eyes gave her pause and he blazed with unparalleled power, but he wouldn't hurt her. Surely he wouldn't.

'Kuin of the Bretani,' he said. 'I am sorry the Desine let you down. But I'm here now. And I will destroy your brother for what he has done, just as I will destroy anyone who dares to deviate from my plans for them.'

Kuin looked down at the palms he spread before her. They were bare of scars.

He had never met a wife.

***

The Desine took his son to the deserts. They did not need the mortal woman who had tried to chain them, who had only wanted them so long as they abandoned a part of themselves.

Again, Kuin of the Bretani walked the dunes. But this time a man holding a baby approached her. They were both gods and there was no one to hold them back.

No one to care for them as they cared for others.

***

Callista rose from the bed that had trapped her with its soft sheets and nightmares. There was a presence near her, around her, suffocating her. She threw out a violent thought and the chair in the corner of the room flew through empty air before shattering against the wall.

'There are many more possible futures that you could see, if you tried to,' the Ine said, completely unharmed and indifferent. 'The same fear that makes you seek these visions also keeps you from seeing them all.'

Callista hesitated, but did not attack him again. She could not defend herself against the Creator God. Instead, she said, 'I can't trust whatever you show me. You have an agenda, Ine. You always did when it came to me.'

His smile wasn't completely patronising or warm, but somewhere in the middle. 'Are you afraid that there is no place for you beside a god? Afraid that once you leave this city, where you are known and have great political power, that you will no longer be *someone?*'

'That's not why,' she said, shivering. It was impossible to maintain eye contact.

'My grandson has come,' the Ine said, heading for the door. 'And soon so will Fayay. Anywhere you go, he will follow.'

'Then stop him!' Callista cried. 'Why won't you stop him?'

He did not need to answer. She already knew why.

The Ine would have a god in the deserts, one way or another.

***

Callista opened her eyes and stared up at the ceiling, confused by the web of dreams she had been catapulted from. Slowly, she began to focus on the faces in front of her. Sandsa. Ala.

'I...what happened?' Callista asked, struggling up against the cushions.

Ala chuckled and patted her on the shoulder. 'You took a nap. Not that any of us can blame ya, pushin' out that kid of yours.'

As Sandsa delivered the dozing baby into her arms, Callista felt a surge of power emanate from her son. He was stronger than her, and so much stronger than his father. Sandsa's smile betrayed his pride. He felt it too.

'I don't know what to call him,' Callista murmured.

'Got plenty of time to sort that out,' Ala said, grinning. 'Now rest. I gotta go tell everyone you're not dead.'

Once her friend left, Callista sighed. *But I have next to no time left in Atsa.*

'My love, are you alright?' Sandsa asked, sitting on the bed beside her. 'Even though you cannot see him, Kuja is here, guarding us. We are safe.'

'I somehow doubt that,' Callista said, gritting her teeth and thinking of the Ine's intrusion into her dreams. Her son stirred in her arms. Tiny chips of blue peeked from beneath his eyelids.

Sandsa's gaze rose to the ceiling. 'We must leave soon. Some of my brothers and sisters may not want to hurt mortals but Fayay has never used a gentle hand when dealing with them.'

Callista's heart shuddered in her chest. The denial remained trapped behind her teeth.

Sandsa frowned at her.

'I know we can't stay! I don't want Ala or Bock or any of them to get hurt!' she burst out, then lowered her voice when her son screwed up his face.

'Your greatest wish was to leave this planet a year ago,' he reminded her.

Callista shook her head. 'Wanting to leave isn't the same thing as actually doing it. I like it here. I have Ala, Bock, Kick...and I did something. I was someone!'

'You will have many more lifetimes to do something and become someone, I promise you,' Sandsa said. He pointed at one of the windows, where they could see a ship streaking towards the sky. 'There are many worlds out there, Callista.'

The sigh tormented her chapped lips. 'So long as they don't have any deserts. Or oceans. Or anything.'

Callista wriggled away from her husband and picked up a techpad. She swiftly began to scroll through the list of planets they were considering for their next destination, steadfastly ignoring the tremble in the hand that held the device. 'Sandsa...nowhere is safe. We will be exposing innocent people to collateral damage wherever we go.'

'But we will be together,' he said.

Callista closed her eyes and built even higher walls inside her mind, shutting him out, hiding the visions of what could be.

Sandsa kissed her forehead and bent to extract her son from her arms.

'No!' Callista protested.

Sandsa paused. 'My love?'

'Stay with me, both of you,' she whispered.

CHAPTER THIRTY-ONE

Callista hovered in the doorway, watching Ala hunch over her desk and stab frustrated fingers into her techpad. After a couple of minutes, Ala's red eye whirred up towards her. 'Come in and sit down before I lose what little patience I got, Cals. Is this about that grunt, Assila?'

Callista clapped a hand over her mouth to catch the sob but knew her friend had to have heard it. Ala immediately dropped the techpad onto her desk and traded it for a bottle filled with golden liquid. Two glasses then appeared from a drawer; their cleanliness was highly disputed.

Ala indicated the opposing seat. 'Looks like you need a strong drink. Too bad I only got this fancy shit that you gave me for my birthday. Piss weak and nothing to rave about.'

The laugh burbled from Callista, wet and uncertain.

But she sat, she drank, and then she said, 'Assila. I had forgotten I asked you to consider her for promotion.'

Ala rested her lips on the rim of her glass. 'What's she got on you? I know my Cals would never let a grunt, much less a starking Alcazaar, get ahead without provin' herself.'

Callista took another sip and winced. 'Ugh. I don't remember it being this bad.'

'What? You bought this one yourself, you said it's fruity.'

'No, not the alcohol. The lying. Keeping things from you.'

Ala knocked back the contents of her glass, licked her lips

and sighed. 'I see. What is it? You really do have a chip after all this time?'

Callista set her drink down. 'Assila threatened to tell the Zatzat what she knows about Sandsa. It could mean another war. One that might not be avoided even if Sandsa and I leave Yalsa 5.'

'Stop dancin' around and get to the point.'

'Ala...'

'Cals. Just tell me what the stark is going on.'

So Callista told her. Ala poured another drink for both of them. They drained two more glasses each in silence.

'Does this make you a god?' Ala finally demanded.

'No! I'm human, like you.' *Except that I will live forever.* Ala wisely made no mention of that. 'You believe me?'

The Maria subofficer's artificial eye continued to grind around in its socket, sounding distinctly disgruntled. Then Ala smiled, revealing teeth. 'You used to look a lot happier. I thought you finally getting a guy was gonna be good for ya. Just got yourself a lot more to worry about.'

'I *am* happy, Ala. I love him.'

'Happiness and love...well, they're like Maria and Alcazaar — one of them always loses,' Ala said, shaking her head. 'Probably why I can't give that little pipsqueak a chance. Someone's heart is gonna get stomped. And it might not be his.'

Callista stared at her. 'You're talking about Bock.'

'Well, who else? The governor?' Ala snorted and swung her legs up onto the desk, knocking over the bottle. It sloshed unhappily but didn't dare spill a single drop in its owner's presence. 'Alright. How can we fight these godly fuckers? Running's not gonna help, you know that, Cals.'

'Sandsa can use his powers to protect us,' Callista said, staring into her lap.

Ala thumped one heel on the table. 'But you think he'll feel that Kuin girl's distress when he uses 'em and will want to go to her. Then the deserts'll snatch him back and turn him into a god.'

'He's a *man*,' Callista insisted.

'Are you sure? Or do you think sayin' it enough times makes it true?'

Callista threaded her fingers together. The stone on the ring Sandsa had given her fell to the side and scratched one of her fingers. 'I don't...I don't want him to be anything else. Is that wrong? I mean, it was exciting when I first met him but...'

Ala stood up and moved around the table. She wrinkled her nose for a few seconds, then bent over her long-time friend and hugged her, muttering, 'There'll always be a place here for ya. Always. Even if you start to look too starking good for your age.'

'Do you think I'm keeping him from being happy?' Callista asked quietly.

Ala drew back and shrugged. 'Don't know that. I only care about you being happy. Just make sure you say goodbye to Bock. That kid will miss you more than I will.'

Callista smiled. 'I think you can replace me in his affections easily enough.'

'I can't do it, I can't risk it,' Ala said. 'Never had your courage, Cals.'

'Courage?' Callista repeated and shook her head. 'I'm not sure that's the word for it. So what will you do if the Zatzat start causing trouble?'

Ala chuckled. 'Are you forgettin' who used to lead this clan before Bolt came along, Clan Leader Dancer? We'll be fine. Now get gone.'

***

'Got you a flight out to some rock,' Bock said, his legs the only part of him that was visible as he twisted his body around to inspect the bottom of the hovercar. Nearby, Kick was keeping silent, arms crossed as he watched the younger man tinker with his vehicle. 'You're like royalty. I'd shoot meself rather than lose somethin' like that.'

Kick cleared his throat. 'Look, mate, I know this is very exciting for you, me letting you fix this machine because you're now better than me at this shit, but it's rude not to talk to someone face to face.'

'He is hurt and upset,' Sandsa told Kick, keeping his voice low. 'I do not believe there has been much permanence in his life. Callista and I leaving will not help matters.'

'Fuck permanence!' Bock cried, kicking a button on the hoversled he was using. He slid back into view, the scar on the side of his face stretched by his scowl. 'What about taking care of Atsa? Huh? Who'll keep the peace now?'

Sandsa kept his eyes on Bock as he felt a vision creep up on him. He could have fought it, but it had been so long since he'd had one that he almost welcomed it. The air shimmered around the teenager, blurring, giving way until the Bock of the future lay there, taller, wiser, older. He wore grim determination along with his fine clothes. The pin on his lapel very clearly read two letters: CL.

Sandsa smiled. 'I imagine you are up to the task, Bock. You will not abandon Atsa.'

'Starkin' right.'

'How's he taking it?' Callista asked, descending the ramp into the garage.

Bock immediately fired off a stream of curses.

'Really, Bock?' she said, shaking her head. 'I'd have accepted all sorts of farewell gifts but that insult about my parentage is not one of them. Even if it is true.'

Bock leapt up from the ground, hurtled over, and then attached himself to her like the prickle of a hardy plant. Callista patted the young man on the back and muttered a few words to him. Whatever she'd said made him nod, an ecstatic grin tearing up his face.

'Oh no, don't you go giving him hope about his chances with Ala,' Kick groaned. 'He'll forget to fill up the tanks in the hovercars if his head is full of lovey-dovey nonsense. Listen, Bock, you better work hard or you'll get kicked out and have to find a *real* job.'

'Holy Creator shit, he's worse than Ala,' Bock complained.

Callista walked over to Kick and hugged him. 'Goodbye, Kick.'

'Stark, I hate that gang moniker of mine — I only got it because they didn't realise it was my last name,' Kick said, winking over her shoulder at Sandsa. 'I was born Kieran Kikke. So, Kieran's a pretty good name for a kid, don't you think? Not that you need help choosing one, of course not!'

***

'Sandsa! Wait!'

He slowed and turned to meet Vom. He'd almost made it back to Maria headquarters, where a hovercar driven by Kick purred in the garage as it waited to take Sandsa and his family to the starship parked on the edge of the city (Atsa didn't have a spaceport, but there was enough space outside it to make up for this). Sandsa had hoped that one last walk through the tranquil streets, one that confirmed the clans were still at peace, would make it easier to leave.

Clearly he'd been wrong.

The Zatzat man stopped short some paces away, his expansive chest heaving with the effort of forcing air into his lungs. It had been far too many years since Vom had raced across sand dunes, Sandsa noted with a small smile, rifling through his friend's memories.

'Bock says you're leaving,' Vom said, panting.

'Don't worry,' Sandsa assured him. 'Atsa City will still be a safe place for your people. We've arranged it so that a new ruler will be elected from the clans from now on.'

Vom nodded. 'A sound plan. Are you going back to the deserts then?'

'No.'

'So you are running from your duties yet again.'

Sandsa opened his mouth, then closed it.

Vom abruptly fell to his knees and raised his palms to the sky, revealing his binding scars. 'My Lord Desine, please, hear me out.'

'What...don't...'

'I know who you are,' Vom said, his eyes filled with pain. 'Assila told me what she saw when you defeated the Alcazaar. You were a wild desert wind, untamed and powerful. She knew at once that you were our god.'

Sandsa frowned, thinking back to when he had stormed into the Alcazaar headquarters. It felt like it had happened aeons, not mere months, ago. But then he remembered that there had been a woman with binding scars. Why hadn't he killed her?

'I am a man, a husband, a father,' Sandsa said, backing away. 'I am nothing else, my friend, nothing more than that.'

'We need you!' Vom rose, his jaw so tight his lips barely moved. 'If you will not return as our god, won't you stay and keep us safe in Atsa? It's the least you can do.'

Sandsa turned his head to the side, trying not to look at him. 'You abandoned the deserts before I ever abandoned you, Vom. I merely wanted what you had. A choice.'

The heat of Vom's bulk drew nearer. 'Did you ever feel anything for us?'

'I was forced to guide you,' Sandsa said, grimacing in shame. 'I did not...truly feel anything for my people until I met Callista. Now I care. I care about every single mortal.'

'You didn't care about us before now?' Vom asked quietly.

The tear squeezed its way out of Sandsa's eye and dashed down his cheek. He lifted a finger to catch it, studying the bead of moisture. 'I...I am sorry. I didn't.'

Vom's expression lost all of its shadows. 'Then maybe you didn't abandon us. Maybe you had to learn to love so you could look after your people properly. Now you can return to us.'

'I will not leave my family for the deserts, Vom,' Sandsa told him firmly.

'Why can't you take them with you?'

'I cannot have both!'

'Why not?'

Sandsa swallowed with difficulty. 'This is what she wants — this!' He smacked his hands against his chest with a decisive thud. 'Flesh and blood! I could not bear her leaving me!'

'You were the wind that howled in the night, the sand that roughened and caressed the hands of those that trusted you,' Vom said, shaking his head. 'Sandsa is not my friend and he is not my god. What is he now?'

Sandsa had no answer for that. Instead, he said, 'Do not take out your anger on the Maria or this city, Vom. This peace was hard won.'

'Don't worry about us,' Vom said, indicating a young man on the footpath who looked so much like him. He had to be Vom's son. 'We will never abandon our responsibilities *or* our families. I pity you, Desine. You will always have to deny some part of yourself.'

Vom turned his back and walked away. Sandsa stood very still, unable to move until Kick leaned on the horn of the hovercar inside the garage, breaking through his reverie. Guilty, and not knowing how to discard that unwelcome feeling, Sandsa hurried towards Callista and his son.

CHAPTER THIRTY-TWO

A clear bowl-shaped shield curved around them, straining, shivering, but somehow it still held. Callista pressed her palms against it, stretching the shield out further, her fingernails digging into its flimsy surface. She would have stayed there, watching, waiting, had water suddenly not sloshed against the shield, sending her stumbling backwards. She looked back up in time to see Fayay's pale eyes appear on the other side of the barrier. The Watine bared his teeth at her. 'You think if you keep running we won't find you?'

Kuja stepped forward and coolly interceded. 'They appear to be succeeding, brother. Turns out I'm pretty good at blocking your sensing abilities, even if I am only seventy-one years old.'

'I will bring them all against you, little one,' Fayay said, his words tinged with the roar of distant oceans.

Callista smiled as a warm hand enveloped hers. Sandsa, now standing beside her, smirked at the god of water. 'You are wasting your time, Fayay. Or do you want our siblings to accuse you of abandoning *your* duties?'

Fayay scowled and vanished.

Kuja returned to pacing the edge of the shield, tirelessly keeping the small family from harm. Callista reached out to touch his shoulder, to thank him, but the rainforest god turned bloodshot eyes towards her.

She woke before she could ask him how much longer he could last.

***

Callista smothered yet another yawn. 'Will your brother ever let me have a decent night's sleep?'

A muffled thud answered her. Sandsa had buried his head beneath his pillow. Callista smiled — then the silence was broken by the wail of a hungry child.

She sighed. 'Now it's your son keeping me up.'

The sheet flowed over and off her skin as she stood to bare her breasts. Sandsa lifted one corner of the pillow and made an appreciative noise, his blue eyes stalking her across their rented room. They were on some mining moon, one Callista had heard about years ago, and its airless surface was so barren that it did not contain any oceans, deserts, rainforests or anything a god might control. Outside the plexiglass window, rocks listed above the mining complex, some thrown there by being bounced away from the domed buildings and their bubble-shaped shields, others having drifted there uninterrupted for aeons. It was constantly night outside, but Callista found that the stars, so much closer and bigger and clearer than they had ever been on Yalsa 5, were a soothing sight.

Callista pointed at the window. 'Look, Kieran. You can pick where we go next.'

Kieran continued to suckle her breast. He did not provide the miraculous answer she needed. Her family had already moved on three times in the past month, chased by dreams that warned them of impending discovery. She vowed not to grow too attached to this view but knew she would miss it all the same.

A warm, wet kiss that promised more touched her neck. 'Is he done? I need to discuss important matters in bed.'

Callista grimaced. 'Not now, Sandsa. I'm too worried, too tense. Kuja feels exhausted.'

'You fear that he will not be able to protect us,' Sandsa noted.

'I'm worried he'll end up neglecting his rainforests and get attacked for that!'

Kieran's mouth popped away from her nipple and he made an unhappy grunt. Callista hurriedly readjusted him, but he fussed for a bit, sensing the conflict between his parents. Once she had settled him again, Callista turned back to Sandsa.

'Kuja would not neglect his duties,' her husband said, eyes shadowed.

'He feels as rebellious as you do, sometimes,' Callista commented.

Sandsa glanced at the window, as though he could see his brother's reflection there. 'Kuja will not renounce his place in the rainforests. He has never...never found any reason to do so.'

'He loves you. He loved your mother. What stops him from loving someone else?'

'I would rather speak of my love for you,' Sandsa said and kissed her forehead. 'Come to bed, Callista. We need not worry tonight. Kuja will last for some time yet.'

***

Cradled against her side, Kieran dozed on. As silent as him but far more attentive to the demonstration the mine supervisor was giving, Callista stared straight ahead, fascinated by the animations crawling across the large suspended vidscreen. The supervisor paused to answer a question. 'Completely safe. All of us wear gear that's high-vis and has markers on it so we can see where you are with both our eyes and our systems.'

Callista shifted in her hard-backed seat, one of many hundreds that filled the lecture hall. Only a smattering of them were taken, mostly by a group of young students who were too busy whispering about the latest lasball game back home to pay attention to the supervisor. She started when she heard them mention they were from Gerasnin, where the Chippers kept their galactic headquarters. It was only a short hop through space from the mining moon.

Callista raised her hand. The supervisor's glassy eyes raked over the students instead of landing on her. He was dressed in sturdy black boots and a matching charcoal jumpsuit which seemed painfully bare without a gang logo. The bulky but manoeuvrable exoskeleton of a mine inspector stood beside him, supported by metal struts. The iridescent orange lights on the exoskeleton made it difficult to look at for too long. Callista gave the supervisor a small nudge with her powers, tipping his chin towards her. He saw her this time. 'Yes?'

'Do you need letters of recommendation?' she asked.

'Oh. No. We prefer our intake to have a clean slate.'

'Yeah, lets you pay a real shit entry-level salary,' one of the Gerasnin students hooted.

'We also offer competitive childcare services and shorter weeks for those who would prefer to spend more time with their families,' the miner said, now eyeballing Callista as though she were the only oxygen tank in a sea of vacuum. 'And if you are hardworking, we are generous with promotion opportunities.'

His lecture moved onto the privately-owned company's relationship with the Galactic Mining Corp. As this mine was independent of the corporation, they did not care about anyone's history with it. Callista felt her spirits rise. She had wanted a job like this for so long but somewhere along the way she had forgotten her dream.

Probably when the Creator God insisted on shackling me to Yalsa 5, she thought in disgust.

Kieran made small mumbling sounds as he woke up. Callista jogged him in her lap, willing him to keep quiet, then stared down at him when she *felt* rather than heard a demand for food. His blue eyes regarded her solemnly. Sighing, Callista left the hall. Once ensconced inside a booth in a nearby communications terminal, she released a breast for her hungry son.

I can do it, she realised. *No one can stop me. Not anymore.*

Kieran tugged a little harder than usual. Callista released a hiss of air, then forced a smile as a pair of miners entered the terminal. They struck up a conversation between themselves, clearly using the room for personal matters when they should have been working.

Callista left them to it.

***

'I want to work here,' Callista said the moment she entered their rented room.

Sandsa lay his techpad flat on the desk, which was a suspended piece of metal that hovered slightly too low for him to comfortably rest his elbows on it. The techpad's small screen featured lines and lines of text informing him of a slew of planets that he might travel to with his family. This updated list had been sent by Bock, who continued to wish them well, though the young man seemed more interested in reporting on his progress with Ala. Three smiles in one day was apparently enough of an improvement that Sandsa needed to be told.

'It is dangerous for us to remain in one place for too long,' Sandsa said, standing to receive his son. He beamed down at Kieran. 'But if you wish to have a job wherever we go, then do so. It is probably a good idea not to rely on the money we took from Atsa.'

Callista's bottom lip disappeared beneath her teeth. 'Mining contracts last an Old Earth year.'

Rubbing his thumb over Kieran's forehead until his child's eyes began to drift close, Sandsa tried to keep his voice even. 'Kuja has stressed that we must move on by next week.'

'I thought you said he could last a little longer,' Callista said, her eyes narrowing.

'That is a little longer,' Sandsa replied, then winced when he felt the force of her anger slam into him. Kieran's eyes shot open and he wailed. Sandsa hurriedly began to murmur to his son, calming him once more. He set Kieran down into the crib and turned to Callista. Her hands were glued to her hips.

'My love,' he began softly, 'we will always be chased.'

'He deserves better than that.'

Sandsa lowered a hand into the crib and stroked his son's face. 'I know. I'm sorry.'

Her response came in a whisper. 'Me too.'

They enveloped each other in an embrace of blame.

***

The moment the scream pierced the air Sandsa threw off the bed covers and flew over to where his youngest brother was curled up into a ball, convulsing, lips parted as he drew tortured breaths. Over in the crib, Kieran wept and complained, his face wrinkled and red.

'Kuja!' Sandsa said urgently. 'Kuja! What's wrong?'

Kuja shook his head, as if to clear it, then grabbed Sandsa's arm and yanked his older brother's ear down to his lips. 'I am too weak. I'm sorry. I'm just…just too weak.'

'How much time do we have?' Sandsa demanded.

'None.'

A gust of wind passed Sandsa — he glanced up in fear, but it was just Callista pulling on her shirt on her way over to the crib. She took Kieran into her arms. His child looked so small against her.

Sandsa cleared his throat. 'Callista…if I…if I use my…'

'No,' she cut in. 'You can't go back.'

Sandsa gripped Kuja's shoulder. 'Will you stand beside me, brother?'

'Standing is all I can do,' Kuja moaned. His body felt limp and heavy when Sandsa pulled him up to his feet.

The door squealed. Designed to withstand the vacuum of space, it gave no resistance to the handful of gods and goddesses that stood behind it. The thick metal was torn from the frame and flung down the corridor, a piece of scrap. As he entered, Fayay's lips gaped into a smile, a terrible one that revealed every single foul and decaying tooth.

Sandsa counted his siblings. There were fewer of them than he expected, but it was still more than two chipless humans and one exhausted god could handle.

'We are here to restore Father's grand design,' Fayay declared.

'Bullshit,' Callista said. Despite himself, Sandsa smiled, finding her more beautiful than ever. A lasgun filled the hand that wasn't supporting his son. 'You don't care about that. You're more worried about what the Ine will do to you if *you* stray. He'll concoct one of his plans for you, of course he will, but those plans aren't without casualties. Or pain. Your father doesn't care about you, only what he needs you to do.'

Several pairs of feet shifted behind Fayay. No one could keep their eyes on Callista for long. Kuja swung an amazed look at Sandsa. *She speaks as if she knows the Ine better than any of us.*

I think she does, Sandsa said, meaning it.

'You could leave, as I have,' he told his siblings out loud. 'He can't punish us if we all stand against him.'

Fayay's laugh was low and sibilant. 'Leave? And neuter myself as well as my powers? Never.'

'Then you will never be as happy,' Callista countered, then lifted an eyebrow when a blast of water smacked the floor at her feet. 'Even I could deflect that!'

The next wave was a mix of powers, fast and furious. Kuja tried to fight back, Sandsa felt him, but then the Rforine staggered backwards, gasping for breath. Callista's lasgun sent glowing red streaks towards the gods and goddesses opposing them. But they had been born with telekinesis to rival, even surpass, her own. The lasbolts slowed, then turned back towards their origin.

Sandsa watched the hypnotic swirl of sand that began at Callista's feet before rising to form a shaky vortex, a surprisingly strong effort given that it was summoned by a mere infant. Her son's shield merged with Callista's own and together they deflected the bolts, successful even without the help of a fully grown god. Fayay scowled and hurled a ball of turgid water that shattered Kieran's shields, both physical and mental. The child screamed.

I will not let my son protect us in my place, Sandsa thought.

He pushed out in front of the people he loved, arms spread either side of him.

Fayay took a step back.

Sandsa grinned. 'You're only second best, Fayay.'

He dove for the coil of power he had stowed away inside himself. And found it. He felt his strength return like hot, molten liquid seeping through his pores and veins, contaminating him, taking hold in every cell.

Sandsa threw himself among his siblings and brawled like he had been taught to in Atsa City, clipping the unprotected chins and temples of gods unused to physical attacks, all the while throwing every iota of power he had at them. They slapped their faces, trying to bat the sand away, but it burrowed into their noses and mouths, choking them.

Sandsa, I cannot watch this...not again... Callista pleaded.

The Alcazaar Clan Leader had once stood before him, accepting the end before he died inside a sandy tornado thrown from the Desine's own hand. Sandsa pushed the images of that night away as soon as she sent them. He would not let Callista distract him. Not now.

Sandsa staggered under the assault of two gods he had missed. One of them was Fayay, who had not gone down as easily as he had hoped. But the Watine was barely a century younger than him and Finara, the goddess of fire, was only a handful of decades Fayay's junior. Flames blistered the skin on Sandsa's forearm and he cried out in pain when salt water ran over the injury, scrubbing it raw. He dug deeper into the wellspring of his powers — and became the desert. He was made of sand. He had no form to hurt, to wound, to maim.

When Sandsa came to himself, he realised he was kneeling on the Watine's back. He smirked and said, 'You will have to do better than that, Fayay.'

He slapped the ground beside his brother's head. Droplets of water showered out of Sandsa's palm and gathered into a puddle the floor, growing with each tug that he felt in his navel. Sandsa ripped his hand away and flexed his fingers until he cupped sand instead. He let the grains trickle over Fayay's half-turned face.

'I will return,' Fayay said, snapping his teeth.

Sandsa laughed. 'I will be waiting.'

The grin that curled the water god's lips made something squirm inside Sandsa's suddenly very human stomach. 'Welcome back, *Desine.*'

Fayay collapsed into a puddle of water, causing Sandsa's knees to hit the floor. Around him, his siblings vanished as well, their deed done. Sandsa glanced up — Kuja was leaning against a wall and Callista was standing over her husband, Kieran in one arm while the other was stretched towards him. Sandsa took her hand, the scar on her palm sliding along the one on his as she helped him stand, then he kissed her, drawing her bottom lip into his mouth. He felt her relax under his touch —

— and then everything went black.

CHAPTER THIRTY-THREE

Sandsa fell against her, a dead weight. Callista's knees immediately buckled, but Kuja limped over and took Kieran from her, allowing her to hold up her husband unencumbered. She dragged her thumb across Sandsa's cheek, readying herself to pursue him into his mind, but then a vine wrapped around her thoughts and tightened — Kuja had blocked her.

She raised her eyes to his.

Kuja shook his head. 'No. I am not sure you could survive it.'

'Why?' she asked.

'He has not listened to the deserts for a long time,' Kuja said, his dimples crawling back into his face as he grimaced.

'A year isn't long to an immortal,' Callista pointed out.

Kieran made a sound of protest and the Rforine peered down at his nephew. A smile transformed Kuja's features. The man that now stood before her reminded her so much of Bock that Callista had to hold in a gasp. Kuja was so young.

'None of us have ever left our domains for more than a few hours,' he said, his smile fading. 'I can feel him. He is a storm. It would even tear me apart.'

Callista sank to the floor, lowering Sandsa into her lap and stroking his slack face. 'He doesn't look like he's in pain but I...' A tear dug its way down her cheek as she began to heal Sandsa's injuries. 'His people can source the Magic from him again, can't they?'

'Yes,' Kuja said, frowning at his brother's body. 'I could never shoulder that burden, giving part of myself to my people. I might die if I let them draw that much from my powers.'

'Is that the reason the other gods don't give powers to their followers?' Callista asked. 'Because it takes too much out of them?'

Kuja extracted an arm from Kieran to make a vague gesture towards the gaping doorway, where his brothers and sisters had appeared earlier. 'No. My older siblings are much stronger than me. But Sandsa...has always had to feel connected. I think he likes knowing that he is not alone, that he is loved and needed, that he is part of a family, even if they are strangers.'

Callista drew a breath and began to armour her mind against the young god. Kuja met her gaze but didn't ask why she was doing it, why she had to hide her thoughts. She had the uncomfortable feeling that he knew.

The word was softly spoken, as if Kuja dared not say more. 'Don't.'

Sandsa jerked out of Callista's hold and flew onto his feet. She eased herself off the floor and walked over to the window that exposed her gaze to space but kept her from losing all the oxygen in her lungs. It was hard enough to breathe right now as it was. She kept very still, even when she felt Sandsa's warmth behind her.

'They need me! Oh, Callista, what have I done?' Sandsa agonised.

She kept her eyes on the stars. Once she had thought of them as constant. Now she might see them burn out completely. 'You chose to live as a man. This is not your problem.'

'Callista —'

'It's not!' She spun back around. 'I refuse — I refuse to let go of you!'

'You do not need to,' Sandsa said, his arms sliding around her waist.

'Sandsa...'

'I can defeat Fayay, no matter what he tries,' he said confidently.

'Will you leave me — leave your *son* — whenever someone calls?' she demanded.

Sandsa reached for her hand. She let him take it. 'Yes, because I must. But understand, I will always come back to you.'

Callista squeezed his fingers. 'It would be easier if we all went to the deserts, wouldn't it.'

'Thank you, my love.' His sigh of relief was cold against her cheek. 'Thank you.'

And then he was gone.

Kuja nudged Callista's side with his elbow. She took back her son and refocused on the rainforest god. 'Did I shackle him needlessly?'

'I...' Kuja hesitated. 'I don't think I'm the one who can answer that.'

Callista laughed and caught her tears with her spare hand. 'I am not entirely to blame.'

'No, Sandsa fell without any urging from you,' Kuja said, digging into his pocket and then producing a scrap of cloth. Callista took the item and dabbed her cheeks with it. 'Please think carefully before you do anything. I have never seen my brother connect to anyone the way he did to you.'

'You've never seen someone hurt him this much either.'

Kuja shrugged. 'Perhaps pain is unavoidable when you love someone. Every memory of my mother hurts and warms me equally. Callista.' He hugged her briefly, making sure not to jostle Kieran. 'I have to leave. But if you call me, I'll hear you.'

Left alone with her son and silence, Callista rocked Kieran in her arms and told him of the dreams in which she had met Sandsa. She spoke of everything they had been through until her throat ran dry and she surrendered to the floor, moisture eking its way out of her eyes.

***

Cloaked in the darkness of night and holding her lasgun close, Kuin of the Bretani stared up at the stars and wondered if she should call upon her god once more. He had been absent in every patch of sand she had travelled to in the past year. She was sure others would have given up by now, but her need was too great to ignore. She had no right to challenge her brother, and a god's wrath could do so much more than one weak girl's hope.

She called. This time he answered.

A man came trudging up the dune. While she was frozen in shock, he took her lasgun from her outstretched hand and hefted it, as though testing its weight. Nodding with approval, he returned it to her. 'Kuin of the Bretani.'

'My Lord Desine,' she gasped and fell onto her stomach, arms splayed out in front of her.

***

Sandsa wondered what it was that Kuin found so amazing about him. He was wearing his usual black pants and shirt and looked like any clansperson in Atsa City. What did she see that he couldn't?

He cleared his throat. 'This will be a lot easier if you stand up and not look at me as though I am some...something better than I am.'

'You have blessed me by showing me your human form,' she breathed.

'It is the least I can do, for abandoning you,' Sandsa said.

Kuin shook her head. 'No, no, it was a lesson from you, I understand it now. We had to learn not to lean on you for every little thing that goes wrong.'

'You make me sound far wiser than I am.'

'Am I arguing with you?' she squeaked nervously.

Sandsa stared down at her prone form. 'What is it you need of me?'

'I want you to crush my brother and save my tribe,' she said, her lips coated with sand.

'Stand, Kuin of the Bretani,' he said and she obeyed, trembling as she did so. 'Did you not just say that you must not lean on me for every little thing?'

Her eyes remained on his bare feet. Where had his boots gone? Sandsa did not care, for the sand danced beneath his toes once more.

'Desine...please,' she begged. 'I am too weak to do it alone.'

He reached for her hand and took it, encasing her chilled fingers with his warm ones. 'But you have always been more powerful than your brother. You remember as well as I do how he was too afraid to face you in a duel that relied solely on the Magic.'

Kuin scowled. 'Doesn't matter. He has priests on his side. They'll outnumber me.'

Sandsa squeezed her hand. 'Then use your words. They also have power.'

'Will you come with me? Speak to them for me?' When he hesitated, she charged on, 'I have heard tales where you made great sandstorms that ran off evildoers for good!'

Sandsa withdrew his touch and turned from her, summoning one of the cloaks he had once worn so often. He drew the hood over his face. 'That is not my way, not now. I have learned how to command respect from those beneath me by caring for them and putting myself in danger for them. Relying on another's interference will not give you the complete love and adoration of your tribe.' He swung his cloak to one side as he moved back around. 'Even though you won't see me, I will be there with you. Don't worry. But this is something you must do. Otherwise how can you prove to your people that you are worthy to lead them, Chief Kuin?'

'You know the hearts of mortals now,' she said softly. 'And you care so much more for us than you did. I can feel it. You will command my respect forever.'

Sandsa was grateful that the hood hid his grimace. 'It was a costly lesson that kept me from you for far too long, but it was one I needed to learn.'

Was this what you wanted, Father?

***

Kuin's steps were steady when she reached her tribe a few hours later. She pointed her lasgun at the sentries on the edge of the camp, challenging them to stop her. Most of them quickly retreated from her path, but one of them brandished his own lasgun, so Kuin ducked and scooped up a handful of sand which she then threw at him. Her Magic kicked it towards his mouth, evoking a cough instead of words.

'The Desine is back and so am I!' she declared.

Her brother stood in front of the largest tent. Other tribes chose to rely on metal and tech to build their shelters, but the Bretani had always considered that a step that brought them too close to the ways of the City Dwellers.

Kuin squared off against her brother, feeling the potent powers of the priests crackle around her.

Desine, are you there? she asked.

Yes. But you need to focus.

Kuin breathed in through her nose before expelling the air over her lips. She should not demand any more from her god. It was honour enough to have been in his presence.

Her lasgun struck the ground. She didn't need it. Instead she made the sand beneath her quake. Priests and priestesses exchanged glances as the tribe converged on them, their faces lean and hungry.

Kuin lifted her chin. 'Hear me, Bretani! You have lost your sons and daughters, wives and husbands, all because my brother does not understand what it means to be chief!'

'Oh and you know?' her brother chortled

He waved his hand and activated his Magic. The ball of sand he tossed at her with his powers exploded into dust before it could reach her. Kuin smiled when fear struck silence into him. 'I do! I know that the more sand you cup in your hands, the harder it is to hold onto it. You have tried to take too much territory from tribes who are our allies — who *were* our allies!'

'What would you do then, outcast?' someone asked.

Kuin spread her arms, inviting her people to attack her or welcome her. 'We must give the land back to our friends and secure what is ours! And we must send fewer warriors and more hunters into the dunes. Or will you only feed yourself and those who can protect you,' she gestured at the retreating backs of the priests and priestesses, 'from the tribe you are starving to death?'

Later, when she watched her brother running out into the deserts, chased by the people he had starved and beaten, Kuin reached out with her senses and felt the Desine. He was everywhere, in every grain of sand. Her tribe buzzed with excitement when she told them this and they shouted their praises to the night sky, led by their chief. Kuin kept smiling.

The Desine was back.

And so was she.

***

Callista nodded along as Sandsa told her what had happened. She did not need the words. She had seen through his eyes as he'd raced to answer every person that had needed his help. His time in Atsa City had given him a new perspective and he had learned to feel compassion and sympathy.

The lesson I bore.

She looked briefly at the steel panel that had replaced the old door when she'd hit the appropriate buttons. It wouldn't protect them any better than the last one. But they didn't exactly need it anymore, did they?

Sandsa danced around her and scooped up his son, playing with and nuzzling him before using his powers to drift Kieran back into his crib.

'I am a better god now,' Sandsa told Callista. 'Thanks to you.'

Callista swallowed. *The Ine plans everything. He planned this so you would care for his creation in a way he never could. Stark, I don't want my son caught up in one of his plans.*

'I told you I would come back to you,' Sandsa said, squeezing her into a hug. His heart thudded against hers. 'I always will.'

'But someone will always need you.'

Sandsa pressed his lips to the side of her neck. Callista fought the pleasant shivers that rippled out from beneath his touch. 'I can guide thousands of them at once when I am one with the sands. And you can come with me. Father will not mind so long as I have returned to my duties.'

'If you're a god again, then what does that make me?' she asked quietly.

'My wife, the mother of my son,' Sandsa said, smiling down at her. 'Together, we will raise a man and a god.'

And what will I be, if you are both gods? she wondered. *Who will I be? Will I have to keep shunting my dreams aside?*

She ran her tongue across the roof of her mouth. 'Will you be able to look after the deserts if we're based here at the mines?'

'I thought we were moving to the deserts,' Sandsa said, stroking her hair.

Callista twisted her lips into what she hoped was a passable smile. 'We will speak of it later. You are tired.'

'I do not feel tired just now.' His eyes were sparkling. 'I only started feeling tired after I met you.'

'Will you stop feeling tired at all?' she asked, taking his hand and leading him to the bed.

Sandsa tugged off his shirt. 'Yes. It will give me more time to attend to my duties and be with you.'

He was a god. Once she had been a grunt, working her way up through the Maria. Then she had been a Clan Leader, making a real difference, helping people. Now she was just a pawn, designed to teach a god how to love so that he could help his people — or to provide a replacement if he failed to return after learning his lesson. Her destiny was this?

Sandsa glanced at her, sensing her discomfort. She performed the smile again and began to shed her clothes. He seemed satisfied.

She curled up behind him, hoping her warmth would help him sleep, but it was a long time before his breaths evened out. Only then could she close her own eyes and follow him into oblivion.

CHAPTER
THIRTY-FOUR

They walked together in her dreams. This time the Ine had brought her straight to the white horizon-less realm at the centre of his power. Sandsa had explained that all of his siblings were forced to meet there every so often to discuss how best to guide their people. Now this realm was barred to him; he was an outcast. Callista could understand why he didn't care about this — it was a cold, unfeeling place.

She latched onto her conversation with the Creator God, unwilling to heed reality which sounded a lot like the cries of her son. Back in that room awaited the Desine, a wild wind she had tried to trap with her bare hands.

'I'm nothing compared to the deserts in his eyes,' she told the Ine. 'If I stay, I'll only be second best. And I can't hang around, not if he expects me to raise his son while he looks after countless other sons. I love Sandsa, I do, but I...I don't even know who am I when I'm with him!'

The figure beside her paused just long enough for her to catch up to him. 'You underestimate yourself, Callista Krendasta. Is it because you do not know your destiny?'

'It's not like any of my dreams of the future have included what happens to me!' she said breathlessly. He kept such a languid pace and it annoyed her that her legs felt too short, too sluggish, to keep up with him.

'It was easy for you to accept Sandsa's love because you foresaw it,' the Ine remarked. 'Now that there is only uncertainty in your future, you believe there is no place for you in Sandsa's. It is short-sighted, Callista. Most mortals do not have the privileges you enjoy.'

Callista swung around in front of him, blocking his path and halting his steps. 'So tell me what happens. Tell me what happens if I stay with the Desine. Will he let me be anything but his wife? Will I still be able to be...me?'

'I will tell you nothing,' the Ine said.

'Please. I need to know what happens.'

The Ine lifted his shoulders and spread his arms. 'Then stay with my son. And see for yourself.'

Callista held a hand over her frantically beating heart. 'I couldn't...I couldn't bear it. I couldn't just be the woman who waits and twiddles her thumbs while she shares her husband with the galaxy.' She lifted her fingers to catch the tear streaking down her cheek before it could touch her lips. 'What if he forgets me? What if he never takes human form again?'

'Those are fears you need to communicate to my son.' The Ine seemed to grow even taller as he stared down at her. 'You must be open with him.'

'Why should I listen to you? You only see me as a *lesson* or an *incubator*.'

'He needed your love.' The Ine's gaze remained as immovable as a mountain. 'It taught him to care for his people, just as his life with you taught him to be a better guide for them.'

'And what about my son? What's his destiny?' Callista pressed.

'He could replace the god of the deserts, should Sandsa ever grow weary of it. Then you could have your husband to yourself once more.'

'No. I won't have it. I want...' Callista closed her eyes and breathed deeply. 'I want Kieran to discover who he is without his powers or any of this...any of this shit.'

His voice was maddeningly calm. 'You are happy for your son to seek the future blindly but will not accept that uncertainty for yourself. Interesting.'

Callista spitted him with a glare. 'Even if I take Kieran away from this, Fayay will still come after him. I don't trust you to stop the Watine, because you clearly set him on us to start with. Is there a way to keep Fayay — and any other god — from sensing and finding my son?'

'Yes,' the Ine replied. 'Although it would severely limit your son's powers.'

'Good. I don't want him to carry that burden. How do I do it?'

When the Ine smiled, it was as though an artist had perfectly chiselled the lines into the face of a marble statue. 'You already know the answer to that question. And so does your father.'

He turned and left her there, his fading footfalls her only company.

She took one last breath before she made her choice.

'Fayay!' she called.

A hot geyser appeared at her feet, spraying hot water over the shield she quickly erected. In the spout's wake stood a smiling Fayay. 'I hear you are ready to surrender the Desine to his duties and withdraw your distracting presence.'

'I have one condition.'

'Name it.'

She hardened her expression. 'If you want Sandsa to stay where he is, you will leave my son alone. He is not a weapon for you to use against your brother.'

'Then your son must forsake the deserts and his powers,' Fayay said, his breath thick and foul against her face. 'I will not abide a threat who can one day raise his hands against me.'

'I know how to temper my son's powers,' Callista said calmly. 'And he will live as a mortal, raised by mortals.'

Fayay's teeth peeked out of the corner of his mouth. 'Very well. But know this. If your son ever uses Sandsa's powers, then our deal is off. I will come for him. And I will take him.'

'Agreed.'

After he teleported away in triumph, Callista inspected the scars on her palms. She could not ask Sandsa to suffer the death of another loved one but nor could she stay at his side. An eternity without him was unbearable, but she would rather take that than look him in the eye and tell him that her insecurity had kept him from his people needlessly.

She had crushed him into a fragment of himself. He could only recover in her absence.

Just as she could only be herself in his.

***

Sandsa set his son back into the crib and smiled over at his wife as she roused herself. 'It is alright. I believe he had a nightmare and no longer requires your services.'

Arching her back and stretching her arms over her head,

Callista held his eyes, even as the sheet fled her naked form. Needing no further encouragement, Sandsa went to her. He felt...her thoughts were steady, resolved. His shoulders slumped in relief. In the morning he would explain how he meant to balance his family with his duties, but for now...her hips lifted from the bed and her knees parted, revealing the moistened lips that awaited his attention.

Sandsa knelt on the bed and worshipped her. His tongue swirled around her clitoris, eliciting moans, then he dove into her core, tasting her desire. Her fingers clawed into his scalp and drew him up into her kiss. He explored her mouth, moaning when he felt her tongue dance in response.

'In me, now,' she ordered.

He obeyed and found that she was tight and tense. Sandsa gently worked his thumb over her throbbing nub until her muscles relaxed enough for him to sheathe himself completely inside her wet heat. She met his deep thrusts with fervour, forcing his rhythm, and it wasn't long before she pulsed around him, once, twice. He gasped and closed his eyes, allowing the cascade of pleasure to overwhelm him.

When he looked down at her again, she was smiling.

He smiled back and kissed her, his lips languid against her own.

Lying on his side, her warmth at his back, Sandsa felt her fingers trail over his thigh, his softened member, his stomach, a sensitive nipple and then to his lips. She was mapping him, leaving her mark in every crevice.

Soothed by her touch, Sandsa closed his eyes and drifted into sleep.

***

She ran.

The flight from the mining moon to Gerasnin had taken two hours. At any moment he might wake and realise they were gone. No matter how far she fled across the galaxy, Callista knew that he would sense their location and be there within a heartbeat. She had left the starship before the docking ramp had even hit the ground, desperate to reach her destination before he came for her.

With each jolt, the precious bundle in her arms made several minute sounds of protests that began to blend into one uniform wail. Callista followed the streetlights as they flared to life beneath the darkening sky and guided her towards the enormous stone temple, both GLEA's headquarters and a place of worship. Callista sobbed with relief when her feet met the white steps. She began to climb, Kieran now silent in her arms, possibly sensing her urgency —

'Colonel Nerani,' Callista said in surprise, halting.

Her son wrinkled his nose in displeasure, no doubt sensing the nest of Chippers in their temple. Unlike in Atsa City where there had only been an outpost, here on Gerasnin, the seat of their power, they had many of these large buildings. To Callista they looked like stone coffins. The soaring arches and cheerful purple banners did little to belie that feeling.

'Clan Leade — Callista,' Nerani corrected herself, pausing on her way up the steps. Her boots were polished enough to reflect the stars and the stubby tentacles on her scalp were lined up perfectly.

'You're a long way from Yalsa 5,' Nerani noted. 'We heard you'd left with Bolt but it's not like anyone bothered to tell us why.' She glanced down at Callista's arms in wonder. 'Your son's really strong. I can feel it.'

'I need your help so people can't feel him,' Callista said.

***

Callista framed her forehead with both hands, keenly aware of the bump caused by the implant beneath the skin on her right temple. She held her breath, reaching for the core of power inside her, the one that had begun in her childhood as a passing distraction and had then become a curse that had lured a god into her bed. She scratched deeper and deeper until...

'How do you feel?' Nerani asked, rocking Kieran in her arms.

Callista wet her lips. 'I can just...make out you and my son, but it's faint. The chip is severely hampering my powers.'

'Next question. How'd you know it would work?'

Callista shrugged. 'Just something my father told me.' *And it was the Ine who told him the chips would nullify our powers and make us undetectable*, she added silently, then said out loud, 'I had no other choice but to try. Can you please give my son a chip?'

A frown filled Nerani's face. 'It seems a shame that you would limit his powers this way. He could be of great service to GLEA without the chip. He feels...immense. Like a god, even...'

Callista tensed. 'By the laws of Gerasnin, I'm his legal guardian and I am giving him over to the care of the Chip...the Galactic Law Enforcement Agency. You can't stop me.'

This way he will be free of the Ine and the deserts.

And he will be free of me. I cannot lead another man astray.

Her palms itched. Callista rubbed them together, but the

irritation persisted. Glancing down at the binding scars, she bit her lip.

'Are you sure about this?' Nerani asked her for the hundredth time.

'No.'

'But you're doing it anyway.'

Callista nodded.

'You would make a fine Chipper yourself, you know,' Nerani told her, holding out Kieran as though to give him back, but Callista stood and retreated from her son, her eyes burning as he began to cry his own tears. 'What'll you do, then?'

Callista stared unseeingly through the ceiling, to the stars that would mock her every night for the rest of her eternal life. 'Be myself.'

***

He woke alone.

Sandsa sat up and stretched out with his senses. Callista was nowhere nearby, nor was his son. He peered frantically into the stars around him — and found nothing. Sandsa tossed the sheets aside and again tried to follow the cords that connected him to his family, but they ended abruptly just beyond his field of vision.

Sandsa breathed deeply, trying not to panic.

Then he saw the techpad on her pillow. He lifted it and read the message she'd left for him.

> *Sandsa, my love,*
> *You never had to choose between the deserts and me.*
> *The Ine made that clear. I should have told you but I was*

selfish. All this time, I kept you from your true self. And I am so sorry.

The Ine also told me that I existed simply to teach you how to love your people — or to provide a replacement if you refused to return after your lesson. This is not the destiny I'd have chosen. I wanted so much more for myself. And this is not what I want for Kieran. If he stays, he'll be manipulated and endlessly targeted. He deserves a chance to live as man.

You won't be able to sense us. I found a way to ensure that. Don't worry about Fayay or the others — even if they do manage to find us, we are safe from them.

I need to find out who I am without you. All I know is that I am not the wife of a desert god.

I love you.

I'm sorry.

'Why didn't you tell me this was how you felt?' he whispered, pressing his lips to the small screen of the device.

He had taken her from Atsa, away from her friends and away from any chance of her having a normal, mortal life. And he had just assumed that she'd wanted this.

Sandsa stood and hurled the techpad at the wall. Pieces of it rained over the floor.

Callista was right. He'd never had to choose.

She'd chosen for him.

His human form disintegrated and he became a tortured wind, howling with eternal fury as he scoured the galaxy. But no matter where he looked, the Desine could not find her.

About the Author

Alyce Caswell lives in Sydney, Australia with zero cats and one husband. When she isn't drinking her way through a giant pot of tea, Alyce is a keen reader and writer of science fiction and fantasy. This is her first novel.

You can contact her via e-mail (alycecaswell@outlook.com) or on Twitter (@alycecaswell).

ALSO BY ALYCE CASWELL

The Galactic Pantheon Series
The Tortured Wind
The Twisted Vine
*The Flickering Flame**
*The Shifting Ice**
*The Whispering Grass**
*The Creeping Moss**

*novella